SHATTERED LIES

JM HUGHSON

Idlebury Books

Cover Art: SelfPubBookCovers.com/mary60
Editor/Formatting: The staff of Victoryediting.com
Printed in the United States of America

DEDICATION

*"Oh, what a tangled web we weave . . .
When we first practice to deceive."*

~Sir Walter Scott

CHAPTER ONE

I T CRASHED ON MY DESK like a meteor hurled to earth from outer space. I looked up. My heart raced. I could hardly breathe.

"Calm down, Emarie," my editor said. "You've been champing at the bit to interview someone interesting. Well"—he smirked—"be careful what you wish for."

"Damn. Next time hand me the file. Don't throw it on my desk. Nearly scared me to death," I replied.

My editor, Jim, chuckled and walked away. When he reached his office door, he yelled across the room, "And by the way, your story will appear in next Sunday's magazine section. You know what that means?"

"A Friday deadline," I yelled back. *Next Sunday? Why the short notice?*

Jim motioned, pointing two fingers at his eyes, then pointing them at me, making it clear he was watching me and that my future was on the line.

I pushed the file aside. I told myself I was too busy to read it. Truth was, I was too scared. "This could be it," I muttered as I tapped my pen on my lips. "This could be my big break." It was Friday afternoon. Only one week to pull this off. Procrastination was not an option.

Nonetheless, I took a few moments to ponder how I'd gotten to be the low woman on the totem pole at one of the most powerful newspapers in the world.

Although I was new to journalism, I wasn't new to life. I was thirty-five years old, single, and thanks to twelve years as an advertising copywriter, I was known to my friends as the Dateless Wonder. Two years ago, as I dragged myself through my morning beautification project, I realized I was tired, discouraged with work, and disgusted with my life. I looked in the mirror at my chocolate-brown eyes with their matching circles. Anxiety washed over me as a bizarre thought zipped through my head. *I'd rather be dead than go to work.* I gasped. But that horrific thought was an inspiration. Yep, at that moment I knew I was through with drama queens, bullies, narcissists, deadlines, secret meetings, new-client pitches, old-client parties, and late nights. I was ripe for a career change. For years I'd hungered to be a freelance feature writer, taking on only those stories that piqued my interest. I wanted to be the queen of my destiny, the keeper of my clock, the comptroller of my wallet. I decided there was no better time than the present.

To everyone's surprise, and hopefully, disappointment, I quit my decent-paying job at one of D.C.'s largest advertising agencies and dove into the world of freelance feature writing. Much to my despair, with no experience in writing anything other than advertising and marketing, the offers didn't materialize.

My wallet was empty.

My refrigerator was bare.

My bills were sky-high.

I needed a J-O-B.

Now!

Nonetheless, I refused to give up my dream. So I queried dozens of newspapers and magazines within a five-hundred-mile radius.

Two months later, after lots of grueling interviews, writing tests, and don't-call-us, we'll-call-you rejections, I got a call from the editor of one of Washington, D.C.'s premier newspapers. An editor at a newspaper in Georgia who hadn't hired me had given me a glowing recommendation. Go figure. Two interviews and one lunch later, I was a cub reporter/writer for the *Washington Intelligencer*'s Lifestyle section. I'd done it. I was back in the world of drama queens, bullies, narcissists, deadlines, secret meetings, and late nights. I felt at home. Now I had to figure out how to climb the ladder of success in one of the world's most cutthroat industries—the Fourth Estate. It wasn't as easy or exciting as I'd thought, but then again, today could be my lucky day.

I lifted the file. It was lighter than I'd expected. A feeling of doom swept over me. *How am I going to write a great story with so little information? Well, I'll never know until I try.* I slowly lifted the file cover, expecting something gross to pop out. I was partially right. A photo of a woman who could be the poster child for trailer trash slid out and landed on my desk. The woman's black eyes stared through me. Her shoulder-length gray hair was sparse and greasy. Her lips were wrinkled due to a bad cigarette habit, missing teeth, or both. She wore a T-shirt that read WORLD'S BEST MOM. The words blurred across her bosom as if they were stretched across gigantic water balloons. Yikes. "I'm glad she's not my mother," I muttered. She looked eighty. She was sixty-five. The same age as my mother, who looked twenty years younger than... I searched for her name... Dorothy Hall.

CHAPTER TWO

F OR THE REST OF THE day, I searched for information on Dorothy Hall of Darrington, Maryland.

I googled.

I printed.

I made a few notes.

Not much to go on.

I wondered why Jim was interested in a story so far out of the D.C. metro area. Dorothy Hall's crime wasn't even big news in Darrington. No one but Jim seemed to care about this sixty-five-year-old woman who'd killed her twenty-five-year-old boyfriend. Was he testing me? Was he setting me up for failure? I decided I didn't have time to foster my suspicions. I needed to jump on the story. It could be my big break.

At five p.m. sharp, I packed up my findings, and with visions dancing through my head of a glass of wine and a plate of chicken wings topped with hot sauce, I rushed home. I shoved my way down the subway escalator of the McPherson Square Metro and jumped on the Blue Line train to the Franconia-Springfield station just in time as a chime rang and a recorded announcement echoed, "Doors closing." Lucky me, I landed a seat facing the other side of the subway car which, if I leaned forward a tad, provided an aisle-long view of the other passengers. In most subway cars, that seat was reserved for senior citizens and persons with disabilities. But in this car, it was for the taking—and a most coveted seat for an avid people watcher such as me.

The subway car bounced and jostled riders, many of whom stood with legs wide for balance and one hand clasped around a narrow metal pole for support. I watched a young woman wearing spikes do an awkward pole dance as she tried to maintain her footing and pride. I chuckled at how her vanity made her look ridiculous. I doubted that's what she was aiming for when she'd slipped into her CFM shoes that morning.

I examined the mass of humanity. Most people looked ordinary. Some looked less than ordinary. I wondered if any of them harbored a deadly secret. I felt like a spy. Then my heart leaped to my throat. "That's her," I whispered. I took a long look at a woman sitting six rows back. I laughed. *No, that's not her.* Part of me felt sorry for the woman. Out of all the people in the world one could look like, that poor woman looked like Dorothy Hall. I doubt she knew she was the spitting image of a killer—a frightfully homely one at that. I glanced at my briefcase. It should have bulged with information-packed papers. It didn't. *There's so little to go on,* I thought. *I smell a big story.* I smiled.

Forty-five minutes later, I was home in my cozy condo. After a quick change into my favorite pair of lounge pants and a sweatshirt, I poured a glass of wine, heated a plate of chicken wings, doused the wings with sriracha sauce, and put the plate and glass of wine on the dining room table. I didn't know what to do first: swig the wine, bite a hot-sauce-soaked chicken wing, open my briefcase, or boot my laptop. I chose a swig of wine. Then I booted my laptop. As it loaded, I snatched a chicken wing. With Neanderthal manners that would shock my manner-maniac mother, I tore off a piece of tender meat. I savored the flavor as I searched for a napkin. There wasn't one within reach, so I licked my fingers and wiped them on my pants. I could hear my mother say, "Oh Emarie, I didn't raise you to be a slob."

I gathered the information about Dorothy Hall and spread it on the dining room table. *Not much,* I thought. *Maybe I don't smell a big story.* "Smells like chicken," I said and laughed to myself. I pushed aside Dorothy's photo and scanned the vague synopsis of the crime that should have kept her behind bars for life but had held her for only one day. *What? No trial? Was it self-defense? Why no trial?* Another document revealed a history riddled with charges of child abuse and neglect for which she'd served no time but had lost all her children. So, she abused seven kids, but she had to kill her twenty-five-year-old boy toy to get noticed?

I had to get to the bottom of the story… fast.

Should I go to Darrington, Maryland?

Should I call the Bingingham County police?

Should I find Dorothy Hall and talk to her in person?

Yes.

Yes.

And yes.

But something other than Dorothy Hall's criminal history was unsettling. It was the fact she lived in Darrington, Maryland. I'd lived there for a few months. But that's another story.

An hour later, I decided I knew everything about Dorothy Hall that was available to the public. I did an Internet search and got the phone number for the Bingingham County police. Then I searched Anywho.com for Dorothy Hall in Darrington, Maryland. Her name popped up, but the age didn't match. "Damn. It's not her," I muttered. I rechecked Dorothy's file. No address or phone number. I turned over Dorothy's photo. A nearly illegible phone number and address were written in pencil. I prayed they were Dorothy Hall's and did a reverse lookup. Nothing. My hands shook. I'm not sure why, but a feeling of doom surged through me.

I rushed to the refrigerator, poured another glass of wine and guzzled it, hoping the fermented nectar would run through my veins and calm my nerves. It didn't. I decided anxiety was a good thing. It meant I was onto something big.

Thanks to a broken GPS I never replaced, I'd have to get directions the old-fashioned way.

Nervous.

Shaking.

I clicked on Google Maps and managed to type the address as my fingers danced across the keyboard. With the directions in hand to what I hoped was Dorothy Hall's house, I went into the sunroom and gazed out the window, feeling as if my life was about to change but not in a good way. "What's wrong, Emarie? Are you afraid you'll succeed and write a Pulitzer Prize-winning story?" But that wasn't it. The truth? I was afraid of Dorothy Hall. A few minutes later, I decided my angst was unfounded.

Back in the dining room, I checked the time on my computer. It was eight o'clock. Was it too late to call Dorothy and set up an appointment? No. As long as it wasn't later than nine, it was socially acceptable to call. Would Woodward or Bernstein care about the time? I didn't think so.

A maniacal search through my handbag resulted in no cell phone. Frustrated, I emptied it on the dining room table. "Where the hell is my cell phone?"

Inhale.

Exhale.

Relax.

"Where is it?" I yelled. "Typical me. I'm an expert at undermining myself."

My home phone beckoned. I looked at it sitting in the charger on a small table in my kitchen. "No, it's unprofessional. Not to mention potentially dangerous." I had to find my work cell.

A room-to-room search turned up nothing. "Oh my God! I left it at work," I said through gritted teeth. I slapped my forehead. "Stupid, stupid, stupid." I went into the dining room and threw everything back into my handbag. I had to get my cell phone and call Dorothy before nine p.m. There wasn't a snowball's chance in hell I could get to the office in time. Then an odd sensation took my mind off my self-loathing thoughts. It was my cell phone, vibrating in my pants pocket. I pulled it out and looked at the screen. My boss was calling.

"Hi, Jim."

"Hi there, Emarie. Just thought I'd see how your story is developing."

"Great," I said as I rolled my eyes.

"What? I can't hear you. It's so noisy here."

"I said, 'great,'" I yelled.

"Okay. Nose to the grindstone. Oh, I gotta go, our table is ready."

He hung up before I could say what I was thinking. That was a good thing because it would have gotten me fired.

So my cell phone had been in my pocket all along. I started to call myself names, but it would just waste more time. Instead, I took a deep breath and dialed what I hoped was Dorothy Hall's phone number.

First ring. Feeling excited.

Second ring. Wondering if she was home.

Third ring. Figured even Dorothy Hall was out having fun on a Friday evening.

Fourth ring. "Yeah," a woman said.

"Are you Dorothy Hall?" I asked.

"Yeah, whaddya want?" Dorothy replied, sounding drunk with sleep or drunk on booze. I couldn't tell.

"My name is Emarie Lukins. I'm a reporter for the *Washington Intelligencer* here in Washington, D.C."

"Did you say you're... Emarie... Lukins?"

"Yes, the one and only Emarie Lukins," I said, hoping I didn't sound immature, or worse, nervous.

"Well, la-di-da. Whaddya want with me?"

"I believe you have an interesting story to tell, and I'd like to be the one to help you tell it," I said.

Silence.

I feared Dorothy would say yes and feared she'd say no. Either way, my career was in her hands. I cleared my throat and said, "Ms. Hall?"

"Yeah, I heard ya." Dorothy gulped something. Water? Wine? I didn't know. "What makes you think I'm so interesting?"

"Well, I've read about you, and I find you fascinating." I cringed, worried what I'd just said would scare her off.

Dorothy laughed, wheezed, and coughed at the same time. "Well, I never... I never had anyone tell me I was fascinating. Whaddya want to know?"

"Well, I have a few questions about the death of your boyfriend," I said, trying not to be accusatory.

"There's nothing more to say about who murdered my boyfriend."

I hesitated. Should I ask her why, or should I ignore her last statement? I chose to ignore it. "I wonder if I could meet with you in person. Of course, I'd come to you."

Silence.

Panic.

"All the reports are from someone else's point of view. Yours would be much more interesting," I said, hoping I didn't sound like I was begging.

"When?" Dorothy replied.

"When what?"

"When do you want to bring your sorry ass over to my house?"

"How about tomorrow?"

"When tomorrow?"

"How about one o'clock?"

"Fine. You coming alone, or are you bringing someone with you?" Dorothy asked.

"Alone."

"Good. See ya at one."

"Is your address 124 South Main Street, Darrington, Maryland?"

"Wow, you are a crackerjack reporter. What's your name again?"

"Emarie. Emarie Lukins."

"Okaaay, Emarie Lukins, see ya tomorrow."

Click. Dorothy was gone.

"Tomorrow's going to be a great day," I sang as I danced around the living room. "Greeeeeeeeaaaaaat," I shouted. *Tony the Tiger, right?*

Despite my excitement, a pit in my stomach revealed a truth I didn't want to face. I was scared to death of Dorothy Hall.

CHAPTER THREE

I TOSSED AND TURNED ALL night. I watched TV reruns of *The Golden Girls*, *Frasier*, and *The Brady Bunch*, all of which increased my wakefulness. I reread Dorothy's skimpy file. I studied the directions to Darrington, Maryland, as if I were preparing for a grad school entrance exam. As the sun rose, my eyes closed. I slept like a baby until I rolled over and looked at the clock.

"Ten o'clock," I screamed as I bolted out of bed. "What the hell is wrong with you, Emarie? Why didn't you set the alarm? Now you're going to be late, late, late for a very important date." I nearly laughed. My career depended on Dorothy Hall—a woman I hadn't met and probably wouldn't like.

Maybe she would forget about our appointment.

Maybe she would be in a drunken stupor.

Maybe I needed to get my act together.

I jumped into the shower… made myself presentable… dressed in slacks, a light sweater, and a jacket that made me look professional but not unapproachable… flung my briefcase and handbag over my left shoulder… held the directions to Dorothy's in my teeth… clutched my keys with my left hand… opened my front door with my right hand… and exited my condo. As I locked my front door, I said,

"Recorder. I didn't pack my recorder."

Keys turned.

Door opened.

I threw everything on the floor.

Then I ran into my pathetically puny office and frantically searched for my recorder. "For God's sake, here I go again," I said. "Where's my damn recorder?"

I searched.

I swore.

I slammed desk drawers.

I admonished myself for poor planning. It was nowhere. I plopped in my desk chair. I wanted to cry. I glanced out the window. I couldn't believe my eyes. There was my recorder sitting on the windowsill, shrouded in sunlight as if it were a gift from above. "Thank you, God."

I ran to my front door... tossed the recorder into my briefcase... reloaded my left shoulder... stuffed the directions between my teeth... and exited my condo. "Keys, keys, where are my damn keys?" I mumbled. I turned the doorknob. I'd locked myself out. I rested my forehead on the blah-tan door and cried.

I reached into my jacket pocket for a tissue. Holy cow, I touched what felt like keys. I pulled them out, looked up, and said, "Thank you, God!" Then I rushed down the stairs and jumped in my car. I jammed the car key in the ignition.

Turn.

Engine on.

"Thank you, God!" God was popular with me today. Then I pulled out of the parking spot, wound my way through my condo complex, and headed toward the Capital Beltway. "Dorothy, here I come."

As I turned right on Commerce Street to take the Tyson's Corner exit, I was struck by a craving for coffee. I knew I didn't have time to stop, but without coffee, I'd be a basket case. I made a U-turn and headed back toward my condo. What was I thinking? I didn't have time to go home and make a pot of coffee.

I mentally scanned the area. McDonald's. Too far away. 7-Eleven. Way too far away. Then I saw it. Starbucks. I gasped. "Oh my God,

I'm going to have to fork over four bucks for a cup of coffee." The cheapskate in me yelled, "No." My brain screamed, "Coffee, coffee, where's my coffee." I had to get coffee. And I had to get it now.

Next thing I knew, I was in Starbucks's drive-through lane. I was tempted to back out. A glance in my rearview mirror made it clear it was too late. There were two cars behind me. *Do I have any cash?* I dug in my purse for my wallet. I checked for money. Fifty bucks! There was no turning back. It was my turn. I didn't even have time to look at the coffee menu.

"Good morning. What's your order?"

"Medium regular coffee, please. Three sugars and extra cream," I said with the expertise of a Starbuckian.

"Our special today is—"

TMI. I zoned out. "Just a medium regular coffee with three sugars and extra cream, please."

"Do you mean a sixteen-ounce Grande fresh-brewed coffee?"

"Yes, Grande with three sugars and extra cream."

"That's two dollars and twenty-three cents. Please pull up to the next window to pay."

"Ah, cheaper than I thought," I mumbled to myself. I pulled up to the next window and waited. *Did I detect annoyance from the young woman behind the order screen? Pay no attention to the woman behind the screen. Ha! Who cares? I'd probably be annoyed with me if I were her.*

One medium regular coffee later, excuse me, one Grande fresh-brewed coffee later, I was on my way to Dorothy's.

The drive was uneventful. I didn't even spill coffee on myself. Small miracle. Then I saw it—the exit sign for Darrington. I fought an urge to turn around and skedaddle back home. Nonetheless, I steered my car onto the exit ramp. According to Google Maps, Dorothy lived only one mile away. I looked at the clock. Twelve fifty-two p.m. Yikes, I didn't have time to get something to eat and calm my nerves.

I turned onto South Main Street. There it was. Second from the corner. Dorothy's house. As I pulled up to the curb, a chill ran through me. The house was dark and drab. If I were scouting for a house to use in a murder mystery, this would be it. It oozed negative energy. I wondered what horrors happened behind its door as visions of blood dripping down its walls danced through my head.

I glanced at the car clock. Twelve fifty-five p.m. Five minutes till the meeting of the minds. Why did I feel as if I were meeting my maker?

I sat in my car and practiced introducing myself to Dorothy. "How do you do?... Nice to meet you... Pleasure... Hi, I'm Emarie Lukins... I'm a mental case..." I looked up and saw someone peering out the front window. She'd spotted me. There was no point in hiding out in the car any longer. I retrieved my briefcase and walked to Dorothy Hall's front porch. My knees shook. I probably looked like a drunk. Nonetheless, I made it. I searched for a doorbell but didn't see one, so I raised a fist and knocked. The person at the window moved. Seconds later, I was face-to-face with Dorothy Hall.

CHAPTER FOUR

"WELL, YOU'RE FASHIONABLY EARLY," a woman said and then sneered at me, revealing a set of black and yellow teeth.

"Dorothy, I presume." Before me stood a three-hundred-plus-pound woman dressed in a stained muumuu. Her hair was straggly and greasy. Her slippers were so grimy I imagined she left dirty footprints wherever she trod. I fought the urge to blurt, "You're even uglier and fatter in person." She was surprisingly tall and revolting. Yet I was drawn to her like an archaeologist to a decaying mummy.

"You presume right." Dorothy moved her gargantuan body to make room for my entrance. "Are you coming in, or are you just gonna stare at my pretty face?"

My legs felt as if they were filled with lead. I lifted my right leg but didn't move forward. *Feet, don't fail me now.* I lifted my left leg. I was paralyzed with fear, but I was sure I hid it well.

"Don't be a scaredy-cat," Dorothy said. "I don't bite."

I managed an awkward smile as I stepped over the threshold into Dorothy's lair. Words of wisdom from the Cowardly Lion popped into my head. *I'd... turn... back... if... I... were... you.*

The door slammed behind me, eliminating the only source of natural light and any hope of escape. I walked into the middle of the dark living room. My eyes struggled to adjust to the lack of light as my nose worked overtime. *God, this place stinks. Smells like animal pee, human sweat, stale cigarettes, and rotten food. Yikes. I think I'm going to vomit. Someone should bottle this stuff as bug repellent.*

A couple of minutes later, my rods and cones sent messages to my occipital lobes and Dorothy's world came into focus. Her furniture was old and worn. The couch was threadbare. A doily on the only chair was yellowed with what I assumed was hair grease. The coffee table was so cluttered it was hard to tell what it looked like. One of the table's legs was sloppily wrapped in duct tape. Dirty dishes littered the coffee table. I got a whiff of cat urine, but there was no cat in sight. The carpet looked brown but had hints of a past life as a green carpet. The kitchen was only a few steps away. The sink overflowed with dirty dishes. Every inch of counter space was smothered in charred, greasy pots and pans, trash, plastic cups, food containers, and God knows what. The refrigerator door and handle were smudged with dirt and food.

"Can I getcha something to drink?" Dorothy asked.

"Oh, no thank you," I replied a little too loudly.

I already had to go to the bathroom. My brain had screamed for coffee, now my bladder was screaming for relief. But the condition of Dorothy's house conjured visions of filth. I imagined a water-, urine-, and feces-stained toilet accompanied by a rusted, stained sink and a bar of soap smeared with dirt. *Why didn't I stop before I got here? I'll have to hold it.* I'd had lots of practice holding my bladder at long rock concerts. I hoped I wouldn't pee myself.

"Well, I'm gonna get a little something," Dorothy said as she waddled toward the kitchen. "Let me know if I can getcha anything."

"Thanks," I muttered. *How about a Pulitzer Prize?* "On second thought, may I use your bathroom?"

Dorothy removed a two-quart bottle of orange juice from the refrigerator, unscrewed the cap, took a swig, and then said, "Down the hall. First door on the left."

I opened the door slowly à la little Dorothy Gale after Toto and she plunged into Munchkinland. But there was a big difference. Little Dorothy was greeted by the sight and scent of fresh flowers. I was greeted by the sight of a filthy rug that hugged the toilet and the scent of years-old urine. Big Dorothy's bathroom was the grossest I'd ever seen. If it were a gas station bathroom, the health department would shut it down. But nature was calling. I checked for toilet paper. Surprise, surprise, there was a full roll. Probably because Dorothy didn't use toilet paper. Yuck. I squatted over the toilet seat so my precious buttocks wouldn't come near the same surface as Dorothy's blubbery butt. *Ah, blessed relief.* I stepped to the stained sink to wash my hands. I turned the cold-water knob. No water. I turned the hot-water knob. No water. I opened the cabinet to the sink and discovered there were no pipes. Instead, the area was stuffed with trash and rags. I quickly wiped my hands on my slacks and exited the stinking hellhole. When I entered the living room, Dorothy was still standing at the opened refrigerator door.

"Want any of my *special* juice?" Dorothy winked and held up the bottle as if to entice me.

"No thanks," I said. "I'm good."

"Well," Dorothy said as she returned the bottle to the refrigerator, "you said I was fascinating." Then she moved her huge muumuu-clad body to the living room chair and plopped.

And she's down.

She motioned for me to sit on the couch and said, "Whaddya want to know?"

"Well…" I caught another whiff of cat urine, so I daintily sat on the edge of the couch and prayed the stink wouldn't get on my slacks. "I would like to get your side of the story as to why you killed your boyfriend."

"Why?" Dorothy asked.

"I think you have an interesting story to tell, and I want to help you tell it."

"What makes *you* think the story hasn't been told?" Dorothy gave me the evil eye. Then she pushed her legs out straight, rolled from side to side and, with all her strength, pushed herself upright. Then back to the refrigerator she waddled. This time she returned with the bottle of orange juice.

I waited for Dorothy to get comfortable. Then I said, "For starters—"

"Yeah, I killed him," Dorothy blurted. "Waddabout it?" She took another swig of her special juice. "If you were sixty-something years old and had as many men as me, you'd kill him too. He was a jerk. Just like the rest of them. All he wanted was sex." She gulped more juice. "Oh, I gave him what he wanted, and he pretended to like me. But I knew he was faking. He just wanted to use me."

"Well, hold that thought," I said, hoping Dorothy didn't detect the look of horror and repulsion on my face. "First, I'd like to get some background information about you. You know, like where you were born, where you went to school, stuff like that. Mind if I record our conversation?"

Dorothy squinted at me. "Go ahead. I'm not ashamed. You want me to paint you a picture of my life, well it's not gonna be pretty. Ha! I suspect you won't be able to handle it."

I ignored Dorothy's comment as I took my recorder out of my briefcase and set it on the right-hand corner of the crowded coffee table. I turned it on and said, "Interview with Dorothy Hall, Saturday, September 12, 2015." I leaned back, remaining on the edge of the smelly couch. "Okay, all set."

Dorothy adjusted herself, pretending to be a queen perched on a throne as she straightened her invisible crown. Then she brushed off the front of her stained muumuu and looked at me as if I were a reporter for *60 Minutes*. She took a breath, leaned in to the recorder, and said, "I was born to two *assholes* right here in this house…" She pointed to a room on the other side of the house without taking her eyes off the recorder. "…in that room back there. I had a prissy sister and a bully brother who, to put it lightly, abused me but told me what they did was '*our little secret*.' I went to school, but I'd burn in hell if I told you what I learned there. Let's just say by the time I was eleven, I'd already had sex with my daddy, his buddies, his buddies' sons, the principal of the school, and the gym teacher. My daddy called me his 'little sex toy.' My momma pretended to see no evil. You know, like one of those stupid monkeys." Dorothy covered her eyes, ears, and mouth to illustrate see no evil, hear no evil, and speak no evil.

She sneered, shook her head, and said, "I suspected I wasn't my momma's child, but no one ever talked about it. Anyway, by the time I was twelve, Jack Daniel's was my only friend. Yep, I was a drunken whore. I guess you could say I found my calling early in life."

"All righty then," I said as I bolted off the couch, silently screaming *I've gotta get out of here. I've gotta get out of here.*"

17

"Leaving so soon?" Dorothy said. "I knew it. You can't handle the truth. *A Few Good Men*, right?" Dorothy looked at me, and then laughed, coughed, and gagged so hard she almost threw up.

I had to gather my thoughts. I needed to control the interview, but I wasn't sure how. *Had I bitten off more than I could chew?* I looked around Dorothy's disgusting living room, stalling for time. Against the wall on the other side of the room, I saw a sofa table. I walked toward it. The closer I got, the worse it looked. It was marred and scratched as if someone had attacked it with a knife. *Now that's distressed wood.* Positioned on top were seven dusty pictures of what appeared to be seven different babies. I picked up the first picture on the left side of the table. *That's one ugly baby.* I looked at it, hoping the baby would get better looking. My mother used to say there was no such thing as an ugly baby. Well, she'd never seen this one.

"Antoinette, Bernard, Catrina, Dwayne, Emily, Freda, and George," Dorothy said from her throne, jolting me back to reality. "That's all of them. All my babies. Seven of them and six different fathers. I know that makes me sound like trash, but it's not true. I'm not trash. I was just hoping to better myself. I thought bringing babies into the world made me a good person. After all, isn't that what a woman's uterus is for? Doesn't the Bible say—" Dorothy hesitated and cleared her throat. Then, as if using the voice of God, she said, "Go forth and multiply?"

Dorothy removed the cap from her orange juice and stared into space as if lost in deep thought. Then she continued. "I held out hope one of the babies' fathers would love me. But I guess I'm just plain unlovable. Nobody loved me when I was a baby. Nobody loved me when I was a smart-mouthed kid. And nobody loves me as a full-grown woman. Not even my children. At least not the ones who know me," she said and then took a large gulp of her special juice.

"Would you tell me about your kids?" I asked, hoping to reveal Dorothy's motherly, loving side, assuming she had one.

Dorothy gulped more orange juice. Then she got up and, clutching her precious bottle of juice, walked over to where I stood. As she leaned toward the table, her right arm brushed my left arm. I shivered. Goose bumps popped up all over me. My scalp itched. I looked at Dorothy to see if she had grown devil horns. I pulled away, pretending to examine another picture. I felt as if I'd been touched by the devil himself. Every nerve in my body screamed. I almost took a swig of Dorothy's special juice to get them to stop.

Dorothy picked up a picture, sneered, and said, "Baby number one, Antoinette, Toni for short. Bullheaded, ugly girl. And I mean ugly inside and out. Wanna know why?"

CHAPTER FIVE

D OROTHY GAZED AT THE PICTURE of baby number one for a few seconds. Then she did something I'll never forget and that burned any hope she was the motherly type. She tilted back her head, made a snorting, guttural noise, and hawked a loogie on the picture of little Toni.

She laughed.

I gagged.

Then she said, "Don't know how she did it, but she got married young—sixteen years young. Had a brood of children too—ten in all. Can't for the life of me imagine why some man would want to bed her. Yikes. You know what they say: put a bag over her head and say you did it for glory." Dorothy saluted the picture of little Toni. Then she cackled.

I watched her, paralyzed with disbelief as to her behavior. Dorothy turned, put her face so close to mine I thought she was trying to kiss me. Her black eyes oozed disgust.

Her voice echoed with pure evilness when she said, "Even with all her mothering experience, she wasn't any better a mother than me."

Dorothy pulled away from me.

I nearly fainted from relief.

As she wiped the blob of spit and mucus off the picture with her muumuu, she said, "I was the worst mother ever. I have six children who'd swear to that." Dorothy paused a moment, put the picture on the table, and walked back to her chair.

The lingering putrid smell of rotten teeth, orange juice, and whiskey made me gag. I kept my distance at the table as I watched Dorothy plop her gargantuan butt in her chair.

"Oh, Toni's kids weren't taken away from her like mine were," Dorothy continued, "but she still wasn't any better at mothering. All but one of her kids grew up to hate her, as did mine. You know what they say: the fruit doesn't fall far from the tree."

That comment put Dorothy in the throes of hysteria. She laughed. She coughed. She wheezed. Her blubber shook. Her face turned beet red. She looked like a heart attack waiting to happen. I ignored her, but secretly I hoped she was suffering.

"Why was Toni taken away from you?" I asked, half-afraid to hear the answer and wondering if Dorothy was right about my not being able to handle the truth.

"Like I said, Toni was ugly inside and out. I can't stand ugly. Not an ugly face and not ugly deeds. She wasn't even a cute baby. And to top it off, all she did was cry all day and all night. Always throwing tantrums to get her way. One day when she was about three years old, I beat her crying behind with a belt. I was just trying to get her to shut up 'cause she was keeping me awake all night." Dorothy grinned and patted her hair. "I need my beauty sleep, you know. Anyway, I guess I swung the belt a little too hard. Little Ugly Toni was trying to get away from me, and the damn buckle hit her in the face. Caused a huge, gaping hole."

I gasped. Memories surfaced of the time when my mother tried to whup me with a paddleball racket. One light tap on my butt and the paddle split in half. We laughed ourselves silly as I promised to never disobey my mother again. The thought of being hit with the buckle end of a belt at any age, let alone in the face at three years old, made me sick. My gut told me Dorothy had only just begun to tell her horror stories.

"You okay there, pumpkin?" Dorothy asked.

"I'm fine," I said. "Just got lost on a trip down memory lane, that's all." *Did Dorothy just call me pumpkin? Was she patronizing me? Oh my God, she has motherly feelings for me. God help me.*

"Okay," Dorothy said. Then she swallowed more of her magic potion. "Anyway… I took the little brat to the hospital. And guess what? She told the nurse I hit her. Next thing I knew, I was trotted off to the police station and fingerprinted, got a mug shot, and eventually went home alone. But one good thing came of it. I never had to look at Toni's ugly face again, at least not until she was twenty-four. That's when she had the nerve to come and tell me she hated me. Boy, she was still ugly." Dorothy looked away. A few seconds later, she leaned into the recorder and said, "I don't give a rat's ass what that liar thinks of me. I don't want to talk about her anymore."

"Okay," I said. I wondered if I'd entered *The Twilight Zone*. My energy drained. I had just enough left to pick up the picture of baby number two.

CHAPTER SIX

I COULDN'T TELL IF IT was a boy or a girl, but at least it was cute. The beautiful baby had the saddest yet most captivating eyes I'd ever seen. I wanted to cry. I put the photo back on the table and turned to face Dorothy.

"Let's see, after Toni was gone, along came Bernard. Baby number two. Cute kid but what a nuisance. Could never sit still. Took after his daddy. Looked like his daddy too." Dorothy tilted her head back and closed her eyes.

This is it. She's having the big one. Please God, make it fast.

"Big, tall guy with black curly hair and the bluest eyes ever." Dorothy's voice softened and took on a dreamy quality. "He was a charmer. I'll never forget Bern's daddy, Wallace. Hated to be called Wally. Always had to call him Wallace like he was more sophisticated than everyone else." Dorothy snapped her head forward and rolled her eyes upward, à la Regan in the movie *The Exorcist*. "Anyway…" She sat up straight, clutched her bottle of magic juice, glared at me, and said, "Wallace had wandering eyes, hands, and other parts. Couldn't keep a damn thing in his pants. Not his privates. Not his money. Not his key to his house. Nothing. But still, he may be the only man I ever loved. Hmm. Hmm. That man was good in the sack."

Visualizing Dorothy in bed with a man made me ill. I slunk back to the couch to avoid passing out and making a fool of myself. Dorothy watched me. I thought she shook her head with disgust, but maybe she was just lost in memories of her last romp with Wallace.

"Didn't stay around." Dorothy interrupted the silence. "Took off as soon as I told him I was pregnant. Anyway, baby number two, Bern, or Sad Sack as I called him, was taken from me when he was just six months old. Some damn fool reported I hit him in the grocery store. All that baby did was cry and whimper." Dorothy raised the bottle of OJ to her mouth and, without taking a sip, lowered it and placed it on the coffee table. Then she leaned into the recorder and said, "Who wouldn't hit him? He knew better. I must have told him a thousand times to *shut up,* and he never paid me no never mind." Bottle of OJ in hand, Dorothy tilted her head back and took several gulps.

Be careful what you wish for. Jim's warning echoed in my head.

Dorothy slammed the bottle on the table and wiped her mouth with the back of her hand. "Social services tracked down his daddy and gave the little crybaby to his daddy's sister. I heard Sad Sack kept running away 'cause nobody treated him right. Wah, wah, wah. Ran away for the last time when he was seventeen to join the Army. He was doing well. Rising in the ranks as they say. Then he got killed in the Middle East. Poor sucker. He was always running. I thought he was running from me but ended up he was running from himself. Well, he ran himself all the way to some foreign country and got killed. Barely lived before he died. I didn't cry a tear though. Knew it was best for him. Sad, restless soul. If the Afghan idiots hadn't killed him, he would've killed himself. He tried lots of times, but he wasn't good at anything, including suicide. Always had to get others to do things for him. Pathetic. Hell, he should have asked me. I would've put him out of his misery."

Whoa! Did I hear what I thought I heard? Dorothy would kill her own child?

"Ha! Isn't that what a mother's for? I didn't want my little one to suffer." Dorothy picked up her bottle of juice, took another swig, and mumbled, "Wallace, where are you when I need you? Hmm. Hmm."

Oh, God! She just admitted she would have killed her son, and all she can think of is frolicking with Wallace? I got what felt like a hot flash. I needed some air. I needed water. I needed to run like my hair was on fire. Nonetheless, I sat on the stinking couch, looking unfazed by the craziness that came out of Dorothy's mouth.

Dorothy nestled in her chair, a bottle of super juice in hand, and said, "Next came Catrina, baby number three."

I was still stuck on poor Bern. I couldn't believe Dorothy thought killing her son was a motherly thing to do. My thoughts were scrambled. *I'm talking to the devil.* I was tongue-tied. I decided to just let her talk.

CHAPTER SEVEN

"I WAS PREGGERS WITH CAT when Bern the Sad Sack was taken from me," Dorothy continued and stopped.

Damn, this woman breeds like a rabbit, but a rabbit would take better care of its babies.

Dorothy leaned forward, elbows on knees, head cupped in hands, and said, "You know… I never had more than one child with me at a time. It's not good for a mother to be without her kids. Seems each one was always taken away while I was preggers with the next brat."

Dorothy looked up and stared me straight in the eyes. The sensation of ice water flowing through my veins caused me to shudder.

"What a hoot," she said. "Those damn social workers were dumb as shit."

Ooh, she cursed. Why am I shocked? Did I actually think she was beyond profanity? Am I really that naïve? I felt like laughing. Instead, I rubbed my temples.

Dorothy shot up straight in her chair and said, "What's wrong? All this truth giving you a headache?"

"No, no," I said. "Just didn't get much sleep last night." *And now I'm living a nightmare.*

"Well, back to me. I mean back to Cat. Don't know where Cat got her red hair. Must have come from her daddy's side. Never knew her daddy well. Just well enough to get knocked up with Cat after a six-pack of beer and a one-night stand. Can't even remember her daddy's face, so I'm sure not gonna remember his name. Cat was just plain stupid. I guess she was nice enough, just *stupid*. If she'd had any sense, she'd still be here with me, but nooo, stupid is as stupid does. *Forrest Gump*, right?"

"Yes," I whispered.

"What? Speak up, girl," Dorothy shouted. "You're never gonna be a success if you don't speak up. Folks gotta hear you."

I returned Dorothy's comment with a smile. *She has the nerve to give me lessons in success. She's got to be kidding.*

"When Cat was four," Dorothy continued, "a nosy neighbor filed a complaint with Child Protective Services about how dirty she was. Liar! Cat wasn't any dirtier than normal kids. Then Cat told the damn nincompoop of a social worker that she'd never had a bath or had her hair washed. Well"—Dorothy slapped her thigh—"is that my problem? She was old enough to take her own bath. Fact was she was just too plain stupid to figure it out herself. She thought I was gonna do it for her. Spoiled brat. Cat the Brat. Cat the Brat. Cat the Brat."

Dorothy's chant chilled me to the bone. I wanted to grab my recorder and run to the comforting arms of my momma. But I knew Dorothy hadn't answered my original question, so I decided to stick it out.

"That's what I called her. Then she went and stole some food from some other kid. When the kid's mother asked her why she did it, Cat the Brat said she didn't have food at home. Liar!" Dorothy screamed into the recorder.

I flinched.

"Scared you there, didn't I, sweetie?" Dorothy grinned and took another swig of juice from the almost-empty bottle. "She could have fixed herself something to eat. She was just too damn lazy. Always wanted me to do everything for her. How was Cat gonna learn if she didn't do anything herself?" Dorothy paused as if she expected me to comment.

I managed a shrug.

"Well, the only thing she learned to do well was lying. She lied so good it got her put in an orphanage. Heard she grew up to be a real prissy pants—always buying expensive clothes, getting her nails and hair done. Even went to college. I guess some of my smarts wore off on her after all."

I nodded my head in support. I couldn't believe I placated this madwoman. I felt myself shutting down. I felt like a captive. I wanted Dorothy to like me. I didn't want her to hurt me. Can you say Stockholm syndrome?

Dorothy glanced at me as if I were the crazy one in the room. Then she continued with her rant about Cat the Brat. "Married a rich guy who could buy her everything—fancy cars, jewelry, vacations to far-off places. Well, la-di-da. It's not as if I didn't give her what she needed. She was just so uppity—thought she deserved the good things in life. Well, I hope the little brat is happy now."

One more swig. The bottle was now empty. *Thank God, maybe she'll sober up in a little while.* It took great effort for Dorothy to raise her drunken body out of her chair. I watched. I was amused and saddened at the same time. Then she lumbered into the kitchen, placed the empty juice bottle on the counter, shuffled over to the refrigerator, opened the door, and pulled out another. *Oh my God. She's got a stash of that stuff. I hope she doesn't pass out before I get my story.*

Lost in my thoughts, I didn't notice Dorothy had wandered back and plopped herself in her chair. I was shocked back to reality when she said, "Had the nerve to hunt me down a few years ago and tell me what a lousy mother I was."

"Who?" I asked.

"Cat the Brat. Stay with the program. Damn, you're never gonna get my story right. I should call the paper and ask for another reporter."

"I'm sorry. I just wanted to make sure I got my facts straight. I wouldn't want to misquote you," I said, trying to sound professional.

"Ha! You think I'm stupid? You're recording this. Just play the damn tape, nitwit. Anyway, I don't have time for this conversation."

Oh no, she was ready to quit! I've completely lost control here. My Pulitzer just flew out the window.

"Cat the Brat never had kids, so how would she know if I was a good mother or not?" Dorothy continued, much to my relief. "I wonder if her rich, fat-ass husband knows she's a liar and a stealer. I'd love to tell him the truth about her." Dorothy stopped. She took a deep breath, appeared calm. "Oh well, enough about Cat the Brat."

My temples throbbed. *How could this woman be so angry one second and so calm the next?* I didn't know if I could mentally, emotionally, or physically handle four more stories about Dorothy's children. I had opened a can of worms, and they were crawling all over me.

"Baby number four was Dwayne," Dorothy said.

I fought the urge to bang my head on the coffee table.

CHAPTER EIGHT

"HE CAME ALONG A FEW months after Cat the Brat left. I called him Dwayne the Pain. The most demanding child you ever met. Thought he was a prince or something. It's amazing, but he always cared how he looked, even when he was a little tyke. Wouldn't wear clothes that didn't match. And his clothes had to be clean and pressed, or he'd throw a fit. What did he think I was, his maid?"

I'm looking at proof you're no maid. I smiled at Dorothy. At least I thought I did.

"And he'd only wear them once. Must have thought I was made of money. I couldn't afford to keep him in the damn prissy clothes he liked so I didn't put clothes on him." Dorothy tapped her temple with her index finger. "Now that's using your noodle. Figured if I couldn't make him happy, he'd just have to run around naked."

Dorothy chuckled.

I waited in horrified silence.

"Well, one day it snowed real hard, piled up fast. Dwayne the Pain insisted he had to go out and play in the damn stuff. But he wouldn't wear his snowsuit 'cause it was a girl's one. You know, a hand-me-down from one of his sisters. You wore hand-me-downs, didn't you?"

I shook my head to answer yes. It was a lie. I'm an only child. I decided to keep that tidbit to myself.

"Anyway, I shoved the brat out the door buck naked. He screamed his stupid head off. Nearly woke the dead. I laughed my ass off. Wouldn't you know, the same nosy SOB neighbor called Child Protective Services and had me arrested for child neglect and abuse. Whatever. Yep, he was taken and placed in foster care. He was three or four. Never kept track of his age. I know he wasn't in school yet. Saw him about five years ago when he came to tell me how much he hated me. He looked damn good. Still a snappy dresser. Mmm. Mmm. I'm proud to say my boy turned out to be a successful businessman. Owns a chain of men's clothing stores. See, I done good. And people tell me I was a lousy mother."

"Baby number five," Dorothy said. "Ah, skip her. I'll move on to baby number six."

I opened my mouth to protest, but Dorothy started talking.

CHAPTER NINE

"**B**ABY NUMBER SIX, FRICKING FREDA. Know why I called her Freda?" Dorothy asked, looking at me with teasing eyes.

"No," I said, trying to recover from the fact Dorothy would refer to a baby as fricking anything. But really, why was I surprised?

Dorothy chuckled and said, "You're gonna love this. I called baby number six Freda 'cause her daddy and I were watching *The Flintstones* when she was conceived. Isn't that a riot?" Dorothy snickered and gulped her tainted OJ. "I heard Wilma say, 'Oh Fred, here we go again,' just as Vernon came. The line stuck in my head, so when the baby was fighting its way out my love chute, I said, 'Oh Fred, here we go again.'"

Dorothy took a gulp of her OJ and laughed so hard the juice squirted out her nose. I didn't think she could disgust me any more than she already had. I was wrong. Dorothy swept OJ and snot off the front of her muumuu, splashing some on my recorder. I thought I'd die. I made a mental note to wipe off the recorder before I put it in my briefcase. The thought of touching something that came out of Dorothy's repulsive body disgusted me. I wish I had my beloved Lysol wipes.

Dorothy didn't skip a beat. "That's when I decided to call the baby Fred if it was a boy and Freda if it was a girl. Well, it was another damn girl. Worse, damn Freda looked just like baby number five. I was pissed. How dare she look like the baby who was stupid enough to get stolen from me?"

"Stolen?" I perked up and sat forward. "Someone kidnapped your baby?"

"Yep, that's the right word. It was the police who kidnapped my baby," Dorothy said.

"Baby number five?"

"Yep." An odd sound like a giggle rose from the depths of Dorothy's sternum. Then in a fake Australian accent, she said, "'The dingo ate my baby.' Elaine. *Seinfeld*, right?"

I nodded in agreement. *Lucky baby number five.* Then the movie *The Wizard of Oz* popped into my head for the third time that day. "He got away. He got away," little Dorothy cried as Toto escaped from the castle of the Wicked Witch of the West. My exact sentiments for baby number five. *She got away. She got away.*

Dorothy screamed at me. "I already told you I don't want to talk about baby number five." Then she glared at me as if she wanted to tell me something. I thought I saw her eyes turn red. "Fuhgeddaboudit," she said. Then she grinned. "Tony Soprano, right?"

"Riiiiight," I said. *Is Dorothy trying to impress me with her knowledge of movie and TV trivia? Well, it's not working.* Her ability to switch moods and topics scared the hell out of me.

"I hated that damn Fricking Freda from the moment I set eyes on her. Attitude. That's what it was. Pissed me off. Like I said, she looked like baby number five. I swear Fricking Freda was impersonating her sister. If she was trying to make me mad, well, it worked. I got so pissing angry that I pinched her—all over her little soft body. Fricking Freda screamed until her precious little face turned beet red. Some damn stupid nurse came in the room and saw me pinching the little bitch. She tried to grab Freda from me. But I wouldn't let go. Freda wouldn't shut up. The nurse screamed at me, 'Give me the baby.' I told her the baby was mine and she'd have to cut off my arms to get it away from me. Damn nurse screamed until a whole bunch of people ran into the room. I stuffed Fricking Freda under the covers and put my legs on top of her. Freda didn't make a peep. She knew what she was doing. She knew if she stayed real quiet, the nurse would think I was trying to protect her. She wanted to go home with me, I could tell. It's just instinct for a baby to want its momma. Next thing I knew, I was pulled off the bed by some burly orderly and the crazy nurse. As they yanked me off the bed, Fricking Freda fell on the floor." Dorothy leaned toward the recorder again and yelled, "Now who's the dumb-ass?" Then she leaned back into the comfort of her chair and said, "The stupid nurse and the orderly dropped my Freda. I screamed and cried for my baby. 'Freda, my precious, Momma will save you. Come to Momma, baby girl.' Next thing I knew, I was hauled off to the psych ward. Whew! There are some real crazies in there. I can't believe they didn't put that screaming nurse in there with me. What a nutcase. I guess someone as smart as you can figure out that Fricking Freda didn't go home with me. I had to sign her over to her daddy's sister. Another stupid move—giving her to a wacko alcoholic. She turned Freda against me. I used to see the child now and then, but Freda acted like she was scared to death of me. Hell, I didn't do anything to her. I barely knew her. That was until she dropped by earlier this year. I was happy to see her, as any loving mother would be to see her long-lost baby. She told me she'd talked to her siblings, as she called them. What a snoot. Evidently, they told her what I'd done to them. She ripped me a new one. Fricking Freda had the nerve to say I was the most evil person in the world. She's damn lucky I didn't slap her. I just laughed in her face. What was I supposed to do?"

"I don't know." *Slit your wrists. Choke to death. Fall down a flight of stairs and break your big, thick neck.* "Sounds like you did all you could."

"Well, thank you," Dorothy said and nodded her head as if to honor my good sense. "Now we're up to baby number seven. Georgie Porgie, Puddin' and Pie, kissed the girls and made them cry." Dorothy laughed and snorted.

CHAPTER TEN

"TRIED TO ABORT THE LITTLE bastard, but he wouldn't come out. He nearly bled me to death and had the nerve to force me to carry him full-term. Nearly grossed me out on account of who his father was." Dorothy leaned forward and yelled into the recorder. "A rapist, that's what he was." Then she relaxed into her chair and continued, "Yes, Georgie's father raped me. That's where the brat came from. That man raped me for years, ever since I was a little girl. He must've been about sixty-five years old, and he could still get it up with the best of them except he wasn't the best by any means. I should know. I've had nearly all the men around these parts. I've even had a few important ones. Never had any babies by them though. The important ones are always impotent. Dorothy slapped her thigh. "Whoa, that's funny. Don't you think?"

I was beyond answering her crazy questions. Like this self-absorbed nut would notice.

"Anywho, Georgie's daddy raped me while I was coming home from the bar after a gang bang with some guys. Made them all use condoms. That's how I knew Georgie was his. He said he was mad I didn't invite him in for the party. Raped me behind the bushes at the church. That man had no couth. Next thing I knew, I was knocked up again. Gave birth to Georgie at home because I was too drunk to get to the hospital. He was scrawny, and his skin was all wrinkled and dark. Looked more like a monkey than a baby. They say drinking affects a baby. I'll drink to that." Dorothy winked at me, raised her bottle of magic juice, said cheers, then took a big gulp. She smacked her lips and smiled at me.

I wasn't amused.

Dorothy didn't notice.

"Believe it or not, Georgie Porgie was another screamer. But I knew how to shut him up. I put whiskey in his bottle. He loved it. When he had his fill, he'd sleep for an entire day. Blessed relief. When Georgie was about four months old, I took his sorry little ass to the grocery store. I propped him in the cart, but he was so drunk he kept falling over. That same nosy neighbor looked in the cart and smiled at him. I swear that woman was spying on me. I'll never forget what the bitch said. She said, 'Your baby is ill.' I said, 'No he's not, he's drunk.' She bent over to take a closer look and smelled booze on the little brat. Would you believe that bitch had the nerve to grab my baby boy and not give him back to me? She kept him. But I didn't care. After all, the brat was no use to me, so I let her have him. Then her husband raised the boy as his own. Had no idea he was raising the son of a rapist." Dorothy laughed, then silenced herself with another long drink of her spiked juice.

"Who was the woman who kept your baby?"

"I'm not telling you that. Stop asking questions that are none of your business."

I ignored Dorothy's attempt to silence me and asked another question. "You said the woman's husband raised Georgie. How come she didn't raise him?"

"Get your nose out of my business."

"Did you ever see him again?"

"I don't want to talk about it. I thought you came to interview me about me killing my boyfriend, and you changed the subject and let me rattle on. You're a lousy reporter. I bet the newspaper sent you…" Dorothy leaned forward and sneered at me. "…'cause you're their worst reporter."

I stared at Dorothy. With one sentence, she'd totally disarmed me. She'd gotten right to my core. My confidence was in the gutter. I was at her mercy.

Dorothy's black eyes oozed hatred. Or was it fear? Yes, she was posturing. I refused to back off. "Okay, I'm the world's worst reporter talking with the world's best mom." I glared back at Dorothy, refusing to break eye contact, intent on gaining control. "So tell me about your boyfriend."

"Who? Bull? Bullshit is what I call him." Dorothy stuck out her tongue, shook her shoulders, and said, "Yuck, talking about him leaves a nasty taste in my mouth. Whaddya want to know?"

I jumped in like Barbara Walters interviewing Monica Lewinsky. "You just said you didn't want to talk about Bull. Then in a nanosecond, you change your mind? Why is that?"

"I don't know. Maybe I'm crazy."

"You can say that again." *Oops. Did I say that out loud?*

"Whaddya say?"

"Nothing. Where did you meet Bull?"

Dorothy leered at me. I feared she was going to press me about my rude, sassy remark. Then she looked away and focused her gaze on the floor. "The first time I met Bull was three years ago in a bar."

Whew! She's going to let it go.

"We were both drunk and took a liking to each other mighty fast." Dorothy lifted her head, looked at me, arched her eyebrows, and grinned. "Know what I mean?"

"Um, no. Tell me about it," I said, feeling confident I was getting this interviewing thing down pat.

"First time we did it was right there at the bar." Dorothy grinned, lost in thought as if she were recollecting happy thoughts. "Couldn't believe nobody knew what we were up to. He was sitting in a chair. I pulled up my dress and straddled his lap, face-to-face. We started kissing. He rubbed my boobs, and I rubbed his dick. Then I whispered in his ear. 'It's yours for the taking.' Of course, I didn't have panties on. He unzipped his pants, and away we went." Dorothy moaned and pumped herself up and down in her chair.

She outdid herself this time. She's truly nuts. I wanted to yell "enough," grab my recorder and run. But I stayed.

"I'm almost sorry he's dead." Dorothy paused, lost in memories. "Anyway, we became a couple. We were happy. Almost like young love. After a few months, he changed. He was always drunk. Not that

I wasn't, but he was a mean drunk. That's when he'd rape me. He raped me every day, sometimes several times a day. Told me he did it 'cause he loved me. Then one day, after he was done doing what he did best, I realized I'd never asked him his last name."

"You dated Bull, and you didn't ask him his last name?"

"Well, it wasn't like we did much talking. Know what I mean?"

Silly me.

"So, one day I asked him his last name. He proudly told me his name was George Jordan, but people called him Bull. I nearly puked. I asked him if his daddy was Dan Jordan. He said, 'Hell yeah. You know my daddy?'"

Holy crapoli! Dan Jordan is the name of the man who raised George as his own? The plot thickens.

"What's up, pumpkin? You know Dan Jordan?"

"No."

"Oh, okay. As I was saying, Bull said, 'You know my daddy?' I said, 'Hell yeah, I know your daddy.' Then I looked him straight in the eyes and said, 'And I know your momma too.' He looked at me like a stupid puppy dog and said, 'You know my momma?' That was it, I lost it."

Dorothy rose from her chair with unusual energy and paced the room. I wasn't sure what had upset her. She gulped her OJ. I noticed the bottle was half-empty. She had consumed a bottle and a half of her magic potion. Then she turned to me and yelled, "I'm your momma, you stupid shit."

I nearly jumped off the couch. I thought Dorothy was telling me she was my mother. I gasped, trying to calm myself.

"Well," she said, her voice softer, her pace slower, "he just stared at me. I couldn't stand the dumb-ass look on his face."

Thank God. This wasn't about me. Then it hit me, Bull, her twenty-five-year-old boyfriend, was her son.

CHAPTER ELEVEN

DOROTHY WALKED OR, MORE CORRECTLY, stumbled back to her chair. She made an awkward turn and fell into its arms. I couldn't believe the chair didn't collapse under the weight of her gargantuan body.

"That's when… Pa… I mean I picked up the poker and beat the living hell out of him." Dorothy's head flopped back. She closed her eyes. "I don't know what came over me," Dorothy said as if she were half-asleep, "but I called 911 and told them my boyfriend raped and beat me and he was in the kitchen getting a knife to kill me with. They tried to keep me on the phone."

A moment of silence passed. *Don't pass out on me now. You're finally spilling the beans.*

Suddenly, her eyes popped open. She licked her parched lips and sat up. "But I'm not stupid," she said, practically yelling. "I hung up. Then I panicked. If I was to plead self-defense, I'd have to look beat up. You know, bruised and bloody. So I beat myself with the poker. Damn thing hurt. Then I decided to light a cigarette and burned my arms, legs, and stomach with it. Did it a lot when I was a teen, so I was used to it. Barely tingled. Then I decided to cut myself with a knife. I was just getting ready to slash myself when the police arrived.

They burst in. Guns drawn. How dramatic." Dorothy rolled her eyes. "You would have thought I was starring in an episode of *Miami Vice*."

My head was spinning. I couldn't keep up with what Dorothy was saying. I hoped the recorder was catching it all.

"You remember *Miami Vice*, don't you?"

"I think it was before my time," I said, yet I had a feeling I'd seen an episode or two at some point.

"Hell, you don't know anything."

"Like I said, it was before my time." *Why was I arguing with this woman?*

"All the good stuff was before your time. Nothing but crap today. Yeah, you look like you're a product of crap," Dorothy said as she snatched the TV remote.

Why am I taking this from a crazy woman? Am I desperate?

Click.

Hum.

Buzz.

Snow.

My attention was drawn to Dorothy's ancient, dusty, dirty TV perched in a dark corner like a spy. It was a piece of crap older than I was. The static from the TV was irritating, to say the least. I looked over at Dorothy, hoping she knew how to stop the madness. She now had a second remote in her hand. She aimed it at the TV as if she were Captain Kirk, ready to zap it with a phaser. *Phaser on stun. Ha! Dorothy doesn't know I've seen every episode of every* Star Trek. *Who am I kidding? I've memorized every episode of* Star Trek. *I loved Captain Kirk, but Jean-Luc Picard was my favorite Starfleet captain. Think I'll keep it my little secret.*

Dorothy punched the VHS remote button for the umpteenth time. Finally, it kicked on. To my horror, I saw a cartoon image of a donkey's mouth. It screeched, "Hee-haw." Dorothy laughed and fast-forwarded the tape.

"You'll love this," she said as she stopped the tape. She pressed the Play button. Now I was staring at two men dressed in overalls, looking like two hillbillies, both deadpan, singing some silly song about finding love and losing it. They ended the song by blowing raspberries, which sent Dorothy into hysterical laughter. But there was something different about her laughter. It was genuine. Was it possible I was witness to a rare moment of happiness for Dorothy? I felt sorry for her. She was a bitter woman who only experienced joy if she could live in a world that no longer existed.

"Now that's real entertainment. Not reality-show crap." Dorothy pointed the remote at the TV and said, "That's real talent. And real talent is timeless."

Click.

Pop.

Silence.

The TV returned to obscurity.

"Now what were we talking about?" Dorothy asked.

"We were talking about your *Miami Vice* rescue after you killed Bull."

"Right. Maybe you're not such a dipshit after all." Dorothy gulped her OJ, dousing any warm fuzzies I had for her. "Well, back to my big rescue," Dorothy said as she tossed both remotes on the coffee table. "I couldn't believe my eyes; damn 911 sent an old, decrepit Barney Fife to save me. I almost laughed. He must have been eighty years old. You know who Barney Fife is, don't you?"

I shrugged. "Name rings a bell." *Why was I goading her? I knew who Barney Fife was. Maybe I was crazy.*

"Mayberry, you nitwit. Mayberry. Heck, sometimes this stupid town is like Mayberry." Dorothy looked at me, waiting for a response. I didn't know what to say, so I kept quiet. She dismissed me with a wave and continued. "Another cop went to check on Bull while my hero came over to me. What a damn fricking idiot. The moron thought I was trying to kill myself. I thought, now there's an idea. So I pretended I was going to slit my throat and wrists. The old bastard tried to wrestle the knife away from me. I kept pleading with him, 'Let me kill myself. I can't believe I killed the only man I ever loved. I killed my love. I can't live without him. I want to die.' I put on an award-winning performance. Hand me my Oscar—"

Dorothy picked up a flashlight off the floor next to her chair, and pretending it was a microphone, she said, "I'd like to thank my mother for beating the shit out of me when I was a kid, my father for teaching me about man-woman kind of love, my brother for teaching me not to cry while his little friends had their way with me, and of course, all the teachers who turned their backs on my bruised body and tearstained face, my minister for telling me Jesus loved me when I knew he didn't, and last but not least, Jack Daniel's for making me what I am today—a drunk, whoring murderer."

Dorothy stopped and took a seated bow. She returned the flashlight to the floor, raised her head, and said, "That damn policeman actually seemed to care whether I lived or died. Something about him made me stop. He wrapped a blanket around my shoulders and escorted me to the police car. He said, 'I'm sorry to have to do this, ma'am.' Can you believe it? Someone calling me ma'am? Then he said, 'But I have to take you to the station for questioning.' For the first time in my life, I felt safe. There I was at the police station with Barney Fife serving me a cup of coffee like I was the queen of England. The old cop's kindness softened me, and I answered all his stupid questions. I told Barney that Bull was my boyfriend and I killed him in self-defense. I said I didn't know anything about him. All I knew was I met him in a bar and I thought he loved me. Then he started abusing me, and one thing led to another and before I knew it, he was trying to kill me. I told them Bull threw me down on the floor and was on top of me, raping me and beating me, and I reached for the poker and hit him with it. Then I put my hands together like I was praying. I cried and said, 'I didn't mean to hurt him, Lord. I didn't mean for him to die.' Then I looked up as if I was looking to heaven and said, 'Bull, Bull, I love you.' What a bunch of bullshit. And that old coot of a cop swallowed it hook, line, and sinker. He thanked me for my time and told me he'd take me to a doctor to look at my injuries. Well, I'm not stupid. You think he would've known that, but I went along with his little charade."

"Did they read you your rights?" I asked.

"What?" Dorothy snapped.

"Your Miranda rights. Did they tell you that you had the right to remain silent?" *Like that's possible.* "That anything you said could and would be used against you in a court of law? That you had the right to an attorney, and if you couldn't afford an attorney, one would be provided for you? Did they ask you if you understood your rights? And did the officer—"

"Barney."

"Did Barney ask you if you wanted to tell him your story?"

"Of course. Do you think I was stupid enough to blabber on if he hadn't?"

"Was a lawyer present?"

"No."

"Why not?"

"I don't need a damn lawyer. I had the judge by the short hairs. He'd never let me stand trial."

"Why not?"

"'Cause I would've revealed the ugly secrets about his lovely wife."

"What about her?"

"Keep your nose out of my business."

"Okay," I said. *Dorothy jabbered on about her children's horror stories and murdering Bull, but she didn't want to discuss the judge's wife. Hmm. What's that about?*

"A lady cop and Barney took me to a doctor. Suspicious man. Kept asking me, 'Exactly how did you get these bruises?' And I kept telling him, 'My boyfriend beat me with his fists while he was raping me.' The doctor looked into my eyes with one of those things and said, 'Hmm. Hmm.' Then he looked over my body like I was a prize pig and said, 'Hmm. Hmm.' I swear he was the coldest man I ever met. I'd been through a trauma, and he didn't even acknowledge my pain. I would've killed him too if it weren't for his prissy nurse, who turned out to be his darling wife, being in the room. Then I was taken back to the police station and put in this little room with nothing but a hard chair and a card table."

"Did the doctor do a vaginal exam?" I asked.

"For what?"

"To check for tissue trauma and semen. To prove you were raped."

"What the hell is wrong with you? I had bruises all over me. It was obvious I'd been raped. And what the doctor did or didn't do is none of your damn business."

"I guess that's a no." *Hmm… No routine vaginal exam? Something doesn't add up.*

"You're as bad as that damn female officer who asked me the same damn questions all over again. I wanted to grab her by her hair and swing her around the room. Then she said, 'I just want to get this straight for the record.' I looked at her, but she didn't say anything, so I said, 'Cat got your tongue?' Then the stupid woman said, 'I know this is hard for you, but can you tell me one more time why you killed your boyfriend?' I was so pissing livid. I stood up, threw the chair across the room, and pushed the table into the stupid bitch. Then I got in her face and said, 'I'll tell you once and only once. I had to kill him.' Stupid bitch had the nerve to ask me why. That's when I went into a rage and screamed, ''Cause, it's not right to have sex with your momma. Is it?'"

"No, it isn't," I said. "Are you saying Bull was your son?"

"Well… duh! Yeah, he was my son. And it's not right to have sex with your momma."

No. It's not right. Not right at all.

CHAPTER TWELVE

"WHAT ABOUT DAN JORDAN?" I said, hoping to relieve some tension.

"Whaddabout him?"

"What role does he play in all this?"

"Well, let see, genius. For starters, he was"—Dorothy raised her hands and made the universal sign for quote marks—"'Bull's daddy.'"

"I got that. What I'd like to know is why you spent only a day in jail and why the murder of Bull didn't go to trial? Didn't Dan Jordan, Bull's father, press charges?"

Dorothy's eyes narrowed. Her jaw tightened. "You're a nosy little bitch."

"It's my job. I didn't mean to offend you. Just trying to get the facts."

"Well, if you must know, Dan Jordan is a big man in this small town. If I went to trial for the murder of Bull, some secrets would come to light. So, to make a long story short, the police held me for a day while they figured out how the evidence pointed to self-defense. It's not that complicated, Einstein."

"How big is Dan Jordan?" I asked, immediately regretting the wording of my question.

Dorothy slapped her knees and howled. "You dumb-ass. I don't share information about my men's private parts. I keep it to myself, so to speak."

Was Dorothy insinuating that she'd had sex with Dan Jordan? Was Dan Jordan Bull's biological father? Was Dan Jordan a rapist? I decided it wasn't a good time to probe that line of questioning, so I ignored her sexually loaded response to my awkward question and said, "Who is Dan Jordan?"

"Ever heard of homework? You're supposed to do it before you start asking stupid-shit questions."

"So who is he?" I asked.

"He's the damn judge in these parts. He's the damn judge who took away all my babies." Dorothy fixed her eyes on me as if she were sending me a telepathic message. Then she continued, "And I don't know what happened to baby number five. A mother needs to know what happened to her babies."

Dorothy cried. I silently waited for her to finish. I felt emotionally blunted. She must have sensed my emotional detachment because she looked at me like a hurt puppy, practically begging for me to feel sorry for her. I decided to take advantage of the moment and plow ahead with my questioning. "Okay, we know Dan Jordan raised your son. But why? Was he Bull's real father? Was he the man who raped you?"

"You're barking up the wrong tree, little lady," Dorothy said as she wiped her crocodile tears on her arm. "Dan Jordan isn't a rapist. Matter of fact, he's a fine man."

"Okay… let me get this straight. A man who you called a rapist was Bull's father?"

"Your point would be?" Dorothy said.

"Is that correct?"

"Yes."

"So Dan Jordan was Bull's daddy?"

"If you were listening, you would already know the answer to your dumb-ass question."

"Refresh my memory."

"I said, he *raised* Bull as his own."

"Oh, so that means Dan Jordan is the husband of the woman who stole little Georgie Porgie, Puddin' and Pie from you?"

"Shut up." Dorothy slammed her bottle of OJ on the coffee table, causing my recorder to bounce to the floor. "Just shut up. You're walking on thin ice. I never told you anything of the sort. None of this is any of your business."

I got up to retrieve my recorder. As I bent down to grab it, Dorothy stepped on it. I can't believe I had the guts to push aside her foot, pick up my recorder, place it back on the table, and take my seat on the couch. Dorothy didn't say a word.

"Okay, I'll ask a different question then. Wouldn't want to get too nosy," I said. "Why did Judge Dan Jordan take all your babies from you except for Georgie, who he raised as his own?"

"You're trying my patience. What makes you think you can come into my home and pump me for information that's none of your damn business?"

"Like I said, you have a fascinating story to tell, and I want to help you tell it."

"Smart-ass," Dorothy said.

I held my tongue.

"Okay, I'll let you in on a little secret." Dorothy leaned forward as if to get closer to the recorder. "Dan Jordan owns this house. He bought it after my dear mother died. Dropped dead one morning several years ago. Think she choked on something. Don't really know or care. Daddy died years ago. Rest his pathetic, abusive soul. House looks the same as it did when they lived here. In fact, all this is their stuff." Dorothy surveyed the room and grunted. "Those damn baby pictures aren't mine. Why would I want pictures of a bunch of brats? My loony momma had a soft spot for babies, so she proudly displayed pictures of her beloved grandchildren. It's pretty funny that I'm the only one who had babies. Ha! My evil sister was barren. Hallelujah! There is a God."

Dorothy paused.

I gave her space. Her happy juice was doing the work for me. She rambled on.

"Due to the nastiness that happened in this house, no one would buy it. Just so happened I needed a place to live and Dan needed to hand over a little hush money. Know what I mean?"

"No," I said, deliberately baiting Dorothy.

"You really are a dumb-ass. It's obvious. Dan bought me this house to keep me quiet about his past. He even threatened me. He said if I told anybody the truth about Bull's father, he'd do to me what I did to Bull."

"He threatened to kill you?"

"Echo. Echo. Didn't I just say that?"

"Bribe money?" I said, ignoring Dorothy.

"Well, whaddya know, scarecrow? You have a brain after all."

I waited for Dorothy to say *The Wizard of Oz*, right? But she didn't, so I pressed on. "Bull was murdered in this house?"

Dorothy sneered at me. I swear I heard her growl. Then she said, "Yep, Bull was killed right there." She pointed to an area that divided the living room and dining room. I scanned the carpet for evidence of a brutal murder. The carpeting was filthy, but I didn't see anything that resembled blood. If Bull's blood had been cleaned, the carpet would be less soiled. But the filthiness was consistent with the rest of the carpeting in the living and dining rooms. Something wasn't right with Dorothy's story. Ha! Something wasn't right with Dorothy.

"Damn shame he died in the same house he was born and where I raised my babies."

Raised your babies? You may have pumped them out, but you didn't raise them. Hallelujah! There is a God. "Who in the police department is part of the cover-up?" I asked.

"Cover-up?" Dorothy yelled and leered at me.

I maintained eye contact, knowing if I looked away, I'd be admitting defeat.

"It's a small town," Dorothy said. "You figure it out, smart-ass. I'm not naming names. I'm no fool."

I decided I'd pushed Dorothy far enough for one day. Heck, I'd had more than enough Dorothy for a lifetime. "Well, Dorothy, thanks for talking to me," I said as I reached for my recorder. "It's getting late, and I have a long drive home."

"I'm not done yet," she said.

I released my grip on the recorder and sank back on the couch.

I watched Dorothy struggle to rise from her chair. Miracles will never cease—she managed to lift her drunken butt and balance on her wobbly legs. She stumbled across the room to the sofa table and picked up a picture. Then she turned. Her face twisted as she burped.

Her next three words made my skin crawl.

CHAPTER THIRTEEN

"BABY NUMBER FIVE," DOROTHY SAID as she held out the picture toward me. "Don't have a clue what happened to her. That really bugs me. A mother needs to know what happens to her babies." Dorothy cried.

I got up off the couch and walked over to her. She handed me the picture of baby number five. *Oh... my... God. It can't be.* I stumbled back to the couch to lie down. I no longer cared about the filth and stench. My palms were white. My mouth parched. I broke out in a sweat. Baby number five looked like a living skeleton. But there was something familiar about the baby's emaciated face. Something I didn't want to admit.

"What's the matter? You look like you've seen a ghost."

It took all my energy to answer with a moan.

"Told you baby number six was baby number five's look-alike. Hell, they could've been twins."

Dorothy walked over to the couch. I tried to sit up. I felt paralyzed. Next thing I knew, we were face-to-face. She grinned and snatched the picture from me. Then she went back to her chair.

"I won't go to my grave until I know what happened to my precious little girl. Never saw her after she turned six months old.

Boy, did she and her sister look like their daddy. Vernon was his name. I couldn't stand him. He was a right nice guy, though. I guess that's why I couldn't stand him. What a sissy. Anyway, every time I looked at baby number five, I got the heebie-jeebies. It was like looking at a tiny version of Vernon. That's why I decided I wouldn't look at her. Do you know how hard it is to take care of a baby without looking at it? Can't do it. So I decided to leave her to herself. Anyway, something about her wasn't like a baby at all. She'd lie in her crib and stare at me like she knew something about me even I didn't know... kinda like you're looking at me now. She gave me the creeps. Spooky. Eerie Emmie, that's what I called her.

Please God, make her shut up.

"Eerie Emmie slept a lot, so I can't say I paid much attention to her. Hell, I'd forget she was there. It's amazing she survived. I'd forget to feed her for days. I guess that's why she never grew much. But she had a set of lungs on her. That damn baby would wail till she passed out from exhaustion. One day a police officer walked by the house. He knocked on the door. Emmie was screaming. I couldn't get her to shut up."

I know the feeling.

"Couldn't she see we had company? That's no way to act in front of company. Then the officer asked why the baby was crying so loud. Nosy bastard. I tried to charm him so he'd leave me alone. He asked if he could see the baby. I said no. That was a mistake. He charged in and stormed into the little brat's room. He gasped when he saw the little bitch. Probably from the smell. That stupid baby would piss and poop all over herself. So I stopped feeding her. Stopped the pissing and pooping." Dorothy pointed to her temple with her index finger and said, "Now that's using your noodle." Then she laughed and coughed so hard that her face reddened and her eyes bulged.

I silently watched and secretly hoped she would choke to death this time. She didn't. She rattled on.

"The shithead cop asked me how old she was. I thought he was just being friendly, so I told him the little weird one was six months old. Next thing I knew, he ran out of the house with her. He went to his police car and called for backup. Can you believe he'd think I could hurt a fly? To make a long story short, I was arrested for child endangerment and neglect or something like that. Still don't understand it. I never hurt that damn baby. They tried to make me feel guilty by telling me the baby only weighed seven pounds. For God's sake, she was almost six pounds when she was born. That means she gained more than a pound in six months. Heck, if I gained a pound in six months I'd go on a diet. Wouldn't you?"

I didn't respond. Dorothy didn't notice. *She's got to weigh more than three hundred pounds. She's delusional.* I remained prone on the couch.

"Well, they took Eerie Emmie away. A couple of months later, a dipshit social worker and a lawyer tried to get me to sign adoption papers. Hell no. Emmie was my baby, and no one was going to have her. I refused to sign. I guess she became a ward of the state." Dorothy paused. Her stare unnerved me. "She'd be about your age now."

I felt myself sinking as if the couch were swallowing me. Part of me wished it would. I desperately wanted to escape the depravity of Dorothy Hall.

"Emily's father, Vernon, got wind of her being up for adoption. He was hopping mad about letting someone else raise his baby. He wanted to find her and get her back. Ha! I put a stop to that. If I couldn't have her, what in hell's name made him think he could? So, I sweet-talked him and had sex with him one more time. This is hysterical—after we finished doing the nasty, he started gasping. Dropped straight to the floor. The frigging asshole keeled over and died right in front of me. Poor thing." Dorothy smirked. "Had a heart attack or something. Only thirty-two years old. Never did find out what killed him. Can't say I really care." Dorothy paused, apparently lost in her memories. "Believe it or not, I got knocked up with baby number six. You remember, Freda. You know, you kinda remind me of her. But I guess that's impossible, right?"

I was speechless. Visions of *The Flintstones* raced through my head. I heard Wilma say, "Here we go again, Fred."

"Yo? What's wrong with you? Cat got your tongue?"

"Well…" I raised my head and forced myself to sit up. "… I have a question."

"Shoot."

"Do you remember Emmie's birth date?"

"Duh! A mother always knows her children's birthdays. Toni, the bullheaded, ugly girl was born on January 8, 1970."

Oh my God, she's going to tell me the birth dates of every one of her precious babies. I'm never going to get out of here.

"Bern, Sad Sack as I called him, was born November 6, 1973. Number three, Cat the Brat, October 31, 1974. A Halloween baby. Should've called her my Halloweenie," Dorothy said and laughed. "After Cat the Brat went to live in the orphanage rather than live with me, I pumped out Dwayne the Pain. It was March 16, 1978. Ah, baby number five. Let's see, Emmie was born August 25, 1980. No! That's not right. She was born in June just like... her momma. Yep, June 23, 1981. Then there's—"

"Um, that's okay, Dorothy. I believe you answered my question."

"What? You don't care about the birth dates of my other two babies?"

I motioned for Dorothy to continue. It didn't make any difference because after I'd heard the birth date of baby number five, I had emotionally and mentally checked out.

"Well, Freda was born only eight months after Emmie. She was what they call premature. I'd call her immature. I swear she was in me when Eerie Emmie was born. She was hiding out, waiting for the right time to pop out. And she did on February 15, 1982. She was almost my Valentine present. But she refused to come early. Last, but not least, Georgie Porgie, Puddin' and Pie came along six years later. Thought I'd never get knocked up again, but lo and behold, he squeezed through my love chute on April 22, 1988. Like I said before, I should have killed him right off. Would've saved me a lot of headaches. But I have to admit, he was my favorite. I know it's not right for a mother to have a favorite child, but I knew him in the biblical sense. Know what I mean?"

"Yes," I muttered. I think I was barely conscious. Heck, I was surprised I was still upright.

For no apparent reason, Dorothy recited an old Mother Goose poem:

"Monday's child is fair of face,

Tuesday's child is full of grace... "

I zoned out.

A few minutes later, there was silence.

Blessed silence, disturbed by the sound of Dorothy maneuvering her huge body out of the chair. Her muumuu rustled as she waddled toward me. Her black eyes fixed on mine. I looked at her. I shook. I tried to grasp the meaning of the thoughts that raced through my head.

Dorothy snapped her grimy fingers in my face. "Yo! Snap to, nitwit."

As if in response to her command, I bolted off the couch and stuffed my recorder and other things in my briefcase. Dorothy didn't protest my leaving. In fact, she escorted me to the door. Before I rushed to the safety of my car, I turned to her and said, "Where did you get the T-shirt you were wearing in your mug shot? You know, the one that read: WORLD'S BEST MOM."

"Bought it for myself," Dorothy said. "May not be much, but I can truly say I'm the world's best mom. Oh, and by the way, you know you can't print any of the stuff I told you."

"Why?" I asked.

"I told you, if you rat on Dan Jordan, he'll kill me. You wouldn't want the murder of the world's best mom on your conscience now, wouldya?"

Like I care. I'd love to give you what you deserve. "Of course not," I said. "Again, thanks for your time."

"Thanks for nothing," Dorothy said. "And remember, you've been warned."

I jogged to my car. As I pulled away from the curb, Dorothy waved at me from the doorway. She swayed as if she would drop. I couldn't have cared less. The security of home and a hot shower beckoned.

As I approached the interstate, I saw the police department. The urge to wash off Dorothy's stink from my body and soul almost kept me from stopping. But I knew a thorough journalist wouldn't leave a stone unturned. Besides, I didn't know if Dorothy had told me the truth about the murder of Bull. There were a lot of holes in her story that needed to be filled.

So I pulled into the parking lot. As I walked to the front door of the police station, Dorothy's crazed cackle reverberated in my head. Visions of her spitting on little Toni's picture made me ill. I wanted to cry. I wanted my momma.

I stood at the door so long an officer thought something was wrong and opened it for me.

"You need help?" she asked.

"Yeah."

The officer helped me in and motioned for me to sit on a bench in the outer office. She walked away. A few seconds later, she returned with a cold cup of water. I guzzled it.

"Tell me what happened," she said.

"I'm a reporter for the *Washington Intelligencer*. I just met with Dorothy Hall regarding the murder of her twenty-five-year-old boyfriend, and I would like to see her police file, please."

"Dorothy Hall?" The police officer squinted, giving me the feeling she was confused.

I looked at her as if she were my savior.

"I'll give you all I can," she said.

"Now that was easy," I said as I smacked an imaginary Staples button. I waited for what felt like an eternity. At first, I was antsy. I wanted to get home. But after a few minutes, I began to relax. The wait was doing me good. Through the glass door, I saw the officer talking to someone on the phone. Then she spoke with a male officer. He appeared perturbed. A half hour later, the officer returned, clutching a file.

"Here's everything," she said as she thrust the file at me.

I took it from her. It felt empty. *Not again.* I took a quick look. One sheet of paper was inside. "This is it?"

"That's it. Case closed," she said. Then she quickly showed me to the door.

Hmm. Dorothy was right. They're protecting Dan Jordan. Like she said, he's a big man in this small town. I pulled out of the parking lot. It was the last thing I remembered until I was safe and sound in my condo. I swear an angel drove me home. Or maybe I said, "Beam me up, Scotty," and it really worked.

CHAPTER FOURTEEN

I STOOD IN MY TINY excuse of a foyer, looking exactly as I did before I left but knowing I was a changed woman. My briefcase, purse, and jacket fell to the floor. I took a deep breath, trying to relax and make sense of one of the most bizarre days of my life. But my moment of silent reflection was soon interrupted by the ringing of the phone.

I struggled to make the few steps to my kitchen to answer it. "Hello," I managed to say.

"Emarie, where are you? I'm waiting for you," a woman said.

"Who is this?" I said, barely above a whisper.

"Emarie, it's Laura. What's the matter?"

"Laura? Oh my God, I forgot. Let me freshen up. I'll be there in a half hour. Please wait for me. I have so much to tell you."

"Okay. You had me worried. See you soon."

It was nearly seven o'clock. I'd promised to meet Laura at six. I couldn't believe I'd forgotten about our standing dinner date. She'd been my best friend since we were infants. Over the years, we'd shared everything with each other: celebrations, heartbreaks, first times, last times, joys, sorrows, birthdays, graduations, births, and deaths.

I took a quick shower... made up my face... changed into something a little sexy (you never know if Mr. Right might be watching from another table)... adorned my ears, neck, wrists, and fingers with complementary jewelry... gave myself the once-over in the mirror... swiped on lipstick... smacked my lips... and rushed to meet Laura for our Saturday night "date."

I walked in the door of TGI Friday's at seven forty-five. Laura was sitting at the bar, chatting up some guy. I hated to interrupt their conversation, but I had a lot to get off my chest. I tapped Laura on the shoulder.

"Hey, Emarie," she said, her face lit with excitement. Then she turned to the man sitting next to her and said, "Richard, this is the friend I told you about."

"Richard?" I said, disappointed to see my nuisance of a coworker glowing at my best friend. "What brings you here this evening? Get stood up again?"

The look on Laura's face was priceless. "You two know each other?"

"Yep," Richard said, obviously bummed that the wonderful woman Laura had told him about turned out to be me.

"We work together. Come on, Laura, let's get a table." I fought my way through the Saturday-evening crowd until I reached the hostess. "Table for two, please."

The hostess scanned her laminated seating chart as if she were Columbus charting a course to the New World. She snatched two menus, said, "Follow me," and hurried off.

Laura was still at the bar gabbing with Richard. I caught her attention and motioned for her to come with me. She gave Richard a quick peck on the cheek. *Please, God, haven't I suffered enough today? Please, not Laura and Richard.* I thought I'd barf. Fortunately, my stomach was empty.

We arrived at our table to a huffy hostess. I almost laughed at her arrogance, but I guess when you're seventeen, being a hostess at TGI Friday's is a big deal. We sat down, and Little Miss TGI Friday's plopped a plastic-coated menu in front of each of us. My eyes focused on the pictures and words, but my mind was deep in thought. *Why did we always come here? We're big girls now. We could afford a more sophisticated restaurant. Maybe one in Old Town, Alexandria, next time. I want a restaurant with white tablecloths, leather-bound menus, an extensive wine list, servers who call me ma'am, and an atmosphere conducive to a quiet adult conversation. TGI Friday's had served us well when we were single twenty-somethings. But as single thirty-somethings, we needed a little* je ne sais quoi, *at least I did.*

I glanced at Laura. She grinned from ear to ear as she scanned the menu. She'd only read it a million times, and every time she ordered the same thing—the low-calorie salmon with a side of plain broccoli of which she ate half and boxed the other half to take home. *What's up with her tonight?*

"I feel like a big hunk of meat tonight," Laura announced.

"Really… What do you call it? Richard?"

Laura lowered her menu and said, "He's a nice guy. Do you mind if I go out with him?"

"He's a creep, but if you want to go out with him, go right ahead."

"Thanks. I'm glad you don't mind," Laura said as the male server bellied up to our table.

"Ready to order?" the server asked.

"Yes," Laura said. "I'll have the bacon and bleu sirloin, medium rare, sweet potato fries, slaw, and a glass of Robert Mondavi cabernet sauvignon."

"And you?" the server asked, barely looking at me.

"We'll start with the Tuscan spinach dip—"

"Oh, thanks, Emarie," Laura giggled. "I forgot we always start with the dip."

I nodded at Laura and continued, "And I'll have the garlic shrimp and a Grey Goose vodka tonic."

"Your drinks and appetizer will be right up," the server said as he scooted off to the kitchen.

"So what's up?" Laura said. "Why were you so late?"

"Well—"

"Oh, don't be coy," Laura snapped. "Richard already told me you're on a big assignment, a murder or something."

"Yeah, or something," I said, growing angry. "Just so you know,

57

my assignment is none of Richard's business." Visions of Laura and Richard cuddled on a couch whispering and laughing about my journalistic skills danced through my head. She hadn't even dated Richard yet, and his opinion already mattered. I felt betrayed by my best friend.

"I'm sorry, Emarie. I am being a bit silly about Richard, but I really like him."

"Whatever."

"Don't brush me off. If Richard is a problem, I'll back off."

"Richard is a jerk, but he's not dangerous. You have a right to decide whether or not you like him. End of the Richard discussion. Okay?"

"Okay." Laura sighed. "Tell me about your day."

I reached for my nonexistent drink. Then, as if on cue, the server arrived with our dip and drinks. I gulped my vodka tonic, held up the glass, and said to the server, "I'll have another."

He nodded and left.

Between mouthfuls of spinach dip and chips, I recapped the entire story of Dorothy with only a few interruptions by the server to deliver my second vodka tonic and serve our meals. Laura did what she did best; she listened. No judgment. No questions. Just a few nods, a couple of giggles, and expressions that ranged from disgust to surprise to concern.

Laura waited a few moments to make sure I was done verbally vomiting my story before she said, "You want to know what I think?"

"Sure," I mumbled.

"I think you're scared," she said. "I think you know who Dorothy is."

I reached for my purse, pulled out Dorothy's mug shot, and handed it to Laura.

"Yep, I see the resemblance," she said as she looked up at me with her usual impish smirk.

I snatched the picture from Laura and stuffed it back in my purse. "Well, I'm not jumping to any conclusions. I need to talk to my mother and father."

"I'm just teasing you. You don't look like Dorothy at all."

"Thanks."

"Dessert?" Laura asked.

"Why not?"

We ordered a Brownie Obsession to share, which we ate in silence, enjoying our dessert and savoring our friendship. Then Laura glanced at the bar. I glanced over too. Richard was gone. I noticed that Laura's gaze lingered a little too long at the bar where she and Richard had met earlier. A feeling of sadness swept through me, for I knew our friendship was about to change. For better or worse was yet to be discovered.

CHAPTER FIFTEEN

I T WAS FINALLY OVER. YES, after one of the craziest days of my life, I was home, nestled in bed, watching *Saturday Night Live*. I should have been fast asleep, but truth be told, I was afraid to drift off. The last thing I wanted to do was to dream about Dorothy. I'd allowed her to infiltrate my waking thoughts, but my dream life was off-limits. So I forced myself to watch TV, but eventually the urge to sleep won.

Hours later, I awoke to the sun streaming through my bedroom window. I looked at the clock. It was nine a.m. I begrudgingly got out of bed. "Time to face reality." I threw off the covers, planted both feet on the floor, and padded my way to the kitchen.

I pressed the button on the coffee maker. I couldn't remember if I'd set up the coffee the night before or not, so I was happy when I heard gurgling water followed by the sight of beautiful brown liquid dripping into the pot. I retrieved my favorite mug, filled it with fresh-brewed coffee, and topped it off with a healthy squirt of whipped cream. Yum, pure heaven. But hell, otherwise known as Dorothy, was beckoning.

I placed my mug on the dining room table, pulled my briefcase to my side, rummaged for my recorder, and pulled out the slim file from the Bingingham County Police Department and the file on Dorothy. The only info in the police folder was typed on a single form. The final judgment was self-defense. No charges filed. No statement from

Dorothy. No mention of Dan Jordan. Case closed. I could hear Dorothy say, "Just the facts, ma'am. *Dragnet*, right?" Problem was, the facts were missing.

I jotted down a schedule to ensure I'd meet my deadline. The usual story deadline was Wednesday, giving Jim adequate time to edit, rewrite, edit... before the Sunday magazine was put to bed on Friday. I needed to get my ass in gear. I held my recorder, dreading having to listen to my interview with Dorothy. The thought of hearing her voice turned my stomach. I took a deep breath and pressed Play. Dorothy's voice boomed from the recorder. "I was born to two *assholes* right here in this house—"

Click.

Stop.

I can't take this. Please, God, don't make me listen to another second of Dorothy Hall. I waited for God to respond. I swear I heard a male voice in my head say, "I've got your back." For a second I thought I was losing my mind, but the voice in my head was the encouragement I needed to plug on.

Click.

Dorothy continued.

I took copious notes including recorder locations for quotes. Two hours later, head aching, I decided I didn't have what it took to be a reporter. Hell, I was ready to quit my job to avoid the Dorothython. I fought the urge to call Jim and back out of the story.

Ring. Ring.

My cell phone diverted my attention. I pressed the Talk icon.

"Hey, Emarie," Jim said before I could even say hello.

"Hi, Jim. What's up?" *You better be interrupting my morning to tell me my story's dead.*

"Just checking to see how your story is going," Jim said. "I know I dumped a tight deadline on you, and I wanted to explain why."

"Okaaay." *Damn, I guess I can't get rid of Dorothy.*

"Well, I originally gave the story to Richard, but when he saw the skimpy file, he chickened out."

"Oh?" *Surprise. Surprise.*

"Then I got to thinking. I should have given it to you in the first place. Do you know why?"

"Nooooo."

"Well, to tell you the truth, I think you've got great potential. I'm sorry a week was wasted on Richard and now you're stuck with mission impossible."

"All righty," I said.

"What I'm trying to say is, I know you can do it. I know you've got what it takes to write a damn good story."

"Well, thanks for the vote of confidence, Jim."

"I'm serious, Emarie. You're a great writer."

"I'm serious too. Your call came at the right time. I needed a little encouragement."

"Well, you've got it."

"Thanks."

"Oh, and by the way, I need the first draft on my desk Tuesday morning."

"Tuesday? I thought the first deadline was Wednesday."

"Yes, but we've lost a week, so we missed last Wednesday's deadline."

I took a deep breath.

"Emarie, I know you can do it."

"I'll do my best."

"Nose to the grindstone," Jim said.

"Yep."

"Bye."

Jim was gone and so was my confidence.

I slammed my cell phone on the table. "Damn you, Richard," I yelled. "You good for nothing, lazy loser." *You better keep your grubby little hands off my friend.*

I wanted to call Laura and tell her what an incompetent jerk Richard was and how he had set me up for failure. I grabbed my home phone and scrolled for Laura's number. *No, it's not right to bring Laura into this. Besides, I've got to get cracking.* I put the phone back in the charger and got to work.

I wrote.

I edited.

I rewrote.

I cried.

I cursed.

At three p.m., emotionally drained and mentally exhausted, I got a brilliant idea. Rather than me telling the story and interspersing quotes from Dorothy, why not let Dorothy tell it? After all, to believe this story, it had to come from the horse's mouth. "Or horse's ass," I said out loud and laughed.

I started the Dorothy interview and began to transcribe the audio. It was a grueling task. *You'd think someone would have invented transcription software, and you'd think one of the country's most well-known newspapers would have it installed on its computers.*

"Aha!" I said. "I believe they have." I clicked and opened my programs. I scrolled. "Yep, there it is." One more click and the software popped up. A few simple instructions and voilà, Dorothy's voice was translated into the printed word. This was a miracle worthy of celebration.

As the software transcribed, I celebrated with a steak, fresh string beans, and a bottle of red wine. While the steak sizzled under the broiler and the string beans steamed, I dashed between the kitchen and the dining room to check on the transcription progress. There were a few errors. *Nothing's perfect.*

I chowed down the entire steak, savored the string beans, and enjoyed two glasses of wine. By that time, Dorothy was discussing baby number five. I stopped in mid-chew. *Lucky baby number five. She got away. She got away.* I let the interview finish. Then I printed Dorothy's words. I was so energized I worked well into the night. The story was developing nicely. I countered Dorothy's statements with my experience of being in her presence. I described Dorothy's depressingly disgusting, filthy home. I discussed the fact there was no trial due to the decision of self-defense. *Ha! The police were too weak to reel in their big fish named Dan Jordan.* I struggled with the implications of not changing the names of Dorothy's babies to protect the innocent. But Dorothy's names for her children were important to the story. As I reviewed my work, I realized Dorothy's statements created more questions than answers. *Damn. I was going to have to talk to her again.*

CHAPTER SIXTEEN

MY ALARM WOKE ME AT six a.m. For the first time in my life, I was excited it was Monday. I couldn't wait to get into the office. I was at my desk by seven thirty. Jim strolled in at eight. He nodded at me and smiled. Richard slunk in at nine thirty. I glanced at him. *For God's sake, Richard, you're a journalist. The whole world's changed before you even get into the office.*

"Whatcha doing?" Richard said as he dropped his briefcase on his desk and booted his computer. Then he leaned over the cubicle wall that separated our "offices" and said, "Writing the story I turned down?"

"Exactly. If you don't mind, I've got to put the final touches on my award-winning story before I show it to Jim." *Jerk!*

"Little overconfident, aren't we?" Richard made a fist à la the Black Panther revolutionaries of the '60s and '70s and said, "Type on!"

Gag me. I ignored him. An hour later, I presented my first draft to Jim.

"Well, I see you've been hard at work."

I tapped my nose and said, "Nose to the grindstone."

Jim laughed. "I'll get back to you." He laid my story on his desk and motioned for me to leave.

I went back to my cubbyhole. I didn't know what to do with myself. I pretended to write as I typed, "All work and no play makes Jack a dull boy." I laughed. I imagined Dorothy saying, "*The Shining*, right?" A chill ran through me. Not because of the movie, but because Dorothy was living in my head.

I looked at my phone. I wanted to call my parents. I had questions. I hoped they had answers. I hadn't told them about Dorothy, which was unlike me because I shared nearly everything with them. I pick up the receiver and quickly put it back in the cradle. Then I picked it up again. For God's sake, my parents needed to know about my suspicions. I dialed.

"Hi, Mom. It's Emarie."

"I know, dear. You're calling early. Everything okay?"

"Fine… I was wondering, do you have my adoption papers?"

"I thought we gave them to you, dear."

"No, you wanted to, but I told you to keep them."

"Well, let me ask your father. You know he keeps track of things like that."

I heard a mumbled conversation, then she said, "The papers are in the lockbox. Are you okay? Is something wrong?"

"No, just curious, that's all," I said. "May I come over this evening and get them?"

"Of course."

"Thanks, Mom. See you later."

"Emarie? You know you can ask us anything."

"I know."

"Well, when you were a child you were full of questions. Some I didn't answer because I thought you were too young. On your eighteenth birthday, I tried to tell you more, but you didn't seem interested."

"I wasn't interested then, but I am now. I'll explain everything this evening."

I hung up, wondering if my questions would hurt my parents' feelings. No, they'd always been open and honest about my adoption. Memories of my mother reading the book *The Adopted Family* comforted me. My parents had always made me feel loved and wanted. I couldn't imagine having any other parents. *What are you afraid of, Emarie? That you can't handle the truth?*

My phone buzzed. It was Jim. I hit the speaker button. "Yes, Jim."

"Come to my office. We need to discuss your story."

"Be right there." I got a pit in my stomach. Was Jim angry, disappointed, or disgusted? I couldn't put my finger on it. I rose from my chair and started my walk to Jim's office, feeling as if I were headed to my execution. *Don't be so dramatic. He probably has a few changes. Yeah, like a few million changes.*

I knocked on Jim's glass door. *More like a glass ceiling,* I thought as I visualized my career crashing to an end. He was on the phone and motioned for me to enter and take a seat.

Jim hung up. "Well," he said as he picked up my story. "You know what you've done here?"

"No," I said, imagining the blade of the guillotine dangling over my pretty little neck.

"Well, you've written the best damn story I've ever read."

"What?" I said a little louder than I'd expected.

"Yep. I was just on the phone with Marie. I got a week's extension for your story so we can flesh it out a bit. Talk to each of Dorothy's children and corroborate her story before this goes to press," Jim said, more animated than I'd ever seen him.

"Okay."

"And one more thing. Find out who's baby number five. See if she's willing to talk. Could make for an even more interesting story. You know, the one who got away."

"Okay." I gulped. *She got away. She got away.*

"Hey, I thought you'd be excited."

"I am."

"Well, I'm excited for you. Now—"

"I know… nose to the grindstone."

Jim smiled and handed me my story. I walked back to my desk and plopped in my chair. Despite Jim's compliment, which meant more to me than he knew, his words, "Find out who's baby number five. You know, the one who got away," caused acid to rise in my throat.

I didn't know where to start, but I had a sneaking suspicion I knew where baby number five was. I hoped I was wrong. I flipped through my story. Jim's edits were extensive. *He thinks this is the best damn story he's ever read, and he ripped it apart?* He added subheads. He moved paragraphs. He rewrote entire sections. He deleted dialogue that presented Dorothy in her true light. *Looks like Jim wrote the best damn story, not me.* I was fuming mad.

I stormed to Jim's office and pushed his door open with so much force the inside handle hit the glass wall. "What have you done to my story?" I yelled.

Jim nonchalantly removed his glasses and pushed back in his chair. "I corrected it."

"Corrected it? You rewrote it."

"Just calm down and have Liz make the changes." Jim put his glasses back on and returned to his work.

I went back to my desk and contemplated what to do with my riddled copy. I decided I'd correct Jim's edits myself. I wrote STET on most of his changes, moved some paragraphs, rewrote others, tightened my sentence structure, and corrected a few grammatical errors. Jim questioned the authenticity of some of Dorothy's statements, so I carefully listened to my interview with Dorothy again.

Hearing her voice didn't give me the creeps. This time I felt sorry for her. She was an abused woman with a miserable life. Like she said, "I guess I'm just plain unlovable. Nobody loved me when I was a baby. Nobody loved me when I was a smart-mouthed kid. And nobody loves me as a full-grown woman." Her words stung. What was it like to go through life unloved? I was glad I didn't know. Nonetheless, she still didn't have an excuse for the fact she abused and neglected her children. But it made it a little more understandable.

A couple of hours later, I delivered my marked-up copy to Liz, our crackerjack copy secretary, and resident den mother.

"You poor baby. This is the worst markup I've ever seen," Liz said.

"It's not as bad as it looks."

"Yeah, I've heard that before. Don't worry, Jim's tough on everyone."

"He needs it back by three o'clock. I'd like to see it before he does. Can you have it done by two?"

"Piece of cake, sweetie." Liz placed my story on her document stand and got to work.

Back at my desk, I checked my schedule. Hmm, why hadn't Jim given me another assignment? Usually, he piled them on until I screamed uncle. I guess he thought my current assignment was work enough.

"Damn," Richard yelled. "Jim dumped four assignments on me. Does he think I'm Superman or something?"

"Or something." *Poor little Richard was overwhelmed. Sweet revenge.*

I decided to focus on locating Dorothy's kids. I made a list: Antoinette (Ugly Toni), Bernard (Sad Sack), Catrina (Cat the Brat), Dwayne (Dwayne the Pain), Emily (Eerie Emmie), Freda (Fricking Freda), and George, aka Bull (Georgie Porgie, Puddin' and Pie). That was all seven of them. But since Bernard and Bull were dead, I only had to find five of Dorothy's children. And if my hunch was right, I only had to find four. *How hard could that be? Where to start? Might as well go right to the source.* I dialed Dorothy. I started to shake. *For God's sake, you've already spent hours with her, how bad can a phone call be?* I was about to find out.

"What the hell do you want?" Dorothy said.

"Dorothy?"

"I said, what the hell do you want?"

"Dorothy, it's Emarie Lukins from the *Washington Intelligencer*."

"I know who you are." Dorothy gulped what I already knew to be her special juice. "You're the idiot who wasted my whole day letting me rant into that damn recorder."

"Dorothy, I need your help."

"With what?"

"I need to find your children."

"You're the goddamned dumbest reporter who ever lived. If you were one of my kids, I'd whack you upside your head. That would knock some sense into you. Don't you remember? You can't print any of what I said, or Dan Jordan will kill me. Maybe he'd even kill you. Ha! There's a silver lining to every cloud."

"You willingly told me your story, knowing I was writing an article."

"Yep, you told me you were writing about why I killed my boyfriend. You didn't say you were writing about my kids."

"I told you I wanted to help you tell your story. Your children are part of your story. And it's a fascinating story."

"Fascinating?" Dorothy asked.

"Yes, fascinating."

"Are you saying I'm fascinating?"

"Yes, you are." I winced.

Silence.

"Dorothy?" I said as I heard Dorothy chugging more juice.

"I'm thinking," Dorothy yelled. "Just how fascinating am I?"

"Very. In fact, you're the most fascinating woman I've ever met," I said, hoping a little charm would work.

"Okay, write the damn story. And it better be damn good."

"It will be. Now, will you help me find your children?"

"Well, aren't you lucky? Fricking Freda came by after you left the other day. Even though I told the hardheaded idiot to never come to my house again, she had the nerve to stop by. She wanted to know about her sister, baby number five. You know, Eerie Emmie."

Beads of sweat tingled on my forehead. I managed to ask, "What did you tell her?"

"I told her to drag her ass down to Child Protective Services and ask them. They were the ones who had the screaming little bitch last."

Hoping to calm my nerves, I took a deep breath and reached for an invisible glass of wine. "Do you know how I can get in touch with Freda?" I said, my voice shaking.

"Nope. Don't know her last name. Don't know where she lives. Don't know her number. You're a smart-ass college graduate, and you claim to be a reporter. Figure it out yourself."

"Okay. I will," I said, furious with Dorothy's ability to instill hope and then pull the rug out from under me.

"Bye. And don't call me again until your stupid story makes me famous." Click.

"Well, she got that wrong," I mumbled. "The story isn't going to make her famous; it's going to make her infamous. But she probably doesn't know the difference."

Liz appeared at my desk. Tears ran down her cheeks. "What a wonderful story about a horrible woman," she said as she handed me the corrected copy and wiped her tears with a tissue. "How could a mother be so horrible to her babies? My kids are all gifts from God. Breaks my heart for her kids. Dorothy Hall will haunt me for the rest of my life."

"You and me both," I said, resisting the urge to give Liz a bear hug.

I scanned the copy. "Thanks. I'll give this to Jim."

Liz nodded, then cried her way back to her desk. I felt bad she had to type Dorothy's dialogue. It had to have been difficult for her. What a trouper. As usual, Liz had done an impeccable job. I had no doubt she was as good a mother as she was a secretary.

I knocked on Jim's door and went in. "Here's the corrected copy."

"Great. I'll look it over tonight."

"Would you mind if I went home early? I'm kind of spent."

"No problem. Oh, by the way," Jim said, "get in touch with Dan Jordan, Bull's father. Get his side of the story."

I gulped. "Okay, will do."

As I wandered back to my desk, I reminded myself what a lousy reporter I was. I should have known to talk to Dan Jordan. I shouldn't have to be told.

I gathered my things, then headed to my parents'—the only place on earth where unconditional love, support, and a warm hug were guaranteed. I needed all three.

CHAPTER SEVENTEEN

THE DRIVE THROUGH MY CHILDHOOD neighborhood brought back memories. Some happy. Some sad. But I had to admit, my childhood was mostly happy. How could it not be? I had great parents and Laura as my best friend.

Laura and I shared the status of being only children. In my neighborhood, that meant you were envied by kids with siblings and hated by their parents. But there was one other status we shared. We were both adopted. Once we discovered that information about each other, we instantly became inseparable soul mates. We were so close that as kids and teens we fantasized about being sisters. Never mind the fact that only a four-month difference in our ages made our fantasy a biological impossibility. Plus I was tall with olive-colored skin, nearly black hair, and what my uncle called suspicious brown eyes while Laura was a cute, petite blonde with mischievous blue eyes. Yep, the eyes have it. I was suspicious, and Laura was mischievous. And we were best buds. We spent hours scouring magazines and imagining our birth parents were among the rich and famous. If we'd known then what we knew now, we wouldn't have wasted so much time fantasizing. For truth be told, we'd both won the parent lottery.

I pulled into my parents' driveway and parked behind their ten-year-old, white Honda Accord. I laughed at how different Laura's parents and my parents were. My parents were practical, hence the Honda. On the other hand, Laura's parents were flashy, hence a brand-new, black Bimmer convertible. My parents were in their sixties and planning for retirement. Laura's parents were in their fifties and planning their next big adventure. My parents paid cash for everything and never owed one red cent to anyone other than the mortgage company. Laura's parents had oodles of credit cards, a beach home, and piles of debt. Our parents couldn't be more different. And despite how close Laura and I were, our parents never socialized.

Even though I knew I could walk into my parents' home unannounced, out of respect for their privacy I rang the doorbell. A few seconds later, I was greeted by my father.

"Emarie, what a surprise."

"Hi, Dad. I'm a little early."

"We're always happy to see you." My father pecked me on the cheek. "Emarie's here, dear," he yelled to my mother.

My mother appeared from the family room, looking as if she'd been crying.

"Mom, what's wrong?" I said as I rushed to give her a hug.

"This came today," she said as she handed me an envelope.

I looked at the return address. It read: Bingingham County Department of Social Services.

My father looked at his feet, obviously avoiding eye contact with me. "You know what this means?"

I started to answer, but my father spoke before I could utter a response. "It means someone is looking for you." He looked me squarely in the eye. His lip quivered as if he was fighting back tears.

"I don't think so. I think this has something to do with a story I'm working on."

"It was addressed to us. We opened it. Someone is looking for you," my father said, concern written on his face. "I feared this day would come."

I sat on the couch while my parents stood. My father put his arm around my mother's shoulders and pulled her close to him. My mother looked down and wrung her hands. They were making me nervous.

I removed the letter from the already-opened envelope. "This is kind of bizarre," I said. "I just called you this morning about my adoption papers, and this arrived on the same day."

72

My parents were silent. Tears streamed down my mother's face.

I unfolded the letter and read it. A biological sister was looking for me. The words blurred. I read the letter several times to make sure I had read it right. I looked up at my parents and said, "Biological? That means the same mother and father." I scanned the words again. "It doesn't say half sister. It says biological sister."

"Yes," my mother muttered, pulling away from my father as she wiped away tears.

I wanted to hug my mother and ease her emotional pain. But I also wondered why this letter was so upsetting for her.

"It's up to you as to whether or not you want to contact her," my father said.

"Contact her? My instinct tells me to throw the letter in the trash and pretend it was never sent." I paced the living room, attempting to control my escalating emotions that ran from anger that someone had the nerve to violate my privacy to fear that the person would intrude on my happy little family to interest as to who she was. *How dare she?* I didn't know what I wanted to do. My parents silently watched, giving me space to reconcile my jumbled feelings. "I bet she wants a kidney," I yelled. "Maybe she wants blood. I hope she's not looking for money because she won't get it from me."

"Maybe she's just curious," my mother said. Then she left the room.

My father wrapped his arms around me while I cried. I felt like a little girl again, safe in Daddy's arms.

A few minutes later, my mother returned with a small stack of envelopes and papers carefully secured with several rubber bands. A piece of paper on top read: "Emarie's adoption papers." I smiled. That was the work of my father.

"I don't want to make a decision right now," I said.

"That's okay. Just know we're here for you," my mother said as she leaned down and hugged me.

"We'll support whatever decision you make," my father said.

"Thanks. I love you guys."

"And you know how much we love you," my mother responded. With that, the Lukins family had a little lovefest.

Hugging.

Crying.

Back rubbing.

Kisses on the forehead.

"Time to get dinner ready," my mother said. "You are staying for dinner, aren't you?"

"Of course, I wouldn't miss it for the world."

My mother and I escaped to the kitchen as my father settled in front of the TV. Mom and I made idle chitchat as we prepared dinner. While the roast was in the oven, I told her I was writing a story that could be my big break. She was happy for me, but when I mentioned Dorothy's name and Darrington, Maryland, she went pale. Suddenly the roast needed her attention. End of conversation. The elephant in the room was suffocating me.

Dinner was delicious but uneventful. Our superficial conversation was killing me. I was sure my parents felt the same. Knowing my father, it took a lot of willpower for him to not discuss the letter. He'd always feared that if I found my bio-family, I would change my loyalties. He needn't. There wasn't a snowball's chance in hell I could love anyone more than I loved my parents. I wished I'd said that to them before I headed home. I had a feeling that after I left, they cried, and my gut told me it had something to do with Dorothy.

CHAPTER EIGHTEEN

B ACK IN MY CONDO, I changed into comfortable clothes, made a cup of tea, and curled up in the chair in the sunroom. I stared out the window. In my hand, I held the letter from Bingingham County Department of Social Services. I read and reread the letter as if to discover a secret message. None found. Anxiety drove me nuts. I picked up my phone and called Laura. No answer. I called her cell phone.

"Yello," Laura said.

"Are you drunk or something?"

"Hey, Emarie. Guess who I'm with?"

"Enlighten me." *It better not be Richard.*

"I'm with Richard," Laura said and giggled. "He says hi."

"Call me when you have a chance."

"Is something wrong?"

"Just my life! But you and Richard have a good time." I hung up. I couldn't believe I'd been so nasty to Laura. Two seconds later, my phone rang. Caller ID showed it was her.

"Yello," I said, imitating her.

"Hey, what's up? I'm worried."

"Oh, it's nothing. I was just upset."

"Upset? Do you need me to come over?"

"No." Instant forgiveness. So typical of Laura. I almost laughed. "It's okay. I'll talk to you about it tomorrow."

"Are you pregnant?" Laura said and nervously laughed.

"I'm the Dateless Wonder. Remember? Unless it happened the other day when a guy rubbed himself on me as I went up the subway escalator."

"Gross," Laura said. "Call me at home later. I won't be out late."

"What if Richard's there?"

"He won't be. Believe me."

"Okay. Bye." *Laura doesn't like Richard. What a relief.*

I poured a glass of wine, nestled on the couch, turned on the TV, and scanned the listings. *The Big Chill* was on. It was one of my mother's favorite movies. My father hated it. I'd never seen it. A half hour later, I was sick of it. Like *St. Elmo's Fire* and *The Breakfast Club*, it was a typical '80s self-indulgent movie. Weren't the stars in *St. Elmo's Fire* and *The Breakfast Club* referred to as the Brat Pack? For the life of me, I couldn't figure out why my mother liked *The Big Chill*. She'd never loan my father to one of her friends for a baby-making session. Even if she would, my father wouldn't do it. Then my phone rang. The on-screen caller ID showed it was Laura.

"Well, that was fast," I said. "What did you do, drop-kick Richard out the door?"

"Sort of. I hate to say you're right but—"

"Richard's a jerk."

"Maybe. What's up?"

"Well…" I said as I picked up the letter off the coffee table. "I got a letter from Bingingham County Department of Social Services."

"Oh no, who wants a kidney?"

"That was my first thought," I said and laughed. "A biological sister is looking for me."

"But I'm your sister."

"I know."

"I wish someone wanted to look for me."

"Really? Have you ever looked for your birth parents?"

Silence.

"Laura?"

"Yes."

I was shocked. I'd thought we shared everything. I guess even your soul mate can have secrets. "What happened?"

"They didn't want to meet me."

"What?"

"They married a few years after I was adopted. They had other children who didn't know about me. They didn't want me to ruin their happy little family," Laura said.

"Why didn't you tell me?"

"Because you were adamant about not wanting to know your birth parents or siblings. I felt like you'd disapprove."

"I'm sorry, Laura. I do feel that way, but it's an individual decision. I'm sorry you felt guilty about looking for your bio-family."

"It's okay. I'm over it." Laura exhaled. "What are you going to do?"

"Well, the ball's in my court. If I want to contact my bio-sister, I have to do it through social services. The letter says if I have any questions, I should call the social worker listed."

"Well? Are you going to call?"

"Yeah, tomorrow."

"Do you think this is related to Dorothy?"

"Nooooo, I think it's a coincidence," I said as a chill settled over me. "God help me if I'm related to Dorothy."

"Did you tell your parents?"

"They gave me the letter. It was addressed to them. My mother was upset, but both my parents were supportive. Oh, I almost forgot the papers they gave me."

"What papers?"

"My adoption papers. Hey, let me read them. I'll call you back."

"I hope there are no surprises like Dorothy listed as your mother."

"Yeah, right. They can't give that kind of information. I'm sure there's nothing I don't already know. I'll call you back."

I retrieved the rubber-band-bound papers and settled into the sunroom chair, then turned the floor lamp on the brightest setting to ensure I didn't misread a word. A copy of my birth certificate, showing I was born to my parents, Andrew and Marie Lukins, was on top. My parents had given me the original when I applied for a passport for a trip to London. I scanned a few letters about meeting times between my parents, social services, and a lawyer, as well as the court date to finalize my adoption. So far nothing too interesting.

I picked up a tattered, yellowed paper and carefully opened it. It was handwritten and read like an instruction manual for the care and feeding of Emmie. "Me? My name was Emmie?" *Eerie Emmie.* Dorothy's voice echoed in my head. "Oh my God."

I read on. Emmie wakes up at six a.m. Emmie likes to eat upon waking. Emmie screams when she sees food. Emmie likes her meals. Emmie sleeps a lot. Emmie cries a lot. Emmie doesn't like a bath. Emmie can't sit up without support. Emmie doesn't like loud noises. Emmie doesn't play. Emmie doesn't smile or laugh. Emmie refuses toys. Emmie doesn't like to be held. Emmie's bedtime is eight p.m. Emmie's suspicious of strangers. And so on and so on. I was struck by my negative review. I sounded like a deeply disturbed, unhappy baby. My parents never complained, although my mother had told me that I screamed and cried at the sight of food, so she put me in another room when she prepared meals. And I did remember my parents commenting on the fact I was nearly ten months old when they adopted me, and I couldn't sit up. Yet I felt detached as if I were reading about someone else.

"This can't be about me. I'm not anything like Emmie." I shuddered.

The paper on the bottom of the pile fell on the floor. I bent over and picked it up. It was another copy of my birth certificate. Whoever copied it was careless, for information from my original birth certificate was visible. I saw my birth weight was five pounds, fourteen ounces. *Wow, I was small.* Then I saw two horrifying words.

"No! No!" I screamed and dropped the papers on the floor. I shook so hard I could hardly dial my phone.

Laura picked up the phone on the first ring. "What did you find out?"

I tried to answer, but nothing would come out.

"Emarie, are you okay?"

"No."

"Tell me," Laura begged.

"My birth name was Emily," I managed to say.

"Okay."

"Emily," I cried.

"So your parents changed your name to Emarie. You said you were named after your grandfather, Emery, and your grandmother, Marie."

"Yes, but this shows my birth name. It was Emily... Emily Hall."

"What's the big deal?"

"Didn't I tell you?"

"Tell me what?"

"Dorothy's last name."

"Don't tell me it's Hall."

"It's Hall," I muttered and cried. "Dorothy Hall. She had seven children. Number five got away. The baby's name was Emily."

"It's a coincidence. Emily and Hall are common names. Anyway, wouldn't Hall be the name of your birth father? Not your birth mother?"

"Not if the mother didn't know the last name of the father. And there aren't many Halls in Darrington. I checked."

"Slow down. You told me your birth mother was married with four children. She had an affair, and you were the product of that affair. She and her husband decided to stay together. So they thought it was best for them and you that they place you for adoption."

"That's what my parents told me. That's the story I grew up believing."

"Was Dorothy ever married?"

"No."

"Then if what your parents told you is true, then she's *not* your mother."

"Well, the first thing to do is call the social worker tomorrow and find out."

"Weren't you in foster care before your parents adopted you?"

"Yes."

"Well, if your mother placed you for adoption at birth, then Hall could be the last name of the foster parents."

"God, I hope you're right. I've got to hang up."

"Emarie, if you need me, call me. I don't care about the time. Call. Okay?"

"Thanks, Laura. I promise."

I hung up. The urge to call my parents was unbearable, but the journalist in me told me to wait until I talked to the social worker and got the facts. It wasn't right to emotionally dump on my parents.

I turned on the TV. Flipping through the program guide took my mind off my adoption papers and a possible connection to Dorothy. Just as I'd started to calm down, I remembered something she'd said. Baby number five was born on June 23, 1981. So was I.

CHAPTER NINETEEN

R ICHARD WAS DRIVING ME NUTS with his bitching and moaning about his workload.

"It might help if you'd stop complaining and get to work," I snapped.

"Ooooh! Aren't we feisty today? Hormonal rage?"

That was it. I'd had it with him. After noisily gathering my adoption file, hoping Richard got the message as to what a pain in the butt he was, I sought refuge in a vacant office. No one had inhabited this primo office for years, so over time, it was where staff went when they needed a little peace and quiet. The glass doors and glass desk made me feel like an animal on display at a zoo. Obviously, this didn't help calm my nerves. Nonetheless, no one was watching me, not even Richard. I opened the red file and took a deep breath, trembling with anticipation as to what the social worker would tell me. The letter from Bingingham County Department of Social Services was on top. The phone number, in bold type, taunted me. I pulled the phone toward me, picked up the receiver, and immediately put it back in the cradle.

"What are you afraid of Emarie? If Dorothy Hall is your mother, it's better to find out sooner rather than later," I said to myself. Another deep breath gave me the courage to dial the number for the social worker.

Ring.

No answer.

Ring.

No answer.

Ring.

"Martha White, how may I help you?"

"Ms. White. My name is Emarie Lukins." Damn. I sounded nervous. I cleared my throat and continued. "You sent a letter to my parents regarding an inquiry from a biological sister," I said, surprisingly emotionally detached and professional. *Good recovery, Emarie.*

"Yes. Please confirm your parents' names?"

"Andrew and Marie Lukins."

"And your birth date?"

"June 23, 1981."

"Let me pull up the file," Ms. White said. "Just a second."

I tapped my pen on my forehead. *What if my bio-sister was ill and really did need a kidney transplant or something? Maybe she won the lottery and wanted to share mega millions with me. Ha!*

"Here we are," Ms. White said. "I must inform you that I can't volunteer information…"

My heart sank.

"…but I can answer your questions."

"Okay," I said, wishing I had prepared a list of questions. "Well, I assume this biological sister has the same mother and father."

"Yes," Ms. White said.

"Why is she contacting me now?"

"It appears she confronted her birth mother regarding the emotional impact of her siblings and her being placed in foster care or with family members. She got into an argument with her birth mother, at which time the birth mother told her about you."

"She didn't know about me?"

"No."

"But she knew about the other brothers and sisters?"

"Half brothers and half sisters, yes. At some point, they met each other and exchanged stories. Most had emotionally and physically abusive childhoods. Your biological sister was raised by an aunt. Evidently, this aunt was a sister of the birth father. The aunt was an alcoholic and abusive to your biological sister. Her half-siblings' stories of abuse prompted her to approach her birth mother. She was angry and gave her birth mother a piece of her mind—"

Dorothy's words—"She ripped me a new one"—flashed through my head.

"She reported that her birth mother said, 'There's one more. She's the one who got away. And you have the same father.'"

I gulped and ran my fingers through my hair. I was surprised the social worker had revealed information for which I didn't ask, but I was grateful for her openness.

"She asked the birth mother about you," Ms. White continued. "But the birth mother said she didn't know what happened to you and told your biological sister to contact social services."

Thoughts raced through my head. "How many children were there?" I managed to ask.

"Seven. Four older than you and two younger."

"How old is she?" I asked.

"She was born in 1982."

"Nineteen eighty-two? I was born in June of '81. We're barely a year apart?"

"Yes, that's true," Ms. White said.

"Freda?" I whispered.

"Excuse me?"

"Nothing. Just talking out loud," I said. "What does she want from me?"

"She's curious. After she found out about you, she's had fantasies you were raised in a wealthy family, driven around in fancy cars, dressed like a princess, and pampered."

"Well," I said and laughed, "I've had a wonderful life with two loving parents, but I certainly wasn't a princess." I paused to gather my thoughts. "Is she married? Does she have children?"

"Yes, she's happily married and has two children."

"I'm glad to hear that. You can tell her I'm single and happy." A moment of silence preceded my next question. "Where do we go from here?"

"If you want to meet her, I'll call her and ask permission to provide you with her name and phone number. It is always up to you as to whether or not you want to contact her."

"I have mixed feelings about this," I said. "I hope this doesn't sound mean, but I'm not interested in meeting her. I have a family. I believe I was meant to be with my parents and my family, and because my parents couldn't have children, someone else had to have me. Besides, part of me thinks she isn't looking for a sister."

"What do you think she's looking for?"

"A mother."

"I think you're right. Nonetheless, it is your decision. You don't have to decide right now. Think about it, and call me back if you want contact."

"Thanks. I will."

"And if you have any more questions, you can—" Ms. White gasped. "Oh... my... God."

"What?"

"Your adoption was illegal."

"What do you mean? My parents went to court to finalize my adoption. My father's boss's wife was the character witness. I have the paperwork in front of me."

"Yes, but no one released you for adoption. Your birth mother refused to sign the papers, and your birth father was deceased. Killed in a car accident. Only thirty-two years old."

"My father told me an ad was placed in the local Darrington-area newspaper in an attempt to find my birth father. No one stepped forward. Was his name Vernon?"

"I can't tell you that," Ms. White replied. "All I can say is that your adoption was illegal. The judge must have pushed you through."

"Oh," I said. "What does it mean that my adoption was illegal?" I asked with a lump in my throat as I nearly burst from my surging emotions.

"It means your birth mother could have taken you back at any time prior to your eighteenth birthday."

"Fat chance," I nearly screamed.

"Do you have any other questions?"

"No, not now. I'm already overwhelmed."

"I understand. If you want more information, give me a call."

"Thanks. I will."

Just as I hung up, I realized I hadn't asked the most obvious questions, such as what is my ethnic background and are there any family medical issues? And I didn't even think to ask if my birth name was Emily Hall. Oh well, she probably wouldn't have told me my birth name anyway. And I could always call back. I was left with a lot of information to digest and jumbled emotions to work through.

I sat in the office, staring at my notes from my conversation with the social worker. Paralyzed by conflicting emotions, I mentally reviewed everything the social worker had said. The story of my bio-sister and Dorothy's story of baby number five and six were similar, making my stomach churn. Was I baby number five? Had I been starved and neglected? Why didn't I ask? Was Freda my bio-sister? Was I the one who got away? Nah! Couldn't be. This was the stuff of movies. My life wasn't that interesting. Or was it? Was my own story the one I'd been waiting to write? *Hold on there, Emarie. You're jumping to conclusions. Your suspicions are probably baseless.*

My adoption had been pushed through the system. Legally or illegally didn't matter now. What mattered was I could have had a different life—a sad life, a horrible life. I could have been raised by Dorothy Hall. *Shiver me timbers!* But lucky me, I was raised by Andrew and Marie Lukins—the best parents in the world.

An emotion I'd read about but had never experienced surged through me like I'd been struck by lightning—pure joy. I felt light. Happy. I wanted to walk down the streets of D.C. and toss my hat in the air à la Mary Richards from *The Mary Tyler Moore Show*. I wanted people to stop and ask about my happiness. I wanted the world to know that I, Emarie Lukins, was the luckiest person in the world.

I looked up and saw Richard staring at me through the glass door. I motioned for him to come in. Joy had taken over my senses. I actually felt close to Richard right now.

"What's going on?" he asked. "You win the lottery or something?"

"I've won the biggest lottery in the world," I said as I gathered my things, pushed past him, and headed back to my desk.

He followed me like a hound after a steak. "What lottery?"

"The parent lottery."

The look on Richard's face was priceless. Was it shock? Was it horror? Then he whispered, "You're pregnant?" It was disbelief.

I laughed so hard I couldn't breathe. I reached for my chair. Richard swooped in and, like the gentleman I never suspected him to be, pulled it out for me. A phone rang.

"That's my phone," he said as he rushed off.

I opened my e-mail and shot off a short note to Laura. "Call me. I have two things to tell you. One of them you won't believe."

CHAPTER TWENTY

I WAITED A FEW MINUTES for Laura to call me back. Thoughts and emotions swept through me like tiny tornadoes. I needed to get myself together. My story was waiting. The clock was ticking. Jim was breathing down my neck. Richard was getting on my nerves. And I needed more info on Dorothy. Then, as if to prove that anxiety is the mother of invention, I had a stroke of genius—take advantage of Richard's newfound concern for me and ask for his help.

I stood up and peered over the cheap fabric-covered wall that separated Richard's and my cubicles. "Richard?"

"Yes?" he said as he quickly closed his computer screen, obviously trying to hide the fact that despite his "hectic workload," he was doing something other than work.

"I know you're busy, but do you have time to help me with some research for my feature article?"

"Sure. Anything for the new momma."

"Great. Would you see what you can uncover on a Dan Jordan from Darrington, Maryland?"

"Piece of cake," Richard said. "Do I get a credit?"

"That's up to Jim, but I'll put in a good word for you."

"Well, if I don't get credit, will you name your baby after me?"

"Yeah, right," I said, barely disguising my disgust.

I plopped in my chair. My e-mail message icon was flashing. Twenty-six new e-mails. *What's going on? Had the president been shot? Was there a terrorist attack?* I clicked the icon. I scanned. *Congrats... So excited for you... You'll be a great... When is it due?... Finally, something to celebrate.*

I felt I was being watched. I looked up to see Liz holding a bouquet of blue and pink flowers. Tears streamed down her plump cheeks. "I hope I'm the first to congratulate you," she said as she handed me the bouquet.

I accepted the flowers from Liz. "Thanks. You are."

Liz leaned over and hugged me. "A baby. That's so exciting. I guess I have a baby shower to plan," she said as she wiped tears from her eyes and departed.

I shot up from my chair, and clutching the bouquet, I leaned over Richard's cubicle wall. "Richard, how could you?" I said as I shook the bouquet. Pink and blue petals showered him like confetti.

Richard looked up at me as he brushed the petals from his hair. "How could I what?"

"Why did you tell everyone I'm pregnant?"

"I didn't tell anyone anything," Richard whined.

"A good reporter gets the facts. They don't spread rumors."

"But you told me you were pregnant."

"I told you nothing of the sort. I told you I'd won the parent lottery. I never said I was pregnant. You're the one who made that assumption."

"You didn't deny it," Richard said.

"Did you get three reliable sources to corroborate your assumption?"

"Are you saying you're not pregnant?"

"Well, I'm not denying it," I said as I disappeared into my cubicle. "Are you working on Dan Jordan?" I yelled across the wall.

"Yep," Richard replied.

"Good, you owe me big."

Silence.

My phone buzzed. It was Jim. I pressed the red button.

"Emarie, come to my office, ASAP," he said and hung up.

I strolled to Jim's office. I didn't have to knock. He was holding open the door for me.

"Well, little momma," Jim said.

"Jim, I can explain."

"Don't bother. I know Richard is just spreading rumors. Unless, of course, the rumors are true."

"No, they're not," I said. "Not that it's anyone's business."

"Good. I'll close down the rumor mill and take care of Richard. You get on with your story."

"Thanks." I turned to leave. Then I quickly turned back toward Jim and said, "Oh, Jim, could you break the news to Liz? She gave me a bouquet of pink and blue flowers and has now set off to plan my baby shower. I feel terrible."

"Of course," Jim said as he waved me off.

I headed back to my cubicle. I'd barely landed my butt in my chair when Liz passed me on her way to Jim's office.

I called Richard.

"What?" he said.

"See what you've done?"

"What?"

"You upset Liz. How could you do such a thing? She's the nicest person in the world." I slammed the phone in the cradle.

I heard Richard laughing or crying. I couldn't tell the difference. But I thought I could safely assume he was laughing. *Jerk. First impressions are lasting impressions.*

It was time to jump on my story, but my conversation with Martha White preoccupied my thoughts. I had a lot of questions, but one question burned through me like tiny sparklers destroying me one exploding cell at a time. It needed to be squelched… now. Despite my burning desire for answers, I agonized over calling the social worker. I knew I had to do it, if not for myself, then for my story. I took a deep breath, picked up the phone, and dialed.

"Martha White."

"Hello, Ms. White. Emarie Lukins again."

"Hi, Emarie. I didn't expect to hear from you so soon. What can I do for you?"

"Well…" I couldn't speak. I trembled. I was afraid to ask the question I knew needed to be asked.

"Emarie? You okay?"

"Yes… I'm fine… I wanted to ask: Why was I removed from my birth mother?"

"Hmm… Let's see." Ms. White paused as she shuffled through papers. "Oh, here it is. I'm afraid this may be difficult for you to hear. Are you sure you want to know?"

"Absolutely," I said, energized by my desire to know the truth.

"Well, to make a long story short. You were removed from your birth mother's home in December 1981 due to abuse and neglect. It appears a police officer was walking by the house when he heard a baby screaming. He noticed an open window, which he thought was odd due to the cold December weather. He looked through the window and saw an emaciated, filthy baby in a crib. He managed to get into the house and remove you. You were taken to a hospital. You weighed in at seven pounds. The medical staff thought you were a newborn, but records showed you were six months old. It was determined you would be removed from the custody of your birth mother, and when your condition improved, you were placed in foster care. Then, obviously, you were adopted by your parents, Andrew and Marie Lukins."

"Thanks… I appreciate it."

"Are you okay?"

"Can you tell me the name of the birth mother?"

"No, I can't."

"Then I have all the information I need. Thanks."

My face felt like it was on fire. Perspiration dotted my forehead. Millions of butterflies flittered in my stomach. I wanted to throw up. *Now you've done it. You've opened the proverbial can of worms. I can't be baby number five. It's just a coincidence. Probably lots of children are removed from bad parents for the same reason.* Again, the words of the Cowardly Lion echoed in my head. *I'd… turn… back… if… I… were… you.* There was no turning back. No way out. If Dorothy Hall was my birth mother, I was in deep. I hoped I wasn't in quicksand.

My e-mail message icon flashed. It was from Laura. Her short message read: "OMG! Richard told me. I don't know what to say. Who's the father? Dateless Wonder????? What time do you want me over?"

I clicked the reply icon and typed: Richard's a jerk. I'm not pregnant. Does seven p.m. work for you? BTW: I just opened a can of worms." Send.

Instant reply from Laura. "See you at seven."

The rest of the day was uneventful with the exception of watching Richard slink into Jim's office and, after getting his tongue-lashing, slink back to his desk. No words were exchanged. As Jim promised, the rumor mill was closed.

At five p.m., a file appeared over the cubicle wall. I took it. A yellow sticky on the front of the file read: "I'm sorry. Hope this helps."

I stood up to thank Richard, but I was too late. He was already gone. His desk was cleared. His computer screen said, "Thanks for the memories." *OMG! I got Richard fired.*

I dialed Jim.

"No, Emarie, Richard wasn't fired."

"How did you know what I was going to ask?"

"People who have glass offices see everything."

"May I ask why his desk is cleared?"

"Let's just say he's been given a new opportunity."

"But he still has a job, right?"

"Yes."

"Thanks, Jim."

"By the way, why was Richard searching for information on Dan Jordan?"

"He's helping me with my story."

"Really? Well just so you know, when I read his name in your article, it rang a bell. Dan Jordan was the judge on one of the most notorious child abuse/neglect cases in Maryland back in the late '80s or early '90s. Lost his job due to a scandal. Don't remember if it was related to the child cases, but it had something to do with his wife. For the life of me, I don't know why I remember all this."

"Thanks, Jim. I'll let you know if they're one and the same."

"Okay, but I need to see your next draft soon... like Monday."

"I know. I'll have it."

"Great. Everything's copacetic."

"Everything's what?"

"Copacetic. You know, hunky-dory."

"Great. Thanks, Jim."

"Emarie?"

"Yes."

Silence.

"Jim?"

Silence.

I stood up to see if Jim was okay. Through the glass wall, I saw him standing at his desk, the phone still at his ear. He pointed two fingers at his eyes and then pointed one at me.

"I know, you're watching me," I said.

CHAPTER TWENTY-ONE

AT SEVEN P.M., THE DOORBELL rang. I pranced to the door as if I were expecting Prince Charming to greet me with a bouquet of flowers and a kiss. But it was just a fantasy. I knew Laura was on the other side of the door. I swung it open, ready to give my best friend a big hug.

"Richard?"

"Emarie, I hope I'm not interrupting anything."

"No. What's up?"

"I wanted to apologize. I've been a bit of a jerk lately. I'm sorry I spread a horrible rumor. It was wrong. I'm sorry, that's all."

"No hard feelings."

"Thanks," Richard said, hanging his head in shame. Then he looked up, suddenly perky, and said, "Did you get a chance to look at the info I pulled on Dan Jordan?"

"No."

"Pretty interesting stuff."

"Richard?" Laura said. "What a nice surprise. Are you staying for dinner?"

Richard looked at me to answer.

Conundrum! If Richard stayed for dinner, I wouldn't be able to

93

unload the details of my phone call with the social worker. But if I didn't ask Richard to stay for dinner, it was obvious Laura would be disappointed. "Yes, Richard, how about dinner?"

"Thanks, I'd love to." Richard bowed to Laura, indicating for her to proceed. As I closed the front door, Laura and Richard made themselves comfortable on the living room couch. I hated to admit it, but Richard staying for dinner was copacetic with me.

Laura and I cooked dinner. Richard set the table and poured the wine. While the clam sauce simmered and the pasta cooked, we sipped wine and enjoyed friendly conversation. I admit I was beginning to have a different opinion of Richard.

The timer rang. I excused myself and went to check on the pasta. Al dente. Perfecto. I placed the strainer in the sink and poured in the pasta to drain. When I looked up, Laura and Richard were sitting side by side on the couch. Laura was radiant. Richard was all smiles. Jealousy had my stomach in knots. I decided it was just hunger pangs as I said, "Dinner's ready."

Laura sprang up and helped me put the pasta and clam sauce in a serving bowl. Richard joined us and took the bowl of steaming yumminess and placed it on the dining room table.

"Smells great," he said.

"Wait until you taste it," Laura replied. "It's delectable."

Delectable? When did Laura use a word like delectable? Richard's gone to her head.

Laura and Richard seated themselves while I carried the salad and dressing to the table. Then I went back into the kitchen and got the fresh-baked bread I'd picked up from Wegmans's bakery. When I returned to the dining room, I heard Laura and Richard giggling as they shared a string of pasta, à la *Lady and the Tramp. Well, isn't that cute? Today must be Richard's lucky day. Two people who thought he was a jerk are having second thoughts. Maybe he's a charming psychopath. Yikes!* Goose bumps crept up my arms.

I took my seat at the head of the table, raised my glass of wine, and made a toast: "To old and new friends." Richard winked at Laura. Laura beamed at Richard. I felt like a fifth wheel. As the three of us clinked glasses and sipped to my toast, I wondered if I was losing a friend or gaining another. Only time would tell.

The dinner conversation was light and entertaining. Richard proved to have a zany sense of humor. Laura was falling in love. I was falling in like. At ten o'clock, Richard announced he had to rest up for his new job. He glanced at me and shrugged, thanked me for a nice evening, and departed.

"I think Richard is nice," Laura said.

"Yeah, me too," I said.

"I can't believe you have warm fuzzies for Richard."

"I wouldn't go that far," I said. "But I saw a different side of him today."

"Speaking of today, what unbelievable information do you want to tell me?"

"Well," I said as I got up and went into the kitchen to get another bottle of wine. "You're not going to believe what I learned about myself today." Pull cork. Pop. I poured two generous glasses of wine, walked back to the living room, and handed one of the glasses to Laura.

"My Lord, Emarie. That's a huge glass of wine," Laura half-heartedly complained as she took the glass and immediately took a gulp.

"You're going to need it," I said.

"Okay, what's so fascinating about you that I don't already know?"

"Well, to start, I'm the fifth child of seven."

"Seven?" Laura said as she took a sip of her wine. "You're number five?" Then her eyes widened. "You're baby number five?"

"Maybe… but it gets better." I gulped nearly half a glass of wine and blurted out the information that bothered me most. "My adoption was illegal."

"What?" Laura gasped. "What did your parents say?"

"I haven't told them."

"Are you going to?"

"Eventually, but there's more."

Laura nodded, indicating for me to continue.

"Well, my birth mother was never married. She had seven babies by six different men. All the children were abused, neglected, or both. All were placed in foster care or with family members except for one."

"Baby number five. You?"

"Yep, lucky number five," I said as the hair on my arms stood up and my face flushed.

"Wow, that's not the story your parents told you." Laura looked straight at me for a few seconds, then said, "Do you think they didn't want you to know the truth?"

Before I could answer, Laura got up and walked to the other side of the living room. She leaned against a chair. "I wonder what my parents haven't told me."

I was surprised at Laura's sudden self-absorption but was glad she didn't notice my obvious discomfort.

Laura turned toward me, still lost in her own little world. Then she said, "What about your bio-sister? Are you going to call her? You still don't know if she needs a kidney."

"She doesn't need a kidney. She's just curious about me. So right now the answer is no. If I change my mind, I can call the social worker to get her phone number."

"Hmm," Laura said as she resumed her place next to me on the couch. "I feel afraid for you, and I don't know why."

"Maybe it's because you're afraid for yourself."

"What?"

"Well, could it be you're afraid if I meet my bio-sister, I won't be your sister anymore?"

"Maybe." Laura took another sip of her wine and stared at me. Her eyes were unfocused, her mouth slightly open. Her expression creeped me out. *Is there something about Laura I don't know?* Then she snapped back to reality and said, "No that's not it. I'm afraid for you to learn the truth about yourself."

"I can handle the truth," I said, surprised that I nervously laughed.

"What if Dorothy Hall is your birth mother?"

I gasped for breath. I couldn't speak.

"Emarie?" Laura placed her glass of wine on the coffee table and leaned toward me. "Are you all right?"

I still couldn't answer. I thought I'd pass out.

"Emarie?"

"I'm okay," I managed to whisper. "I swallowed wrong." Cough. Cough.

"Yeah, sure."

"I'm not Dorothy Hall's daughter. I'd rather burn in hell than be her daughter."

"Be careful what you wish for," Laura said. "Did you ask the social worker if your birth name was Emily Hall?"

"I asked her if she could tell me the name of my birth mother. She said she couldn't divulge that information." I nervously sipped my wine. "Oh, I just remembered that Richard did some research on Dan Jordan. I hope there's something juicy in there." I reached for my briefcase at the side of the couch, pulled out the file, and flipped through the pages. "Hmm. It's a whole lot thicker than Dorothy's file. Looks like I have some reading to do."

"Well, since you've obviously changed the subject, I'll thank you for a lovely evening," Laura said. "Plus it's getting late, so I'll leave you to your reading."

"Wait just a minute," I said. "You're not driving home after all the wine you drank. I think you should stay here tonight."

"I'm fine." Laura rose from the couch and fell back down. "Whoa. On second thought, I think you're right."

"The guest room is always ready," I said, pointing to the couch. "I'll get you a sheet, blanket, and a pillow."

Laura smiled, looking as if she were three sheets to the wind. I stumbled to the linen closet, surprised that I'd felt fine sitting down but loopy when I stood. By the time I'd walked the fifteen steps back to the living room, Laura was out cold. I put the pillow under her head and covered her with the blanket. Then I took her wineglass into the kitchen.

On my way to my bedroom, I picked up the Dan Jordan file. I managed to change into my pj's and get into bed. I set the alarm for six a.m., positioned a pillow behind my back, opened the file, and promptly fell asleep. On my way to Dreamville, I heard Jim say, "Dan Jordan was the judge on one of the most notorious child abuse/neglect cases in Maryland back in the late '80s or early '90s."

Three o'clock in the morning—the witching hour. I was wide-awake. I propped myself up with two pillows, hoping a new position would help me fall back to sleep. As my eyelids grew heavy, I saw a black shadow at my bedroom door.

"Laura?" I whispered.

CHAPTER TWENTY-TWO

F OR A MOMENT THE SHADOW was still. Then it moved across the room and through the furniture. It stopped and hovered in the corner by the window. Was my sleep-deprived, wine-infused brain playing tricks on me? I hoped so. I squinted. The shadow took on a more solid form. It looked like a man. I watched it. For some reason, I wasn't afraid. The figure pointed two fingers at its nonexistent eyes, and then it pointed its index finger at me. Now I was scared. My saliva dried up, causing my upper lip to stick to my front teeth.

"Jim?" I whispered.

The figure stepped toward my bed. I felt its eyeless stare. Then it moved its head as if to look at the file next to me on the bed. I noticed it wore what looked like a black robe. *Is it in a choir? Is it a professor? Is it... Oh my God... It's a judge.* I mustered the courage to reach for the lamp. I fumbled with the switch. Light filled the room, casting strange shadows. Poof. The figure was gone.

"What the—?" I glanced at the Dan Jordan file. There were two pictures of Dorothy Hall dressed in what looked like a garish, filthy, old-fashioned housedress. "I don't remember these pictures," I mumbled.

I flipped through the file. Another picture of a nice-looking man fell out. His black hair was slicked back. He was impeccably groomed. He looked sophisticated, yet he had an uncharacteristic twinkle in his eyes as if he were trying to say, "I'm not as serious as I look." I turned over the picture—nothing. No name. No date. No photographer's imprint. I studied the man's face. His features disappeared. *He's trying to tell me something.* "Holy crap, that's the man who was in my room."

I couldn't read fast enough. The file had been put together in sequential order. "Thank you, Richard. I owe you one." First was a copy of a newspaper article dated December 15, 1981. The headline read: *POLICE SAVE INFANT FROM ABUSIVE AND NEGLIGENT MOTHER.*

I kept reading.

Police rescued a malnourished and dehydrated infant from the home of the infant's mother, Dorothy Hall. The child was examined by doctors at Darrington Memorial Hospital where it was determined the female infant's condition was life threatening. Nonetheless, the infant is expected to make a full recovery, after which she will be placed in foster care or in the care of relatives until it is determined if Dorothy Hall is a fit mother.

The infant appeared to be approximately one month old, but records show the infant was, in fact, six months of age. Child neglect and endangerment charges have been filed against the child's mother, Dorothy Hall.

Anyone who knows the whereabouts of the child's father should call Detective Kilpatrick at 301-555-2100.

"Wait a minute. If this is about Emily Hall and if I'm Emily Hall, then the father would be dead. If social services knows this tidbit, how come the police didn't know? And there's no mention of Dorothy's other children. Maybe I'm not Emily Hall."

Coldness.

Shivers.

Goose bumps.

Was the ghost still in my room? Or was I creeped out at the thought that the article was about me?

The next item was a hospital report that stated the seven-month-old infant was released from the hospital into the care of foster parents on January 25, 1982. The name of the child was not listed. A psychiatric evaluation of Dorothy was ordered, following which she was found not guilty due to insanity. She was released to a psychiatric hospital where she remained for six months before she was discharged to return home.

A batch of papers piqued my interest. They were court papers on the individual hearings about Dorothy Hall's abuse and neglect of her six children. The information was scant, stating only the charge of harm to a minor as well as the date and time of the hearing. All charges were finalized with no jail time, only psychiatric evaluations and removal of the minor child from the defendant's care.

"Hmm, no info as to what she did to her children? That's suspicious. No mention of the children's fathers. Do I smell a cover-up? Did she tell me the truth? If I am her daughter, what did she do to me?"

I leaned back in bed, clutched a collection of newspaper articles dated 1990, took a deep breath, and read the first one.

LOCAL MOTHER ON TRIAL FOR ABUSE OF SIX CHILDREN.

The article described the atmosphere of the courtroom as tense for the trial of Dorothy Hall. *So there was a trial.* Judge Jordan was calm. *Oh my God, Dan Jordan was the judge.* Dorothy Hall was agitated and spat statements regarding her innocence. Judge Jordan silenced Dorothy several times and threatened to have her removed from the court if she had another outburst. It was like reading about the Salem witch trials. A description of the horror Dorothy Hall perpetrated on baby number one followed. It was the same story Dorothy had told me about Ugly Toni. My curiosity got the better of me, and I skipped ahead to Dorothy's testimony about baby number five. I shot up in bed when I read Dorothy's comment: "The bitch next door starved the little brat. She's the one who should go to jail. Not me." My emotions reeled, but I found the energy and focus to carefully read all the articles. With the exception of Dorothy's statements about baby number five, the stories of her babies were exactly as she told them to me. How could she use the exact words today that she used more than twenty-five years ago? And who was the nosy neighbor? Was she the same person who called the police about Dorothy's first four babies and stole baby number five?

My cell phone rang. I looked at the clock. Five thirty a.m. Who in their right mind was calling so early? I snatched my phone from the night table and said, "Hello?"

"Emarie?"

"Richard?"

"I'm sorry to call so early, but I found some information you need to know regarding Dorothy Hall."

"What?"

"She's dead."

"What?" I began to twist my hair. It was a bad habit I'd developed as a child. It had taken me years to break the habit but only seconds to fall back on the immature, self-soothing behavior.

"Her body was found in a pond not far from her house," Richard said.

"When?" I threw back the covers, got out of bed, and engaged in my other self-soothing behavior—pacing.

"Two years ago."

"Two years ago?" I nearly yelled.

"Yep. Right after she murdered her boyfriend Bull, aka George Jordan."

Richard's statement stopped me dead in my tracks. "Then who did I interview? Who would have had such detailed knowledge of Dorothy's child-abuse trial?"

"I don't know," Richard said. "But I do know Judge Jordan died from a heart attack ten months ago."

"Crap. Why didn't the police officer tell me that?"

"What police officer?"

"The Bingingham County police officer who gave me the skimpy file about Dorothy's arrest for the murder of Bull."

"Beats me. But I found out something else."

"What?"

"Dan Jordan owns Dorothy Hall's house and the house next door."

"Dorothy told me Dan Jordan bought her the house, but I didn't know he owned it. Why would he want to own her house? Why would he want to live next door to her?"

"He didn't."

What do you mean?"

"I got suspicious, so I looked up marriage records for Dan Jordan.

He married Patricia Goodwin in 1970 when they were both in college. The happy couple lived next door to Dorothy."

"Okaaaay?"

"The current resident is Patricia Jordan," Richard said. "The original house was torn down in 1999, and a larger house was built on the lot in 2000. But in 1983, Judge Jordan built a house across town on the other side of the tracks, so to speak. He's the only listed resident of that house. Looks like he and Patricia went splitsville. But they never divorced."

"Richard, are you thinking what I'm thinking?"

"What are you thinking?"

"I'm thinking I need to pay a little visit to Patricia Jordan."

"I'm following you," Richard said.

"Don't follow me. Come with me. I need the support… and maybe even protection."

"You're on! See you in an hour."

I jumped in the shower. Thoughts bounced around my head. *Who did I interview? Why didn't anyone tell me Judge Jordan was dead? Heck, why didn't I look up the information? Why didn't his obituary pop up when I googled his name?* I wrapped myself in a towel and stepped out of the shower. Then I remembered what Jim had said about Judge Jordan. "Lost his job due to a scandal. Don't remember if it was related to the child cases, but it had something to do with his wife."

I got dressed in record time, finishing up right as the doorbell rang.

"Richard, you're early. Wonderful. Let's go."

"Emarie? Richard?" A voice from the couch startled me.

"Laura. I'll explain later," I said as I slammed the door.

In a matter of seconds, Richard and I peeled out of the condo parking lot. A confused Laura watched from the sunroom window.

CHAPTER
TWENTY-THREE

A T NINE A.M., RICHARD AND I arrived at Dorothy's house. Richard opened his door and got out, but I sat in the car thinking about the Dorothy Hall gabfest that had gone on for the entire drive to Darrington. Richard had asked lots of questions. Some I answered. Some I evaded. Richard was like a dog with a bone. Funny how he didn't want to write this story, and now that it was mine he was all over it. I wanted to yell at him to shut up. But I must admit, Richard asked questions I should have asked. I learned more about being a journalist from Richard in two and a half hours than I'd learned on the job for the past two years. Who would have thought Richard the Nitwit would prove to be a more competent journalist than I? I guess that made me a bigger nitwit.

A vision popped into my head of Richard standing before a camera, gripping a microphone as he covered a news story. On the screen, I saw a blue banner with the words: "Richard Bader, Investigative Reporter." Then he said, "Cut. We're out." He hands off the microphone to me. "Thanks, Emarie. You're my favorite gofer."

"Yo, Earth to Emarie. We're here," Richard said as he knocked on the passenger side window. "Where are you?"

"I'm sorry." I opened the passenger window and leaned toward Richard. "Just lost in thought. Why don't we get something to eat first?"

"Good idea. I'm starving."

A few minutes later, I spotted the Golden Arches. I took a spin around Mickey Dees. No spots. Then a car shot out and almost hit my car.

"Idiot," Richard said. "He didn't even look."

"Yeah, but lucky me, I got a parking spot."

Richard and I waited an eternity for our food. The server must have thought we were a couple because as she pushed our tray of Egg McMuffins, hash browns, and coffee toward us, she said, "Here ya go, lovebugs."

I turned away, but I heard Richard chuckle. Then we fought our way to a private table in the corner and ate in silence. *The calm before the storm?*

I have to tell him. Bite of Egg McMuffin. Chew. *It's not right to keep him in the dark.* Swallow. Gulp coffee. Smile at Richard. *Does he have a right to know my business?* Bite of Egg McMuffin. Chew. *Will I open another can of worms?* Swallow. *If this story doesn't work out, will he have information he can use against me?* Gulp coffee. Smile at Richard. *Bound... ar... ies. Oh, screw boundaries.* "Richard, there's something I want to tell you."

"Shoot, my little lovebug," Richard said, sounding unusually playful.

"Um... we... I..."

"Go on. Say it." Richard leaned forward, elbow on the table, chin resting on his hand, his head tilted to the left.

Cripes, he thinks I'm going to profess my love for him. "Well, I think it's important to my story that..."

Richard sank back in the chair, obviously disappointed that my big news was work related.

"...you know a little about me."

Richard straightened up and leaned toward me. Then he took a sip of coffee. "I'm all ears."

"Well, for starters. I was adopted."

"Ooookaaay," Richard replied.

"And I was born here in Darrington, Maryland."

Richard's eyes widened. "In...ter...esting."

I nodded and lifted my coffee cup. I was surprised when my sip developed into a noisy slurp. "A few days ago, my parents received a letter from Bingingham County Department of Social Services informing them that a biological sister was looking for me."

"Biological?" Richard asked. "Clarify biological."

"Biological means we share the same mother and father. Otherwise, the sister would be a half sister."

"Okay. Proceed."

Was Richard making fun of me? Is it a good idea to open up to him? "I was born to a woman who had seven children by six different men."

Richard sank into his chair again. He looked up and moved his head side to side as if he was in deep thought. Then he leaned forward and said, "Please don't tell me you're baby number five."

"Okay. I won't."

"You are. You're baby number five." Richard lifted his coffee cup to his mouth and then put it down. "Holy cow. Did you know this before you took on this story?"

"I didn't exactly take on this story. I was assigned it after you refused it. Remember?"

Richard didn't respond to my verbal spanking.

"To answer your question, no, I didn't know." I fiddled with the empty Egg McMuffin wrapper. "Remember the day I told you I'd won the parent lottery and you *assumed* I was pregnant?"

"Yeah. How could I forget?"

"That was the day I found out the details of my birth. That was the day I began to wonder if Dorothy Hall was my birth mother."

"That must have scared the crap out of you."

"Yep," I said. "In the adoption paperwork my parents gave me, there was an envelope. Inside, there was a copy of my new birth certificate, which showed I was born to my parents. Whoever copied it was sloppy because part of my original birth certificate was visible." I picked up my coffee only to find it was empty. "I need another coffee."

"I'll get it." Richard practically jogged to the counter. In minutes, he was back with two piping hot coffees. "Okay, what did you see on your original birth certificate?"

"My birth name," I said. *I'm going too far. I feel it. This is on a need-to-know basis.*

"So?" Richard said.

Open can. Let out worms. I looked around the restaurant to make sure no one else could hear what I was about to say. I leaned toward Richard and whispered, "Emily Hall."

"You're shitting me," Richard yelled. "Your birth name was Emily Hall?"

Oh my God. He just yelled my secret. Now all of Darrington knows. Jerk. "For God's sake, Richard, keep it down. Remember where we are." I sipped my coffee as visions of Dorothy gulping her happy juice ran through my head. I wished I had some of her happy juice right now.

"I'm sorry," Richard said. "Wait. Wouldn't your last name be that of your birth father rather than your birth mother?"

"Now you sound like Laura," I said. "I don't know. But there's something even more intriguing."

Richard raised his eyebrows, eyes wide in anticipation of hearing something juicy.

"My adoption was illegal."

"Illegal? Why?"

"Because my birth mother wouldn't release me for adoption and my birth father was dead."

"Dead?"

I gulped more coffee, instantly regretting my decision as the hot liquid burned its way down my esophagus. I put my hand to my throat as if it would soothe my pain. I managed a feeble "Yep."

"Was it…" Richard leaned forward. His lips formed a smirk. Then he whispered, "… murder?"

"No, nothing that interesting. Car accident."

Richard leaned back in his seat. He sighed and took a bite of cold hash browns. *I'm losing him.* "But what's interesting is how I was removed from the birth mother's custody."

Richard stared at me, obviously lost in thought.

Is he so bored with my story that he hopes I'll shut up? "I was found by a police officer who heard a baby screaming. The officer looked through a window and saw me in a crib. I was filthy, naked, and…" *Did Richard just smile? Does the mere mention of the word "naked" excite him? Cripes, he's visualizing me naked. Creep!* "…emaciated. Then he forced his way into the house and removed me from the premises. I weighed only seven pounds. I was six months old." I paused. *Why can't I stop myself? I bet his next comment will be, "Thanks for sharing."*

"Holy crap, Emarie," Richard said. "That's the same as Dorothy's story of baby number five."

"I know, but I'm not jumping to any conclusions. It's a common child-neglect story."

"Really? It's common for children to be nearly starved to death by their mother and rescued by a police officer who just happens to walk by the house?"

"Well, it doesn't jive with the story my parents told me. And I don't think they'd lie to me."

"And what was it they told you?"

"They told me my birth mother was married. That she and her husband separated. While they were separated, she became pregnant with me by another man. My birth mother decided to get back together with her husband and thought it was best for me to be placed for adoption."

"Sounds like someone whitewashed your story. Sounds like your parents were lied to."

"I hadn't thought about that," I said, holding back tears. "Oh God, I just remembered something."

"What?"

"On my eighteenth birthday, my mother told me I had four siblings. But I wasn't interested in hearing the rest of the story so she didn't tell me anything more."

"What happened to the other four children?" Richard asked.

"According to the social worker, all of them were removed from their mother's care and either placed in foster care or with family members."

Richard cleared his throat and took another sip of his coffee. "You were the only one who was adopted?"

"Yes."

"Well, whether you're Dorothy's child or not, you're the one who got away." Richard choked out the words.

Something glistened in his eyes. I couldn't believe it. Richard was holding back tears. The more time I spent with him, the more I liked him. But didn't I just call him a creep? Could I have been wrong about him?

"What happened between the time you were removed from your birth mother and the time your parents adopted you?"

"After I was given a clean bill of health and discharged from the hospital, I was placed in foster care. I was adopted by my parents when I was almost ten months old. But because my birth mother refused to sign the adoption papers and my birth father was dead, legally I couldn't be adopted. It appears the judge pushed me through the system and placed me for adoption."

"And that's wrong?" Richard asked.

"It's not wrong, but it is illegal."

"Who was the judge?"

"I don't know. I wish I could find out. I'd like to give him a big hug and kiss."

"Wasn't the judge's name on your adoption paperwork?"

"Ooh, let me check." I reached for my handbag, hoping I'd brought my adoption papers with me. I took out the file Richard had given me and put it on the table. Then I continued to search my handbag like a dog digging in the dirt to recover a long-buried bone.

"Emarie?" Richard said. "Where did you get these two pictures?"

"Umm…" *Oh great. He found the pictures the robed man left on my bed last night. Should I tell him the truth? Yes. Honesty is the best policy.* "They were in the original file."

"No, they weren't. The only photo I remember was this one," Richard said, pointing to the picture from the original file of Dorothy Hall decked out in her WORLD'S BEST MOM T-shirt. "Which one of these lovely ladies is Dorothy?"

"What?" I said, momentarily giving up my dig. Richard was studying the photos the caped being had left on my bed. I glanced at them and said, "They're both Dorothy."

"Which woman did you interview?" Richard asked.

I snatched the photos, picked one, and tossed it back at Richard. "This one. But it's obvious it's the same woman in both pictures."

"I don't think so," Richard said as he thrust the photo back, placing it side by side with the other. "Look. Their hairlines are different. The eyebrows on this woman are arched. This woman's nose is narrower. And one has dark brown eyes and one has blue eyes. These are not the same person."

I examined the photo of the blue-eyed woman. Chills coursed through me as I remembered when Dorothy stared me down with her coal-black eyes. "You might be right," I said. "Or maybe the blue-eyed woman wears brown contact lenses."

"Maybe, but it's not easy to change facial features. So I guess I'm right. These are two different women."

My hands shook as I held the photos. *How could two people who look so different look so much alike?*

"Which one did you interview?" Richard asked.

I handed a photo to Richard. "This one. The one with the brown eyes."

"Hmm." Richard studied the two photos again. "Interesting."

"What's interesting?"

"Well, they're both wearing the same dress."

"Okay? I guess it's possible they both bought the same dress somewhere."

"That's not it. It's the *same* dress." Richard got up and moved to my side of the table. He turned the photos around and pointed to the picture of the brown-eyed woman. "See this stain?"

"Yeah, looks like a bleach splatter."

Richard pointed to the same area on the picture of the blue-eyed woman. "Well, unless they went to the same Oops Sale, I'd say they're wearing the same dress. And notice the print is equally faded on each. What are the chances of that?"

I was speechless.

"Wait a minute," Richard said. "If I remember correctly, the article I read stated Dorothy Hall was wearing a T-shirt with the words..." Richard paused.

I couldn't tell if he was trying to remember what he read or if he was teasing me.

"…'World's Best Mom' when she was found in the pond—dead." Richard picked up the photo of the woman clad in the WORLD'S BEST MOM T-shirt. "See?" He pointed to the woman's eyes. "Brown eyes. So if this brown-eyed woman is Dorothy Hall, and Dorothy Hall is dead, then who did you interview?"

"The question is: What was the color of the eyes of the woman who was found dead in the pond?"

I felt someone staring at us. I looked up and saw a red-haired woman sitting at another table. I looked away and pretended to examine the photos. Richard went back to his seat. Next thing I knew, the woman was standing at our table.

She looked at me and glanced at the photos. "I hope you're not putting your nose where it doesn't belong." Then she hurried out of Mickey Dees. A scent of lavender was all she left behind.

CHAPTER TWENTY-FOUR

"WHAT THE HELL DID SHE mean?" I quickly gathered the photos and papers and stuffed them back in my briefcase. When Richard didn't answer, I looked up to find he was gone.

I rushed out of Mickey Dees and spotted him standing in the parking lot. "What are you doing?" I yelled.

"I was hoping to catch a glimpse of the woman's car so I could get her license plate number." Richard walked back to where I stood. "No such luck. She's gone."

"What do you think she meant about us putting our noses where they don't belong?"

"Don't know, but it sure does make this story even more intriguing," Richard said.

"Did you get a good look at her?"

"Nope."

I walked to my car. "I hope she wasn't threatening us."

"Us?" Richard said. "She was talking to you."

"Me?"

"Yep."

"She doesn't scare me." I looked away, hoping Richard didn't detect my lie.

"Good. Are you ready to find out if Dorothy is dead or alive?"

"I'm ready."

As I put my briefcase in the back seat, Richard slapped the roof and said, "I hope you can handle the truth."

His comment stung. *Why does everyone think I'm so delicate?* "I am woman. Tougher than you'll ever be." I muttered. As I pulled out of the parking spot, I turned to Richard and said, "Are *you* ready to find out if Dorothy is dead or alive?"

"Of course. Why wouldn't I be?"

"Just checking. Wouldn't want you to chicken out on me."

"Not a chance."

We drove the short distance from McDonald's to Dorothy's house in silence. I didn't know what was going through Richard's head, but mine was about to explode from conflicting thoughts and emotions. With all the confidence I could muster, I walked up to Dorothy's front door as Richard tagged behind. The house looked dirtier if that was possible. I glanced at Richard.

His nose flared. He looked at me and said, "Yuck."

The anxiety of seeing Dorothy again was overwhelming, but there wasn't a snowball's chance in hell that I'd back out now. So I took a deep breath and reached for the doorbell, forgetting there wasn't one. One more deep breath gave me the courage to knock on the front door. My face was so hot I was sure I was beet red. Richard looked as cool as a cucumber. *What does that mean? Who comes up with these sayings?* I pounded on the door. No answer.

"She's not home," I said, half-relieved and half-disappointed.

"Maybe it's because she's dead," Richard cheekily replied.

"A few days ago I would have hoped you were right, but now I want the story. Even if it means I have to face that disgusting woman again, whoever she is." I knocked on the door again. After a few seconds and no answer, I said, "Okay, let's try next door."

"Patricia's house?" Richard asked. "Are you sure?"

"I've never been more sure. She's got some explaining to do."

The grass was definitely greener on the other side. I noticed well-manicured shrubs. The scent of flowers tickled my nose before my eyes captured their beauty. Flowers, flowers everywhere—in beds, nestled around trees, and lovingly cradled in ornate ceramic pots. The yard burst with color. The front porch looked freshly painted. Two red Adirondack chairs welcomed us. I half expected a bluebird to land on my shoulder. *How could two people who look so alike be so different?* I reached for the doorbell. Then I hesitated.

I smiled at Richard. "Well, here we go."

He glanced at the doorbell and nodded as if to say, "Go on. Press it."

I pressed it. The doorbell version of Beethoven's fifth symphony echoed through the house.

"What the hell do you want?" a woman screamed from inside.

Instantly, my skin crawled. My scalp retreated and tightened. I answered with another ring of the doorbell, knowing the person on the other side of the door would be forced to open it. I was right. Before me stood the woman I knew as Dorothy Hall.

"Oh, it's you. What the hell are you doing here, Emarie Lukins?"

"Ms. Jordan?" I said. "Ms. Patricia Jordan?"

The woman I knew as Dorothy arched her brow, smirked, and rubbed her chin, obviously thinking how she was going to explain herself.

Gotcha!

"So little miss smarty pants, college girl, ace reporter figured it out, did she?" Then the woman leaned toward me and sneered, revealing yellow and brown teeth. Her breath stank.

Yep, this was definitely the same woman—the woman who'd presented herself as Dorothy Hall. I was about to find out why.

"You must be *real* proud of yourself," she continued. "Who's the nincompoop you brought with you?"

"His name is Richard. He's a colleague of mine," I said. "May we come in?"

"Oh sure." Patricia moved her muumuu-clad blubber body aside and slightly bowed. "Enter, Emarie and Nincompoop. Take off your shoes. I wouldn't want you to dirty the pretty carpet."

"Holy moly," Richard whispered.

The foyer was huge. We kicked off our shoes and arranged them on the hardwood floor. I looked up and was stunned. If I hadn't seen it with my own eyes, I wouldn't believe it. Patricia's house was as neat as a pin and beautifully decorated. To the right of the foyer, a sparkling crystal chandelier hung over a polished mahogany dining room table. Fine crystal and antiques were protected in a large breakfront. To the left, a formal living room with antique furniture and beautiful oil paintings looked like a room in a world-class museum.

Richard and I walked around the spiral staircase. Ahead, we peeked into a magnificent family room. A large flat-screen HD TV took center stage. Surround sound speakers were inconspicuously located throughout the room. A stone fireplace conjured images of cold winter evenings warmed by its flames. Fine leather furniture invited relaxation. Plush carpeting begged to be walked on. I buried my toes in its pile. *Ah! Pure luxury.*

I looked for Patricia but didn't see her, so I glanced toward the kitchen. Cherry cabinets lined the walls. The countertops were granite. The floors hardwood. The appliances stainless steel. Then a whiff of lavender reminded me of the red-haired woman. Patricia's house even smelled good. I suddenly felt out of place, as if I needed to be on my best behavior. My mother's words flashed through my memory. "Now Emarie, don't touch anything and don't take any candy without being offered."

But what struck me was how out of place Patricia seemed in the house. She was better suited for Dorothy's sty.

Patricia emerged from a back room I assumed was a bathroom. I looked away and noticed a sunroom off the kitchen. Through the windows, a huge deck jutted over the large yard. When I looked back, Patricia had made her way into the kitchen and had her head buried in the stainless steel, side-by-side refrigerator.

"Oh no," I whispered to Richard. "She's going to pull out a bottle of her happy juice."

"I could use some happy juice," Richard replied.

"Want some?" Patricia said, waving the bottle of her special-blend orange juice at me, seemingly happy at the thought of having a drinking buddy.

"No thanks," I said.

"How about you, Nincompoop?"

"Name's Richard, and no thank you."

Patricia poured her juice into a crystal glass worthy of twenty-one-year-old Glenlivet scotch, shuffled over to a leather chair, and plopped down, sloshing juice on her muumuu. "Don't get huffy with me, young man," she said as she brushed the happy juice onto the immaculate carpeting. "Sit down. Or do you need an invitation?"

I sat on the love seat, putting me closest to Patricia. Richard took a seat on the couch.

"Nice place you have here," I said, hoping to change the topic and atmosphere.

"Well, whaddya expect from the wife of a well-respected judge?"

I would expect his wife to be better groomed and well-spoken. I kept that thought to myself.

"So whydya come back?" Patricia asked. "Miss me?"

"I think there's a bigger and better story to tell," I said.

"How big?" Patricia leered at me, waiting for my response.

Words failed me.

"Well, don't just sit there. Get your stupid recorder and get to work." Patricia glanced at the clock on the table next to her chair. "I don't have all day." Gulp. Swallow. Burp.

I pulled my recorder from my briefcase and placed it on the end table next to Patricia. I pressed the Record button and said, "Interview with Patricia Jordan, aka Dorothy Hall. September 16, 2016." Then I took my place on the love seat. Richard examined a picture he'd lifted from the end table next to the couch.

Patricia noticed too. "Get your grubby man hands off my things."

"Yes, ma'am," Richard said as he carefully replaced the photo of what looked like a woman with short red hair.

I hesitated, not sure how to start the interview.

"Well, go ahead," Patricia blurted. "Ask me."

"Ask you what?" I said.

"For God's sake, girl, don't you see the elephant in the room?"

I turned to Richard. He shrugged. *Not getting any help from him.*

"Don't check in with Nincompoop," Patricia said. "He's no better a reporter than you."

"Okay," I said, hoping to get my bearings. "Why did you pretend to be Dorothy Hall?"

"I don't pretend to be anybody," Patricia said. Then she looked away. I thought I heard her laugh and say, "Yeah, that's the ticket." Then she leaned into the recorder and yelled, "Because I hate her."

"Why do you hate her?" I asked, pretending to be cool, calm, and collected despite my shaking hands and churning stomach.

"Because she had what I wanted. She had what I couldn't have. And then when I got it, she took it away."

"What did she have that you didn't?" I asked.

"Babies," Patricia spat. "She had babies out the wazoo. Seven of them. She pumped them out like a damn rabbit. And she didn't give a rat's ass about any of them. Hell, if it weren't for me, none of her kids would have survived."

"You were the nosy neighbor, weren't you?" I asked.

Patricia rolled her eyes and shook her head. "You're getting smarter by the minute." She leaned forward and held her head in her hands. "Bull's dead. And it's all her fault."

"What do you mean it's all her fault?" I asked.

Patricia snapped to attention but didn't say anything. Was she going to tell the truth or weave a tall tale? Then she relaxed into the comfort of the chair. "I told you I killed him," she said. "Didn't you listen to your stupid tape?"

"Yes, but I thought you were Dorothy Hall. So I assumed Dorothy killed Bull."

Patricia laughed and croaked like a frog. "What makes you think I'm not Dorothy?" Then she lifted her glass and swirled her magic juice.

"Because Dorothy's dead," Richard said.

Patricia stopped swirling her drink and gave her full attention to Richard. "Really? How did she die?"

"You tell me," Richard said.

Patricia gritted her teeth and glared at Richard.

He didn't flinch.

"I wouldn't know," she said.

"Why not?" Richard asked. "You seem to know everything else about Dorothy."

"I wouldn't know because she's not dead… at least not to me."

Richard smirked. Obviously, Patricia's hesitation had piqued his interest. "Are you telling me that you, Patricia Jordan, killed Bull?" he said, sounding more like a drill sergeant than a reporter.

"Guess so, brainiac."

"Why did you kill him?"

"I told you, it was Dorothy's fault," Patricia spat. "That whore. Once a whore always a whore."

"Why was it Dorothy's fault?" I asked.

"Well, in case you didn't know, Dorothy had seven children by six different men. I don't know about you, but to me, that makes her a whore." Patricia's face turned red. Beads of sweat formed on her forehead. "Worse, she was a lousy mother, and she had sex with her son—her own flesh and blood. If it weren't for me, she'd be in jail."

"If it weren't for you, she'd be alive," Richard said.

"Who?"

"Dorothy," Richard replied.

"Bingo." Patricia winked at Richard, snapped her fingers, and pointed at him.

"So who kept you out of jail?"

Patricia looked and me and grinned. "Ooh, Nincompoop isn't as stupid as he looks." Then she sneered at Richard. "Like I said, I'm the wife of a big shot judge."

"Am I to assume the legal system in Darrington is in cahoots to keep your involvement in Bull's death a secret?" Richard asked, leaving me feeling like a very, very bad reporter.

"Hell no," Patricia said. "They don't give a rat's ass about me. They're in cahoots to keep themselves out of trouble for what they know."

Richard raised an eyebrow, indicating he wanted to hear more.

"Ooh, I like you. You know how to pump a lady…"

Richard raised both eyebrows.

"…for information," Patricia said. She leaned forward, eyes fixated on the floor, and said, "Well, I guess it's time the world knew the truth." Then she slowly raised her head and looked at me. "Can you handle the truth, little lady?"

I was mum, but I did manage to nod in the affirmative. *This is it. The worms are out of the can. Why do I feel as if I'm about to hear the truth about myself?*

CHAPTER TWENTY-FIVE

"WELL, LET'S SEE, WHERE DO I start?" Patricia said as she hauled her gargantuan body to the edge of the chair. In her struggle to lift herself, she nearly tipped it over.

What happened next was unbelievable. Richard shot up, ran over to her, and helped her up. Patricia leaned on Richard and gave him a rotten-toothed smile. I got the feeling she thought her smile conveyed gratitude, but there was something sinister about it. Then she shuffled to the refrigerator to refill her cup of courage.

Richard wiped his hands on his pants as if to clean himself of Patricia's evilness. Then he walked over to the love seat, sat next to me, took a deep breath, and looked at me. I swear his eyes said, "What the hell did you get me into?"

My heart started to race. I felt like I had cotton balls in my mouth. *You? What hell did you get me into?* I looked at Richard and whispered, "multiple personality disorder."

"No such thing," he said. "It's called dissociative identity disorder." Then he got up and returned to the couch.

Thud. Patricia had returned and she managed to plop herself in her chair with no help from Richard. She gulped her magic juice and proceeded as if there had been no break in our conversation. "Let's see, how do I say this without hurting your sissy-girl feelings?" Then she reached into her crotch and scratched like a dog with fleas.

Richard crossed his legs in revulsion. I squelched a laugh.

"Okay," Patricia said. "For starters, I'm not gonna play your stupid game."

"Game?" Richard asked.

"Dipshit," Patricia said. "I'm not Patricia Jordan. I'm Dorothy Hall."

I looked at Richard, but he was focused on Patricia. *Is she dissociating, or is she telling the truth?*

"I'm all ears," Richard said.

"That bitch, Patricia Jordan, stole baby number seven," she said. "That bitch took my baby boy, Georgie Porgie, Puddin' and Pie."

Patricia, or more accurately, Dorothy, scanned Richard and me for a response. Richard leaned forward, indicating for her to continue. I was lost in my thoughts; wondering why, if she was Dorothy Hall, whose house was this and why was she so at home in it?

"When Patti's husband, the right honorable Judge Dan Jordan found out, he stormed into his loving wife's house and took the baby away. I never saw my baby again. I cried myself to sleep every night, longing for my babies. I cried not knowing what happened to baby number five…" Dorothy stopped and swigged her juice.

I gulped.

She continued, "…and baby number seven." Dorothy wiped a tear from her cheek and yelled, "A mother needs to know if her babies are safe, now doesn't she?" She burped and took another gulp of juice. "And everybody in this stupid town knows what happened to baby number five, my sweet little Eerie Emmie." Dorothy glared at me, and I felt the hair rise on my arms. "And they know what happened to baby number seven. Secrets. Secrets. Damn secrets. All to protect crazy Patricia Jordan. She's a lunatic. Crazy as the day is long." Dorothy looked straight at me. "But you, you smart-ass college grad, already knew that. Didn't you?"

I didn't know how to respond. Why was I so afraid of this woman?

Richard came to my rescue. "What happened to baby number seven?" he asked, apparently unfazed by Dorothy's rant.

"Ms. Lukins may think you're charming, but I think you're a dumb-ass."

Richard remained silent.

Dorothy slammed her glass on the end table. The glass shattered, spewing her special juice across the room. Richard and I didn't move. Blood ran down Dorothy's arm. She didn't appear to notice as it dripped on the beautiful carpet. Once again, she dragged herself out of the chair, smearing blood on its fine Italian leather. She waddled like a penguin into the kitchen. Richard and I watched her get another glass of her special juice.

Neither of us moved. Heck, I didn't even breathe. I watched Dorothy like a hawk, contemplating how I could retrieve my recorder and get the hell out of the house at the first sign of danger. She returned to her bloodstained chair. I reached for my cell phone.

"Sissy," Dorothy spat. "Whaddya gonna do, call the police? I'm not gonna hurt you. I wanted to the first time I saw you, but I didn't. I'm sure not gonna hurt you when your lover boy is sitting next to you."

Dorothy's juice had worked its magic. She was a mean drunk. I was terrified.

"Why did you want to hurt her?" Richard asked.

I couldn't believe it. Richard was baiting her. Now I was horrified.

"Because I knew who she was the moment I laid eyes on her."

"So who is she?" Richard asked.

"Boy, don't make me throw this glass at you. You're not that stupid. Or hasn't she told you?"

"Told me what?" Richard had the guts to ask.

"You're her lover. Doesn't she whisper secrets to you under the covers while she's having her way with your private parts?" Dorothy closed her eyes, tilted her head back, and moaned.

I was beyond horrified. I was angry. *Richard, say something. She's making me out to be a slut. Ooh... and with you!*

Dorothy lifted her head, provocatively gyrated her hips, and let out a maniacal laugh.

Richard wasn't amused, but he wasn't afraid either. "So who is she?" he calmly asked.

Dorothy hesitated, looked at Richard as if he had two heads, then shook her head as if to bring herself back to reality. "Back to baby number seven," she blurted. "Stupid shit, Patricia, stole that baby from me. Know what her dearly departed husband did?"

Richard shook his head to say no.

"He kept him. Raised the damn brat himself." Dorothy rubbed her face, smearing it with blood and making herself look like Heath Ledger's version of the Joker. I felt as if I were in a real-life horror movie.

"Did he take good care of him?" Richard asked.

"I guess so," Dorothy said. "Bull grew up to be a big strapping man and one of the best sex toys I ever had. He was even better than his daddy."

"Did you know Bull was your son when you started dating him?" Richard asked, ignoring Dorothy's comment about Bull's sexual skills.

"Nincompoop," Dorothy said to Richard. Then she pointed at me. "Nitwit there already asked me that question. Listen to her stupid tape." She paused and seemed to think about her next statement. "But how was I supposed to know? Hadn't seen him since I pushed him out of my love canal. I had too many men to even know who Bull's real daddy was."

"Pushed who out of your love canal?" Richard had the nerve to ask.

"Bull," Dorothy yelled. "If you're trying to get my goat? Well, it's working."

Aha! She just contradicted herself. She knows the rapist was Bull's father. Her comment about how many men she'd had sex with made me shiver with disgust. I hoped Dorothy didn't notice.

"Don't be so shocked," Dorothy said to me, making me wonder if she could read my mind. "I was quite a looker when I was young."

Put a bag over her head and say you did it for glory. Dorothy's words ran through my head.

"Dan Jordan raised Bull?" I said.

"Yep," Dorothy spat out.

"Did Patricia know?" I asked.

"Of course. She was part of the cover-up."

"What cover-up?" Richard asked.

"The cover-up of what Judge Jordan did with baby number five and baby number seven. Get with the program, idiot. Patricia's eggs were hard-boiled. She couldn't have babies. That's why she hated me. She was crazy jealous. That's why she stole Bull from me. She begged her sweet husband to let her keep Bull. You know, a present for his darling, barren, batshit-crazy wife who he couldn't stand to live with, let alone do the hokey-pokey. But instead, he kept Bull for himself and hid my baby boy from me. That really got up Patricia's craw. She couldn't stand the fact her husband loved a whore-born baby more than he loved her."

"You never suspected Bull was your son?" Richard asked.

"No."

"Why not?" Richard asked.

"Well, I didn't see a resemblance to anyone I knew in him. Like I said, I can't remember who his daddy was."

Liar, liar, pants on fire.

"Okay, so everyone but you knew Bull Jordan was your son?" Richard asked.

"Well, you're a regular Matlock, aren't you?"

"Matlock?" Richard said.

"You doofus, don't you know anything? *Matlock* was one of the best detective shows on TV." Dorothy gave Richard a dismissive wave, indicating her annoyance with his ignorance of everything she found important. "Ah, you're too young to know good TV. I can show you some good TV."

Oh no, Hee Haw *reruns here we come.* Surprisingly, there wasn't a DVD or VHS player. I relaxed.

"So am I to believe that everyone in this town kept their mouth shut and no one told Bull you were his mother?" Richard said.

"Yep. That's what you're supposed to believe."

"So why did Patricia kill him?" Richard asked, not taking Dorothy's bait.

"Well, nosy Patricia just happened to walk in on Bull and me while we were doing the nasty." Dorothy broke out in crazed laughter. "You should have seen her face… her eyes all bugged out and all. Then she went berserk. Crazy woman. Been committed to the loony bin at least a dozen times."

"So why did she kill Bull?" Richard asked.

Dorothy directed her response to me. "I think the speechless wonder already knows why."

"Why?" I said.

"Oh, you're a useless piece of shit. How did you ever become a reporter? You know why Patricia killed him."

"Refresh my memory," I said.

"Because it's not right to have sex with your momma," Dorothy screamed. "Patricia went batshit crazy when she saw Bull on top of me. She yanked his naked ass off me and yelled, 'She's your mother. Dorothy's your mother.' Then she went into the kitchen, got a knife, and stabbed him to death. EEE… EEE… EEE…" She made stabbing motions. Then she looked at me, smiled, and said, "*Psycho*, right?"

"Right," I muttered.

"So there you have it."

"Okay," Richard said. "But according to the court records, your body was found floating in a pond two years ago. Yet here you are. So whose body was found in the pond?"

"Who do you think?" Dorothy said.

"Patricia Jordan?" Richard said.

"Oooh, you're good. But do you know who killed her?"

"Dan Jordan?" I asked.

"Ha! She speaks," Dorothy said, belittling me again.

"Yes, and I believe I speak the truth."

"Pfff." Dorothy blew me off. Then she stared at me as she tried to gather her thoughts. "Ever heard the phrase 'opportunity knocks'?"

"Of course, but what does it have to do with the murder of Patricia Jordan?" I asked.

"Well, the whole situation gave good old Dan an idea… Oh, I can't tell you. I'm not supposed to be talking about any of this."

"Too late," Richard said.

"Well, if you insist," Dorothy said. "Dan decided if Patricia was dead, he could finally have a life."

"Hmm, interesting," Richard said. "So how did Dan kill Patricia?"

"He didn't," Dorothy said. Then she gulped her juice and said, "I did. He made me."

I leaned forward and stared at Dorothy. "No one can make you kill someone."

"You're obviously not from these parts."

Yes, I am. But I hope I'm not from you.

"So how did you kill her?" Richard asked.

Dorothy smiled and rubbed her hands together, obviously happy to tell her story. "The best way to kill a crazy pig is with food," she said. Then she smiled to herself and continued, "It may have been Dan Jordan's idea to kill her, but it was my idea how. I came here to her house and knocked on the door. Old pig peered through the peephole. What she saw was me standing there with a big, juicy steak on a plate. 'Peace offering?' I said. She was so predictable. She opened the door and invited me in. Piggy Patti gladly accepted the steak and headed to the kitchen. That's when I grabbed her. She stumbled and fell to the floor. I took the steak and jammed the bloody hunk of raw meat down her throat. She choked to death on her last meal. Made it look like she died of natural causes." Dorothy laughed and shook her head. "Now that's using your noodle."

Is it possible for two three-hundred-pound women to engage in that type of struggle? I don't think so.

"Then how did her body end up in the pond?" Richard asked.

"I called Dan and told him the job was done. Then he dragged Patricia's lard-ass corpse to the lake and threw her in."

Incredible Hulk, right?

"Who dressed Patricia in your WORLD'S BEST MOM T-shirt?" Richard asked.

"Oh, that was Dan's idea," Dorothy said. "A few weeks before pig wife's unfortunate choking, her loving husband took pictures of her wearing my T-shirt. She didn't want to do it, but Dan bribed her by promising if she did, she wouldn't have to deal with me anymore. Ha! So you see, he didn't lie to her. Most folks thought Patricia and I looked alike, but because we were both social outcasts, everyone was afraid to make eye contact. If they had, they would have seen we were different people. Anyway, Dan figured if her body was found clad in my T-shirt, everyone would think it was me. And if people thought I was dead, no one would care. No one would ask questions. It worked."

"And then Dan died?" I said.

"Yep." Dorothy grinned at Richard and me. I wasn't sure what response she wanted. Then she laughed until she coughed and hacked.

"So you poisoned him?" Richard asked.

"Don't put words in my mouth, idiot," Dorothy said. "Fact was he couldn't bear how things ended up. He loved Bull. God only knows why. That boy was dumb as dirt. Dan also knew the jig was up. He couldn't live with the cover-ups and secrets. He was haunted by what he'd done. So a year or so after he lugged his wife's big dead ass to the lake, he popped himself with his revolver. Made sure he didn't ruin his handsome face. I have to admit, he was a good-looking corpse."

"So it wasn't a heart attack that killed him?" I asked.

"No. Where did you get that information?"

"Don't know. Doesn't matter," I said.

"When did Dan buy your house next door?" Richard asked.

"You really are a nincompoop," Dorothy said. "The information is in the public record. Look it up yourself."

"It would be faster if you told me," Richard said.

"He bought the house in 1982. It was a keep-your-mouth-shut gift. It worked. I never told anyone—not even his darling wife—what I knew about baby number five."

"What about baby number five?" Richard said.

Dorothy shook her head and sneered. Then she transformed into an image of evilness and said, "Eerie Emmie."

CHAPTER TWENTY-SIX

I HYPERVENTILATED AND MOMENTARILY PASSED out. Richard ran over to me, concern in his eyes. Or maybe it was annoyance. I wasn't sure. I felt light-headed and disoriented. I wanted to go home, get in bed, and pull the covers over my head to ward off the boogeyman.

"Ha! I knew it," Dorothy said. "You're pathetic."

"Low blood sugar," Richard replied.

"That's a hell of an excuse," Dorothy yelled. "I know you two ate before you came. You stank like poster children for Mickey Dee's. Practically wilted the flowers."

"I'm fine," I said. "As you were saying?"

"I wasn't saying anything." Dorothy maneuvered herself out of the chair and headed into the kitchen.

Richard reached toward me and touched my hand. "It's almost over."

It took my last ounce of strength to smile at him. I took a deep breath and slowly released it. My moment of relaxation was interrupted.

"I'm bleeding like a stuck pig," Dorothy yelled from the kitchen. "Why the hell didn't you tell me?"

"Thought you knew," Richard said.

"Thought I knew, huh?" Dorothy slammed the refrigerator door. Bottles rattled. "It's your fault if anything broke," she said. Then she wiped off her bloody hand with a kitchen towel, but she only managed to smear it more. She didn't notice the blood on her face. She still looked like the Joker.

I watched Dorothy sway on her way back to the family room. *Please fall and break your neck. Put me out of my misery.*

"Baby number five?" she said. "Yes, let's talk about Eerie Emmie. Little shit got herself stolen from me." Dorothy stared at me and continued, "Ooh, I've got an idea. Why don't you tell me what happened to Eerie Emmie?"

"Me?" I said. "I don't know anything about baby number five."

"Don't play stupid with me."

"I don't understand what you're saying."

Dorothy threw her glass across the room. It crashed against the stone fireplace. Shattered glass and beads of happy juice sparkled on the carpeting.

"I knew who you were the moment I saw you," Dorothy said. "You look just like... She cleared her throat and coughed. Her voice cracked when she said, "...your daddy."

She sounded like a man. I looked at Richard. He looked at me and shrugged.

The front door slammed. Richard rose. *My knight in shining armor.* Dorothy remained still as her eyes darted back and forth. Footsteps echoed in the foyer.

"What are you doing here?"

I looked toward the voice. A woman with short red hair stood, staring at Dorothy. I wasn't sure if she even noticed Richard and me.

"Just dropped by to say hi, but you weren't home," Dorothy said, sounding like her old self. "Then these two nitwits dropped by to see me."

"I'm sorry," I said. "I thought she was Patricia Jordan."

The red-haired woman turned her angry glare on me.

"My name is—"

"I know who you are." The woman stepped into the room. She stood in front of Richard and me.

She looked familiar, but I couldn't place her. Then it hit me. She was the woman from McDonald's.

She pointed at Dorothy and said, "She told me all about you. And I know who you really are. Recognized you the moment you walked into McDonald's. There was no mistaking you. You look just like your father. You've got his black hair and coal-black eyes."

"Vernon?" I muttered.

"Vernon? Who's Vernon?"

"Dorothy said—"

"Don't believe a word you heard from her." The woman shot a glance at Dorothy. I thought I heard her grunt. Then she stood in front of me and said, "You're not Dorothy's child."

I shot up straight as if a bolt of lightning energized me. "Then whose child am I?"

The woman walked over to the couch and sat on the end as far away from Richard as she could. Then she leaned forward and rubbed her hands together while she gathered her thoughts. "You're the daughter of—"

"*No*," Dorothy screamed. She tried to get out of her chair but only managed to fall back into the safety of the leather cushions. "Don't tell her anything. You'll ruin everything."

"You're the daughter of Dan and Patti Jordan."

"What?" I said. "After what Dorothy told me, I had a horrible feeling I was her daughter."

"I'm sure she told you an incredibly convoluted story. One that's nothing more than the ranting of a crazy person. I assure you the truth is much simpler."

"How simple," I asked.

"Wait," Richard said. "How do you know she's Dan and Patricia Jordan's daughter?"

Instant anger. Not at Richard. At myself. Once again, Richard asked an obvious question.

The woman looked at me and said, "Is your name Emarie Lukins?"

"Yes," I said.

"Are your parents Andrew and Marie Lukins?"

"Yes," I barely said aloud.

The woman clapped her hands. "Then it's settled. You're Dan and Patti's child."

I noticed a twinkle in the red-haired woman's eyes. Was it joy? "Prove it," I said.

"Only a blood test could prove it. But if I told you why you were placed for adoption, I think it might be all the proof you need."

"Okay."

"Some of this may be hard for you to hear, but as they say, sometimes the truth hurts."

I nodded, giving her permission to continue.

"Well, as you know, Dorothy Hall slept with every Tom, Dick, and Harry. And she was quite fertile. To top it off, she was a horrible mother."

"That's not the half of it," Dorothy blurted.

"Your birth mother, Patti, was horrified by how Dorothy treated her children," the woman continued, ignoring Dorothy's comment. "She complained endlessly to Dan, or as people around here knew him, JJ, short for Judge Jordan. In 1981, Dorothy was hauled into court after social services responded to an anonymous call from—"

"Anonymous, my ass. You know who called," Dorothy yelled.

The woman looked at Dorothy, and then she looked back at me. "As I was saying, *Dorothy* was hauled into court after social services responded to an anonymous call from a person who reported the horrible living conditions of Dorothy's four children." She glared at Dorothy. "Social services intervened. The children were immediately removed from Dorothy and placed with either family members or foster parents. Unfortunately for the kids, the situation wasn't much better than living with their mother."

Hmm. Didn't Dorothy say she only had one child living with her at a time?

"I was a good mother. I was the world's *best* mom. I've got the T-shirt to prove it."

Once again, the woman ignored Dorothy. "Soon after, and after many years of longing for a baby, Patti gave birth to her first child—you. Your father was present for your birth, but he couldn't handle the demands of work, marriage, and fatherhood, so he moved out, leaving you in the care of your mother. Your mother, Patti, was never quite normal, and the raging hormones of pregnancy and birth threw her over the edge—she had a mental breakdown. Why Dan married her is beyond me. But why your mother lived here and your father lived on the other side of town made perfect sense. Your father didn't visit often, so he was unaware of your mother's mental and physical condition. Worse, he was unaware of *your* condition. One day he dropped by to check up on your mother and you. Your mother was home, but you were gone."

"Shut up," Dorothy yelled.

"No. She has a right to know," the woman said. "So you shut up."

I glanced at Dorothy. I thought I'd see rage. Instead, she appeared calm. The woman seemed to have power over Dorothy.

"Your father questioned your mother as to your whereabouts. She laughed and said she traded you to Dorothy Hall for a box of chocolate candy."

"Those were damn good candies," Dorothy said. "Life is like a box of chocolates. *Forrest Gump*, right?"

The woman ignored Dorothy. "Your father ran next door and pounded on Dorothy's door—"

"Nearly knocked it off the hinges," Dorothy said. "Idiot."

"Dorothy refused to let him in the house," the woman continued. "He ran around the back, saw an open window, and heard you screaming at the top of your lungs. He looked in the window and was horrified. You were naked, covered in feces, and deathly thin. He knew you were in medical danger, so he ran back to the front door, forced his way into the house, and then called the police. When they arrived, he had them arrest Dorothy and rush you to the hospital. We feared you would die, but you didn't. Thankfully, you got the family's hardy gene. You survived and started to thrive. Your mother, Patti, was admitted to a psychiatric facility. Dorothy was charged with child endangerment, but nothing became of the charge. She was released. With your mother in the psych ward, your father knew he couldn't take care of you, and he knew your mother couldn't and shouldn't take care of you. He wanted you to grow up happy and healthy, so *he* placed you for adoption."

"According to the social worker I spoke with, my adoption was illegal."

The woman flinched and scratched her lip. Obviously what I said unnerved her. "Why?"

"Because my birth mother refused to sign the adoption papers and my birth father was dead. Therefore, I wasn't legally released for adoption. So, if my birth father was deceased, how could Dan Jordan be my father?"

"Well, I wouldn't know anything about that. I don't know how he…" The woman glanced at Dorothy. "I mean, I don't know all the details. All I know is your father, Dan Jordan, begged Andrew and Marie Lukins to adopt you."

There was something wrong with the red-haired woman's story. I wanted to scream "Liar" and tell her I'd seen part of my original birth certificate and that my birth name was listed as Emily Hall, but something told me to keep my mouth shut. I knew I had to keep that information a secret. At least for now. So I decided to pick up on her last statement. "Dan Jordan knew my parents?"

"Shut up," Dorothy screamed. "You promised you'd never tell."

The woman glared at Dorothy. "Dan is dead. Therefore, Emarie has a right to know who she is." Then she looked at me and said, "Yes, he knew your parents. Dan and your father were best friends in college. They pledged to be best friends forever. When Dan asked your parents to adopt you, they were overjoyed. They had longed for a child for years. They came to Darrington to meet you. It was love at first sight. There was no question as to whether or not they would welcome you into their lives."

"Okay, I need a break," I said. I got up, put on my shoes, and went outside. My mind raced. Questions and emotions nearly paralyzed me. I was surprised Richard joined me.

"Are you okay?" Richard asked as he wiggled his foot into a shoe.

"I don't know. I'm relieved I'm not Dorothy's daughter. But my parents lied to me."

I buried my head in Richard's chest. He rubbed my back and let me cry until I pulled away and sat in one of the red Adirondack chairs.

"They lied to me," I said, wiping my tears with my hands.

"They did it because they love you," Richard said.

"I've always believed they loved me, but still, they lied to me. I'm not baby number five. I'm the only child of Dan and Patricia Jordan. That's a big difference."

"Yes, it is," Richard said. "But your parents never told you that you were baby number five."

131

"In so many words, my mother did. She told me my birth mother was married and had four children. She and her husband separated, she met another man and got pregnant with me. She and her husband decided to reconcile and thought it best to put me up for adoption. That's the story I grew up with. That makes me baby number five." I thought I heard the woman arguing with a man inside the house, but I was too upset to mention it to Richard. Besides, he didn't seem to notice. "And why would the social worker tell me I was the fifth child out of seven?"

Richard looked at me. I couldn't tell if he was confused or concerned.

"And why was my birth name Hall rather than Jordan?"

CHAPTER TWENTY-SEVEN

T HE FRONT SCREEN DOOR CREAKED, diverting my attention. The red-haired woman appeared, carrying a tray on which a pitcher of lemonade and a plate of cheese and crackers rested.

"I thought you might need some nourishment." She put the tray on the table, looked at Richard, and said, "There's a chair on the back deck. Could you get it, hon?"

Once he'd left, the woman sat in the chair next to mine. She poured a glass of lemonade and handed it to me.

"Thank you," I said. One sip was heaven. It was the most delicious lemonade I'd ever had. "This is wonderful."

"It's fresh. I always keep a bottle of fresh lemonade in the fridge."

"Dorothy always keeps a bottle of her special juice in the fridge," I said, instantly regretting my comment.

The woman squinted. She seemed confused as to who I was talking about. Then she offered me the plate of cheese and crackers. "I know."

"What, no chocolate?" I said, hoping to relieve the tension.

She smiled. "I have chocolate cookies, but I thought better of it. Besides, cookies don't taste good with lemonade."

"Where's Dorothy?"

133

"Who? Oh… yes. I sent her home. She's more trouble than she's worth."

I couldn't help but laugh. "That's the truth."

"You don't know the half of it."

Richard appeared holding a chair. He put it down so he faced me and the woman. She poured him a glass of lemonade and offered him cheese and crackers, which he happily accepted.

As the woman placed the plate on the table, she glanced at me and said, "I can see this is difficult for you. If you want, we can stop."

"No, I want to know the truth." But deep down, I didn't trust that she would tell me the truth.

She sighed and went back in the house. Richard and I sat in silence, sipping lemonade, both of us lost in thought. I was about to say something when the woman returned carrying my briefcase. She placed it next to me. Was she hinting for Richard and me to leave?

She reached into her pocket and handed me my recorder. "You may want to record our conversation."

I guess she wanted to tell me more.

"Oh, thanks." I placed the recorder next to the tray of cheese and crackers and started the interview. "Interview with… I'm sorry, I don't know your name."

"Anonymous," the woman said.

I wanted to argue the importance of knowing who she was, but I decided to let it go for now. "Okay… let's begin at the beginning," I said. "How do you know Dorothy?"

"Dorothy? Oh… um… I know Dorothy through Patti. She and Dorothy had been friends since before they could walk," she said. "Their relationship was always contentious."

"Tell me about… my birth mother… Patricia," I said.

"Contentious?" Richard interrupted. "Why was their relationship contentious?"

"They were in love with the same man."

"Dan Jordan?" Richard asked.

"Yes."

"Seems to me he didn't love either one of them," Richard said.

Oh, he loved one of them… dearly. But I don't want to talk about it."

Richard glanced at me. I wondered what the woman was hiding, but I decided not to pursue the subject. I didn't want to anger her. What I wanted was more information.

"So, Emarie, you want to know about your birth mother, Patti. Well, I'll skip her childhood dramas and get to what I think would be of most interest to you."

"Okay."

She took a deep breath, exhaled, and like a well-rehearsed robot, she said. "Patti met Dan during her sophomore year of college. Patti was madly in love with him. A few months later, they married. She was happy. I don't know about Dan. He didn't seem to take to marriage, or maybe he didn't take to Patti's moods, delusions, and paranoia. After a few years, Dan landed his dream job as an assistant state's attorney. He got busy. Patti got crazy. After more than a decade of marriage, your father thought if Patti had a baby, she would mature and be normal. Men always think motherhood makes a woman happy and normal. Go figure. Well, the stress of motherhood didn't help. Your father moved out. Your mother decompensated. You already know how you ended up with Dorothy. When you were released from the hospital, your father took you, but his busy life wasn't conducive to fatherhood. Your father knew his old college buddies, Andrew and his wife, Marie, struggled with infertility, so he asked them if they would adopt you. They said yes. The rest I already told you. End of story." The woman looked at me as if she expected me to ask her a question she feared to answer.

"And *your* friendship with Dorothy?" I asked.

"I was *never* and am *not friends* with Dorothy."

"How did you know Dan and Patti?" Richard asked.

"We all went to college together."

"Who is we all?" Richard asked.

"Dan, Patti, Andrew, Marie, and me." The woman stood. "This conversation is over."

"Richard's question seems to have angered you," I said. "Why?"

"It's my secret… I mean it's my business, so stay out of it."

I was taken aback by the abruptness and tone of her reply. I wasn't ready to stop, so I decided to change the topic. "Why does everyone in this town keep so many secrets?"

The woman sighed and sat down. "Other than Bull's and Dorothy's deaths, there were no secrets, just cover-ups."

"One and the same," I said.

"Not exactly."

"How so?"

"Well," the woman cleared her throat. "A secret implies not everyone knew everything or anything for that matter. In other words, a secret can be kept by one person or a few, but a secret kept by a whole town? Now that's impossible."

"Okaaay," I said. "How would you describe a cover-up?"

"A cover-up, in this town at least, means there's no secret. The truth is there for the taking if you have the time and energy to dig through the BS."

I paused to gather my thoughts. "So what you're saying is the truth is out there but a few people can make it so hard for someone to discover it that eventually the person or persons will lose interest and give up the search?"

"Sort of." The woman smirked. "What I mean is everyone in this town knows the truth, but if they wanted to prove it, well, it would be nearly impossible."

"So after a while, everyone just shuts up and doesn't ask any questions," Richard said.

"Yes, and everyone goes about their business. You know, live and let live."

"More like live and let die. Bond. James Bond," I said as the movie's theme song by *Paul McCartney and Wings* rattled through my head.

"What?" the woman asked.

"Oh, nothing. Just thinking of lyrics to an old song."

"So what's the truth?" Richard asked.

"Which truth?"

"Well, for starters, if Dorothy is still alive, then whose body was found floating in a pond?"

The woman straightened up and furrowed her brow. "You have the articles. You tell me."

"Well, if Dorothy was just here, then obviously she's not dead."

The woman didn't respond. I couldn't tell if she was contemplating what to say or if she was angry.

"But a newspaper article dated a few days after Bull's death stated Dorothy's body was found floating in a pond," Richard said.

"I believe if you read the newspaper article again, you'd see it stated a body, *presumed* to be that of Dorothy Hall, was found floating in a pond."

"That's what I just said," Richard nearly yelled.

The woman poured Richard another glass of lemonade apparently stalling for time to calculate her next response. "I beg to differ. Finding the body of a particular person floating in the pond and finding a body presumed to be that of a particular person are two different things. The former indicates Dorothy was dead. The latter indicates she may be alive. Be very careful with how things are worded, and you'll begin to see how clever the cover-up was and is."

Richard looked at me and shrugged. I was about to ask a question, but he beat me to the punch. "We already know that Dorothy killed Patti and Dan Jordan threw Patti's body in the pond. So I guess the body presumed to be that of Dorothy Hall is really Patti's."

"Who told you that?"

"Dorothy," Richard and I replied in unison.

"Dorothy is an emotionally and psychologically unstable person. She's bound to say anything for attention."

Richard leaned forward and reached for a piece of cheese. "Is she lying or not?"

"I'm not going there." The woman picked up the pitcher and poured herself a glass of lemonade.

"Why not?" I asked.

"It's best left unanswered. End of conversation."

I felt angry and disrespected. I'd thought the woman was being open with me. Now she shut me down. I wasn't going to let her get away with blowing me off, but I didn't speak up soon enough.

"What about Judge Jordan?" Richard piped in. "Is he dead?"

The woman diverted her gaze as if she was embarrassed about what she was about to say. "Sadly, yes."

"Heart attack?" I said.

The woman glared at me. "You probably read that in the newspaper too. Better check again."

"Richard? Did you give me the article about Judge Jordan's death?"

"I put it in your briefcase. It's in a red folder with the newspaper article about Dorothy's death."

I rummaged through my briefcase until I found the red folder. The two articles in question were there. Sure enough, the two-year-old article about Dorothy stated a body presumed to be that of Dorothy Hall was found in Watson's Pond. And the ten-month-old article covered Judge Jordan's death in Darrington Memorial Hospital.

I looked at the woman. "He committed suicide, didn't he?"

"Is that what the article says?"

"Well, it says he died from a heart attack following the treatment of wounds consistent with a gun-related incident."

"Okay." The red-haired woman smiled at me, but it wasn't a kind smile; it was more of a know-it-all smirk. I felt uneasy. Then she said, "Therein lies the truth. Now find it."

Richard grabbed the article out of my hand. "He shot himself, didn't he?"

"Is that what the article says?"

"Well, it implies he did."

"Or it implies someone else shot him," I said.

The woman grinned. "Such as?"

"Such as his wife," I replied.

"That's a good point." Richard handed me the article and stared at the woman, obviously trying to gather his thoughts. "If Dorothy isn't dead and you won't or can't confirm it was Patti's body found in the Watson's Pond, then where is Patti?"

The woman took a deep breath and without a word, she went into the house.

Richard gave me a fake, closed-lip smile. I didn't know what his smile meant, and I didn't feel like asking because although I was silent, my brain was screaming. Everything I knew about the story of Bull's death rattled through my head. Dorothy's stories of her babies haunted me. I didn't trust the red-haired woman anymore. I wanted to run. I wanted to go home. I wanted my parents. Then a strange feeling buzzed through me. I didn't know if I could trust my parents.

I looked up. Dorothy was standing at the front door staring at me. A chill ran through me. Hadn't she been sent home? Richard appeared to be lost in thought again. *Doesn't he see Dorothy? What is he thinking? Does he know something I don't know?* When I looked back at the door, Dorothy was gone.

I was about to ask Richard a question when the woman returned. In her hand, she held a picture. She sat down and handed the picture to me. Richard leaned in to get a look at the photo of a bedraggled woman wearing a T-shirt with the words WORLD'S BEST MOM stretched across her huge breasts. I glanced at Richard.

"Not Dorothy Hall," he said. "Dorothy has brown eyes."

I looked at the woman and noticed she had green eyes. I returned my attention to the woman in the photo. *How can two people who look so different look so much alike?*

"Patricia Jordan?" I said.

"No." The woman arched her eyebrows and shrugged. "What you hold is the key to the truth." She stood up, indicating our time was up. "Well, we've wasted enough time here. I need to get on with my day." Then she thrust a limp hand toward me.

Does she want me to kiss it or shake it? I shook it.

"You have *no* idea how nice it is to finally meet you," she said. Then she picked up the pitcher of lemonade and the plate of cheese and crackers and went back inside the house.

But I had two more questions. Through the screen door I yelled, "Wait, what's your name? And why does my birth certificate say my birth name was Emily Hall instead of Emily Jordan?"

"You'll figure it out," the woman yelled back.

I was dumbfounded. I turned the doorknob. It was locked. I'd been shut up by being shut out. Now what?

CHAPTER TWENTY-EIGHT

RICHARD SNORED THE ENTIRE TRIP home. I wasn't sure if he was exhausted or if he was avoiding conversation. Either way, I was happy for the solitude. Although my brain was obsessed with the day's events, I wasn't in any mood to discuss Dorothy Hall and Patricia Jordan.

I pulled into my condo parking lot, partly happy to be home and partly anxious about rewriting my story.

"Richard," I said as I shook him. "We're here."

Richard yawned and stretched. "That was fast." Then he looked at me as if he wanted me to ask him to stay.

"I'd better jump on my story," I said.

"You still need more information."

"What do you mean?"

Richard looked at me like a scornful parent. "I think you know what I mean."

"I know. I need to talk to my parents."

"Ob...viously," Richard said, à la Professor Snape from the *Harry Potter* movies. He walked toward his car. Then he turned toward me and said, "Who do you think the red-haired woman is?"

"I don't know."

"Hmm." Richard sighed. "She seemed more at home in the big house than Dorothy. See you at work."

As Richard drove away, I thought about the red-haired woman. I remembered her saying I'd figure out her name. *Do I already know it?* I wondered as I dragged my weary body up the stairs to my condo. As I tossed my things on the dining room table, an envelope caught my eye.

"Oh no, Laura's mad at me." I tore open the envelope. The typewritten note read: *Emarie, I know you have a lot of questions about your adoption. You can ask me anything. I've got your back.*

I immediately called Laura. Ring. Ring.

"Hi, Emarie. What's up?"

"What's up with this note?"

"Oh, I forgot about the note. It was delivered by courier."

"Courier? Who sent it?"

"How would I know?"

"What time was it delivered?"

"Around ten this morning, just before I left," Laura said. "Why?"

"Did you sign for it?"

"No, the courier handed it to me and left."

"Did the courier ask who you were?"

"Emarie, why all the questions?"

"Never mind. It's not important. I've gotta go."

"Emarie? What were—"

"Gotta go. I'll call you later. Bye."

I read the note again. Something about the phrase "I've got your back" made me pause. It sounded like something Jim would say. But how would he know anything about my adoption? And why would he send me an unsigned note? Richard? No, it couldn't be. He hadn't known I was adopted until I told him at McDonald's this morning. Why didn't the writer sign it? What was he or she hiding?

As the day's events whirled through my head, I mindlessly ate some leftovers. I needed to talk to my parents, but I was exhausted. No, that wasn't it— I was afraid to talk to them. Maybe I couldn't handle the truth. Maybe I didn't want to write the story. No, I was lying to myself. I wanted to know the truth, and I wanted to write the story… no matter what the consequences. I dialed my parents' number.

"Hi, Dad."

"Did you get my note?" he whispered.

"That was from you?"

"Yes. Who did you think it was from?"

"Well, you didn't sign it, so my imagination ran wild."

"Oh, I'm sorry. I didn't realize I hadn't signed it."

"Why did you send a note? And why are you whispering?"

"Because I don't want your mother to know I'm talking to you. I don't know if she has already gotten with you."

"About what?"

"Your adoption questions."

"Why didn't you call?"

"Because she'd see it on the phone screen."

"You can erase that info, you know."

"Well… I don't know how."

"Dad, I need to talk to you and Mom, but right now I'm overwhelmed, emotional, and exhausted. How about tomorrow?"

"That's fine. But I'm warning you, your mother's a wreck."

"Why?" I asked, then immediately wished I hadn't.

"We had an agreement."

"An agreement? With whom?"

"We'll talk about it tomorrow. Get some rest. I love you, Emarie," my father said.

"I love you too. See you and Mom tomorrow."

My mother's nervousness and my father's sneakiness had my stomach in knots. Their reactions were the opposite of their usual responses to life's challenges. Something was up. And what was about to transpire could hurt my parents… and me.

I poured a glass of wine, hoping it would calm my nerves. Glass in one hand and briefcase in the other, I went to the living room and carefully placed the glass of wine on the coffee table. With my briefcase on the floor between my knees, I retrieved my recorder and folders. On top was a small manila envelope I hadn't seen before.

"Where did this come from?" I mumbled.

Inside the envelope, I found something wrapped in tissue paper. It felt like a picture frame. I tore off the paper. I was right. From a plain gold frame, a man and a woman smiled at me. I studied the image of a happy bride and groom. Nice-looking couple, I thought. The man was sandy-haired and handsome, yet somewhat effeminate. The woman had black hair. As I turned over the picture and removed the backing from the frame, I wondered who they were. I gasped.

Written in pencil were the words: Dan and Patricia Jordan's wedding day, July 11, 1970. There was no doubt the red-haired woman had put it in my briefcase. But why? Did she want me to have a picture of my parents when they were in love—before they had me? The photo ripped a little as I fumbled to get it out of the frame. I scrutinized the faces of Dan and Patricia Jordan. Both had chipmunk-like cheeks. I laughed at the thought that their cheeks were stuffed with Jordan almonds. As I chuckled, my thumbs accidentally covered the bride's and groom's hair.

"Oh… my… God." I felt dizzy. Despite their differences in hair color, Dan and Patricia Jordan looked like twins. I studied the picture the woman had given me—the one of Dorothy she said was the key to the truth. I put the photos side by side. The photo of Dorothy looked like an older version of the bride… and groom. But there was a discrepancy. The bride had brown eyes. In the photo I held, Dorothy had blue eyes.

I pulled out the two pictures Richard and I had debated over in McDonald's. I looked at the photo of the blue-eyed Dorothy. Then I looked at the photo of the brown-eyed Dorothy. Then I compared the picture of the blue-eyed Dorothy with the one the red-haired woman had given me. It was definitely the same person. I compared the pictures with that of the brown-eyed bride. There was no doubt now. The woman I knew as Dorothy Hall was really Patricia Jordan. That meant Dorothy Hall *was* dead. And that meant… No, I refused to jump to conclusions. I sat back. "Mom and Dad, you've got some explaining to do."

Before I returned the photo to its frame, I looked at the back again. Something I hadn't noticed caught my eye—a faint stamp in the left-hand corner of the photo read: Vivian Jordan Photography.

I rushed to my computer, googled the photographer, and clicked on the link. A professional photo of the red-haired woman popped up. *How is she related to Dan Jordan?* I quickly clicked through her photos. *Nice work,* I thought.

I went back to Google and scrolled for more information.

Nothing.

I picked up the frame and, to my surprise, a small envelope was taped to the inside of the back. It was sealed. *Should I open it? Or should I return it to the red-haired woman?* My imagination ran wild. My curiosity was killing me. I opened it. Inside were two brief newspaper articles. The headline of the first article read:

POLICE CALLED TO INVESTIGATE INFANT'S SAFETY.

Vivian Jordan called the police regarding the safety of an infant in the possession of her sister-in-law, Patricia Jordan, wife of the Honorable Dan Jordan.

"Well hello, Aunt Vivian."

I read on: *Ms. Jordan was concerned as to the identity of the baby's parents and feared her sister-in-law had kidnapped the infant. It was determined the infant male was, in fact, the child of Dan and Patricia Jordan.*

"Bull, aka Georgie Porgie, Puddin' and Pie?" I mumbled. "The baby Patricia Jordan stole from Dorothy? How was it determined? Were there birth records? Did Dan and Patricia Jordan legally adopt Bull? Why would Vivian question the identity of the baby's parents? Was this just another piece of the cover-up puzzle?"

The second article was dated six months after the first regarding the baby found in the possession of Patricia Jordan. I quickly scanned the story. Aha! The article said: *Dan and Patricia Jordan adopted the infant male in question in a private adoption. No information regarding the adoption was released to the media. Attempts to obtain copies of the child's original birth certificate were denied to protect the identity of the birth mother.*

"Yeah… right. I smell cover-up all over this. Why did the newspaper run this story? Was it to shut up Dorothy Hall, Bull's birth mother?"

I stared at the pictures of Dorothy. *Who are you? Are you as bad as you're made out to be?* Whether Dorothy's eyes were blue or brown, they expressed sadness. Maybe she was to be pitied rather than hated. Maybe she was a bad mother because she couldn't help it. I felt sorry for her. No, that wasn't it. I felt an attachment to her as if she were begging me to tell her story. I couldn't wait to talk to my parents. I was now overcome with energy no bottle of wine could quench.

The time on my cable box read eleven p.m. Time for bed. I had a big day ahead of me. A few minutes later, I was tucked in, cozy under the covers. The darkness of my room and the comfort of my bed had no effect on my inability to fall asleep. The story I'd written about Dorothy swirled through my head. Something was wrong. There was a clue I'd missed. Or there was information yet to be uncovered. *Come hell or high water, I am going to get to the bottom of who is the real Dorothy Hall. I am not afraid of the truth.*

I jumped out of bed and ran to the living room, got my recorder, and listened to Patricia/Dorothy's version of Dorothy. I rewound and forwarded the tape over and over. Then I read my story. I was confused and enlightened at the same time. Based on my first meeting with the woman I thought was Dorothy, I tried to make sense of the information. What did it tell me? I couldn't figure it out.

It was now one a.m. I went back to bed. Despite the thoughts clamoring to keep me awake, I fell asleep. I know I did because when I awoke it was three a.m.—the witching hour. I wondered if my ghost friend would pay me another visit. The thought had barely cleared my mind when the temperature in my room dropped. I was freezing. I sat up and looked around, but I didn't see anything. I pulled up my covers to warm my shivering body and felt an invisible force pressure me to fall asleep. I fought to stay awake. Then I saw him. The robed man stood in the same corner as before. This time I wasn't scared. I knew he wanted to tell me something. He pointed two fingers at his eyes the same way he had before. Then he pointed at me.

"What are you trying to tell me?"

He pointed at his eyes again and then pointed at me.

"Help me understand," I begged.

But he was gone. And I was now wide awake. It was only 3:04 a.m. I felt as if an hour had passed. I snuggled under my covers. As I drifted off to sleep, I remembered my father's words: "We had an agreement." I was too tired to care.

At seven a.m., my alarm blasted me out of a deep sleep. I begrudgingly got out of bed, seemingly having lost my energy and enthusiasm for my story during the night. I shuffled to the kitchen, pressed the button to start the coffee, and then went into the living room. I picked up the pictures of the two Dorothys and studied them, hoping for a revelation.

Nothing.

I visualized last night's ghostly visitation and pondered what the ghost had tried to say.

Beep.

Beep.

Beep.

Coffee was done.

My attention was broken.

As I sipped my first cup of java, I was struck by an idea. The ghost was trying to tell me something about the eyes.

In the wedding picture, the bride, Patricia, had brown eyes, and the groom, Dan, had blue eyes. Is Dorothy the woman with the blue eyes? Was Dorothy's body recovered from the pond or not? Okay, Mr. Ghost Man, what are you trying to tell me? Is there something about my eyes? I remembered what the red-haired woman had said. "There was no mistaking you. You look just like your father. You have his dark hair and coal-black eyes." Coal-black eyes? In the wedding photo, Dan Jordan had blue eyes. What the hell was going on? Was I being gaslighted? If someone was trying to confuse me, it was working.

I clutched my cup of coffee to warm my cold hands as I entered the living room. The photos of Dorothy/Patricia dressed in identical stained dresses welcomed me as I sat down. It was hard to tell which was which.

"Good morning, ladies." I looked at the picture of the brown-eyed woman. "Are you my momma?" Then I looked at the picture of the blue-eyed woman. "Are you my—? Oh my God."

I snatched both pictures and ran to the guest bathroom. I flicked on the light and positioned myself in front of the mirror. Then I held up the picture of the brown-eyed woman. I scanned her features one by one, looking for a match with mine. There wasn't any resemblance. Then I held up the photo of the blue-eyed woman. I didn't need to scan her feature for feature. There was no doubt; we had the same nose—longish with a bump that caused the nose to hook slightly. If the body in the pond was Dorothy Hall, then Dorothy Hall was my mother.

I returned to the living room. My head was spinning. I called Laura.

"Good morning, stranger."

"Laura, I'm sorry to call you so early, but I think I have the evidence that Dorothy Hall is my mother."

"Really? What is it?"

"Well, I was studying the photos of the two Dorothys and realized the blue-eyed Dorothy and I have an identical nose."

"Such as?"

"You know, a huge hooked nose with a hideous bump."

"Ooh, that describes you perfectly."

"Laura, I'm serious."

"I'm afraid you are, Emarie, but the reality is, your nose is not unusual. Lots of people have the same-shaped nose as you. Heck, you and your cousin Susan look so much alike you get mistaken for each other… and you aren't even related."

"Sort of like Dorothy Hall and Patricia Jordan."

"For God's sake, Emarie, you're losing yourself in this story."

"No, I think I'm about to find out who I really am."

"You mean who your birth parents are?"

"Yeah, something like that." I glanced at the clock. "Hey, I have to go. I'm going to my parents' to discuss my findings with them."

"Okay, I hope you hear what you want to hear."

"I want the truth."

"Well—"

"Don't even say it, Laura."

"What?"

"That you hope I can handle the truth."

"No. I was going to say… if your parents won't tell you the truth, then no one will."

"Oh… sorry. Gotta go."

"Call me and tell me what you find out."

"Okay." I almost hung up the phone. "Oh, Laura?"

"Yes."

"I want you to know that no matter what, you're still my sister."

"I know."

CHAPTER TWENTY-NINE

T HE PICTURES OF THE TWO Dorothys preoccupied my thoughts. Something was amiss. But what? As I examined them again, I was drawn to their eyes. Brown-eyed Dorothy's eyes were closer together, and she had a bit of a Neanderthal brow. Blue-eyed Dorothy's eyes were softer, her eyebrows slightly arched. *How can two women who look so different look so much alike?* Then I remembered the photo the red-haired woman had given me. Or should I say the picture Aunt Vivian had given me? She said the picture was the key to the truth. I pulled it from my briefcase and laid the three pictures of the women dressed in the WORLD'S BEST MOM T-shirt side by side on my dining room table. Blue eyes, brown eyes, blue eyes. I placed the photos of the two blue-eyed women side by side. Not the same woman. Then I placed the photo of the brown-eyed woman next to the photo of the blue-eyed woman the red-haired woman had given me. Bingo. I had a match. Now, according to Dan and Patricia's wedding picture, Patricia had brown eyes. There was only one photo of a brown-eyed woman, so I assumed it was a photo of Patricia. Why was there a picture of her with blue eyes?

I called Richard.

"Richard, do you know anything about Photoshop?"

"Well, good morning to you, Emarie. What do you want to know?"

"Can you tell if a photo has been photoshopped?"

"If it's obvious, anyone can tell."

"And if it's not?"

"Then you need to talk to Carl in graphics."

"Do you know his number?"

"Emarie, Carl works weekends, so today is his day off. Even Carl deserves a little peace and quiet on his only day off."

"Do you know his number?"

"Yeah, hold on."

I held for so long I almost forgot who I'd called and why.

"Okay, but before I give you Carl's home number, tell me what this is about."

"It's hard to explain."

"Try me."

"Okay. Remember the photo the red-haired woman gave me?"

"Yeah."

"She said the photo was the key to the truth."

"Okay."

"Well, I was looking at the two file photos. I wanted to see if I bore any resemblance to either woman. I looked in the mirror and held up each picture."

"Which lovely lady do you resemble?"

"The blue-eyed one. I have her nose."

"Your point would be?"

"Wait, I'm not done. When I got home, I found a wedding picture of Dan and Patricia Jordan in my briefcase. I can only guess the red-haired woman put it there. There's no doubt the bride had brown eyes. So I deduced Patricia Jordan had brown eyes and the woman known as Dorothy Hall is really Patricia Jordan. Dorothy is the one with the brown eyes in the photos from the file. But the woman in the photo the red-haired woman gave me has blue eyes. If you put the photos of the women with blue eyes side by side, you can see it's not the same person. But if you put the photo of the blue-eyed woman the red-haired woman gave me side by side with the photo of the brown-eyed woman from the file, it's obvious it's the same woman. Therefore, I think someone photoshopped the photos."

"Or… Dan Jordan married Dorothy Hall."

"That's nuts. I think the person who messed with the photos was the red-haired woman, who by the way is a photographer and Dan Jordan's sister."

"Sister? She said Dan had a younger sister and brother. She never said she was the sister."

"Well, get this. On the back of the wedding photo, there was a photographer's stamp. The name was Vivian Jordan. I googled the name and up popped a photo of the red-haired woman."

"Okay, so what makes you think she's Dan Jordan's sister?"

"It gets even better. There were two articles in an envelope attached to the inside of the picture frame. Both were dated from 1988. One reported that Vivian Jordan called the police with concerns about an infant male in the possession of Patricia Jordan, her sister-in-law. I think that makes her Dan's sister. So she's lying by omission. But why?"

"Ha! It appears everyone is lying to you."

"Well, I hope my parents tell me the truth. Now, how about Carl's phone number?"

"It's 703-555-3498. And don't tell him I gave you his number."

"Ooh, another lie."

"Yeah. Good luck."

I hung up and called Carl. To my surprise, he was willing to get together immediately. Even better, he said he'd meet me at his place, which was only ten minutes away. And yes, he wanted to know how I got his number. I lied and told him I got it from the employee directory. He believed me. Never mind that there is no employee directory.

I gathered my files, pictures and all, and headed to Carl's. I was greeted by a sourpuss, middle-aged man.

"Carl?" I asked.

"Just a minute," the man said. Then he yelled, "Carl, you have company."

The thumping of someone running down the stairs shook the house. Then a boy who looked about sixteen years old emerged at the bottom.

"Hey, Emarie. Richard said you wanted me to help you with a story you're working on. Come on up."

The man I presumed was Carl's father moved aside and motioned for me to follow Carl. I nodded and trudged up the stairs.

"In here," Carl said.

I followed his voice to a back room and stood in the doorway, trying to take in the mounds of papers, magazines, and books nestled next to equipment I'd only seen in a TV production studio.

"Wow, this is some setup," I said.

"Thanks," Carl said, his eyes wide with pride. "Show me what you've got."

"You work at the paper?" I asked.

"Yeah, been there five years."

"I've never seen you before."

"Never seen you either, but I've heard about you."

"Oh… well, I have some pictures I want you to look at. Richard said you're good at this stuff, you know, with Photoshop."

"Sure am."

I gave Carl the two photos of the brown-eyed and blue-eyed Dorothy dressed in the bleach-stained dress that the robed ghost left on my bed. Then I gave him the original file photo of brown-eyed Dorothy in her WORLD'S BEST MOM T-shirt as well as the photo Vivian Jordan gave me of blue-eyed Dorothy in the same T-shirt.

"Whoa, these are some scary-looking chicks."

"I wouldn't call them chicks."

Carl ignored me as he studied the photos under a bright desk lamp. "Hmm… these are all the same person."

"No, they're two different people."

"No, they're definitely the same person made to look like two different people. I'll show you."

Carl scanned all four photos and pulled them up on his computer screen. I took the opportunity to show him the differences between the file photo of Dorothy and the photo Vivian gave me. I pointed out the differences in their eyebrows, their noses, and their hairlines. Carl wasn't impressed.

"Still the same person," Carl said. "Wait a minute. You *do* have two people here and…"

"And what?"

The images on the screen zoomed in and out as Carl scrutinized every inch of the pictures. Then he picked up each one and eyed it through a loupe. "Whoever manipulated these photos is damn good... but not as good as me." Carl twirled his chair around, nearly knocking me over with his feet. Then he handed me the picture of the brown-eyed Dorothy wearing the bleach-stained dress. "Can you guess why this one's so interesting?"

"Because she's one of the homeliest women I've ever seen?"

"No." Carl smiled at me. Then he stabbed the photo with his finger. "Because she's a he."

"What?"

"Yep, definitely a man. Let's compare *Mr.* Brown Eyes with Ms. Blue Eyes." Carl put the two photos of Dorothy clad in the stained dress side by side. "Although Ms. Blue Eyes is one beefy-looking woman, she's still a woman. See, her upper lip is a little fuller than Mr. Brown Eyes. Her jaw is less pronounced than Mr. Brown Eyes's jaw. Her neck is narrower than Mr. Brown Eyes's. And notice the eyebrows. Ms. Blue Eyes's brows are curved and above the brow line. Mr. Brown Eyes has a heavier brow on which his eyebrows are thicker and arched in an inverted vee."

Carl scrutinized the photos on screen again. "The nose is interesting. Usually, a woman's nose is thinner and flatter, but if you notice, it's hard to distinguish gender by Ms. Blue Eyes's nose. It's more like a male nose, although it's longer than Mr. Brown Eyes's nose. Also, notice Ms. Blue Eyes's facial fat deposits. She is definitely morbidly obese, yet Mr. Brown Eyes doesn't appear to be obese, just naturally fuller cheeks. I'd say it's a good makeup job. And if you notice, the neckline of the dress on Mr. Brown Eyes looks as if it was pulled up a bit. Probably to hide an Adam's apple."

"I've seen the brown-eyed woman. I didn't notice an Adam's apple. But she's definitely obese. Looks like she weighs nearly three hundred pounds."

"I just call them how I see them," Carl said.

"Anything else?"

"In general, a female face is considered more attractive. But in this case, it's a toss-up. Neither is attractive. I've seen men who are beautiful in drag, but why any man would want to look this unattractive is beyond me."

I gulped. "Me too."

"I must say, Ms. Brown Eyes, or more correctly Mr. Brown Eyes does a great job of impersonating a woman. I don't think anyone would suspect she's a he."

"I know I didn't."

"What about her voice? Does she sound like a woman?"

"Yep, a nasty, uneducated one at that."

"Hmm."

"What?"

"It's much harder for a man to disguise his voice than his face. Unless, of course…"

"Of course, what?"

"Unless he is a low-testosterone male or he already had an androgynous voice. Haven't you heard someone speaking and thought it was a woman and was shocked to find out it was a man or vice versa?"

"Yes. Dan the high talker. *Seinfeld*, right?"

"Who?"

"Never mind."

Carl pulled up the photo Vivian had given me and, pointing at the computer monitor, said, "Now, this other photo is Mr. Brown Eyes photoshopped with Ms. Blue Eyes's eyes. And if you look closely, Ms. Blue Eyes's nose has been airbrushed and inserted on this photo. Makes them look even more alike. But notice the jaw, neckline, and brows are definitely male."

"That's what I suspected. But why were they mistaken for each other? Even I mistook them."

"You've seen both of them? Together?"

"No, only Mr. Brown Eyes."

"Then how do you know they were mistaken for each other?"

"Because when I saw these two photos, I thought it was the same person."

"Someone went to great lengths to make Ms. Blue Eyes look like Mr. Brown Eyes. A good photographer and makeup artist could make these two look similar. But you can't change facial features without surgery… or Photoshop. I don't see any evidence of surgical manipulation."

"You don't think it was the other way around."

"What do you mean?"

"You think someone went to great lengths to make Ms. Blue Eyes look like Mr. Brown Eyes. Not the other way around?"

"Absolutely. Someone wanted the woman, Ms. Blue Eyes, to look like the man, Mr. Brown Eyes."

"But why?"

"That's the million-dollar question."

"And why was Mr. Brown Eyes photoshopped with blue eyes?"

"Have you met Ms. Blue Eyes?"

"No."

"Do you know who she is?"

"I think so."

"Do you know where she is?"

"Yep... I think so." My mind wandered as I recalled something Dorothy had said. "Well, I still think both these people are women."

"Think what you want, but this photo is the key to the truth," Carl said, handing me the photo of Dorothy that Vivian had given me.

"What did you say?"

"I said this photo is the key to the truth. Part man. Part woman. A he/she so to speak."

I had a sudden urge to leave. "Thanks for your help, Carl."

"Anytime." Carl watched me grab my things. "I hope I helped."

"I believe you did. And you can read about it in the Sunday magazine."

"Cool."

Carl escorted me to the front door, and like a gentleman, he opened it for me. "See you at work."

I smiled at Carl. "Yeah, see you."

"Oh, by the way," Carl said, "the blue-eyed World's Best Mom looked like she might have been in a fight or something. Looked like whoever covered up her bruises and swelling missed a few spots."

"Thanks. I'll take a look at the photo when I get home."

Carl's conclusion that one of the Dorothys was a man raised lots of questions. It was time to interrogate my parents. Did they know the truth? Would they tell me the truth? Could I handle the truth?

CHAPTER THIRTY

FRIDAY MORNING.
Butterflies.

Energy.

Anger.

My gut was trying to tell me something. I wanted answers—now. I knew I should be in the office. Instead, I set out for my parents' for a little Q & A. Two and a half hours later, I pulled into Mickey Dees... in Darrington. My parents would have to wait.

I entered McDonald's—the same one where Richard and I first met the red-haired woman. Everyone, even the children, looked as if they harbored a secret. They gave me the creeps. I swear I got the evil eye from several people. At the table next to mine, a man and woman glared at me.

"She looks like that crazy judge," the woman whispered.

"Yep, looks just like him," the man replied.

I wanted to give them a piece of my mind, but I thought anything I said might confirm their suspicion that I was related to the crazy judge. I managed to hold my tongue. But I couldn't hold my temper. I threw my food in the trash and stormed out. *That'll show them.*

Back in my car, I tried to gather my composure. After a few

156

minutes, I decided a good cry might help release my pent-up emotions. But as hard as I tried, I couldn't muster a tear. A knock on my car window ended my attempted pity party. I looked up and saw a well-dressed man. He motioned for me to roll down my window.

"Hey, sorry to disturb you, but I thought you might want this," he said as he handed me an envelope.

"Who are you?"

"Dwayne. Dwayne Martin. I knew you'd come back. I've been here every day for the past week waiting for you."

I looked away for a moment as I searched my memory. *Dwayne. Dwayne. Oh my God, Dwayne the Pain.* When I looked up, he was gone. I scanned the parking lot. No sign of Dwayne.

The envelope was addressed to Mr. and Mrs. Frank Martin. No return address. Inside, there was another envelope addressed to the Honorable Daniel Jordan. I opened it and withdrew a single piece of paper. It was a letter from Mr. and Mrs. Frank Martin. Red crayon scribbles obscured the type, but I managed to read the short but not-so-sweet letter.

> *Dear Judge Jordan:*
>
> *This letter is to inform you that despite your efforts to thwart our adoption of Dwayne Hall, we have succeeded in legally adopting him. We are happy to announce that we and our three sons welcomed Dwayne into our family on July 21, 1981. Dwayne is a loving, intelligent, and creative little boy. He adores his new brothers, and they adore him. We know he will thrive in our loving home.*
>
> *Sincerely, Frank and Marianne Martin*

My eyes focused on the red crayon. My first thought was Dwayne had scribbled on the letter when he was a little boy. I was shocked when I realized the scribbles formed words that read: *Fuck You. Sincerely, the Honorable Daniel Jordan.*

Holy crap. Another little lie had surfaced. Judge Jordan was a vindictive man. Obviously, Dwayne wanted me to know this tidbit about my birth father. But why? How did he know about my assignment? I'd been thrown into a maze of lies. "Truth will out. Shakespeare, right?" I almost laughed. But in reality, I hoped Shakespeare was right.

Dorothy's house was only a mile away. I had more questions. Something told me now wasn't a good time for a confrontation with the vile woman. So I headed home. *I must be nuts. I drove all the way out here, and now I'm going back home.* But deep down, I knew it was time to face my parents—the two people who loved and adored me. The two people who had always been open and honest. The two people who wouldn't hurt me for anything in the world. Or would they? Truth will out.

After a pit stop at my condo and a bite to eat, I headed to my parents'. Friday evening rush hour traffic was horrendous. By the time I got there, it was nearly seven. I pulled into the driveway and parked behind their Honda. The house was dimly lit in a comforting way. I stood at the front door, took a deep breath, and rang the bell.

"Who could that be?" I heard my father say. The door opened ajar. When he saw it was me, he smiled and yelled to my mother, "It's Emarie, dear."

"Emarie?" my mother said.

"Yeah, Mom, it's me."

"What a pleasant surprise."

"Mom, Dad, I have something I need to talk to you about."

"Anything, dear," my father said.

My mother glanced at my briefcase, turned, and went into the kitchen. My father headed for the dining room table. I followed. Meanwhile, my mother was doing something I'd never seen her do in my entire life—opening a bottle of wine.

"Want any?" she asked.

"No thanks, dear," my father said.

"Sure," I said.

My mother entered the dining room holding two wineglasses in one hand and the bottle of wine in the other. She placed a glass in front of me and poured a generous portion. Then she filled her glass and sat down.

"I don't know where to start, sooo…" I pulled the photos of the three Dorothys from my briefcase and said, "I guess I'll start with these."

"Oh God," my mother said as she looked up at my father.

My father cleared his throat and looked at me. I could see

discomfort and sorrow in his eyes. "Um… Emarie… we can't tell you anything about these photos."

"Why not?"

"Because we don't know anything about them," my mother said.

I looked at my father, making it clear with my angry stare that I knew my mother was lying.

"Well, that's not the truth, Marie," my father said as he picked up the picture of the brown-eyed Dorothy. Then he returned the photo to the table. "We know the truth but…"

I swear my blood rushed to my head with the thought that he was going to finish his statement with, "But you can't handle the truth."

"…we can't tell you."

I looked from one parent to the other. "Why not?"

"It was part of the adoption agreement," my father replied.

"Part of the adoption agreement?" I yelled. "Well, now it's part of my life story, and I think I have a right to hear it."

Tears ran down my mother's cheeks. She wiped them away with her hands. Then she rose from her chair and leaned toward me as if to give me a hug. I pulled away and walked into the living room. My parents stayed in the dining room. I was surprised they weren't consoling each other. For the first time in my life, I wondered if everything I believed about them and everything I believed about us was a lie. Hurt and anger consumed me.

I walked into the dining room, gathered my things, yelled, "Liars," and stormed out of the house. As I peeled rubber on my exit from the driveway, I glanced at the front door, the same door that had always been so welcoming. The door I'd entered more than thirty-four years ago, cradled in my mother's arms when my parents brought me home for the first time. The door I skipped out, holding my daddy's hand, filled with excitement about my first bicycle ride. The door where my father stood guard, waiting for me to come home from dates. The door at which my mother waited for me to arrive when she knew my heart was broken about not getting a job I'd wanted more than anything. I looked at the door, hoping for confirmation my mother and father felt my pain, but they weren't there. I guess I was right after all—they didn't care about me. The truth hurt.

I drove like a crazy woman.

I cried.

I cursed.

When I got home, I threw my briefcase so hard against the wall it left a large hole. I couldn't give a crap. The pit in my stomach confirmed my worst fear—I'd been betrayed by the two people I trusted most. My life was a fraud.

"Who the hell am I," I screamed to no one. I sobbed so hard I snorted and croaked. Instantly, I broke out in laughter. "I am Dorothy's child," I said, remembering how Dorothy laughed until she snorted her magic juice and coughed so hard I thought she'd throw up. Pounding on my door silenced me.

"Who is it?"

"It's me, Richard."

I opened the door. "What are you doing here?"

"I have something to show you," he said as he waved a manila envelope in my face.

Richard looked around my condo as if he expected to be attacked. "What's up with the hole in the wall?"

"Nothing."

Richard arched his eyebrows. He wasn't buying my answer. "Have you been crying?"

"No… allergies."

"I think this is the answer you're looking for," he said as he handed me the envelope.

Inside was a photo of a bald man with dark brown eyes. He looked familiar, but I didn't know why. "So?"

"Look closely," Richard said. "Who does he look like?"

"Oh my God, he looks like me and—"

Richard snatched the photo out of my hand and said, "Oh, I didn't notice." Then he handed it back to me and said, "Who else does he look like?"

I stared at the photo for a few seconds, noticing similarities between the man in the picture and the man with slicked-back black hair in the disappearing photo the robed man had left on my bed. I decided not to mention this to Richard. Then I noticed something else. "Crap, he's a male version of Dorothy. Do you think he's related to her?"

"No," Richard said. "For God's sake, turn over the picture."

I turned it over. "Dan Jordan? 2015? He died in 2014," I said incredulously. "Death becomes him." The stamp on the bottom read: Vivian Jordan Photography. "Where did you get this?"

"Someone put it on my desk this afternoon."

"Carl?"

"Nah… Maybe… Nah."

"Then who?"

"I don't know."

"Then we need to find out."

Richard pulled his cell phone from his pants pocket and dialed. "Carl? Hey, it's Richard. … Richard Bader. … Fine thanks. Did you put an envelope on my desk this morning? … No? … Okay. … Uh-huh. … Uh-huh. … Uh-huh. Oh. Thanks, Carl."

"Well?"

"He said he didn't see anyone go in my office, but he saw Jim come out."

I was about to say, "Why the hell didn't Jim put it on my desk?" when my cell phone rang. "Hello?"

"Emarie, so nice to hear your voice. When am I going to see your face? Even better, when am I going to see your story?"

"Hey, Jim. I'll be in tomorrow. I'm still working on my story." I looked at Richard and shrugged.

"Well, it would be nice if you reported in once in a while. You missed your deadline."

"I know. I'm sorry. But something big has happened… with my story, of course."

"Tomorrow's Saturday, Emarie. I want your next draft on my desk by Monday."

"Fair enough, Jim. You'll have it on Monday."

Jim hung up without saying good-bye.

"Crap. I have only two days to get to the bottom of this story. Worse, Jim sounded angry."

"Hustle your bustle," Richard said. "I've got to go. Got to get up early. I have a very important job, you know."

"Tomorrow's Saturday, Richard."

"Oh."

I showed Richard to the door. "Say hi to Laura for me."

As he exited, he turned and said, "By the way, I think you know why Dorothy and Dan look alike." Then he smirked and left.

I held the door open and watched Richard hurry down the stairs. I wondered what he meant. *Was Richard playing games with me? If so, why? And why now? What did Richard know that I didn't?*

After Richard left, I stretched out on the couch and recapped every detail of my story. At least I thought I did. The reality was, I fell fast asleep. I awoke Saturday morning, knowing exactly what I needed to do.

CHAPTER THIRTY-ONE

M Y MORNING RITUALS, WHICH HAD felt burdensome lately, seemed perfectly relaxing today. I felt like myself again. Or maybe I didn't. I felt light, happy, and carefree—something I didn't think I'd ever felt before. Nonetheless, I realized how out of sorts I'd been... how my obsession with my story had begun to rot the essence of who I was. I had an urge to call my parents and apologize for my behavior the evening before. I decided to wait until I gathered more information. I needed to talk to Dorothy.

I took my time getting ready. I even fooled around checking Facebook and my personal e-mails. Nothing interesting there. I showered. Dressed. Enjoyed a couple of cups of coffee and a light breakfast. On the off chance Jim would be in the office on Saturday, I dialed his work number. No answer. So I left a voice mail message stating I would be out of town today and reassured him my story would be on his desk Monday morning. I had never felt so at peace in my entire life.

I pulled out of my condo parking lot... sunroof open... music blaring. I didn't care if I woke the dead. I wanted everyone to know that I, Emarie Lukins, was alive and ready to take on the world. At eleven a.m., I entered Darrington, Maryland, for what I hoped would be the last time.

I drove past the McDonald's. "Ha! I bet those people think they know everything about me."

Farther down the street, I saw a store sign I hadn't noticed before: "Martin's Menswear—World-class Clothier... Neighborhood Prices."

"It's got to be Dwayne's place. Looks like he's done well for himself." I needed to talk to him but now wasn't the time.

I rounded the corner and parked in front of Dorothy Hall's house. I smiled to myself, knowing this would be the last time I'd have to face her. I was going to tell her everything I knew. And I was about to throw her a curveball.

The front door of Dorothy's house opened before I even got out of my car. And there she was in her muumuu and happy-juice glory. She screamed something at me, but I couldn't hear over the top of my music. I shut off my radio, closed my sunroof, and got out of my car. "I'm sorry, Dorothy, I couldn't hear you."

"I said, 'What the hell are you doing here?'"

I climbed the three steps to the porch on which crazy Dorothy stood. "I've got something to tell you."

"You don't have anything to tell me, 'cause you don't know anything."

"This time you're wrong," I said. "May I come in?"

"Help yourself, bitch."

Despite the warm welcome, I entered Dorothy's dump. I spotted her bottle of magic juice on the coffee table and noticed it was more than half-empty. Only a little after eleven a.m. and Dorothy was already pickled.

Dorothy motioned for me to sit on the couch. "Have a seat. You better have a good reason for interrupting my quiet time."

"Oh, I do." I took my place on Dorothy's stinky couch and dug through my briefcase for my recorder.

Dorothy plopped into her filthy, body-oil-stained chair. "What the hell is so important?"

"Well... I think I've figured out who you are."

Dorothy flinched. She looked at me and held my gaze. Did I detect fear? Then she laughed, coughed, and hacked up a loogie. She spat it on the carpet. "That's what I think of you."

I wasn't fazed by her disgusting behavior. I was in control. "Okay, let's stop playing games and get to the truth."

"Game on," Dorothy said. "You tell the truth, and I'll dole out the consequences."

"Are you threatening me?"

"Just tell me *your* version of the truth."

"Okay," I said. "This is what I know. You're not Dorothy Hall."

Dorothy swigged her juice but didn't respond. I detected disgust in her eyes. If looks could kill, I'd be dead.

"You're Patricia Jordan."

Dorothy broke out in maniacal laughter. She gasped for breath. For the first time, I didn't want her to croak. I wanted her to hear the truth… my truth.

"Go on," Dorothy said. "You're so entertaining."

"Let's see, where do I start? Well, I'll tell you what I know in chronological order. Ready?"

"Shoot."

"You met and fell in love with Dan Jordan when the two of you attended the University of Maryland from the fall of 1969 until spring of 1973. Dan, you, and my father and mother, Andrew and Marie Lukins, were friends in college. Dan knew you were emotionally unstable, and he thought marriage and motherhood would improve your situation. So on July 11, 1970, despite being sophomores, Dan and you married. You tried for many years to have children, but you were unable to conceive, unlike your neighbor, Dorothy Hall, who pumped out babies like a rabbit. She was an abusive and negligent mother. You reported Dorothy to the police regarding her treatment of her children. One by one, Dorothy's four children were removed from her care and, under a court order, each was placed with family members or in foster care. Then, by some miracle, you got pregnant… with me. The hormones of pregnancy drove you over the edge. Dan moved out. You gave birth to me, but in a state of insanity, you traded me to Dorothy for a box of chocolate candy. Dorothy treated me the same as she treated her own children and nearly starved me to death. Dan found out I was in Dorothy's care and went to Dorothy's house looking for me. He found me in medical danger and had me removed. Then he committed you to a mental hospital. Dan couldn't care for me. He knew my parents were an infertile couple and longed for a baby. He asked them to adopt me. They were thrilled. But you refused to sign the adoption papers, so Dan concocted a story of how

165

I was another of Dorothy's babies—baby number five. To legitimize my adoption, he ran an ad in the local newspaper to find a birth father he knew didn't exist. Then he made up a story stating the birth father had been killed in a car accident. He then pushed me through the system, allowing my parents to adopt me as long as they vowed to never reveal my true identity."

Dorothy adjusted herself in her chair and glared at me. I'd expected her to interrupt. She didn't, so I continued. "Over time, your mental health issues destroyed your relationship, and you and Dan separated but never divorced. To save his sanity, Dan built a house on the other side of town while you remained living next door to Dorothy. She had two more babies. Your envy of Dorothy's fertility reached a peak when Dorothy had baby number seven, a boy. In a rage, you stole the baby. When Dan found out, he knew you couldn't take care of the baby and he knew he couldn't give the child back to Dorothy for her to abuse. So he concocted another story explaining the baby was yours and his biological son. He took the baby and raised him as his own. The baby grew up to be Bull. Bull took Dorothy as his lover, not knowing she was his mother. When she found out Bull was her son, she went nuts and killed him. But Dan and his cohorts convinced a judge that Dorothy killed Bull in self-defense. Dorothy was sprung after only one day in jail. Secrets were safe again in Darrington. But Dan was seething with anger over the death of his son. He swore to get revenge. Now here's the kicker."

Dorothy leaned forward in her chair and exhaled as if she was about to say something. I refused to let her butt in, so I kept talking. "For some reason, Dorothy and you had always been confused for each other. So Dan and his sister, Vivian, hatched a plan to kill Dorothy. Vivian took photos of Dorothy and you wearing the same T-shirt. You know, the WORLD'S BEST MOM T-shirt. Then Dan killed Dorothy and threw her body in the pond. When the police found the body, Dan identified her as Dorothy Hall. It looked like a simple drowning of a pathetic woman. No foul play was found. The murderer of Bull was dead. Case closed. But Dan couldn't live with what he did, so one evening he put a gun to his head and pulled the trigger, leaving you the sole survivor of a history of child abuse, neglect, incest, and murder. The entire town knows the truth, but they've kept your dirty little secrets for more than two years."

I looked to Dorothy for a response. She sat with her elbows on her knees, staring at the floor and rubbing her hands together. It was obvious she was at a loss for how to respond. Had my plan worked? Would my story force out the truth from this vile person? A few minutes passed. Then she turned to me, or should I say she turned *on* me?

"You stupid shit," Dorothy said. "You come here with a cockamamie story you think is the truth about who I am, who you are, and what happened. Well, that's the most convoluted piece of bullshit I've ever heard. It's a twisted fantasy. But even a stopped clock is right twice a day, so I'll admit you're right about one thing—I'm not your mother."

Dorothy tugged at her thin gray hair. To my surprise, she pulled it off, revealing a bald head. Her transformation was shocking. There was no doubt she was a he. Masculine posture. Deeper voice. He looked ridiculous clad in a Hawaiian muumuu. I stifled a laugh. *What is wrong with me? I could be in danger, and I find this funny?* With a little help from bald Dorothy, the wig flew across the room and landed on the table where the seven baby pictures were still displayed. Suddenly, he turned and faced me. Then he chugged his happy juice.

"And you are?" I asked.

Red in the face and trembling with anger, he yelled, "I'm your father, you stupid shit."

I remained calm and in control. I'd finally gotten the best of Dorothy Hall, or I'd finally gotten the best of what's his name. The other possibilities were I was paralyzed with fear or too stupid to run. "What's your name?"

The man laughed and said, "Dan Jordan. Nice to meet you, baby girl."

"Dan Jordan? I thought you were dead." I remembered the photo Richard had given me of Dan Jordan dated 2015.

"Well, you got that wrong too. You really are a nincompoop… dumb as the day is long… not the brightest bulb in the box. And you call yourself a reporter. You're nothing but a nothing. You never were anything, and you never will be. I'm glad I didn't have to raise you because I would have had to beat some sense into you."

I was a jumble of feelings with no words to express them. I hated him. I was repulsed. I was fascinated. I wanted to know this crazed man better. *The fruit doesn't fall far from the tree.*

"I suppose you're recording this," Dan said.

"Yep."

"Give me the recorder."

"No."

"I said, give me the recorder."

I handed it to him.

He yanked it from me, held it to his mouth and said, "I, Judge Jordan, do solemnly swear to tell the truth, the whole truth, and nothing but the truth, so help me God."

I leaned back and waited. For a few minutes, Dan stared at the floor. Elbows on his knees. Head supported by his cupped hands. Silent. I thought he was crying. Again, I was wrong.

He was laughing. I heard him mumble, "Yeah, that's the ticket." He lifted his head and looked at me. His stare was blank as if he were looking through me. His expression appeared to reveal sadness, but it could have been relief. Then all hell broke loose.

CHAPTER THIRTY-TWO

D AN ROSE FROM HIS CHAIR with the grace of Mikhail Baryshnikov. No pushing himself forward to the edge of the cushion. No grunting. No struggling with his gargantuan body. I almost expected him to do a plié, a pirouette, and leap across the room with the majesty of a gazelle. Instead, he paced like a caged lion. He looked at me and then looked away. I remained on the couch.

He approached me, leaned in so we were face-to-face, and said, "Emarie, you ignorant slut, I'm going to tell you the truth… Ha! Can you handle the truth?"

His breath was horrid, but I didn't retreat. I held his gaze. He broke eye contact and pulled away from me. Cage door open. Wild animal out. Dear Old Dad raged.

"Okay, I'm gonna make it short. Then I want you to get out of my face and never, ever come back. Do you hear me?"

Dan waited for my reply. I remained calm and quiet. That didn't sit well with him.

He screamed at the top of his lungs, "Did you hear me?" He stared at me. When I didn't answer, he screamed like a Marine Corps boot camp sergeant, "I… can't… *hear*… you."

"Yes," I whispered. "I heard you."

Dan paced. He looked ridiculous—a bald man in a muumuu. But now I didn't feel like laughing because he looked like what he was—pathetic. I felt sad for him. He breathed heavily while he struggled to find the right words. When he did, he hurled them at me.

"There is no Dorothy Hall," he said. Then he pushed his index finger into his chest so hard I thought he'd actually stab himself. "I'm Dorothy Hall. I'm the genius who pulled off the biggest lie in the world."

"So tell me the truth about your big lie," I said.

Dan glared at me. "Smart-ass." Then he grabbed his juice, chugged, burped, and wiped spittle off his lip with the back of his hand.

God this man is disgusting. I can't believe I share his genes.

"Patti, your dipshit mother, kept getting pregnant. I never wanted any damn kids, but she never took precautions. Pumped out babies like a damn rabbit. I swear she was messing around with other men. She had to have been because she had seven kids and we hardly ever did the nasty. Do you know what it's like to have sex with a whale?"

When I didn't respond, he waved me off.

"She never told me she was pregnant, and because she was a tub of lard, no one ever knew, not even me. Then she'd get cramps and whammo, she'd pump out a baby. Seven in all. Had all the babies at home. Never reported their births, so there were no birth certificates. Patti was batshit crazy. She had no business raising babies, so I took them. Or should I say, Dorothy took them?"

Dan walked over to the table on which the pictures of Patti's seven babies were displayed. He picked up a picture. I swear it was the picture of baby number five. Me?

"God, I hate kids," he said. "Damn little brats." Dan swept the pictures of all seven kids off the table and watched them crash to the floor. The sound of shattered glass angered him. He kicked the pictures across the room, then paused and spat on them. Finally, he walked over to the chair and sat down. Surprisingly, he spoke calmly, as if he were telling his life story to an empathic reporter from *People* magazine. "Well, my career was booming. I was busy. Too busy to take care of little crybabies. And when I was home, I didn't have the patience for their stupid, childish, selfish ways. Fortunately, Patti's pregnancies were spaced out so I only had to care for one kid at a time. Anyway, she spied on me. She didn't like how I raised them; thought I was harming the precious little brats. One by one, she reported me, or I should say she reported Dorothy Hall to Child Protective Services. And guess who was assigned to preside over the five child abuse and neglect cases?"

"Who?"

Dan's tone changed. "Me, you nitwit. God, I can't believe someone as stupid as you is my child."

And I can't believe someone as disgusting and depraved as you is my sperm donor.

Dan reverted to a state of calm and continued, "Anyway, the first case was Ugly Toni. Dorothy was scheduled to appear in court in three weeks. Now, I was neck deep in shit. I had to do some fast thinking. So I called my sister, Vivian. We devised a brilliant plan. Since no one knew I was Dorothy Hall and people who knew us thought Patti and I looked like brother and sister, we dressed Patti to look like 'Dorothy.' All she had to do was agree to sign the papers to release parental rights." Dan slapped his thigh. "Ha! I really am a genius. Being a judge has its perks. I was able to get a friend at the Department of Vital Statistics to create a birth certificate showing Dorothy Hall was the mother of Ugly Toni and backdate the certification stamps. Now that's using your noodle. We pulled off this charade *five* times. Fortunately, Patti never refused to play along and she kept her mouth shut."

"Did you keep the pictures of Patti dressed as Dorothy up to date?"

"Yep. Every year or as needed."

"How come you only had to pull off your charade five times?"

"I think you already know the answer, but since you're as dumb as a doorknob, let me refresh your memory. We pulled off the charade five times because I kept Bull and raised him as my son, and I placed you for adoption."

"Why did you place me for adoption?"

"You were the spitting image of me," Dan said.

I wanted to tell him I didn't see the resemblance, but I kept my mouth shut. His face turned red. He rubbed his bald head. Anger had returned.

"I couldn't give you to some foster care nincompoops. Do you know what goes on in some foster care homes? Disgusting. But I couldn't stand you. You always gave me the eeriest look... Eerie Emmie. You disgusted me, so I ignored you. I left you naked in the crib so I wouldn't have to change your damn diapers. I would toss food into your crib, but you were too stupid to eat it."

"I was an infant," I whispered as I choked back tears.

"Oh, shut up. You were just plain stupid. It's your fault Patti thought you were being starved and called the police. They removed you from my... Dorothy's care. Again, I had to tap dance as fast as I could. I knew if you went into the foster care system, I'd lose track of you. I decided come hell or high water I would place you for adoption with someone I knew. I contacted six of my"—Dan made quote marks in the air and sneered at me—"'best friends.' Not a one of them wanted you."

Thank you, God.

"Then I remembered my college buddy, Andrew Lukins. I hadn't talked to him for years. What an asshole. But I guess you could say he was a nice guy. Besides, he knew I was a cross-dresser and he never judged me or told anyone. He was married to Little Miss Goody Two-Shoes, Marie. I knew they were childless. I figured it was because Saint Marie had refused to open her legs and give up her virginity."

Dan laughed and coughed. Drool splattered his muumuu. I took a deep breath and managed to fight the urge to defend my parents' honor. He wiped off the drool and continued his insensitive tirade about my parents.

"I thought twice as to whether or not I wanted them to be your parents, but I decided at least I would know where you were. I looked them up and found them living in Maryland, just outside Washington, D.C. I told them about you, but I didn't tell them whose child you were."

"My parents don't know that you and Patti are my bio-parents?"

"No. I thought about telling them, but then the hoax would be exposed. So I made up a story. Don't even remember what it was."

I do.

"They were thrilled to adopt you. I had the paperwork drawn up and had Dorothy Hall's name listed on your original birth certificate as the mother. Father unknown. Ran an ad to find him. Hot damn, I'm good. But goddamned Patti refused to sign the paperwork. Evidently, she took a liking to you. She thought you looked like her. Now I had to think of something else. I looked up a judge in Prince Georges County, Maryland. Bingo. He owed me a favor. So during the Easter holiday when no one was in the office, I presented paperwork showing your father was deceased, and Judge Name Withheld to Protect the Not So Innocent pushed you through the system. Case closed. Andrew and Marie Lukins were now the proud parents of Eerie Emmie. God only knows who Patti was screwing while I was busy getting rid of you because a few months later she pumped out another brat. Got rid of it fast."

"Fricking Freda," I muttered as images of Fred and Wilma Flintstone flashed through my head.

"Yeah, you did pay attention," Dan said. Then, in the voice I'd come to associate with Dorothy Hall, he said, "Oh Fred, here we go again." He laughed as if he were recalling the most hysterical joke. "Oh God, I remember that day like it was yesterday. Anyway, six years later Patti birthed Bull. He could have been my clone. The moment I set eyes on him, I was in love."

"Narcissus?" Dan was so lost in his memories of Bull he didn't hear what I said.

"Bull was the only kid whose birth certificate lists Patti and me as the parents. I loved him that much. And I raised him as my child, not Dorothy Hall's."

"Did Bull ever meet Dorothy?" I asked.

"What? I'm not that stupid. I kept that part of my life secret. I told him Patti was his mother and she was in a mental hospital."

"He never met his mother, Patti?"

"Not officially. Since she constantly spied on me, she saw Bull and me several times in the grocery store or in a restaurant. She made a few nasty remarks to him. When he asked me who she was, I told him she was just a crazy, nosy neighbor. He was none the wiser."

"How did you pull off having sex with Bull?"

"Who said I had sex with Bull?"

"You did. You said you met him in a bar and you two got into it right then and there."

"Are you accusing me of incest? That was Dorothy, not me. Get your facts straight. Besides, Bull was so drunk he didn't know what he did or didn't do."

"Why did you kill him?"

"Because the dumb shit tried to have sex with Dorothy again. When you're desperate, you don't care with whom you get your rocks off."

"That still doesn't explain why you killed the son you loved."

"Okay, Dorothy messed around with Bull. Then Bull went too far and discovered Dorothy wasn't all woman if you know what I mean?"

The idea of Bull and Dorothy messing around was nauseating. I nodded my head, indicating I knew perfectly well what Dan meant. Not wanting to explore that further, I said, "And you killed your son why?"

Dan leered at me and yelled, "Because the nitwit blew my cover and he threatened to out me. So I got a knife and stabbed him." Dan made a fist, jabbed the air with an invisible knife, and said, "EEE… EEE… EEE. *Psycho*, right?"

I remembered him using the same gesture and words when Dorothy had told me about killing Bull. "I had to kill him," Dan continued. "My life and Dorothy's life were on the line."

Dan just confessed to murdering Bull. Maybe he isn't as brilliant as he thinks. "Then what?"

"Again, I had to act fast. I got cleaned up and put on my man clothes. Then I ran next door and forced Patricia to dress in Dorothy's clothes. I dragged her to Dorothy's house. When she saw Bull's body, she went nuts and tried to kill herself. Superficial wounds. She was too much of a coward to really hurt herself. Then I used my Dorothy voice and called the police. I told them I killed my boyfriend because he beat me and tried to rape me. Then I gave the police the performance of a lifetime and told them I couldn't believe what I'd done and I was going to kill myself. After I hung up, I noticed Patti didn't look as if she'd struggled with Bull, so I beat her. Then I left the scene, hoping Patti would pull it off."

"Oh… my… God," I said as I remembered Carl saying, "Ms. Blue Eyes looks like she may have been in a fight or something. Looks like whoever covered up her bruises and swelling missed a few spots."

"Stay with the program," Dan yelled. "The police came. An officer asked her why she tried to kill herself. She told him Bull beat her and tried to rape her and in self-defense she stabbed him. When she realized he was dead, she tried to kill herself. She told the police she had killed the only man she ever loved and she didn't deserve to live. She was brilliant. After the coroner declared Bull dead, his body was removed from the house. The police called to inform me my son had been killed. The suspect's name was Dorothy Hall. They asked me to go to the county morgue and ID Bull's body. I played the grieving father, cried, and told the police I couldn't bear to see my son dead, so I would send my sister, Vivian, in my place. As soon as I hung up, I called the coroner, a buddy of mine, and asked if he had written his report on Bull's death. He hadn't. I told him to determine Bull had died from trauma to the head and neck when he fell on top of Dorothy and to state the knife wounds were superficial and were *not* the cause of death. When he squawked and told me he couldn't put his job on the line, I said, 'Remember 2011?' He owed me big, and he knew it. And guess what? He took it one step further and stated Bull's blood alcohol level was .15, fall-down drunk. That's what friends are for."

"Looks like you owe him big now."

"Everybody in this town owes somebody big. Anyway, in the meantime, Patti, otherwise known as Dorothy Hall, was taken to the emergency room and examined, then to the police station for questioning. Patti as Dorothy refused her right to a lawyer. That was her first brilliant move. Then she was questioned and held overnight. Her hearing was the next day. The judge reviewed the coroner's report and Patti's statement, or I should say Dorothy's statement. He determined she superficially stabbed Bull in self-defense and the cause of death was injury due to alcohol intoxication. In other words, it was an accidental death. She was free to go. Patti had done it. I couldn't believe it. End of story."

"It's not the end. There are lots of holes in your story. And if it got out that your buddies covered for you, they'll go to jail right along with you."

"I said it's the end of the story." Dan rose from his chair and walked into the kitchen. He probably thought removing himself from my presence would shut me up. He was wrong. As he peered in the refrigerator, I asked another question. "Why did you kill Patti?"

CHAPTER
THIRTY-THREE

DAN SLAMMED THE REFRIGERATOR DOOR. "I didn't...," he yelled as he made his way back to the chair, clutching another bottle of his magic juice. "I killed Dorothy Hall."

"But it was Patti's body that was found in the lake."

"Who told you that?"

"Figured it out myself." I pointed to my head and said, "Now that's using your noodle."

Dan's face and bald head turned so red I thought his head would explode. Instead, he said, "Okay, so I *killed* Patti. I had to."

"Why?"

"Because I had to kill that bitch, Dorothy Hall." Dan got up and walked over to where the photos of the seven babies lay on the floor. He pushed them with his foot. Then he bent down and picked up one. "She killed my boy. She killed my Bull." He turned toward me and said, "I hated her guts. She deserved to die."

"You hated whose guts? Patti's or Dorothy's?"

"Dorothy's, you nitwit. She's the one who killed my son."

"How did you pull it off?"

Dan tilted his head and arched his brow, the look on his face indicated he thought I was a complete moron, but I wanted the words to come straight from the horse's mouth. No conjecture. Just the facts.

"Okay, I'll tell you." Dan pulled at his muumuu, adjusted his private parts, and gracefully sat down. He took a long drink of his juice and placed the bottle on the table. Then he leaned forward, rested his elbows on his knees, and rubbed his hands together. "It's really simple. That murdering bitch Dorothy had to go. People thought Patti and I looked like brother and sister. And even though our features were different, they mistook Patti and Dorothy as the same person. So I came up with a brilliant idea. I asked Vivian, a talented photographer, to take photos of me dressed as Dorothy wearing Dorothy's favorite T-shirt. Then we dressed Patti in the T-shirt and took her photo. My whiz of a sister photoshopped the pictures so we'd have a composite picture of Patti and me as Dorothy—just in case."

"In case of what?"

"In case..." Dan looked at me. The hatred in his eyes turned to sadness. He turned away. Then he looked back at me and yelled, "In case I needed a body, you stupid shit."

"I don't get it," I said.

"I'm not surprised," Dan muttered.

"Enlighten me. Why would you need a composite photo of you and Patti dressed as Dorothy wearing Dorothy's WORLD'S BEST MOM T-shirt?"

"To save my ass. Anybody with half a brain could study the photo of Dorothy and figure out it was me. So when they found Patti's body in the pond in a state of decay, I would have proof the body was Dorothy Hall, but the photo wouldn't easily implicate me."

"So you planned to kill Patti?"

"Well, duh. Someone had to be the scapegoat. Besides, Patti was just taking up space. She didn't serve a purpose. No one, especially not me, would miss her. So you could say I gave purpose to her pathetic existence."

"What would that be?"

"She died so Dorothy could live."

"I see. Hmm." I tapped my forehead à la Columbo. I nearly laughed when I realized I was copying the mannerisms of a TV detective from a show I watched with my parents when I was a toddler. "I'm confused. When did you have the pictures taken of you as Dorothy and Patti as Dorothy?"

Dan squinted at me. "What are you getting at?"

"Well, did you have them taken before or after Dorothy killed Bull?"

"What difference does it make?"

"Just wondering." Then a horrifying thought zipped through my head. I visualized the two photos—one of Dan dressed as Dorothy in the WORLD'S BEST MOM T-shirt and one of Patti wearing the WORLD'S BEST MOM T-shirt. Then I visualized the photo Vivian had given me. The one she said was the key to the truth. The one Carl had said was a he/she. Then I remembered something that for some reason I had ignored. The stamp on the back of the composite photo read: Property of Bingingham County Maryland Police Department. Yikes. I felt beads of sweat tickle my forehead. If Dan knew what I suspected, I could be in trouble.

He got up and paced the room, then turned and glared at me before continuing to pace. Did he know what I was thinking? Maybe not. After all, he thought I was as dumb as a doorknob. You lied," I yelled. "You were there. You were at the crime scene when the police arrived. The pictures were taken after the fact. Vivian did the makeup, and a police photographer took the photos. They covered for you."

"You're nuts. I wasn't there. I told you I left the scene before they got there."

"Liar," I yelled.

Dan was paralyzed by my anger. He didn't say anything, and I was relieved he didn't do anything to harm me.

"You vowed to tell the truth, the whole truth, and nothing but the truth."

Dan reached for my recorder. In my head, I screamed, *No, no, no. Don't shut it off.* He must have read my mind because he removed his hand. Then he picked up his bottle of happy juice, drank until he had to come up for air, and said, "There's no easy way to say this, but…"

CHAPTER THIRTY-FOUR

"IT WAS *YOUR* FATHER'S IDEA."

Electricity surged through me. I sat straight up. That wasn't the response I'd expected.

"Don't look so surprised," Dan said. "You knew. No one asks a question unless they know the answer or think they know the answer."

I didn't say anything. My mind raced. I wanted to ask another question, but I didn't know which one. Just when I was about to talk, Dan blurted, "He told me when I was dressed as Dorothy that Patti and I looked so much alike I could kill her and no one would know the difference."

I gasped. "When did he say that?"

"I don't know… years ago. In college, I guess."

I took a deep breath and slowly released my tension.

"So you see, it's your father's fault Patti is dead." Dan screamed into the recorder, "Murderer. Murderer. Andrew Lukins is a murderer!"

"No," I yelled. "You're just trying to get off the hook for killing Patti and Bull."

"Are you calling me a murderer?"

"I call them as I see them." I shook with fear. I was treading on thin ice. This enraged crazy man could kill me.

179

Dan sank in his chair. Then he covered his face with his hands and cried. I couldn't believe it. I had slain the dragon. But there was something phony about his crying. I decided to ignore his emotional display and change the line of questioning.

"Let's get back to the scene of the crime," I said.

Dan didn't respond. He appeared to be lost in space. *It's about time. It's about space. It's about time to slap your face.* It never ceases to amaze me how childhood memories pop up during the most serious conversations. Maybe I'm nuts. After all, there's no doubt my bio-parents were loony. At least I could blame my genes.

Dan looked at me, grabbing my attention, and in Dorothy's voice said, "Whaddya want to know?"

"Why was Dan in the house when the police arrived?"

"Dan wasn't there. I was."

"Was Patti there?"

"Yep," Dan as Dorothy said.

"Why was Patti there?"

"Because I called her and told her what I'd done. I didn't expect her to show up, but she did."

"Why were you there?"

"Dipshit, Patti called the police. They were just down the street when she called. There was nothing I could do. They took us both in."

"Who? Patti and you?"

"Yep."

"Hmm. Dilemma. What did you do?"

"Well, since crazy Patti told the police she was Dorothy Hall, there was nothing I could do but say I was Patti Jordan. So while Patti, now known as Dorothy, was at the hospital having her bruises and cuts taken care of, the damn police questioned me. I told them all I knew—I heard Dorothy yelling, ran next door, and found Dorothy standing over Bull's body with a knife in her hand. Then I became hysterical. I cried and screamed about how Dorothy had killed my son. I should have won an Oscar for my performance."

"Anyone think you looked like Dan Jordan?"

"Shut up." Dan was back.

"Well?"

"Like I said, I killed Bull because he was going to rat on me. If he hadn't made me kill him, no one would have recognized me. But there I was in the police department, talking to officers I'd worked with for thirty years, and damn if they didn't figure out that Patti was me. My cover was blown." Dan stopped and looked at me. Then he laughed and said, "Isn't that a hoot? Dumb-ass died in vain. And Patti and I looking alike paid off big-time."

"What did you do when you were recognized?"

"I whipped off my wig and begged for mercy. I begged them to keep my cross-dressing a secret." Dan stopped and looked at me.

"Well?"

"Well, what?"

"What happened then?"

"They let me go. I didn't kill Bull. Dorothy, aka Patti, did. Patti took the rap. I was just a cross-dresser who dressed as his wife. A little role reversal never hurt anyone."

"Who helped you with the cover-up?"

"What cover-up?"

"Obviously, there was a cover-up." I waited for Dan to spill the beans. He didn't. I decided to push things along. "Well, let me think this through. You and Patti were both taken in, as you say, and questioned regarding the death of Bull. Patti identified herself as Dorothy Hall. You identified yourself as Patti Jordan until it was discovered she was you, Dan Jordan, in drag. Now, I would suspect in any murder investigation, the suspect would be fingerprinted. And I would imagine the fingerprints would reveal Dorothy Hall was actually Patti Jordan. I guess you had some tap dancing to do in explaining yourself to your cop friends. So this is where the cover-up starts."

I glanced at Dan before continuing. "The police department and the court system would be turned upside down and inside out if it was revealed a prominent judge was a cross-dresser and he killed his son during an indecent act while dressed as a woman named Dorothy Hall. Worse, Dorothy Hall had a long history of abuse and neglect of five children, all of whom were removed from her care—your care. And you were the judge who ruled on the child abuse cases against Dorothy, in reality against yourself, while your wife disguised herself as Dorothy Hall. Imagine the public uproar if this was leaked."

I waited for Dan to respond. His silence spoke volumes. So I rattled on. "Ooh, what a humiliating scandal. Hence, you and your cronies in the police and court communities agreed to let Patti—otherwise known as Dorothy Hall—take the rap. Then one of your judge buddies, Judge Cornelius, I believe, presided over Dorothy's, aka Patti's, hearing and declared that according to the coroner's report, George "Bull" Jordan's death was an accident. Dorothy, aka Patti, was not a murderer. The stabbing was superficial and in self-defense. She was free to go. You agreed to never dress as Dorothy Hall again. Case closed. You went back to being the Honorable Daniel Jordan. All is well in Darrington... until..." I tapped my forehead à la Columbo again. "Patti becomes obsessed with the death of her son and the abuse and neglect of her other six children. Patti repeated the story of her seven babies to everyone and anyone. She had become a problem. She had to be eliminated."

"Shut up!"

"I'm not done. You couldn't live without Dorothy. So you killed Patti and threw her body in the pond. But you didn't do it alone. Your sister, Vivian, helped. Then you waited for the body to surface. When it did, your cop buddies knew it was your wife Patti, but they reported the badly decomposed body found in the lake was '*presumed* to be Dorothy Hall.' And no one questioned anything, leaving you a free man."

"I said shut up."

"Hold your horses. I'm not finished. You couldn't live without Dorothy. In fact, Dorothy may have been the only woman you've ever loved. So you plotted with your police friends to kill yourself off with the promise you'd never indict them in the case. You disappeared for a while, just long enough for the people of Darrington to forget you. Everyone assumed you were distraught over the death of your son and you decided to retire. Then a story ran in the local paper stating you died from wounds consistent with a gun accident. I can hear people now: 'Ah, poor Judge Jordan. I bet he killed himself because he couldn't get over the murder of his son.'"

Dan rose and began to pace. I momentarily shut up. When he didn't speak, I continued. "A month or two goes by, and everyone forgets about you. You're going nuts. You miss Dorothy more than anything. But because no one knew Patti was dead, you dressed up again and took on Patti's identity. Your cop friends were mad, but since people thought you were Patti, they let it go. But still, you couldn't give up Dorothy. So every day you went to the house next door and played Dorothy. At night you went home to Vivian, who pretended to care for her dead brother's crazy wife. Your little charade worked until I came knocking on Dorothy's door."

I took a deep breath and waited for Dan to respond. He seemed a little too calm. Then he said, "Well, little lady. You think you're so damn smart. What do you think I'll do next?"

Was he going to hurt me? No, he was going to destroy the tape. I nonchalantly glanced at my watch. In that split second, Dan took the recorder.

"You know you can't print any of this," he yelled as he tried to erase the recording. "You'll ruin the lives of a lot of people. You wouldn't want to do that, would you?"

I tried to get the recorder from Dan. Big mistake. He grabbed me, twisted my arm, and flung me to the floor. "Leave me alone," I screamed.

Dan backed off and glared at me. Was he going to hurt me or let me go? He threw my recorder across the room and yelled, "Get out before I kill you."

Instinct told me this was no idle threat. I snatched my things and ran for the door, grabbing my recorder from the floor while simultaneously opening the door. I bolted to my car with the speed of an Olympic athlete. "Keys, keys, where are my keys?"

"Looking for these?" Dan said.

I turned toward his voice. He was next to me, my keys dangling from his hand. I watched them sway, feeling like a scared, starving dog too afraid to snatch lifesaving food from the hand of its abuser. I reached for my keys. He yanked them back and then threw them into the street. I scurried after them, jumped in my car, and burned rubber on my way out of Darrington.

It was an hour before I settled down. How I didn't get stopped for speeding is beyond me. Another hour and a half and I was home. I raced upstairs, only to hear voices coming from my condo. Worse, I heard a woman giggling.

"Damn, I don't need this," I muttered. "Some stupid high school kids have broken into my condo." I flung the door open. Laura and Richard bolted from the couch. "I don't even want to know what you two were doing."

"We weren't doing anything," Laura said. "My God, Emarie, we've been worried sick about you. We came over to see if you were okay and decided to wait."

"Thanks," I said. Then I broke down in tears.

Laura rushed over to console me. "What happened?"

I reached into my purse, pulled out my recorder, and handed it to Richard. "It's all on here. At least I hope so."

Richard turned on the recorder. Dan's voice boomed, "Get out before I kill you." Richard looked at me, his face as white as a ghost. "What the hell have you done?"

CHAPTER THIRTY-FIVE

"I CAUGHT A KILLER... AND..."

"And?"

"He's my father."

Laura's eyes widened. "Your father is a killer?"

I shook my head and whispered, "Yes."

"Oh... my... God, I thought your father was the nicest man in the world."

"Not my father, my bio-father."

"You met your bio-father?"

"Yes, and so did Richard."

Richard looked at me, his brow scrunched in confusion. Then he grinned and said, "Holy crap, Carl was right."

"Way to go, Carl," I said. "Laura, don't take this personally, but I've got work to do."

"I understand," Laura said, but her eyes said her feelings were hurt.

"And Richard, I need your help."

"No problem."

While Richard escorted Laura to the door, I turned my briefcase upside down. Within seconds, my dining room table was covered with photos, papers, and tapes.

Richard picked up a picture of Dorothy and looked at me. He shrugged his shoulders and tilted his head, indicating he expected me to say something.

I held his gaze for a few seconds and said, "I think this story was a plant."

"A plant?"

"Yeah, it was given to me on purpose."

"How would anyone know you had anything to do with this story? Certainly Jim…" Richard paused, his eyes as wide as saucers.

"Are you thinking what I'm thinking?"

"What are you thinking?" Richard said.

"Well, for starters, I think Jim has been a little too patient with my deadlines. He hasn't complained. And although he destroyed my first draft, he's been hands-off on a hot, hands-on story."

"Okay."

"And what about you, Richard?"

"What about me?"

"How convenient that you were reassigned to another department that evidently keeps you so busy you have time to run back and forth to Darrington with me."

"Uh-huh."

"Strange. You're one of Jim's best writers, yet he cut back on your workload and reassigned you because you told everyone in the office I was pregnant. That's hardly a fireable offense. Maybe a slap on the wrist and an HR report. But reassigning his best writer? Something's fishy."

"Uh-huh."

"And you know what's even stranger?"

"No."

"This story was originally yours, but you turned it down."

"I turned it down because there wasn't much info to go on."

"True, but you managed to find information about Dorothy's and Judge Jordan's deaths."

"Your point would be?"

"You and Jim are in cahoots."

"Emarie, that's totally paranoid."

"Really? Let me google something and see." I opened my laptop and booted it, then got Richard and myself a glass of wine. "Cheers," I said as we clinked glasses. Then I sat down and googled James Keane. Voilà, there he was, third listing, Wikipedia, James Keane, editor, *Washington Intelligencer*. I scanned the information. Something caught my eye. It was a family listing. Wife: Elizabeth Keane, deceased. Two children: Donald Keane and Maria Keane. Mother: Lydia Keane. Father: "Aha! His father is the Honorable Warren Keane, deceased. Damn, his father was a judge."

"So what?"

"Come on Richard, give it up."

"Okay. Jim knows Dorothy Hall is really Judge Jordan."

"How?"

"His father was the judge who pushed baby number five through the system."

"Jim's father is the judge who placed me with my parents?"

"I guess so."

"How did Jim know I was baby number five?"

"He didn't." Richard paused and looked away as if to hide his lying eyes. Then he looked at me and said, "He gave me the story about Dorothy killing her twenty-five-year-old lover. I thought it was intriguing. In my research, I discovered the history of Dorothy's six children, but I couldn't find birth certificates or other information. Among the papers was a handwritten note from Judge Jordan thanking Judge Keane for helping place Emily Hall with Andrew and Marie Lukins. When I saw the last name of the adoptive parents, I wondered if they had any connection to you. Then one day I heard you ordering something on the phone. You told the person to send it to Andrew and Marie Lukins at an address in Maryland. At first, I thought it was just a coincidence. I didn't say anything to you, but I mentioned it to Jim. That's when he remembered his father telling him about a friend who was the judge on the case of a woman who had abused her children. Jim's father told him that years ago he helped the judge get one of the babies adopted. I did a little digging through Maryland birth records and found a birth listing for an Emarie Lukins born to Andrew and Marie Lukins. If I wanted more info, I'd have to order it. But I knew I'd seen more than I wanted. I knew you were connected with the story. How? I didn't know. I told Jim I couldn't work on the story anymore. He blew up at me, and then he gave the story to you."

"That was cruel," I said.

"That wasn't Jim's intention. In fact, despite the evidence, he still thought your being baby number five was impossible. He knew you wanted a break. He knows you're a good writer. And..." Richard paused to go into the kitchen and pour himself another glass of wine.

"And what?"

"And he knew if you were baby number five, you would write the story from an emotional point of view no other writer could. In other words, he knew you'd write a damn good story."

"And what if I refuse to write it?"

"You and I both know there isn't a snowball's chance in hell you won't write the story."

I walked into the living room. I was pissed. I felt used and disrespected. Whether I wrote the story or not, Jim had no right to discombobulate my life and my parents' lives. It should have been my choice to discover my life story. It shouldn't have been thrust on me. I turned around and shouted at Richard. "Jim's a bastard. He had no right to play with my emotions or capitalize on my life story. He doesn't care about anything but his next big promotion." I went back to the dining room and got my cell phone. Richard grabbed it from me.

"Emarie, don't call Jim. Don't let him win."

"What do you mean?"

"Okay, Jim gave you the story knowing if what I'd discovered was the truth you'd either be thrilled or devastated. He figured, either way, he'd win. You'd write an award-winning story under his guidance, and he'd be the hero. His buddies would congratulate him, and the paper would get lots of positive press. And your career would soar. As far as your feelings and your parents' feelings were concerned... well... he figured you and your parents would get over it. No harm done. Everyone wins."

"No harm done?" I yelled. "What a jerk. What about Dan Jordan? What about Vivian?"

"They'd get their comeuppance."

I almost laughed when I heard Richard use the word comeuppance.

It was so old-fashioned. But I was still too full of rage to comment. "And what about my… No, there's something else going on here. This isn't about me."

"Who is it about then?"

"It's about Jim. He's ratting on his father."

"Not necessarily."

"What?"

"Jim doesn't have to run the story."

"Then why does he want the information?" I said. "For himself? To ruin his father? To bribe his father?"

"Jim's father is dead, so you can rule out bribery."

"So why is this story important to Jim?"

"I don't know."

I pushed Richard aside on my way to my computer. I googled Judge Warren Keane. I scrolled… nothing… click on page two… scroll… nothing… click on page three… scroll… "Aha! Here it is. The obituary for the Honorable Warren Keane. He died in 2014." A quick scan revealed nothing too interesting, just information about his illustrious legal career culminating in his appointment as the general circuit court judge of Prince Georges County, Maryland. The final paragraph held the shocker. It read: *The Honorable Warren Keane is preceded in death by his parents, William and Charlotte Keane. He is survived by his wife of forty-five years, Lydia Keane (née Wilkinson), his son, James Keane, his daughter, Joyce Keane, and a brother, the Honorable Daniel Jordan.* "Oh… my… God."

"What?" Richard turned my laptop toward himself and scanned the article. "Holy shit. Judge Warren Keane and Judge Dan Jordan are brothers."

"That means Dan Jordan is—"

"Jim's uncle."

"Richard, have you seen a picture of Jim's father?"

"Yep. It's on his desk."

"Can you make a copy of it for me?"

"Sure, but why?"

"Nothing yet, but I'd like to see a picture of him. You know, for comparison."

Richard paused. "I just remembered something."

"What?"

"Well, one evening after Jim and I had put a long story to bed, he and I went to a bar in Georgetown and knocked back a few drinks—beer for me, scotch for Jim. Anyway, we started talking about our families. I told Jim I was an only child. He told me he had a sister and they were pretty close. Then we got to talking about our parents. He told me his father had been adopted and had an identical twin brother. They didn't know about each other until they went to college at the University of Maryland. He said his father was constantly stopped by people saying hi to him and calling him Dan. Then one day a mutual friend introduced them. They became pals for a while, but they had a falling out. Jim laughed when he told me his father couldn't stand his identical twin. That's almost like not liking yourself."

"Who was the mutual friend?"

"Jim didn't say."

"I bet I know who it was." I dialed the phone. Ring… ring… ring…

"Dad, I have a question. When you were in college, did you know two guys who didn't know they were identical twins?"

Silence.

"Did you introduce Dan Jordan to Warren Keane?"

Silence.

"Dad?"

"Yes. Why do you want to know?"

"Did you know my boss, Jim, is Warren Keane's son?"

"No. You're kidding!"

"No, he is."

"Oh, that's great, Emarie."

"Did you know Dan Jordan is a cross-dressing murderer?"

"Cross-dresser, yes. Murderer, no."

"When was the last time you had contact with Dan Jordan?"

"When we got you. I never spoke to him again. Couldn't stand him or his wife. I think her name was Patti."

"Thank God."

"Why, Emarie?"

190

"It's important to something I'm working on."

"Okay. Hope it's nothing to do with Dan Jordan."

"It's fine, Dad. Say good night to Mom for me. I love you both."

Back in the living room, I was greeted by an ashen Richard.

"Richard, what's the matter?" I reached for his arm.

"Emarie, if Dan Jordan is your father and Warren Keane is his brother, then—"

"Oh my God, Warren Keane is my uncle and Jim is my cousin."

"You know, now that you mention it, you and Jim resemble each other."

"Don't even go there."

"Okay. Just an observation." Richard looked at the clock, put his half-full glass of wine on the counter and said, "Oops, I've gotta go."

I was surprised by Richard's sudden urge to leave, but I escorted him to the door and, out of habit, almost kissed him good-bye. He didn't seem to notice as he turned to leave. I shut the door and leaned with my back against it.

"Awkward." I wondered why he was in such a rush. "Laura." I rushed to my sunroom, flung open a window, and caught Richard just in time to yell, "Don't you tell Laura anything."

Richard waved and said, "My lips are sealed." Then he hopped in his car and off he went to Laura's for makcup whatever. Had their friendship turned into a relationship? Not with my little sister, you don't.

CHAPTER THIRTY-SIX

E XHAUSTION IS THE BEST SLEEP aid. But excitement is the best alarm clock. Like a baby, I slept hard and rose before the sun. Sunday morning was usually the start of a lazy, carefree day for me, but not today. I was charged and ready to expose Dorothy Hall for who she truly was—a demented, dangerous man.

Cup of coffee in hand, I sat down at my dining room table, opened my computer, and started to write. I wrote like a crazed woman, completely lost as to time and space.

I laughed.

I cried.

I cursed.

I listened to every tape and jotted down quotes and notes. I typed, edited, and typed some more. I talked out loud as I tried to organize a disorganized story. The more I wrote, the more questions I had, only to discover the answers buried in something Dorothy, Dan, or Vivian had said. Every time I thought my story was done, I'd remember something, causing me to rewrite entire sections. I felt pressured and excited as I solved the massive puzzle of lies and unraveled the truth about the despicable Dorothy Hall. I reread my article and manically scribbled changes. While I incorporated the changes, a bright light diverted my attention.

Holy cow, the sun was coming up. I had written all day and night. But I wasn't done yet. I wanted the story to culminate in an explosive ending, and I couldn't see how to light the fireworks. As I looked up to glimpse the rising sun, I saw my ghostly friend standing in the corner of my living room. He motioned, indicating he was watching me. I wanted to divert my eyes, but I couldn't. He wouldn't let me. He was trying to tell me something.

"What? What do you want?" I screamed.

Even when he approached me, I wasn't scared. Then all the papers and photos on my table formed a mini tornado and gently gathered on the floor. Only two items remained. One was the photo of Dan Jordan that Jim allegedly left on Richard's desk. The other was a printout of Warren Keane's obituary. I didn't remember printing it, so I picked it up and read it. That's when I noticed one simple word—the first and most crucial word in the obituary. It was the word *suddenly*. I looked toward my ghostly friend. He was gone. But his message was loud and clear. "Oh my God. Dan Jordan killed his brother, Warren Keane. Dan killed Jim's father." But how could I prove it? I thought it through. This was a piece of information for another story. No, wait. Maybe Jim's father wanted me to tell his son who was responsible for his death. But Jim would think I was nuts. I didn't know what to do with the information, so I put it out of my mind and finished my story. It ended with the last words Dan, my bio-father, said to me, "Get out before I kill you." Fireworks.

I couldn't believe it. I was done—with my story. I set the coffee to brew. On my way to shower, I pressed the Print button on my computer and waited until I heard the printer come to life. A bit later, I downed several cups of coffee while I reviewed the printout of the final draft, only to be startled by a knock on the door. I looked out the peephole. A man dressed in a black suit was at the door. *Oh my God, it's the FBI.*

"Who is it?" I said.

"D.C. Limo, ma'am. I'm sorry to knock on your door, but you didn't answer your phone."

I opened the door. "Who sent you?"

"Jim Keane from the *Washington Intelligencer*."

"Really? Why?"

"I'm to escort you to work this morning."

"Oh… hold on a minute. I'm not quite ready."

"Take your time, ma'am. I'll wait in the car."

From my sunroom, I watched the limo driver get back in his car as I called Jim on my cell phone.

"Good Monday morning, Emarie. I suppose you're calling about a limo driver waking you up bright and early this morning."

"Yes, Jim. But for your information, I was already up, dressed, and ready to head to the office."

"Can I assume your story is finished?"

"Yes."

"Good. I'm eager to read it."

"I'm eager *for* you to read it."

"Good. See you in a few."

"Bye."

My cell phone beeped, demanding attention. I had messages. I scanned my recent call list. Sure enough, there were four calls from the limo driver and one from a number I didn't recognize. Then it hit me. It was Dorothy's number. I checked my voice mail, deleted the limo driver's messages, and listened to dear old Dan's message.

"Emarie? Remember me? It's Dan, your dad. I know where you live. I'm on my way to retrieve what is rightfully mine, namely every bit of information you have on me, everything you've written about me, and your lovely tape recorder with all your recordings of Dorothy, Vivian, and me. Capiche? Oh, and don't forget the photos. I'll need them too. See you soon."

I checked the time. The call had come in at five a.m. "Holy crap, it's seven fifteen. He'll be here any moment."

I ran to the limo, jumped in the back seat, and said, "Hurry up! Someone's trying to kill me."

Without a word, the limo driver followed my instructions. An hour later, thoroughly frustrated by D.C.'s infamous rush hour traffic, I walked into the office, only to find Jim was in his office with someone.

My nerves were getting the best of me. I couldn't tell if I was eager or anxious. It didn't matter. I wanted to see Jim—now. So I stood up and made sure he saw me. He looked my way but didn't acknowledge me. Then Richard showed up.

"Story done?"

"Yep. Right here," I said as I pointed to the stack of papers and gently stroked my hand across the top sheet.

"Whoa. That's a hefty article."

"I know. It's a big story about murder and deception in a small town."

"Okaaay," Richard said, diverting his eyes toward Jim's office. "Who's with Jim?"

"I don't know. But Jim is eager to read my story. He sent a limo for me this morning."

"Superstar treatment," Richard said. "I think I'll walk by Jim's office and see who he's talking to."

"He's wise to that trick, you know."

Richard winked at me and walked away just as my buzzer went off. I picked up the phone. "Hello?"

"Hey, Liz, this is Jim. Be a dear and go downstairs and get a couple of donuts? My *uncle* and I are starving. And while you're down there, would you tell Roger to come to my office?"

"No problem." I gulped. Richard was long gone. I stuffed my story in my briefcase. Then my briefcase and I quickly left and took the elevator to the ground floor. Surprise, surprise, Richard was waiting for me, gasping for breath.

"I already know who's in Jim's office," I said.

"Dan Jordan," Richard said as he tried to catch his breath.

"It must be serious. Jim addressed me as Liz, asked for donuts, and requested I tell Roger to go to his office."

"Roger? The head of security?"

"The very one."

"You brought your briefcase?"

"I didn't want to leave the goods behind. What if Dan looks for it? He's seen it enough to recognize it."

"Good thinking. You buy a few donuts, and I'll go talk to Roger."

The donut vendor was in his usual place. I scanned the baked goodies and chose five—four for Jim and Dan and one for me. Richard hadn't returned, so I grabbed the latest edition of *People* magazine off the rack and flipped through it.

"Seen this yet?" A woman said.

Crap, it was the red-haired woman—Vivian Jordan. Our eyes locked. I was speechless.

"Did you think you'd get away with writing your crap of a story?"

"Excuse me?"

"You heard me. Dan's not about to let your story run…"

Where the hell were Richard and Roger? I wanted to warn them, but I couldn't—not without raising the suspicions of Vivian Jordan.

"…so you might as well hand over your briefcase."

I was about to protest when the magazine cart overturned, spilling its contents at my feet, knocking Vivian to the floor, and eliciting screams from several shoppers. Just when I turned to run, a man pushed me down and ran off with my briefcase. Only his legs were visible as he charged out of sight.

"Stop him," I screamed. An instant later, I was pulled to my feet.

"You're under arrest," a man said.

I glanced at him. To my relief, it was Roger. He winked at me. I protested my arrest as he dragged me to his office. Roger slammed the office door and quickly locked it, revealing a person hiding behind the door.

"Richard?"

He was holding my briefcase. This time I wasn't the least bit embarrassed to give him a hug.

"Wow, that was fun," Richard said.

"Fun?"

"Yeah. Roger and I had to do some fast thinking when we saw you and Vivian standing at the magazine rack. Roger didn't know who she was, but I knew what she was up to. Tipping the rack was an act of genius."

"Well, I hope you didn't hurt her. She could charge you with assault."

"Okay, you two," Roger said. "Now I have to save Jim. Who did you say was in his office?"

"Dan Jordan, Jim's—"

"He's a murderer," I blurted. "He could harm Jim."

Roger moved his hand over his .38. "Stay here. I'll check on him."

Richard and I obeyed like two children in the principal's office.

"Wonder what happened to Vivian," I said.

Richard shrugged.

"By the way, who tipped the cart?"

"Roger."

"Hope he doesn't get in trouble."

"We'll see." Richard paced. I could see the little wheels in his head turning. "Don't you want to get the rest of the story?"

"What do you mean?"

"What's going on in Jim's office is part of the story."

"You're right. Let's go."

We charged up the stairs. We huffed and puffed. At the fourth floor, I stopped to catch my breath.

"Come on, sissy. There isn't a minute to spare."

"I'm coming," I said.

"Only four more flights. You're halfway there."

Richard charged ahead of me. I admired what great shape he was in and vowed to get more exercise. On the fifth floor, I heard voices. On the sixth floor, I couldn't believe my eyes. Liz huddled with and consoled several employees.

"Where's Richard?" I asked.

Liz pointed and said, "I wouldn't go up there if I were you."

I crawled over my coworkers and climbed the last two flights of stairs.

Richard sat with his back to the stairwell door. "Took you long enough."

"So what's the plan?"

"Plan? What use is a plan when everything's in chaos?"

"Is Roger in there?"

"Yeah, didn't you hear the gunshot?"

"No."

"Scared the staff. They're hiding on the sixth-floor stairwell."

"I know."

Bang… another gunshot.

"Holy crap," Richard said.

"We've got to help Jim." I dialed 911.

"What's your emergency?" the dispatcher asked.

"Gunshots on the eighth floor of the *Washington Intelligencer* building."

"It's been reported, ma'am. Police and rescue are on their way. Are you or anyone else injured?"

"I'm fine. But I'm concerned about my boss and our security guard."

"As I said, police and rescue are on the way. Are you in a safe place?"

"A bunch of us are in the stairwell. I don't know how safe it is."

"You need to get out of the building."

"Okay." My trembling hands caused me to drop my cell phone. I snatched it and said, "The police are on their way. It's not safe here. We need to tell Liz and the others to get out of the building. Let's go."

"I'm not going anywhere."

"Are you nuts?"

"No, I'm a reporter," Richard said. "I'm getting the story."

"Well, I'm going to tell Liz and the others to get out. Wait here."

I raced down the two flights of stairs. No one was there. The sound of blaring police sirens motivated me to scurry up the stairs and catch up with Richard. He was gone. "Damn him. This story's mine." I opened the stairwell door and crawled out into the lobby area just as the police burst out of the elevators. They ignored me. One officer jumped over me and ran toward Jim's office. Despite the seriousness of the situation, I laughed and said, "I'm an idiot. This is something Inspector Clouseau would do."

I got up and followed the cops. Roger opened the door as Jim and Richard held up their hands to show they were unarmed.

"Where is he?" I yelled. "Where is that murderer, Dan Jordan?"

"Ma'am, you need to leave the area," a young, and I must say handsome, police officer said.

"It's okay," Jim said. "She's with us."

"Where is he?" I said.

"He's gone. Roger scared him off," Jim said.

"How did he get out? I didn't see him run down the staircase."

"Back staircase, Emarie," Richard said.

"Oh… I didn't know there was a back staircase."

"And you've worked here how long?"

"Okay, you two," Jim said. "Cut it out."

Reprimand. Ouch. Instant regression to a little schoolgirl. I hoped my hurt feelings didn't show.

Jim spoke with the officers. A few minutes later, the police and Roger left. At that point, Jim turned his attention back to Richard and me. "Okay, I'll catch you two up on today's excitement later. Right now I want to read your story."

"It's in my briefcase"—I gulped—"in Roger's office."

Richard and I looked at each other and charged for the elevator. The eight-story ride felt like an eternity. The door to the lobby opened, and we ran to Roger's office. The door was locked. And a hand was on my shoulder.

CHAPTER THIRTY-SEVEN

"WELL, WELL, IF IT ISN'T Eerie Emmie."

The hair on the back of my neck spiked. I turned. Dan Jordan, looking dapper in a black suit, white shirt, and charcoal-gray-and-white-striped tie, smiled at me. I was struck by his charming good looks and shiny white teeth.

"And good morning to you, Mr. Bader," Dan said.

"What are you doing here, Mr. Jordan?" Richard said.

"Just having a little chitchat with your boss." Dan faced me, sneered. "You know, about your story, babycakes."

"What about it?"

"Well, it looks like your little story about me was nothing but a big waste of time." Dan chuckled. Then he lowered his head until we were face-to-face. "Because it's never going to see the light of day. Capiche?"

I stared into Dan's coal-black eyes. "Yeah, capiche."

To my surprise, he turned and walked away. He met up with Vivian, who was rubbing her elbow. Then they got in a cab and were gone.

I sighed with relief. Then I banged on Roger's door again.

"If you hit it any harder, you'll break it," Roger said from behind me.

"Roger, please tell me my briefcase is in your office."

"If that's where you left it, then that's where it is." Roger pulled out a massive keychain heavy with keys. He put a key in the door and pushed it open.

I rushed in. *Please God, let my briefcase be there.* To my relief, it was right where I'd left it. I looked inside. My story was safe and sound.

"Come on, Richard. Jim's waiting to read my Pulitzer Prize-winning story."

Richard glanced at Roger and said, "Humble, isn't she?" Then he followed me to the elevator for another silent, eight-story ride. We stepped into an empty, quiet elevator and stepped out into an office buzzing with chatter.

Liz rushed toward me. "Emarie, are you okay?"

"I'm fine. Is everyone else all right?"

Liz's eyes sparkled with excitement. "Yeah, the most exciting day we've ever had."

As if on cue, Jim yelled from his office door, "Okay, fun's over. Everyone back to work. And Emarie, hand over your story."

I was taken aback by Jim's use of the phrase "hand over your story." What was he saying? Was he going to confiscate my story? Was Dan Jordan right about my story not seeing the light of day? I walked to Jim's office, clutching my story to my chest so tight that if Jim tried to take it from me, he could be charged with inappropriate touching.

He reached for it, obviously expecting me to give it to him. I tightened my grip. He smiled and gently tried to take it from me, but when he realized he'd have to fight me for it, he pulled away.

"I know this story is your baby, but are you going to let me read it?"

"Are you going to print it?"

"If it's good enough, I will."

I released my grip.

Jim snatched my story and handed me another file. "In the meantime, get hopping on this."

I nodded and walked back to my desk, my next assignment in hand.

"Well, what did he say?" Richard asked, peering over the divider between his old desk and mine.

"Who?"

"Jim. What did he say about your story?"

"He's not a speed reader, Richard."

"Did he say he's going to print it?"

"He said if it's good enough, he will."

"That's a relief. I guess good old Dan didn't sway him."

"I hope not."

"Whatcha got there?"

"My next assignment. I'm afraid to open it. Hey, Richard, did you notice something different about Dan Jordan?"

"Well duh."

"Like what?"

"Well for starters, he was dressed mighty fine. He was much thinner. Wasn't as ugly as a man as he is as a woman. In fact, he was nice-looking, for a guy. Why?"

"He didn't have bad breath or black and brown teeth either. His teeth were movie-star white."

"Hmm. Maybe he wasn't Dan Jordan," Richard said.

"Who was he then?"

"Warren Keane."

"Jim's father? He's dead."

"Maybe… and… maybe not. Maybe there's more to Dan's story."

"If that was Jim's father, then who's the ghost that keeps visiting me?"

Richard looked at me like I had three heads. "Ghost?"

"Yeah, ghost."

Richard squinted. He looked uncomfortable. He disappeared behind the divider and reemerged at my desk.

"You've seen him, haven't you?"

Richard sat on the edge of my desk and whispered, "I may have seen something I can't explain. Why?"

"I thought the ghost was Dan Jordan until I found out he was still alive. Looks like him. So if Warren Keane is alive, then who's the ghost?"

Richard thought for a few seconds and said, "Have you seen a picture of Bull Jordan?"

"Nope. I looked but couldn't find one. There wasn't even a picture of him in the newspaper article."

"A newspaper didn't run a picture of a local murder victim?"

"The Darrington newspaper barely covered the story, and other newspapers didn't bother to pick it up. Odd, don't you think?"

Richard thought for a moment then said, "What about TV news?"

"Nada. Nothing. I already checked." We were both lost in thought until I broke the silence. "Richard, do you think the ghost could be Bull Jordan?"

His eyes widened. "You could be right," he said. "Remember when Dan said Bull looked so much like him that he fell in love at first sight?"

"Yeah."

"Did the ghost look like Dan Jordan to you?"

I tried to recall my ghostly guest's features. "His face wasn't distinct, but somehow I knew he looked like Dan, and he was thinner, possibly younger. I've got to get a picture of Bull but how?"

"Maybe a photographer who has pictures of her nephew," Richard said.

"Vivian Jordan?"

"Yep."

"No. We'll have to find a picture some other way."

"Like how?"

"Like through a high school yearbook."

"For God's sake, Emarie. Do you think Bull still looked like his high school yearbook photo? Do you look like yours?"

"You've got a point." I pondered my dilemma. "Richard, we missed the obvious."

"What?"

"Social media. You know, Facebook and Twitter."

"I don't picture Bull as a social media kind of guy."

I logged on to my computer and opened my Facebook page.

"Ooooh, pictures of Laura," Richard said.

"Back off. This is serious."

I typed in Bull Jordan in the search bar. Only one Bull Jordan popped up. Definitely not him. I typed in George Jordan. There were a lot. I quickly eliminated a few and then clicked on one. The image of a smiling surfer dude bore no resemblance to Dan Jordan. I clicked on a few more, but none were Dan Jordan look-alikes. I wasn't about to give up my search, so I decided to click on another George Jordan. Bingo. Looking back at me was Dan Jordan with a head of thick black hair. That had to be him. I clicked the About link. Yep, he lived in Darrington, Maryland. There was only one photo, no friends, and few posts. Not very revealing. But his last post caught my attention.

"Richard, look at the date of the last post."

Richard pushed his head in front of me to see the screen, forcing me to roll my chair back. "Last week? Bull's been dead for two years, so who posted on his page pretending to be him?"

"Who else? Daddy Dan."

"Maybe and maybe not. Could be Vivian. Could be Jim. Heck, it could be the dead Mr. Warren Keane."

"Richard, you're scaring me." I looked at him, thinking he could be right.

Richard leaned back. "If the ghost is Bull, what is he trying to tell us?"

"Haven't got a clue," I said. "But he does the same thing Jim does—you know, the *I'm watching you* motions."

"Yeah," Richard said as he pointed to his eyes and then pointed at me. "Maybe we should forget about Bull's ghost for now. I think we're getting hung up on something that may mean nothing."

We sat in silence for a few minutes as I mentally went over the details of Dan Jordan's story.

Finally, Richard broke the silence. "Emarie, something just occurred to me." He made weird faces as he mulled over his thoughts.

I was getting impatient. "Richard, just spit it out."

"Okay. Let's assume Warren Keane, Jim's father, is dead. That would mean the man in Jim's office this morning was his Uncle Dan. Under that assumption, how would you explain the changes in his appearance? Weight loss? Whitened teeth?"

"No padding or fake teeth. Dorothy is Dan with padding and fake teeth. That would explain why, when Dorothy revealed herself to be Dan, she became agile. She wasn't three hundred plus pounds. She was all padding." I paused as I visualized Dorothy. Then I realized something else. "Plus her arms weren't saggy like those of someone who is morbidly obese. They were toned, and she had man hands."

"Okay. But what if that was Jim's father this morning? How do you explain the fact he spoke to you in the same manner as Dan Jordan? You know, telling you your story wouldn't see the light of day. Calling you Eerie Emmie and babycakes."

"Why would Jim lie about his father being dead?" I thought about it for a moment. "Doesn't make sense to me. Besides, we saw his obituary."

"I think the man in Jim's office was Dan Jordan. I think Warren Keane, Dan's identical twin, is dead. I think Dorothy Hall is the creation of someone who is a Hollywood makeup artist. Hence, I think there's more to Vivian Jordan than we know."

I was about to respond to Richard's analysis when Jim flung open his office door and yelled, "Emarie, get in here."

I got up and sheepishly looked around the office. Everyone's eyes were on me. Liz looked like she was about to cry. I walked to Jim's office, feeling like a very bad little girl about to be lectured by mad daddy. Jim held the door open until I was fully in his office. Then he let it shut. He sat in his desk chair, picked up my story, and leaned back so far I thought his chair would flip over and dump him on the floor. Then he sprang forward, grinned at me, and said, "Stellar story, Emarie. I couldn't be happier with what you've written. Therefore, it pains me to tell you I can't run it."

"What?"

"I can't run it."

"Damn Dan Jordan. I know he was in your office this morning. I know he's your uncle. I can't believe you're kowtowing to him."

"Hold your horses, I wasn't finished. I can't run it until I contact the police."

I took a deep breath, trying to squelch my suspicion. "Why?"

"It isn't just a story. It's a murder confession by my uncle. It reveals my Aunt Vivian to be an accomplice to murder, and it implicates my father in an illegal matter. So you could say it's personal."

"Dan threatened you, didn't he?"

"Yes, but what worries me more is he threatened you and your parents. And I believe he'll follow through with his threats."

I gulped. The thought that Dan Jordan would harm my parents made me sick.

"I've made a few edits." Jim leaned forward and handed my story to me. "Review them and make the corrections yourself. Do not give this to Liz to retype."

"Don't you trust Liz?"

"Of course, but this information is between you and me."

"And Richard?"

"Yes."

"I understand," I said as I rose and started to leave Jim's office.

"And when you bring your final copy, give me everything you have in your files for this story: tapes, photos, everything. Leave absolutely nothing regarding this story in your personal possession. Got it?"

"Got it."

"Oh Emarie, one more thing."

I turned and faced Jim. "Yes?"

"I'm happy to call you 'cousin.'"

I smirked and opened the door.

"Please tell Richard to come see me."

"Sure, coz."

I left Jim's office feeling elated and scared. When I got back to my desk, Richard was waiting for me.

"Well?"

I scanned my story, revealing pages of red ink.

Richard peered over my shoulder. "Yikes, Jim was heavy-handed with the red pen."

"Yep. And he wants to see you."

"Me?"

"Yep."

Richard slunk his way to Jim's office. He opened the door, glanced back at me, and entered.

Meanwhile, I got cracking on Jim's edits. My imagination ran wild with thoughts of what harm Dan might do to my parents. Tears ran down my cheeks.

Liz came over and gave me a hug. "Don't feel bad. Jim's hard on everyone."

I looked at Liz and smiled, wishing I could tell her the truth.

CHAPTER THIRTY-EIGHT

I T TOOK ME MOST OF the day to incorporate Jim's edits. His changes boiled my blood. Some were nitpicky. Some were drastic. Two huge chunks of copy he deleted—one which implicated Dan and Vivian in Patti's murder—nearly threw me into a hissy fit. At the bottom of the last page, Jim had the nerve to write a few final remarks: *Dynamite story. Well written. You've got what it takes.*

"Oh sure," I muttered. I'm probably the only person in the world to be suspicious of positive feedback. My final copy and my background information in hand, I knocked on Jim's door. He motioned for me to enter. Barely able to hide my anger, I placed the copy and background materials on his desk. "Here's the evidence."

"Emarie, you do understand, don't you?"

"Absolutely," I said, hoping my red cheeks and expressionless stare didn't reveal my lie. "What's the next step?"

"I'm turning the story over to a lawyer this evening. We'll see where it goes from there."

"Is it okay if I share this with my parents?"

"Not yet. Wait a few days. And by the way, I told Richard what I told you. So both of you are to keep quiet about what you know."

"Loose lips sink ships." I motioned that my lips were sealed.

"Or get people hurt or killed."

I got a pit in my stomach, but I managed to smile as I left Jim's office. Then I ran down the stairs to Richard's office. I barged through the stairwell door, controlling an urge to scream for Richard. I didn't see him, and I didn't know which desk was his. I finally spotted a young woman chatting on the phone and blurted out, "Do you know where Richard is?" When I saw him come into the office, I rushed toward him.

"Emarie, for God's sake, what's wrong?"

"Did you tell Laura anything about my story? Other than what *I* told her?"

He didn't speak. He didn't have to. His eyes screamed yes.

"Richard, you didn't."

"I may have told her a little. Why? Is she in danger?"

"I don't think so. Dan doesn't know who she is, but you know Laura. She may have told her parents, her other friends, and God knows who."

"So?"

"Six degrees of separation."

Richard picked up his desk phone and hit speed dial number two. I pressed the speakerphone button just in time to hear, "Hi, this is Laura Simmons, marketing manager at Simmons Technology Consultants." So Richard had Laura on speed dial. Those two were definitely too cozy.

Richard quickly hung up and hit speed dial number one. The phone rang five times and went to Laura's home voice mail. He hit speed dial number three. Again, a phone rang several times and finally went to Laura's cell phone voice mail. Richard didn't leave a message. He turned and looked at me.

"I have an awful feeling something is wrong with Laura," I said.

"Me too. We need to find her." The words were barely out of Richard's mouth when his phone rang. The screen showed Laura's home number. "Laura?"

"Hey. What's up?"

"Um, I'm here with Emarie. We're on speakerphone."

"Um, I can't talk right now. I have company."

Richard ran his free hand through his hair. "Are you all right?"

"Um…" Laura hesitated. I thought I heard a man's voice whisper, *"Tell him you're okay."* "Um, I'm fine. F-i-n-e… fine."

"Oh, that's good to hear," Richard said as I frantically motioned for him to hang up. "Hey, I've got another call. I'll catch ya in a few."

"Fine," Laura said. The phone clicked, and she was gone.

"Emarie, what the hell was that about?"

"Fine is our code word for trouble. Laura's in trouble."

Richard raised a brow. "Fine is a code word?"

"Yeah, it means effed up, insecure, neurotic, and emotional."

"That's for sure."

"Shut up. Laura's in trouble. I'm afraid Dan and Vivian paid her a little visit."

Richard and I charged out of the office. After I retrieved my briefcase, we ran to the McPherson Square Metro station. Once we were settled into seats and had caught our breath, I said, "What are we doing?"

"We're going to check on Laura."

"I know, but we could be putting her and ourselves in danger. I think we should call the police."

"Listen, if Dan is at Laura's, and that's a pretty big if, he's not going to hurt us."

"You figure that how?"

"Because we've already got the scoop on him. We can implicate him in murder."

"Yeah, so what are one, two, or three more murders to him?"

"Emarie, relax. We need to be in control."

I didn't feel like continuing the conversation, so I sat and looked out the window at the subway tunnel wall and listened to the clickety-clack of the subway train wheels on the track. It reminded me of long trips home from the beach when I was a child. I'd stretch out on the back seat of the car, stare out the window at the stars, and relax to the comforting sound of the car tires as they sped over the seams in the road. But instead of feeling relaxed, my mind raced with thoughts of Laura being tortured by Dan and Vivian.

The train burst into the sunlight. A few moments later, it stopped at the Arlington Cemetery station, and a mob of middle school kids boarded. In an instant, the energy level rose a thousand percent, and I have to admit it was a welcome relief. I watched the pimply, gawky, noisy adolescents as they pushed and teased each other, but for the most part, they were well behaved. I spotted two girls sitting together and giggling over a magazine. Memories of Laura and me doing the same years ago nearly brought tears to my eyes.

"Laura and I are more than friends, we're sisters, you know."

Richard nodded to acknowledge what I'd said, but his eyes were focused on a person sitting at the back of the car. I glanced back. The guy was dressed in black, his face concealed by a hood. Ice ran through my veins. We'd been followed by the robed man.

The teenagers disembarked at the King Street-Old Town station, emptying the train. But Richard and I were not alone. The man in black was still at the back of the car, staring at us. He raised his hand, pointed at his eyes, then pointed at us. Then he disappeared. Richard looked at me. Neither of us spoke until we were in my car at the Franconia-Springfield station. As I backed out of the parking spot, I glanced in my rearview mirror. Someone was in the back seat. I slammed on the brakes and threw the car into park. The car jerked, throwing Richard forward.

"What the hell—" Richard yelled as he turned around to look out the back window. "Holy shit," he said as the man in black disappeared like millions of stars being sucked up by a giant interstellar vacuum.

"We need to find out who that is," I said.

"No shit, Shylock."

"It's Sherlock."

"What?"

"Doyle, not Shakespeare."

"Your point would be?"

"Never mind." My tires squealed as I sped out of the garage. "Laura, here I come," I screamed.

"Ditto," Richard said.

CHAPTER THIRTY-NINE

T WENTY AGONIZING MINUTES LATER, RICHARD and I pulled into the parking lot of Laura's apartment complex—Riverside Park, conveniently located near the exit to the famous, or I should say infamous, Wilson Bridge. I secured a parking spot that couldn't be seen from Laura's apartment. Then Richard and I hustled to the lobby door.

As I reached for the door handle, Richard said, "Wait. We need a plan."

"Okay," I said. "I'll go up first. Laura will be expecting me. If I don't come out of her apartment within five minutes, you come in and save us."

Richard took a deep breath, obviously expressing his annoyance with me. "That's not a plan."

"Okay, Sherlock, what's our plan?"

"Well, Watson. I'll go in first. Dan won't expect me. It will throw him off."

I nodded my consent.

Richard didn't move, leaving me to wonder why he wasn't racing to the elevator to save Laura. "On second thought, you go first," he said.

"Sissy. Wait until Laura finds out you can't leap tall buildings in a single bound."

Richard didn't respond to my snide remark. He was lost in thought, no doubt hatching a plan to save Laura. Then he said, "Okay, we'll go together."

"That's our plan?"

"We'll improvise," he said as he headed for the elevator.

"I don't like that plan." Nonetheless, I followed Richard. He pressed the button for the tenth floor, and a minute later, we exited the elevator and headed toward Laura's apartment. We stood at the door, listening for chatter, noise, screaming, anything to indicate she and whoever were inside. All we heard was silence.

Richard knocked on the door. No response.

I rang the doorbell. "Laura, it's me, Emarie. Open the door." Still no response.

Richard grunted and did something shocking. He pulled out his key ring, located a key, and unlocked the door to Laura's apartment. Those two were definitely up to something, but now wasn't the time to probe.

The apartment was small, so other than a closet, there was nowhere to hide. As always, Laura's apartment was neat as a pin. There was no evidence anyone had been in her apartment. Heck, there wasn't any evidence anyone lived in her apartment. It looked like a model home.

Richard walked back to the bedroom while I snooped around the living, dining, and kitchen areas just in case there was a clue as to Laura's whereabouts. On my way to scout out the bathroom, I caught a glimpse of Richard standing in Laura's bedroom examining something.

"Found this on the bed," he said.

"Oh God, what is it?"

"A note."

"What does it say?"

"It says, 'Daddy took me to the sty in the sky.'"

"They've gone to my place," I screamed as I raced out of Laura's apartment and down the hall to the elevator. I frantically punched the elevator button. *Hurry up. Open.* Richard caught up with me. I pressed "L" and down we went.

"How do you know they went to your place?"

"Because when I lived here on the twelfth floor, my apartment was a mess. Laura used to call it the sty in the sky."

"Oh," was all Richard said. "So who's daddy?"

"Boy, you're no Sherlock Holmes. It's Dan. Dan Jordan. My bio-daddy."

"That's what I thought."

"Yeah, sure."

Once the elevator opened, we ran through the lobby and across the parking lot to my car. I sped to my condo in record time.

Laura's car was in a reserved parking spot. *Hmm, she knows better than to park in a reserved spot.* "There's Laura's car. They're here. Let's play it nonchalantly. You know, like I just happened to come home and I'm surprised to see her."

"And where do I fit in?"

"You don't."

"What?"

"Just stay here. If you hear any screaming, call the police."

"I don't like that plan."

"Well, at least it's a plan. But in case anything goes wrong and you need to save your scaredy-cat ass, here are the keys to my car," I said, dangling my car keys in his face.

Richard snatched the keys from me. He was angry, but I didn't care. I ran up the stairs to my condo. Through the door, I heard two people—a man and a woman—in a heated discussion.

"Keep looking. That damn story's in here somewhere," the man said.

"Give it up, Dan. There's nothing here. We need to get out of here before she gets home."

Dan and Vivian were in my condo. I didn't hear Laura. Time to follow through with my plan. I walked in, right as Dan entered my office. I didn't see Vivian, so I assumed she was in there with him.

The sunroom seemed like a good place to hide. I squeezed into a small concealed area that gave me a full view of the parking lot.

That's when I saw Richard and Laura kissing and hugging. Her car trunk was open. *Oh my God... they stuffed Laura in the trunk of her car. Nobody messes with my sister without answering to me.*

"Well, look who's here. If it isn't my baby girl," Dan Jordan said.

The sound of Dan's voice sent chills through me. Nonetheless, I casually turned around. "Hi, Dan. What are *you* doing here?" I said as I pushed past him and exited the sunroom, hoping he couldn't see the parking lot from where he stood. Then I walked into the kitchen, forcing him to turn his back on the sunroom windows. I opened the refrigerator door and peered in. "Get you anything? Water? Soda? Happy juice?"

"Don't get smart with me, bitch."

I was about to respond when Vivian appeared from the back room.

"Nice to see you too, Vivian."

"I wish I could say the same."

"Well, what brings you two here today?"

"That's the dumbest question I've ever heard," Dan said. "I want that story, and I want every piece of information—every fact, figure, contact, computer file, memory stick, photo, phone number, everything. Oh, and I want that damned tape recorder and every tape. And I want them now."

"I don't have them. Everything's at the office."

"Bullshit! Jim told me you work from home."

"I never took Jim for a liar. I guess I was wrong."

Dan stared at me with the coldest dead eyes I'd ever seen. "Well, there's only one thing to do."

"What?" I said.

"Escort you to your office and get what's rightfully mine."

"Beats taking the metro." Hopefully, I appeared calm because if Dan and Vivian could see the bottom half of my body hidden behind the kitchen counter, they'd see me struggling to balance on shaking knees.

Vivian picked up my purse that I'd stupidly left on the dining room chair. *No wonder Dan had found me.* As we left my condo, Dan grabbed my arm and dragged me along. I spotted Laura's car and noticed the trunk was closed. I looked for my car. It was gone. Richard and Laura had gotten away. *Way to go, Richard.*

Dan shoved me in the back seat of Laura's car while Vivian took her place in the passenger seat. I expected Dan to drive like a maniac. Instead, he drove like a little old lady. In fact, he drove so slow I wanted to jump in the front seat and drive myself. At this rate, it would take us hours to get to the office. On second thought, that may be a good thing. It would give Richard and Laura time to find a safe place, probably Richard's house. And hopefully, Jim would be well on his way to the lawyer's office with the evidence.

Dan took the scenic route down Route 1 to Old Town, Alexandria, to Washington Street, past Reagan National Airport, over the Memorial Bridge with a view of the Lincoln Memorial, up Constitution Avenue past the Ellipse on the left and the Washington Monument on the right. He turned left on 15th Street, passed the Treasury Department, and continued until he pulled into the parking garage at the *Washington Intelligencer*. Surprisingly, his driving like a tourist didn't seem to bother the other drivers. Not one horn honk nor obscene gesture. Even more interesting, he and Vivian didn't make a peep.

Dan and Vivian got out of the car, but I refused to move until told to do so. Without a word, Dan dragged me out of the back seat like I was a giant stuffed animal.

"Damn," I screamed.

"Shut up or I'll give you something to scream about."

Dan gripped my arm and pushed me to the garage elevator. Vivian took up the rear. As the door closed, I caught a glimpse of Jim struggling to walk to his car with an overstuffed briefcase and an armload of what I assumed was the backup evidence for my story. I almost screamed to get Jim's attention. But I realized that I didn't trust him either, and I didn't want the evil duo to spot him, so I kept my mouth shut and tried to gather my wits.

Dan shoved me to the back of the elevator. Then Vivian and he stood in front of me, blocking my view and any possibility of escaping if the doors opened on another floor. Overwhelmed with anxiety at the thought of being trapped with two crazies who had no qualms about killing people, I started to tremble.

The door opened to the lobby. Vivian moved slightly, giving me a sliver view of the world outside the elevator. I quickly scanned the area, hoping to see Roger, but he wasn't there. Just then, a woman stepped sideways into the elevator as she waved to a friend. She pressed the button for the ninth floor. *Damn.* She hadn't seen me, dashing all hope for a rescue or a witness. Then I realized we were getting off on the eighth floor. The other passenger would have to see us when we exited the elevator. I needed to get her attention without Dan and Vivian noticing. The elevator arrived at our stop. No time left—I had to think fast.

As the door opened, I took a deep breath and prepared to bump into the woman, hoping to force her to look at me. Dan moved forward, making me believe he was departing. Instead, he pushed a button and said, "Oh, my mistake. We want the tenth floor."

A few seconds later, the door reopened on the ninth floor, and the woman got off without comment. Dan, Vivian, and I rode the rest of the way in silence on our way to the tenth floor. There was nowhere up from there. The door opened, but not one of us made an effort to exit.

As the door began to close, Dan thrust his hand out and stopped it. "Oops!" he said. "Almost forgot to get out."

Vivian exited first, and Dan pushed me out. Then we took the stairs down to the eighth floor. Dan grasped my arm and pushed me forward into the empty office. *Hmm. Everyone went home early. Must have been due to the day's excitement.*

"Where's your desk?" Dan said.

"Right there," I said, pointing.

Dan pushed me forward with so much force I stumbled and nearly fell. "Hey, take it easy."

"Don't tell me what to do. Now get what I want and I'll let you go."

"I told you I don't have anything. I gave it to Jim."

Dan dropped my arm and rushed into Jim's office. My arm tingled as the circulation returned. Dan ransacked Jim's office like a crazed gorilla. Papers fluttered in the air and gently fell to the floor. Desk items flew across the room and crash-landed on furniture, against the window, and on the floor. Jim's office looked like a giant snow globe. I almost laughed, but the sight of Roger entering the office made me sigh with relief.

"Looking for something," Roger said, peeking into Jim's office.

"I left my Cartier pen on Jim's desk this morning. I was hoping it was still here."

Roger eyed Jim's once-immaculate desk and said, "Don't see any pen here."

"He probably found it and put it in his drawer for safekeeping," Dan said as he searched through the already-opened top drawer of Jim's desk.

Roger reached in and removed one of Jim's famous red Bic stick pens. "This it?"

Dan growled. "No."

"Well, I can't let you rummage through Mr. Keane's desk. You'll have to call him in the morning."

Dan drew a gun on Roger and said, "I'm not leaving without what is rightfully mine."

"And what might that be?" Roger calmly asked.

"The information he's using to write a story about me?"

"Oh, is that the story Emarie is working on?"

"Yeah, what about it?"

"Well, all background information for feature stories is kept in the safe."

"Who has the key?"

"The CEO of Henderson Publications."

"Who's that?"

"Malcolm Henderson."

Dan waved his gun toward the phone on Jim's desk and said, "Call him."

"Can't do. He's out of town for the next week. Like I said, call Jim in the morning. I'm sure he'll accommodate your request."

"Who has the key while good old Malcolm is out of town?"

"No one."

"Why?"

"No one needs it. Besides, I hear the story's been canned."

Dan grunted, lowered his gun, put it in the inside pocket of his suit coat, and left Jim's office. He looked at me. "Find your own way home, Eerie Emmie." Then he and Vivian left the office.

I waited until they were in the elevator, safely cloistered behind its metal door before I ran to Roger and hugged him. "I didn't know you were such a good liar."

"Me neither."

I pulled away from Roger, feeling uncomfortable with the level of intimacy I'd instigated.

"Need a ride home?" Roger asked.

"I live in Alexandria. Fairfax County, not the city."

"Great. Wife and I have a place in Old Town. Just a hop, skip, and a jump from you."

"I can take the subway. I live close to the Franconia Station."

"Hey, after the day you've had, you deserve a chauffeur-driven ride home."

"Thanks, Roger. I appreciate it."

Roger closed the drawers of Jim's desk and tried to straighten it a bit. "He'll have a fit when he sees this."

I shrugged. "Oh well, he needs to see it."

Roger and I walked through the garage in silence. I scanned the cars, trying to predict which one suited a security guard. He walked to the driver's side of a dilapidated car. *No surprise here.* As I positioned myself at the passenger door of the rusty car, I thought it was odd that Roger had his back to it and was leaning toward the car next to the old clunker.

"Are you coming?" he said.

I went to the other side of the car and stood next to Roger.

"Hop in," he said as he opened the passenger door to a brand-new Audi A8. I sank into the lap of luxury and allowed the new-car smell to captivate my senses. Roger slipped into the driver's seat and pressed a button. The engine ignited, resulting in a low purr.

"Gorgeous car," I said.

Roger smiled.

On the way to my place, not a word about work escaped our lips. Instead, Roger entertained me with historical tidbits about Washington, D.C. and Alexandria, Virginia. I began to relax, and for the first time ever, the D.C. rush hour traffic was enjoyable. Who knew the building security guard was so educated, informative, and charming? Not me. My stereotype of security guards had been shattered.

CHAPTER FORTY

H OME AT LAST. I CHECKED my office. To my surprise, nothing was out of place. I wished I could say the same for Jim's office. I picked up the phone to call Laura and wandered into my sunroom. Hmm, a window was open. The faint scent of cigarette smoke lingered in the air. *Laura?*

As I scrolled for Laura's cell phone number, I spotted her car entering my condo parking lot. *Damn.* Dan and Vivian had arrived. Obviously, slowpoke Dan was behind the wheel. He opened the trunk of Laura's car and looked in, then slammed it shut.

"She's gone," he said to Vivian.

"What a surprise," Vivian yelled over her shoulder as she walked toward a red Lincoln MKZ. She opened the door to the driver's side and got in. *Imagine that, Dan Jordan not in the driver's seat. I see who wears the pants in their relationship.* As the car backed out of the parking spot, the passenger side of the car faced me. The window rolled down and a hand popped up, middle finger raised. Dan had seen me. I sighed with relief as the red Lincoln disappeared around the corner.

I dialed Laura's cell phone number. A phone rang from the back room.

"Hello," Laura whispered.

"Where the hell are you?"

"In your bedroom closet."

A few seconds later, I opened the closet door to find Laura and Richard huddled in the corner.

"What the hell are you two doing in here?"

"Hiding," Richard said.

"You can come out now. The big bad wolf is gone."

"Well?" Richard asked as he and Laura emerged. "What happened?"

"Let's see…" I quickly brought my friends up to speed. "…Then I found you two huddled like Hansel and Gretel in my closet. TGI Friday's, anyone?"

"Sounds good," Laura said.

"By the way, where's my car?" I asked Richard.

"Parked it around the corner," he said as he handed me the keys.

"Good thinking."

The restaurant was packed. Richard put his name on the hour-long wait list. Pager in hand, the three of us went to the bar. Laura and I landed stools, but Richard had to stand. I ordered my usual, vodka tonic. Laura had a glass of house chardonnay. Richard went for a beer. We raised our drinks.

"Cheers to friends," Richard said.

"Cheers to the most interesting man in the world," Laura said.

Richard smiled, clinked beer bottle to wineglass, then gulped the cold, amber liquid. The deafening noise of chatter and music made it frustrating to hold a conversation, but the energy of young professionals gathered after a hard day's work was exhilarating. It was exactly what we needed. For the first time in weeks, I felt normal.

Fifty-five minutes, two drinks, and a more detailed recap of the day later, our pager was flashing and vibrating. We made our way to the host's stand where we were greeted by the same seventeen-year-old with a chip on her shoulder. Laura and I looked at each other and laughed.

The dining area was noticeably quieter than the bar. As I handed my menu to the server, my cell phone rang. I dug in my handbag but didn't get it in time. The screen read: "One missed call. Jim."

"It's Jim. I'll be right back." I hurried outside and called him back. Our conversation was short and sweet. Very sweet. I rushed back in the restaurant to tell Laura and Richard the news.

"You're not going to believe it."

"Try us," Richard said.

"Jim's lawyer said there's a strong possibility my story can run. The information is conjecture until proven otherwise, but not to be surprised if it results in Dan and Vivian being hauled in for questioning. And it will definitely ruffle some feathers in the Darrington police department. The lawyer is going to do some investigating and get back to Jim in a week or so."

"Great news," Richard said as he gulped his beer. But something about the look in his eyes raised my suspicion. Was he happy for me or not?

"What about my being kidnapped and stuffed in the trunk of my car? Does anyone care about that?"

"Oh, Laura, I forgot about that," I said.

"Nice to know my sister cares about me."

"Did they hurt you?"

"No."

"Were you scared?"

"No."

"That's not like you," I said.

"I knew they wouldn't hurt me. They just wanted to use me to get to you."

"How did they find you?" Richard asked.

"Internet."

Richard and I stared at each other. "Don't say I told you so," he said. Then I profusely apologized to Laura for putting her in harm's way.

Laura broke out in laughter. "You nitwits," she said. "They didn't put me in the trunk of my car. Dan and I got in my car, and he drove us to your condo. Vivian followed behind in her red Lincoln. Of course, Dan needed directions, which I was happy to provide. I drove him all over creation until he got wise to what I was doing and threatened me. It was hysterical. Wish you were there."

I inhaled and wondered about Laura's sanity. It wasn't the first time.

Richard downed the rest of his beer. "How did you end up in the trunk?"

"Dan told me to stay in the car when Vivian and he went into Emarie's condo. I wanted them to think I ran away, so I pulled down the back seat, crawled into the trunk, and pulled the seat up. Unfortunately, I got stuck." Laura grinned at Richard and stroked his hand. "Mr. Bader came to my rescue."

Gag me! I changed the topic to the repercussions of today's events. "Think Jim will press charges against his Uncle Dan?"

Richard shook his head and swallowed a mouthful of steak. "No. Know why?"

"Enlighten me," I said.

"Because Dan didn't fire a gun. He had a starter gun. He's all bluff."

"Didn't Roger fire his gun?"

"Hell no," Richard said.

"So the gunshots I reported to 911 were from Dan's starter gun?"

"Yep. Jim told the police there was no problem. Roger confirmed there were no gunshots. The police left."

"That's why Roger wasn't afraid of Dan when he confronted him ransacking Jim's office."

"Yes… well… um… The good news is your story will run."

I smiled. "I hope so. It's a damn good story if I must say so myself."

Richard looked at me as if he was stifling a remark. I held his stare and changed the topic. We spent the rest of the evening chatting about mindless things. Blessed relief. It was obvious Richard and Laura were smitten with each other. But that was a conversation for another time.

I returned to my condo, tired but refreshed. Just as I was getting into the latest episode of my favorite TV show, my home phone rang. The on-screen Caller ID read: Unknown Caller. I let it go to voice mail. At the next commercial break, I retrieved the message.

"Hey, *Eerie* Emmie," Dorothy Hall said. "I'm baaack. You know that man you saw today? The one you thought was Dan Jordan? Well, did you do a double take? I hope so because he wasn't Dan. Dan died two years ago. Remember? And there's nothing anyone can do to me because I'm dead too. Ask your buddy, Jim. Besides, everyone thinks I'm that fat ass, Patti. I've covered my ass. So run your damn story. There's no way anyone can prove anything about what you say I said. Bitch."

Was Dorothy/Dan insinuating the man I saw today was Jim's father, Judge Keane? It would explain the drastic difference in looks. But if it was Jim's father, why did he threaten Jim and create chaos? Why did Jim refer to him as "my uncle?" Why was Vivian with him? And if it was Jim's father, why had he and his family faked his death? I forwarded the message to my work voice mail. Jim had some explaining to do.

Finally, exhaustion got the better of me, and I went to bed. At three a.m., I was awakened by a loud noise in my kitchen. My heart nearly beat out of my chest as I tiptoed down the hall. Ready to face my intruder, I courageously turned on the hall light and glanced in the kitchen. No one was there. Maybe I was dreaming.

As I reached to shut off the light, I saw him—the robed man. He stood in the corner of the dark dining room. Light from the street lamp shone through the sunroom, shrouding him in soft light. He held something out to me. Was it real? As I approached him my nervousness eased, allowing me to accept the item. I looked straight at him, hoping to see his face. Fat chance. Once again he motioned, indicating he was watching me. Then he stepped back into the darkness and disappeared.

I turned on the dining room light and studied what he'd given me. "What the hell?" It was my story. I ran to my bedroom, jumped in bed, and began to read. The first few pages were how I'd written them. Dorothy's evil descriptions of her babies were the same. But my suspicion that Dorothy was my birth mother and the details of my adoption were deleted, eliminating my identity as baby number five. My story had been depersonalized. Why? Any mention of Dan having an identical twin? Gone. Dan's confession had been rewritten from Dorothy's point of view only, sounding like nothing more than the ranting of a crazy person. Dan's identity as a cross-dresser was erased from history. Vivian's involvement was minimalized and decriminalized. Someone had whitewashed my story. Who? Why? Oh my God. Jim?

I dialed Richard's home number. No answer. I called his cell phone. No answer. I dialed Laura.

"Hello," a sleepy Laura said.

"It's me, Emarie."

"It's the middle of the night. Everything okay?"

"Yeah, I need to talk to Richard. Is he there?"

"No. Why would he be here?"

"Well, I thought you two were… you know… lovers."

"He's not here. And this is not the time to discuss our relationship. Good night, Emarie."

Where the hell was Richard?

CHAPTER
FORTY-ONE

I DIDN'T SLEEP THE REST of the night. I paced. I read and reread my story. I fumed. At five a.m., I got dressed. By five forty-five I was at the Franconia-Springfield Metro station. I couldn't believe how many people were waiting for the train.

After an uneventful ride, I arrived at the office at six thirty. Not a soul was there. Quiet time in my office was a luxury, so I took the opportunity to read e-mails and work on one of my new assignments. At eight, I glanced at Jim's office and noticed something odd. He wasn't in, yet his office was in pristine condition. No sign of yesterday's ransacking. And where was everyone else? Normally, the office would already be bustling at this time. Something was up.

According to my calendar, I hadn't forgotten an important meeting. Now my suspicion radar had gone off. I checked my e-mail again. Nothing new or important. I went to the lobby for a reality check. Everything was normal. People hustled for coffee, donuts, and newspapers. The elevator doors opened and closed as passengers embarked and disembarked. I went back to the office and checked my cell phone. No calls. No texts. No voice mail. I called Richard. No answer. I called Carl. No answer. Where the hell was everyone? At nine fifteen, Liz walked in. She strolled past me to her desk without a glance... without a word.

Jim entered his office, sat in his chair, grabbed his phone's receiver, and started talking. Yet the phone didn't ring. He didn't press a button to call anyone. My suspicious mind worked overtime.

A few other employees wandered in. The energy in the office was heavy. "Did someone die or something?" I said, loud enough for everyone to hear.

"Not yet," Liz replied. A few seconds later, she walked past my desk and inconspicuously dropped a piece of paper. She continued out the door. On the paper, four words were written: "Ladies' room. Second floor."

I waited a few minutes so it wouldn't look like I was following her. The elevator door opened. Out of habit, I stepped back to make room for people to exit the elevator. It was empty. A ripple of fear made the hair on the nape of my neck stand up. Once on the second floor, I entered the ladies' room. A woman stood in front of a sink, grooming herself in a mirror.

"Cripes, why can't people get dressed before they get to work?" I muttered.

She put on mascara, mouth wide like a newly caught grouper gasping for air. Then she put on lipstick, smacked her lips, grabbed her purse, and left. She didn't even look at me. I guess I was invisible. I checked each stall. No Liz. A few minutes later, she entered, looking ill. She grabbed my arm and guided me to the far end of the bathroom.

"I'm probably going to get fired for this, but I can't live with myself if I don't tell you what's going on," Liz said. Tears welled in her eyes. "It's Jim. He's out to destroy you. He used you. He figured out who you are. Then he assigned you the story."

"He used me for what?"

"To expose his uncle for what he really is."

"Okay?"

"He never intended to run your story. He used you to get the information he wanted to destroy his uncle for what he did to his father. Well, it looks like you dug too deep. You revealed family secrets. And in the process, you discovered Jim and you are related. He didn't think you'd figure it out. And he's made everyone pledge to keep their mouths shut about the existence of the story and any information they may know."

"Why would anyone other than Jim, Richard, Carl, you, and I know anything about my story?"

"Gotta go. I've told you too much already." Liz rushed out of the ladies' room, wiping away her tears.

I waited a few minutes before leaving the bathroom, hoping no one would link me with Liz. This gave me just enough time to ruminate about what she'd told me. *Why did Liz tell me about the meeting? Did everyone in the office know about my story? They shouldn't, so why did Jim warn them to keep their mouths shut?* Suspicion consumed me. Comfort food was what I needed to calm my nerves. I went down the stairwell to the lobby, bought a donut and a cup of coffee, and headed back to the office. I'd barely sat down when Jim buzzed me.

"Yes, Jim."

"Come see me."

"On my way." This was it. I had to confront Jim about my story. I'd have to stifle my emotions and keep a clear head. Mission impossible.

Jim didn't welcome me at his office door, as was his custom. Instead, he waved me in. I opened the heavy glass door and walked over to his desk.

Without looking up from what he was reading, he said, "Have a seat." Then he gathered the papers and handed them to me. "Here's the final copy of your story."

I glanced through the pages, hoping Jim couldn't tell I'd already seen it and was seething with disgust. Oops! I couldn't control myself. "How could you?" I said as I threw the story at him. "You've taken the truth and made it bland. There's no story here."

Jim leaned forward, making no attempt to arrange the pages scattered on his desk, his lap, and the floor. "Emarie, just so you know, in our family we don't air dirty laundry. That's for someone else to do and us to deny."

"You've twisted the truth. We're journalists. We're supposed to expose the truth."

"You're so naïve. There's no truth, Emarie, only media manipulation."

"You gave me this story on purpose. Didn't you? You knew everything about your dear old Uncle Dan."

"I had my suspicions. I needed proof."

"What didn't you know?"

"I didn't know who you were."

"Bull. I think you figured it out. And I think the fact I was in your life scared the crap out of you because you didn't know what I knew about who I was. You were afraid I'd figure out who you were and talk. So this is your way of shutting me up… to protect your shameful family."

"Our family."

"No, Jim. It's your family. Andrew and Marie Lukins are my family. I'm proud of my family."

Jim got up and paced his office. "There was no Bull," Jim spat out. "There were no other babies. Only you."

"Oh please, do you think I'm such a lousy reporter that I can't tell a lie when I hear one?"

"What do you mean?"

"You're lying. I have proof others exist."

"How many?"

"Two plus Bull, aka George Jordan, makes three. Plus me makes four out of seven."

"You don't have proof of anything. You don't even have proof Dan Jordan is your father."

"Then why did you call me cousin?"

Jim paused, cleared his throat, and rubbed his chin. "Emarie, it's over. The story will run as is."

"Why are you protecting him?"

"I'm not protecting him."

"I know. You're protecting your father."

"My father was a good man."

"I don't doubt that. But he got himself caught in a cover-up."

"That's not the half of it." Jim shook his head and sighed. "I can't discuss this anymore. The story runs as is."

"As is, it's a piece of crap. I wouldn't run it at all."

"Good idea." Jim picked up the phone and dialed. "Hey, Bill. Change of plans. Can Emarie Lukins's story and run Richard Bader's story on the revival of the good old American bicycle."

"It all makes sense now." I turned and left Jim's office.

"Wait just a second."

I turned around, hoping Jim was going to apologize for using me.

"Do you have any copies, hard or digital, of the story?"

"No."

"I trust you gave me *all* the backup—tapes, photos, notes, etcetera."

"Yes."

"You didn't discuss anything about the story with anyone, did you?"

"Like who?"

"Your parents… your friends… coworkers other than Richard."

"No."

"Good. Now get to work on your new story assignment."

I was so angry I thought my head would explode. Jim thought I'd want to continue working with him after what he'd put me through? What chutzpah. I spent the rest of the day deleting personal files and e-mails from my office computer and packing my personal desk items. No one appeared to notice. After all, they'd been warned.

At 4:55, Liz dropped by my desk. "It's obvious you're not coming back. I just wanted you to know I enjoyed working with you."

"Thanks, Liz. I've enjoyed working with you too."

"Does Jim know?"

"Not yet. Tomorrow."

"I understand."

Liz slowly walked back to her desk. I wondered what stories she could tell. That thought would have to wait. It was time to face my parents.

CHAPTER FORTY-TWO

FOR THE FIRST TIME IN my life, I was afraid of my parents. Not afraid they would hurt me, but afraid of their reaction to what I was about to tell them. So I sat in my car outside their house and rehearsed what I'd say. The living room curtain moved, revealing my father's face. Then the front door opened, and like the protective father he is, my dad came to check on me. He knocked on my driver's side window.

I rolled it down and said, "Hi, Dad." Those two words resulted in a guttural sob and a torrent of tears.

My father opened the door, bent down, and hugged me. "Come, come. Nothing can be so bad your dad can't fix it."

I laughed through my tears, remembering myself as a five-year-old tree climber. My mother had yelled for me to come down from a large mimosa tree in the backyard for fear I'd fall and break something. The tree was in full bloom, and I loved its wispy pink flowers that I imagined had magical powers.

I yelled back to my mother, "I'm not afraid of anything because Daddy can fix anything."

"Well, he's not here, so get down from that tree."

I ignored my mother's demand.

"Emarie, if you don't get down now, you won't have TV privileges for a week."

"I don't like TV," I sassed back.

"Okay, then no TV and no playtime with Laura for two weeks."

The thought of not seeing Laura was too much to bear. So I took a flying leap off the tree limb. As I hit the ground, I heard something snap a split second before excruciating pain coursed through my body. It was the worst pain I'd ever experienced—a thousand times worse than falling down the basement stairs and banging my head on the two-by-fours of the unfinished walls, which had resulted in a black eye and an osteoma above my right ear that grew so large I had to have it surgically removed when I was sixteen. My mother rushed to my side. I just held my left arm and wailed.

"Your arm is broken. We have to go to the emergency room."

"No, no," I screamed. "Wait for Daddy. He can fix it."

My mother ignored my plea and rushed me to the ER. By the time we got home, I was exhausted, drugged, and paralyzed by the weight of a cast that covered my arm from the base of my fingers to my elbow. A little later, my father came home. He kissed me on the forehead and said, "Couldn't wait for me to get home to fix your arm, huh?"

I screamed at my mother, "I told you Daddy could fix it." Then I cried as my father consoled me.

"Well, I couldn't get home in time," he said as he dried my tears with his handkerchief. "Good thing your mother took you to the emergency room. Looks like the doctor did a pretty good job."

"Emarie?" my father said, rescuing me from a long trip down memory lane. "Come on. Let's go inside."

Arm-in-arm, my father and I walked up the sidewalk. As we entered the house, I knew everything was going to be all right because Daddy could fix it.

My mother emerged from the back bedroom. "Emarie, it's good to see you," she said as she gave me a tight hug. "We've been worried."

"Just a little," my father said, already fixing the situation.

I sat on the couch, my mother next to me. My father sat in his recliner. Neither asked me anything.

"Well, I have something I need to tell you."

My mother took my hand, and my father nodded, indicating I had their attention and support.

"I quit my job."

"Emarie, why?" my mother said. "I thought you loved your job."

"I do. I mean I did," I said. "But something happened, and I can't in good conscience continue to work there."

"Why?" my father said. "What happened?"

"Well, remember the story I was working on? The one involving Dan Jordan?"

My parents glanced at each other. My mother removed her hand from mine and looked away.

"Yes," my father said.

"I have plans, Dad. I'm going to ruffle some feathers. It may not be pretty, and I don't want to pull you and Mom into anything. So if what I'm going to do will hurt you, I won't do it."

"Just what are you planning to do?" my mother asked.

"Write a book. One that could send a few people to jail, namely Dan Jordan and Vivian Jordan. And I want to be one hundred percent sure that you and Dad had no knowledge of anything illegal with my adoption or the abuse of any of Dan and Patti's six other children."

"Abuse?" my mother said.

"Yes, Dan Jordan as Dorothy Hall abused his and Patti's seven children, of which I was one."

"Oh God." My mother moaned.

"Do you want to hear about it?"

"I guess we need to," my father said.

"Well…"

For the next two hours, I regurgitated the past six weeks of my life. My parents listened intensely and surprisingly unemotionally until I told them about my abuse at the hands of Dorothy Hall, aka Dan Jordan. My mother cried. My father said, "Oh my God" a half a dozen times. I didn't want to get caught up in the emotions of the moment, so I let my parents sit with their feelings while I continued. The only break in my story occurred when my mother got up and returned with a bottle of wine and three wineglasses.

I finished with a question. "Did you know Dan Jordan was a cross-dresser?"

"Yes," my father said as my mother nodded in agreement. "We knew when we were friends in college."

"Did you know Dan Jordan disguised himself as a woman named Dorothy Hall?"

"No, absolutely not," my father said. "In college, he didn't give himself a name. He was just Dan in drag."

"Did you know Judge Warren Keane was Judge Dan Jordan's identical twin brother?"

"Yes, you asked me that before. I told you I introduced them to each other in college. I didn't find out until later they were identical twins."

"I know, I'm just confirming." I took a deep breath and continued. "Did you know... I was... Dan and Patti Jordan's child?"

"No," my mother said. "That's news to us."

Disgust shadowed my father's face. "Horrible news."

"But it doesn't change our love for you," my mother said.

My father cleared his throat. "That's right, dear."

"So you'd swear you knew nothing other than the fact that Dan Jordan and Warren Keane were identical twins, both were circuit court judges in Maryland, and my adoption was completely legal."

"All we knew was Dan Jordan had a child he wanted to place with a loving family. He remembered us from college, looked us up, and asked his brother Warren Keane to help with the process, which we certainly believed to this day was completely legal," my father said.

"And we didn't know you were Dan and Patti's child," my mother said. "We were thrilled to get you."

"I know, Mom. I'm not questioning your love for me. I just need to know how much you and Dad knew about the truth of my birth and adoption." I took a sip of wine. "I'm glad to know you didn't know anything that could jeopardize you or me. Oh, by the way, since my boss... ex-boss... Jim, is Warren Keane's son, believe it or not, Jim is my cousin."

My father rose from his recliner, stretched, and went into the kitchen. I followed him. My mother followed me, an empty bottle of wine in hand. As my father searched the refrigerator for his favorite snack—hard Italian salami and smoked Havarti cheese—my mother opened another bottle of wine. *Hmm, Mom never drank before I mentioned Dan Jordan's name a few weeks ago. Is there something I don't know about my mother?*

"Mom, may I ask you a question?"

"Sure," she said as a pop signaled that another bottle of wine was ready for consumption.

"I've never seen you drink before I showed you Dorothy Hall's photo a few weeks ago."

My mother looked at my father. "You tell her," she said as she gulped wine.

"Are you sure?"

"Yep," my mother said. "She needs to know."

"Well…" My father stuffed his mouth with a hunk of cheese wrapped in salami. "Your mother dated Dan Jordan. That's how I met her."

"You're kidding, right?"

"No. I dated that jerk for six months. Your father rescued me from his clutches."

"Mom, this may be highly personal, but—"

"No, I never slept with him."

My father chuckled and said, "She saved herself for me."

"Okay. TMI," I said. "But thanks for your honesty."

My mother and I finished off the second bottle of wine as the Lukins family reminisced about life.

"Well, I better get going. I have a big day tomorrow. I have to officially quit my job. I haven't told Jim yet, so I need to get to the office early."

"You're not driving home after all the wine you've had," my father said. "You'll stay here tonight."

"No argument, Emarie," my mother said. "Your room is always ready."

CHAPTER FORTY-THREE

I ROSE WITH THE SUN, energized by the excitement of my new adventure. As I walked from the subway to the *Washington Intelligencer* for the last time, I hummed, "Another One Bites The Dust." Queen, right?

The elevator ride seemed like it took forever, but John Deacon's lyrics kept me company. I walked into the office and spotted Jim at his computer. He didn't look up. I knocked on his office door. He jumped up and opened it for me.

"Good morning, Emarie. I was hoping you would arrive early."

"Here I am."

I sat in the front of Jim's desk facing him as he continued to type. He quickly reviewed what he'd written and hit the Print button.

He snatched two pages from the printer, sat in his chair, and looked at me. "Is there something you want to say to me?"

"I think you know why I'm here."

"You're here to resign."

"Yes," I said, looking Jim square in the eye, hoping I was exuding confidence.

"Good," he said.

I raised an eyebrow. "Not exactly the response I was expecting, but I'm glad you're glad."

"What I'm going to tell you is between you and me. Nobody, not even Richard, can know what I'm about to do. Agreed?"

"Agreed."

Jim handed me a sheet of paper. "Read it."

I quickly read the document. "Why would *you* resign?"

"Because you and I, cousin, are going to air our dirty laundry in grand style."

I gulped. *Was Jim about to butt into my plan?* "What do you mean?"

"Emarie, I'll be honest. I never intended to publish your story."

"So you did use me."

"Yes, but when I assigned you the story, I had no idea who you were. I had no idea the story would be personal for you. I only knew you were a good writer. I took a chance there was an investigative reporter in you."

"And just in case there wasn't, you had Richard babysit me."

"Okay, I'll level with you. When Richard suspected that Dorothy Hall was Dan Jordan and that Dan Jordan was my uncle, he didn't want anything to do with the story. To tell you the truth, he wasn't right for the story anyway. That's why I gave it to you. Because he already knew some details, I asked him to review your first draft." Jim raised his hand to stop me from commenting. "I know that wasn't right or fair. Richard was left with the impression that your emotions were in the way of your ability to ask necessary questions. I agreed. I was going to ask him to help you, but you beat me to the punch. Richard told me you asked for his help, and I approved. I knew with a little help, you would write a great story."

What? Richard knew that Dorothy was Dan? He played me. He took me for a fool. Memories scurried through my head of Richard calling me in the middle of the night with news about the deaths of Dorothy Hall and Dan Jordan as well as the fact that Dan Jordan owned three houses, one of which Dorothy inhabited. And what about his analysis of Dorothy's pictures when we were in McDonald's? In retrospect, Richard's reaction was a bit artificial when I told him I suspected I was baby number five. Hmm, he already knew. But how?

Richard, you liar. I held my tongue so I could hold my temper. For the first time ever, I was furious with Laura. She had to be the leak. She's the one who had Richard's ear. Oh my God. Was he playing her too? Was he pumping her for information, so to speak?

Jim didn't seem to detect my ire and rattled on. "I temporarily reassigned Richard and made him promise not to tell you about our arrangement. I knew if you found out, you'd be angry. I couldn't let your emotions get the best of you. I needed you to dig up solid information and write a dynamic story about my evil Uncle Dan and Aunt Vivian so I'd have the information I needed to destroy them and restore my father's good name. You did a stellar job. You uncovered more information than I could have imagined and distilled it into an intense, concise, and captivating story. Probably one of the best I've ever read. When Uncle Dan showed up threatening to kill everyone who had any knowledge of your story, including me and your parents, I thought the story was dead. My gut said I had to tell the story. But how? For several days, I combed through every detail you gathered. I listened to the tapes over and over. There was too much that needed to be included. Way too much for a feature story—"

"Particularly one you had no plans of printing," I said.

Jim smirked. "But I want the story told. So here's my offer. I'll give you *all* your story backup if you'll write a *book* about Dorothy Hall. I'll be hands-off, pay all expenses—office supplies, travel, editing, publishing, your mortgage, gas mileage—everything."

"What's in it for you?"

"Just the satisfaction that my Uncle Dan and Aunt Vivian get their comeuppance."

The word "comeuppance" gave me pause. I remembered nearly laughing at Richard when he used the old-fashioned expression. Now I knew where he got it. "You didn't take the story to a lawyer, did you?" I said, hoping Jim didn't notice my hesitation.

"Yes and no."

"I don't know what to make of all this, Jim. I'm angry you used me. Yet I'm excited about the opportunity to tell an almost unbelievable story."

"There's one more thing, Emarie." Jim handed me another piece of paper. "This is why I visited a lawyer."

I hesitantly took the document and quickly scanned it. My blood boiled. "You want me to be your ghostwriter? Absolutely not. If I do the work, I want the credit… and the royalties."

"You have to write it under my name."

"Why?"

"So you're not connected with the story. It's for your protection."

"Yeah. Sure. Besides, Dan isn't stupid. He'll know you got the information from me."

"Don't worry about that. Dan isn't going to do anything. He's not going to get himself involved in a lawsuit. He'd be laughed out of court."

"But he knows we both work for the newspaper."

"Yes, that's why I didn't want to print it. I want to keep the newspaper out of this."

"But he knows I interviewed him as a representative of the newspaper. He can make a big stink about it."

"He won't. I guarantee it."

"How?"

"I have my ways."

Jim's statement raised my suspicions. *What kind of information did he have that would shut up Dan Jordan? Did he have evidence Dan killed his identical twin, Warren, Jim's father?*

"I don't care. I won't do it."

Jim leaned forward. "But I have the backup files, tapes, photos, copy—everything *you* need to write the book." He flopped back in his chair. His stupid gotcha grin told me he thought he was holding all the cards.

I stood up. "Get yourself another ghostwriter. How about Richard?" I handed Jim my resignation letter. "Effective immediately." Then I turned to leave.

Jim rushed to the door. "Emarie, we've got something here. Think about it."

"Your desperation is unflattering for a man in your position."

"Just think about it," Jim pleaded.

"Survey says: NO! *Family Feud*, right?" I waited for an answer that never came. My head ached. My past was a confusing mess, and my future was unsettled. My life was rapidly becoming a soap opera. All I could think of was an old comedy sketch, *As the Stomach Turns. The Carol Burnett Show,* right? Ha! I'd just quit my job based on the premise I was going to write an award-winning, tell-all book about Dorothy Hall. Time to put on my big-girl pants and move on.

I rode the elevator, thinking about how it was symbolic of life's ups and downs. Then I laughed. Because going down in life was what I needed in order to rise. Hmm. Emarie Lukins, award-winning advertising copywriter, so-so newspaper journalist, world-renowned, Pulitzer Prize-winning author of *Daddy in Disguise.* The elevator stopped on the fourth floor. *Good-bye, Fourth Estate.* A man and a woman stepped in as the man said, "It's nothing but a pipe dream." *You talking to me? Robert De Niro.* Taxi Driver, *right?*

Finally, I exited the building. "Well, Emarie, there's nowhere to go but up." I headed toward the Metro station, feeling free and not understanding why. Someone grabbed my arm, and I turned around and almost smacked Richard with my briefcase.

"Emarie, I've been calling for you since you left the building. Where are you going?"

"Well, hello Richard the Liar Hearted."

"What do you mean by that?"

"You lied to me."

"About what?"

"Oh please, don't play dumb."

"About what?"

"Fuhgeddaboudit."

"Okay, Tony, let's talk."

"Okay. My place. Six o'clock. Leave the blonde at home."

Richard shook his head and headed toward the office. I watched him disappear into the morning business crowd. *Why did I invite him over? Can I trust him? Too late now.*

On my drive home from the Metro, I stopped at Staples and bought reams of paper, notebooks, memory sticks, red Bic pens, sticky notes, paper clips—everything to supply my new career as an author. On the way to the checkout line, a display of laptops caught my eye.

"Oh crap. I didn't return my work laptop." I broke out in a sweat.

Not because I was in possession of the newspaper's property, but because I couldn't believe my stroke of luck. My drunken lovefest with my parents had made me completely forget about deleting my personal data—e-mails, contact list, pictures, website searches, etc. *Yikes, I shouldn't have mixed business and pleasure.* So there I was, unemployed, nearly broke, forking over a chunk of change for a new laptop and software. An hour and a half later, I strolled out of Staples more than two thousand dollars poorer but no less excited about my self-employment.

I spent the afternoon tidying up the files on my office laptop, setting up my new, personal laptop, and getting my home office organized for my new career. I stepped back and admired my labor.

"This is where the magic happens."

I glanced at the clock. It was already five thirty. I needed to prepare for Richard's arrival. I didn't have much food, but luckily I had plenty of wine. I set out a bottle of red wine, two wineglasses, and a few hors d'oeuvres. Perfect. Not too much food. That should discourage Richard from overstaying his welcome.

At six p.m. sharp, my doorbell rang. I opened the door to find Richard... and Laura.

"I told you to come alone," I said, à la a spy from an old movie.

"You told me not to bring the blonde," Richard replied, playing along.

"Correct. So why did you bring her?"

"Because she's not a blonde," Richard said and smiled. "Take my word for it."

"Only two wineglasses?" Laura said, giving me the evil eye. "What are you two up to?"

"Business," I said in a tone I hoped conveyed Laura wasn't welcome.

"Oh, and you don't want me here? Why not?"

"Because what Richard and I need to discuss is not for sensitive ears and loose lips." The hurt in Laura's eyes made me regret my insensitivity toward my best friend. "Laura, I'm sorry. I didn't—"

"I know when I'm not wanted. So I'll go."

"Me too," Richard said. "But before I leave, I've been instructed by Jim to pick up your laptop."

Head lowered in shame, I went to my office and returned with the laptop and handed it to Richard.

"I hope you had the brains to clean out your personal stuff," Richard said.

"I did, but I'm sure Jim can get Carl to retrieve it."

The door closed. Richard and Laura were gone.

I was mad at myself. I'd unintentionally hurt my best friend's feelings. I opened the bottle of wine, chugged, sat on the couch, chugged, wallowed in my sorrow, chugged, wallowed wallowed, chugged chugged, opened a second bottle, chugged, wallowed some more, chugged, and passed out—until someone pounded on the door at ten thirty p.m. *Who the hell was knocking at this hour?*

"Hello, Richard," I said, hoping I didn't sound as incoherent as I felt.

"I smoothed things over with Laura," he said. "Thanks to me, she may forgive your rudeness. Now, what is it you wanted to see me about?"

"Did you smooth things over with a little kissy-kissy?" I said before I stumbled to the couch.

"Something like that," Richard said. "Besides drinking, what have you been up to this evening?"

"Just me and a bottle of chardonnay doing the kissy-kissy," I said as I raised the wine bottle and gulped.

"I see the fruit doesn't fall from the tree."

"Say what?"

"You remind me of Dorothy and her special juice."

"Don't ever compare me with that monster."

"Sorry," Richard said. "Maybe we should take a rain check."

"Good idea. How about tomorrow? Same bat time. Same bat station. *Batman*, right?"

"Can't do. I'm busy tomorrow." Richard shook his head and left.

The next morning, I awoke on the couch, clutching an empty bottle of wine, head pounding, mouth so dry my tongue stuck to the roof of my mouth. I felt like a fool. I probably looked like one too.

CHAPTER FORTY-FOUR

FIRST DAY OF MY NEW career as an author. I sat down at my perfectly organized desk, opened my virgin laptop, and retrieved my e-mail. Hmm, nothing but junk mail—someone from Canada trying to sell me Viagra; a man from India desperate to send me four million dollars of lottery winnings if I immediately wired three thousand dollars to cover his cost of handling the exchange; one from an unknown address titled: "You're next." I deleted the first two and opened the third. There was nothing in the e-mail, only an attachment. I have no idea what possessed me to open the attachment, but I did. I was greeted by a picture of Dan Jordan holding a gun to a picture of a baby. I leaned in to get a better look. It was a picture of baby number five. "Thank you, deranged Dan. I now have the cover shot for my book." I printed the photo and saved it as a new file titled Daddy Dearest.

I had no idea how to start a book, but I figured a review of information was in order. I pulled out my secret file and flipped through the pictures of Dan dressed as Dorothy and Patti dressed as Dorothy.

I smiled. I had fooled Jim. I'd had Carl make copies of the photos. I gave Jim the copies and kept the originals for myself. He was none the wiser. And of course, I had copies of everything—every version of my feature story, notes, tapes, photos, newspaper articles, Dwayne's parents' letter, website shots—you name it, I had it.

I started to type. I immediately decided I didn't have what it takes to write a book. I went to the kitchen, poured myself a mug of coffee, and cried. A few minutes later, I wasn't in the mood for a good cry, so I wiped my tears and went back to work. I printed a copy of my article before Jim whitewashed it, then read it for the umpteenth time.

"This is it. This is the outline for my book." I could take it piece by piece and build on what I'd written. I felt energized. I wrote nonstop until six p.m. It was Saturday night—Laura's and my night out. I called her.

"Hello, Emarie," Laura said, her tone unwelcoming.

"Hey, Laura. I owe you an apology for last night. How about TGI Friday's? Seven? My treat."

"What? Are you kidding?"

"You're mad at me."

"No."

"Then what?"

"Like you don't know?" Click. Laura was gone.

I was stunned. Laura had never hung up on me. Not even when she had good reason to. I wandered into the kitchen. The calendar hanging on the side of the refrigerator caught my eye. "Oh my God, I missed Laura's birthday."

I got dressed. Forty-five minutes later, I appeared at Laura's front door with flowers, Chinese food, two bottles of wine, and her favorite ice cream. I knocked. I waited but didn't hear anything. I felt like a jilted lover. Knock, knock. I heard footsteps, and then someone peered out the peephole. The door opened. Laura looked like a wreck. She burst into tears and threw her arms around my neck. We stumbled inside, looking like long-lost lovers. Laura stretched out on the couch.

I took a few moments to put the ice cream in the freezer, then I returned to console my friend. "Laura, I'm sorry I forgot your birthday."

"Oh, it's okay."

"What's wrong?"

"Richard."

"What about Richard?"

"You haven't heard?"

"No. What?"

"He was in a horrible accident."

"When?"

"Last night. Some crazy woman ran him off the road. His car flipped four times."

I inhaled. "Oh my God. What happened to the woman?"

"I don't know. But Richard is in critical condition and only family is allowed to see him." Laura sat up. "I'm scared, Emarie."

"Me too."

"I can't bear the thought Richard could die."

"Is there a description of the woman?" Before Laura could answer, I pulled my cell phone from my purse and dialed Jim.

"Hello, Emarie. I suppose you want to know about Richard."

"Was there a description of the woman who ran him off the road?"

"Where did you get that idea?"

"He was run off the road by some crazy person, right?"

"No. According to the police report, Richard was drunk and lost control of his car."

"What time did the accident happen?"

"Hold on." I heard Jim shuffling papers. "Okay, it happened at approximately nine-thirty last night. Not too far from your place."

"No way was Richard drunk."

"How do you know?"

"Let's just say I know. Thanks for the info, Jim."

"Emarie, if you know something, you need to call the police."

"I know. I will. Thanks again."

"Are the police claiming Richard was drunk?" Laura asked.

"I guess so. Where did you get the information a woman ran Richard off the road?"

"From his mother. She said Richard kept repeating, 'Dorothy did it.' She asked him who Dorothy was, and Richard said, 'A crazy...' Oh no... Dorothy is your Dorothy. Dorothy is Dan."

"Yep, I believe you're right. And I believe I'm next."

"What?"

"May I use your laptop?"

"Sure."

I got Laura's laptop and sat next to her on the couch. I signed in to my e-mail account and opened the e-mail titled "You're next." The horrifying photo of Dorothy holding a gun to a picture of baby number five popped up.

"You're next? Oh, Emarie. What are you going to do?"

"I don't know."

"You can't go home. You have to stay here."

"Dan knows where you live, and he'll figure out that if I'm not home, I'm probably here. I'll go to my parents'. I don't think he's stupid enough to follow me there. I'll stay there until I can come up with a plan. But first I have to go back to my condo and get a few things."

"I'm going with you."

"No. And don't answer the door unless you know for a fact the person on the other side is your parents or me. If someone knocks, ask who it is. If it's me, I'll say the name of your first pet.

"My hamster, Beanbag?"

"Yes."

"Okay. Now I'm really scared."

"For some reason, I'm not—not anymore. I'm going to get dear old Dan if it's the last thing I do."

"That's what I'm afraid of."

My heart made a liar of me. It raced and skipped all the way back to my condo. I thought I'd go into cardiac arrest. I entered my condo and scanned for anything out of place.

"All clear," I said.

I packed clothes, personal items, laptop, and everything for my book. Then I headed to my parents'. The twenty-minute drive felt like an hour. Hypervigilance took over my senses. I raced ahead of every car that paced me. I scanned everyone in cars next to me at red lights. I thought I saw Dorothy following me. Thankfully, I was wrong.

As I pulled into my parents' driveway, my cell phone rang. "Hey, Jim."

"Emarie, it just occurred to me you have something that doesn't belong to you."

"Like what?"

"Like your cell phone. Return it tomorrow."

"Sorry, I forgot."

"Well, remember tomorrow. Give it to Roger."

"Okay."

"Bye. Crap! Now I have to buy a cell phone and get a new phone number complete with a new plan."

I looked up to see my father standing at the front door.

"Emarie, you okay?"

"I'll explain when I get inside."

My father helped me carry my things into the house. The sound of the front door latch engaging lifted the weight of the world off my shoulders.

My mother hugged me. "I'm sorry about your coworker, Richard."

"What?"

"It was on the news, dear." My mother hugged me tightly. "He was so young."

"Are you telling me Richard died?"

"I'm afraid so."

Now the weight of the universe engulfed me. All I could do was cry. I pulled away from my mother. "I've got to call Laura and see if she's okay. Richard and she were dating."

She picked up almost immediately.

"Laura, are you okay?" I said, trying to hide my sadness and tears.

"I feel much better. Richard's mother called to tell me he's improved. He's expected to be okay."

"Are you sure you talked to Richard's mother?"

"Yes. Why?"

"You know her well enough to recognize her voice?"

"Yes."

"Are you one hundred percent positive it was Richard's mother who gave you the news about his condition?"

"What are you getting at?"

"Well, the news just reported the opposite."

"Meaning?"

"The news reported Richard died."

"Well, it's a mistake," Laura yelled. "I just hung up with his mother, and she said he's improving."

"Okay. As long as you're sure, then I'm sure."

"Hold on. I'll call her on my cell. I'll put it on speaker."

I waited while Laura placed the call. I could hear Richard's mother's phone ringing. No answer.

"Laura, what number did Richard's mother call from?"

I heard Laura sigh. "301-555-1955."

"Is it her cell phone number?"

"I don't know. She never calls me."

"Where do his parents live?"

"Chevy Chase."

I got my cell phone and checked the number for Dorothy. It was different. Relief. "What's the number again?"

"It's 301-555-1955. What's with the twenty questions? Who do you think you are, Columbo?"

"It's the reporter in me. I just want to check it out. I'm at my parents'. Call if you hear anything different."

"Okay, but I know he's going to be okay."

I rushed to my parents' computer and looked up the phone number. It was a landline assigned to David Bader of Chevy Chase, Maryland. What a relief. So was Richard dead or alive?

CHAPTER FORTY-FIVE

D ESPITE A RELAXING EVENING WITH my parents, I was still on edge. I turned on the local news and hung on to every word the announcers said. No mention of Richard and his accident. At eleven p.m., I watched all the local late-night news channels. No mention of Richard. I googled his name. I clicked on a *Washington Intelligencer* link about Richard's accident. I gasped. The story had been removed. I logged on to NBC4. An article link turned my stomach. "Car Overturns on Beltway. Local Man Killed." My hands shook. I could hardly click my mouse. The headline read: CAR ACCIDENT KILLS PROMINENT DOCTOR. Although I knew Richard wasn't a prominent doctor, I scanned the story anyway. Then I leaned back in the chair and exhaled. "Not Richard." *Why the cover-up?* I decided I was too exhausted to continue my investigation.

At three a.m., I awoke from a disturbing dream. The streetlight shone through my window, imitating sunrise. I wanted to e-mail Jim about Richard. I went to the bathroom instead. That's when I saw him. The robed man was in my room. He'd followed me to my parents' house.

"What the hell do you want?" I said.

He didn't respond. My cell phone rang. The robed man dissipated.

"Jim? What the—"

"I'll explain later. Meet me at the office at six a.m."

"I don't work there anymore."

"Emarie, just do it."

I went back to bed but couldn't sleep. At five a.m., I packed my things and dressed, forgoing a shower so I wouldn't wake my parents. I left a note on the kitchen table and quietly left.

The drive to the office was surreal. It was as if I were living in the first episode of *Life After People*. Then I hit the Capital Beltway. Holy crap! I couldn't believe the number of people already on the road. Despite the traffic, I made it downtown in record time. The Capitol and monuments lit the city, shrouding it in a rare moment of innocent tranquility. I pulled into the *Washington Intelligencer*'s garage and spotted Jim waiting at the elevator. I joined him, and without a word, the two of us rose to the office.

It was eerily dark. Jim flipped on the lights. The fluorescent tubes hummed and flashed as they warmed up. Jim motioned for me to follow him to his office. He sat at his desk, and I took a seat on the couch.

"I guess you want to know what's going on."

"No shit, Sherlock," I confidently said, belying my nervousness as I ran my hand between the couch cushions. My fingers touched something that made my skin crawl. It felt like human hair. My imagination ran wild. I had visions of a decapitated head attached to the hair. I withdrew my hand.

"Well..." Jim got up and paced his office.

When his back was toward me, I slipped my hand between the cushions and yanked on the hair, pulling out a wig. I quickly stuffed it in my handbag.

"As you know, Richard has been involved in a serious car accident."

I mouthed the words, "No duh," but since Jim wasn't looking at me, he didn't notice.

Jim turned and smiled at me. "The good news is... he's going to be okay."

"You asked me here at six a.m. to tell me that?"

"No. I asked you here to secure a promise from you. What I'm about to tell you must be handled with the utmost clandestineness."

Secure a promise from me? Handled with the utmost clandestineness? Yikes, why the eighteenth-century language? I rolled my eyes and said, "You want me to keep a secret?"

"Yes."

"Let me guess, the secret is about your Uncle Dan; my daddy dearest."

"Not exactly." Jim ran his hands through his hair, took a deep breath, and exhaled. "Dan Jordan is my uncle, but…" The sadness in his eyes repulsed me. I'm sure that's not what he intended, but I recognized it for what it was: manipulation with fake emotions.

I raised my eyebrows, opening my eyes wide with anticipation like a schoolgirl about to be let in on a deep dark secret. "But what?"

"He's not your father."

"What?" *Who the hell is my birth father?*

"He's not your father."

"I heard you the first time." I kept my voice calm, hoping Jim would think that nothing he could say would shock me. Then I tilted my head, looked him in the eyes, and cheekily said, "Do enlighten me."

"Okay." Jim made himself comfortable behind the security of his desk. "I've harbored a family secret my entire life." Jim leaned forward. "Dan and Patti Jordan tried to have children to no avail. Dan was infertile. He wanted to adopt children, but Patti refused. She insisted any child of theirs would be born of her. So she took on a series of suitors and gave birth to seven children."

"Now you tell me?"

"One of those suitors was…"

"Let me guess. One of the suitors was your father, the Honorable Warren Keane."

"Yes." Jim nervously strummed his fingers on his desk. "Patti had two children by him."

"Bull and me?"

"Yes."

"So I'm the one Dan gave away, and Bull is the one he kept. Why?"

"He had some harebrained idea that since my father was his identical twin, then any child of his brother's was also his."

"So I'm your sister?"

"Yes."

"Why are you telling me this?"

"Well…" Jim pushed away from his desk. Next thing I knew, he stood over me, forcing me to look up at him. I felt like prey. "As my sister, you're entitled to an inheritance from our father's estate."

"Inheritance?" I said, not hiding my suspicion.

"Yes. You'd be financially secure."

"Really?"

"Really." Jim walked back to his desk and sat down.

"How much?"

Jim wrote something on a memo pad, ripped off the top page and pushed it to the corner of his desk, forcing me to rise from the couch, indicating he had taken control of the situation. I picked up the piece of paper and read it, masking my shock as I counted the zeros to ensure what I'd read was true. Then I folded it, went back to the couch, and put it in my purse.

"Well?"

"What do you want in return?" I asked.

Jim pushed a manila envelope toward me. The return address was one of D.C.'s most prestigious law firms. I picked up the envelope and removed three papers, which I scanned. My scalp tingled from anger, but I managed to carefully return the papers to the envelope and put it in my handbag. Then I got up and said, "I'll have my lawyer call yours."

"Wait," Jim said as he aggressively pulled my arm.

I turned and faced him, shaking off his grip. "I don't take bribes."

"Do you want to end up like Richard?"

"Is that a threat?"

"Not from me… from Uncle Dan."

I left Jim's office. He didn't follow me. As I waited for the elevator, I glanced back. Jim sat at his desk, his head resting on his arms, his body heaving. I walked back to his office and knocked on the door.

Jim looked up. I couldn't tell if he was laughing or crying, and I didn't care. I had a question, and Jim was going to answer it, come hell or high water.

"Change of mind?" Jim said.

"No. I have a question."

Jim arched his eyebrow and said, "What?"

"Who's the man in the black robe?"

The blood drained from Jim's face. He looked like the leader of the zombie apocalypse.

"I don't know what you're talking about."

"I think you do."

"I said I don't know what you're talking about."

"He doth protest too much. Shakespeare, right?"

"The lady doth protest too much, methinks. Shakespeare right."

I smirked at Jim, exasperated by his snide remark. I turned to leave. Jim's closet door was ajar, revealing something shocking—women's clothing. Jim lunged at me and grabbed my handbag.

"Give it back," I said as I tried to get my purse from Jim's clutches.

Jim managed to open it and get the envelope. He shook the envelope at me. "Sign it."

"No."

Jim threw my handbag to the floor. "You're a fool to turn down half a million dollars."

"You're a fool to bribe me."

He came at me, his face twisted into a snarl as he yelled, "Get out before I kill you."

Dan Jordan's words coming from Jim scared the crap out of me. I ran for my life.

Once I left the Metro station, I had calmed down and regained my senses enough to drop in on Richard at the hospital. Fortunately, his condition had been upgraded and he was able to receive visitors. Laura sat on the edge of his bed, holding his hand. They were lost in a lover's gaze. I was lost in the urge to gag.

"Emarie," Laura said as she rose and hugged me. "Richard's doing much better. I'm so relieved."

"Yeah, me too."

"Hi, Emarie," Richard said.

"Hey, feel like talking?"

"Sure. Shoot."

"Do you know who ran you off the road?"

"Yep. It was Dorothy. I'd bet my life on it."

"Well, I'd bet my life it wasn't Dorothy."

I opened my handbag and pulled out a wig. "I found this in Jim's office this morning."

Richard gasped. "Oh God. The car. I can see it now. It was a silver Mercedes. Just like Jim's."

"Why would Jim want to hurt you?" Laura asked.

"Because I know too much," Richard said.

"Exactly," I said. "And since you're not family, he can't bribe you with a five-hundred- thousand-dollar inheritance from dear old dad."

"He bribed you?"

"Yes. He tried."

"And?" Laura said.

"I refused. I think I could make more off book sales and movie rights to my book about Dorothy."

"I think you're overoptimistic, but I'm glad you refused the bribe," Richard said.

"Yep, five hundred thousand dollars is tempting, but now that I know Dan Jordan isn't my father, the story has a new twist."

"What?" Richard said. "Dan's not your father?"

"Nope. And Jim isn't my cousin."

Richard pressed the button to raise the back of his bed. "Who is he?"

"He's my brother."

"Is Patti your mother?" Laura asked.

"Yep."

"You mean to say Warren Keane fathered you with Patti Jordan?" Richard asked.

"Yep... and Bull too."

"Oh, what a tangled web we weave."

"Damn," Laura said. "You have one screwed-up family."

"And it's going to make for an interesting book."

"Have you thought through the implications of publishing your book," Laura said.

"So now you're the voice of reason?"

"Yes, you need to examine the options. Maybe it would be better to accept Jim's bribe."

"No way. The book needs to be written. Dan Jordan has the blood of Patti and Bull on his hands. He needs to be accountable for what he's done."

"Emarie?" Richard said. "If you need help writing your book, keep me in mind."

What? Does he think I can't write? Is he trying to take control of my book?

"Get well, Richard."

CHAPTER FORTY-SIX

F OR THE NEXT THREE MONTHS, I holed up in my condo.
I wrote.

I edited.

I cried.

The book was almost finished, but something was missing. It haunted me for two days until I realized the story wasn't all about baby number five, me. The other children had survival stories that needed to be told. So I decided to call Dwayne. Along with the letter he'd given me at McDonald's, he'd also given me his business card. I hoped he'd be happy to hear from me.

Sure enough, thanks to Dwayne, a week later, I was electronically face-to-face with my siblings. My stomach was in a knot as I listened to their stories and tried to feel connected to the people with whom I shared a mother. Their abuse at the hands of Dorothy, and for some at the hands of relatives or foster parents, made me embarrassed to talk about how easy my childhood had been. When I thought I saw Freda mouth the word "princess," I decided to shut up and listen. Besides, with few questions asked of me, it was obvious that my great life was of no interest to any of them. With a promise to keep in touch, we ended our call. Deep down inside, I knew that promise would be broken.

During that time, there was no word from Jim, Dan… or Richard.

Laura popped in off and on with take-out treats, wine, and consolation. My parents visited bearing homemade and canned food, toilet paper, and love. Laura and I didn't talk about Richard. My parents and I didn't talk about my book.

I managed to shower every third day.

Occasionally, I broke away from my computer and watched TV.

I barely slept.

I was obsessed with Dorothy.

I never returned my cell phone to the *Washington Intelligencer*. So for the first month, I enjoyed its use. One day it occurred to me that Jim hadn't cut off my phone for a sinister reason. He was monitoring my call activity. I stopped using it. Call it paranoia. I called it good judgment. Laura reminded me that Jim probably had connections that would allow for a tap on my home phone. I stopped using that too.

As paranoid depression took over, my imagination became my only friend. And it was running wild. One afternoon, I spent four hours writing down license plate numbers of every car, truck, and motorcycle that drove through or parked in my condo parking lot. I kept a snow shovel next to my front door. During fits of paranoia, I'd hold the shovel and stand guard like a medieval knight at a castle door.

I had slipped into madness.

I'd become one with Dorothy.

Her words were like worms eating away at my sanity.

One Friday evening an unexpected knock on my door ignited my fight-or-flight instincts. Adrenaline rushed through my veins. With nowhere to run, I had no choice but to fight. Armed with my trusty snow shovel, I yelled, "What do you want?"

"Emarie, it's me. Laura."

I peered through the peephole. Laura was smiling back at me. I opened the door ajar. "What do you want?" I repeated.

"I'm concerned about you. Let me in."

"I don't trust you. Go away."

"It's me. Laura. Your best friend. Your sister."

I opened the door. I was greeted by Laura… and Richard. "I knew

I couldn't trust you," I screamed as I tried to slam the door. Richard saw to it that I didn't. Then they both pushed their way in.

"Get out," I yelled.

"Emarie, calm down," Laura said as she tried to hug me.

I jerked away and raised the snow shovel. "Get out."

Richard pushed me. The snow shovel and I crashed to the floor. I looked up at Laura and sobbed. Then she sat on the floor next to me, held me, and like the best sister in the world, cried with me.

"It's okay," she said.

A few minutes later, feeling calmer yet still emotionally numb, I rose from the floor and hugged Richard. Then I went to my office and returned with the first draft of my book. I handed it to him. "Peace offering? Will you be my beta reader?"

"I'd be honored," Richard replied.

"Thanks." I handed him a red pen. "And while you're at it, feel free to use this."

Richard smiled. Laura sighed. I stared at them, not knowing what to say or do.

"Anyone for TGI Friday's?" Laura said, her eyes wide with enthusiasm.

"Not tonight," I said, feeling bad about rejecting her offer. "It's going to take a little while for me to recover from my trip on the Writersville Express to crazytown."

Laura gave me a reassuring hug. "How about takeout Chinese food?" she asked.

"Sounds good," Richard and I said in unison, making me smile.

An hour later, after a quick cleanup of my dining room table and me, the three of us shared Chinese food from our favorite restaurant and, of course, wine. Conversation was nil.

Richard broke the silence. "I scanned your manuscript. It looks fantastic."

"Really? You're not just saying that to make me feel better?"

"I honestly think it's fantastic."

My spirits rose. Yes, approval is the glue for a shattered ego.

"Richard, how long will it take you to read my manuscript and get it back to me?"

"Give me a week."

"That soon?"

"Well, since I'm no longer employed, I have time on my hands."

"What happened?"

"Jim and I had it out. So I quit."

"I hope it didn't have to do with me… and the book."

"It had everything to do with you and the book."

"What do you mean?"

"Jim is bent on destroying you to protect his father's honor. I stuck up for you. He flew into a rage and gave me two options—quit or be fired. I chose to quit."

"You told Jim you know he ran you off the road, didn't you?"

"Yep. And guess what? He didn't deny it. By the way, do you still have the evidence?"

"If you're talking about the wig, yeah, I still have it."

Richard shot me an impish grin. "Well… I've got the rest of the ensemble."

"You're kidding."

"Nope."

"You're my knight in shining armor."

"Yes, and I know where I can get a snow shovel to protect my little damsel in distress."

I wasn't sure I liked being referred to as a damsel in distress, but I smiled and let Richard's remark slide. "All kidding aside, I'm sorry you quit. What are you going to do?"

"I'm a cheapskate," Richard said as Laura shook her head in agreement. "I've saved enough money to live comfortably for a couple of years. So I'm not worried."

I was falling in like with Richard again.

We three best friends spent the evening catching up on the past three months. I didn't have much to say, but it was obvious Laura and Richard had been busy with each other. The more I heard, the more worried I became that at any minute they would announce their engagement. I looked at Laura's hand. No ring.

"Shall we tell her?" Laura said.

"Tell me what?"

"I don't think this is a good time," Richard replied.

"Oh come on, Richard. We're sharing it with our best friend."

Oh my God. Here it comes. They're engaged. No, they're pregnant. I downed my glass of wine, smiled, and said, "Well?"

Richard nodded his approval to Laura. "We've decided to move our relationship to the next level. We're moving in together."

Whew! What a relief. "I thought you said you'd never live with anyone before marriage. I believe your exact words were, 'I'm single until I say I do.'"

Laura laughed and patted her belly. "I've eaten a lot of words lately."

"Okay, I don't want to know what else you've eaten. Let me just say I'm happy for you."

Richard forced a smile. His eyes said he wasn't happy.

"I think it's time to call it a night," I said.

Laura insisted on helping me clean up the dishes while Richard watched TV.

After they left, my stomach churned. I couldn't decide if it was the food, the thought of Richard and Laura living together, or a bad omen.

Suddenly, my condo became eerily quiet. It was as if I were the only person in the entire building. I looked out the window and saw that most of my neighbors' cars were in the parking lot—a good indication at least some of them were home.

Out of habit, I went to the refrigerator and got a bottle of wine. Yuck. I couldn't stomach the thought of a glass of wine. I put the wine back and had a glass of water on the rocks.

I nestled on the couch, picked up the TV remote, and scrolled through the program guide. A movie listing caught my eye—the 1945 movie *Mildred Pierce* starring Joan Crawford. I'd seen the HBO miniseries with Kate Winslet. It was wonderful. I was curious as to how well Joan Crawford played the role, so I clicked.

The movie popped on to reveal the iconic actress as Mildred Pierce standing in a room next to her daughter, Veda. I didn't pay much attention to the words until she said: "Get out before I kill you." I gasped. Then the soundtrack stuck and repeated "Get out before I kill you" over and over. That was no coincidence. I attempted to change the channel. Nothing. I turned off the TV and turned it back on. An announcer said, "The next film in our Joan Crawford film festival is a biographical movie in which Joan is the main character, played by Faye Dunaway. It's titled *Daddy Dearest*."

"*Daddy Dearest?*" I screamed. "It's *Mommie Dearest*."

The announcer continued. "In this movie, Emarie Lukins, a lowly reporter looking for her big break, accidentally discovers the identity of her birth parents while researching a story about a sixty-five-year-old woman who killed her twenty-five-year-old lover. The movie builds to a shocking ending—one so horrifying that she regrets ever exposing the ghastly deeds of the man she believes is her biological father."

The screen went black. I clutched my pounding head. I looked up. The robed figure was in the corner, next to the TV.

I'd had it with this elusive being. What I did next was either pure genius or pure idiocy. I got up, charged at the robed man, and grabbed him. I couldn't believe he was solid. Was he a real person?

I shook him and screamed, "What do you want?"

He pushed me away and did his usual I'm-watching-you gesture. I pulled his hand away from his face. Then I pushed his hood back. The robe fell to the floor. The man was gone. I eyed the robe, too terrified to touch it. Nonetheless, I leaned over and picked it up. I threw it on the living room chair. I paced. I wanted to call someone, but who?

Then I did something I'd regret until the end of time. I put on the robe. Emotions, more painful than I could ever imagine, surged through me. I experienced the thoughts and feelings of everyone I knew—Jim, Richard, Laura, my mother and father, my grandparents, friends, neighbors, coworkers, Dan Jordan, Vivian Jordan, Patti Jordan, and each of Patti's babies. Jim was right; babies one through four weren't Dan's.

I saw Patti as an attractive young woman with the ability to charm any guy she wanted. And sex and lots of it was all she wanted. She was in like with Dan and would have been in love with him if he could have given her the one thing she wanted most—babies. So Patti decided if Dan couldn't deliver what she wanted she would get her needs met elsewhere. She became pregnant by one of her many sex-buddies with baby number one, Antoinette, aka Toni, in March 1969. Toni was born in off-campus housing in January 1970 while Dan and Patti were in college.

But once Patti entered motherhood, her charm and her hold on sanity slipped away. It was obvious she was emotionally unstable and unable to take care of a baby. Dan didn't want the responsibility for a baby that wasn't his, so he told Patti to get rid of it. She refused and begged him to marry her. He complied, and they married in the summer of 1970. Two's company. Three's a crowd. Patti was a lousy mother. So Dan took matters into his own hands and illegally obtained a social security number and driver's license in the name of his alter ego. Dressed in drag, he went to the courthouse and registered Antoinette's birth to his new persona. Hence, thanks to the birth of Ugly Toni, Dorothy Hall was born.

Patti continued to get pregnant, and Dan continued to run from his manhood in the guise of Dorothy Hall. Who knew something that started as a joke would end up as a lifestyle?

While Patti was out raising hell with a multitude of lovers, Dorothy Hall raised little Toni. But Dorothy's emotional and physical abuse of Toni didn't go unnoticed. In early1973, Toni was removed from Dorothy's care and placed in a worse situation with the mother of her bio-father.

Just before graduation in 1973, Patti discovered she was pregnant with baby number two, Bernard. He was born in November of the same year and removed from Dorothy's care just six months later after she went on a rampage when Patti announced she was pregnant with baby number three, Catrina. Bernard spent his childhood in five foster homes where he was physically and emotionally abused. He was killed in Afghanistan. His soul was free at last.

Poor Catrina was born in late 1974. She suffered for three years with Dorothy as her mother until she was rescued when Child Protective Services was tipped off by an anonymous caller. Child Protective Services placed Catrina with her grandparents, who didn't have the time, energy, or desire to raise a child. Throughout her childhood, she was miserably lonely.

By the time Catrina was placed in the care of her grandparents, Patti was already pregnant with Dwayne, baby number four by father number four. Dorothy neglected Dwayne, and after three years he was removed from Dorothy, placed in foster care, and eventually adopted into a loving home by the Martins.

Then Patti did something despicable. She wooed Dan's identical twin brother into having sex with her. In her twisted mind, she figured identical twins were the same person. Wooing him was her way to get Dan to give her what she wanted—his child. So along came me, Emily, baby number five, fathered by Dan's identical twin brother, Warren Keane. Dan was furious with what his brother had done and pressured Warren to get rid of me. Warren refused. Once again, Dan took matters into his own hands. He starved me and waited for someone to find out. Fortunately, Vivian Jordan did and called the police.

I relived my trauma of neglect and starvation. I don't know how I survived, but I did. The emotional and physical pain was excruciating. Warren Keane felt guilty about my situation. He remembered my parents from college and knew they were a childless couple. He contacted them about adopting me. When I thought I couldn't endure the pain any longer, it dissipated in the arms of my parents. I was engulfed by the warmth of their genuine love. Life had never felt so good.

In 1982, Freda was born. Despite the fact the letter from the Bingingham County Department of Social Services stated we were biological sisters, we weren't. We had different fathers. Freda was placed with an alcoholic aunt who neglected and mistreated her. She grew up alone, sad, and bullied by kids at school. No wonder she wanted to meet the sister she believed to have been raised like a princess.

Then, of course, six years later George, aka Bull, was born. He was sired by Warren Keane, not out of desire but out of blackmail by his brother, Dan, who promised not to reveal Warren's role in my birth and adoption if Warren would have sex with Patti until she became pregnant again. Dan also promised to keep quiet about Warren's role in my illegal adoption to my parents, thus upholding the high esteem of the Honorable Warren Keane in the Prince Georges County judicial system. Yes, Bull and I were siblings. Bull's childhood was a mixture of happiness and sadness. The older he got, the further happiness slipped into the past, and sadness and anger festered his present and future. No surprise he buried his emotions in sex, drugs, and alcohol. But I was surprised at one thing. He died ignorant of the fact that Dorothy was his father, Dan.

I wondered how I could publish my book when so many would be emotionally tormented. But then again, how could I not tell the story of a man and woman who'd abused seven innocent children? That thought instantly changed the scenario.

I saw myself as a hero. I saw Dan and Vivian get their due. I saw Jim, who was the only person in his family who knew of his father's indiscretions, smiling after his father was vindicated of any wrongdoing in my adoption. I saw each of Patti's children happy they knew the truth. I saw Richard and Laura holding hands and walking on the beach, happy in love.

Everything went black. I was exhausted, yet I managed to throw off the robe. It dropped to the floor and disappeared as if something had pulled it through an invisible hole. I sat on the couch, my mind in turmoil, my emotions running amok. What was the robed man trying to tell me? Then it struck me—the robed being wanted me to see the truth. I had.

And it was a double-edged sword.

CHAPTER FORTY-SEVEN

A FEW DAYS WENT BY. I was bored, so I started writing another book. This time it would be fiction. No more reality for me. As I got lost in my story, the doorbell rang. I looked through the peephole and saw Richard smiling at me. I opened the door. He wasn't alone.

"Richard. Jim. What a surprise. Do come in."

Richard and Jim entered my condo just enough for me to close the door. I motioned for them to have a seat. Neither took me up on my offer.

"Okay, let's cut to the chase," Jim said. "I've read your book. No way will I allow you to publish it."

"I don't think that's your decision, Jim," I said as I glared at Richard. I couldn't believe he had betrayed me and shown my book to Jim.

"You gathered the information while working on a story for the newspaper. Therefore, you don't have rights to it."

"The story wasn't published."

"What part of 'the info belongs to the newspaper' do you not understand?"

"Oh please, Jim. You broke every rule of journalism. Heck, you even broke your own rules. You let my deadlines slide. You told me my story was great when it wasn't up to basic journalistic standards. You didn't ask for my sources. Nothing Dorothy said could be corroborated. Do you think I'm stupid? As soon as I knew the story was personal to me, I knew you'd put me up to it. I knew you weren't going to run it. Besides, you'd have to reveal your role in the story, not to mention a five-hundred-thousand-dollar bribe to ghostwrite it for you. And the pièce de résistance? The crime you committed while dressed as a woman."

"What the hell are you talking about?"

"Please, Jim. Feigning innocence is unbecoming. Don't you agree, Richard?"

Richard looked at me. His eyes pleaded for me to shut up.

I would have none of it. "I believe Richard had a few days off, thanks to your driving skills."

Jim seethed. He looked like a stroke waiting to happen. He turned and opened the front door. Then he looked back at me and said, "If you publish the story, I'll make sure it's the last thing you ever do." He slammed the door behind him.

"Emarie, what's up with you?" Richard said as we both moved into the living room. Richard sat on the couch. I sat in the chair.

"Nothing."

"You're baiting a crazy man."

"He's not going to do anything to me."

"Don't be so sure."

"He's just scared. He's in too deep."

"I think he's afraid of Dan Jordan."

"Probably," I said. "Why the hell did you show him my manuscript?"

"I didn't."

"Then how did he read it?"

"Let's just say he paid me a visit at home."

"And?"

"He duped me. He dropped by to…" Richard raised his hands and finger-quoted. "…'have a little chat about my returning to work at the paper.' I went into the kitchen to get us a drink. When I went back into the living room, Jim was gone… and so was the manuscript."

"You didn't keep it in a safe place?"

"It was in my office. Jim had no right to snoop."

I gritted my teeth and uttered, "Sometimes you're sooo naïve."

"No, I wasn't naïve. I didn't expect Jim to drop by. And I certainly didn't expect him to rummage through my things. Besides, how did he know I had your manuscript?"

I was dumbfounded. I alphabetically went through the names of everyone who knew about the story. It was a short list—much shorter than the twenty-six letters of the alphabet. When I got to the *L*s I said, "Laura? No. Liz?" I nearly choked. "Richard?"

"What?"

"Do you trust Liz?"

"I don't trust anyone. Why?"

"Oh my God. It was Liz. She told Jim you had the manuscript."

"How would she know I had it?"

"A few days ago she called to see how I was doing. She said everyone at the office was asking about me." I paced and wrung my hands.

"And?"

"I told her I'd finished my book. She said she hoped she'd be the first to read it."

"And?"

"I told her you already beat her to the punch. I told her you were my beta reader."

"Damn, Emarie, sometimes you can be sooo naïve."

"Or plain stupid. I thought Liz was the most trustworthy person in the world."

"No one's completely trustworthy. Everyone has a breaking point… and a few secrets."

"Not Liz."

"Then you are naïve. I guess you don't know about her relationship with Jim. Do you?"

"You're kidding."

"Nope. Jim and Liz have been an item for years. Everyone knows… with the exception of you."

I wanted to cry. I hated feeling stupid. And I hated being duped. I hated myself. "How come no one told me?"

"Why would they? It was obvious."

"Oh Richard, I'm devastated."

"Don't be."

"Where is my manuscript?"

"I guess Jim has it."

I flopped in the chair. "Crap. He could publish it."

"I don't think he will."

"Now *you're* being naïve... even stupid."

"No, he won't publish it."

"Why not?"

Richard took a deep breath and looked at me as if I were ignorant. "It would cost him too much. He would be exposed as a cross-dresser. Not to mention his harboring information about child abuse and murder in his own family. It would cost him everything—his career... reputation... family loyalty. He'd lose his power in one of the most power-thirsty cities in the world."

"Why didn't he give it back to you?"

"I guess he thinks it was the only copy."

"No, that's not it." I leaned forward and rested my head in my hands. "He's using it as leverage."

"For what?"

"To shut up his Uncle Dan and Aunt Vivian."

"Why would they talk about the information in your book?"

"Why did Dorothy talk to me to begin with?"

Richard shrugged.

"I think Dan wanted to be outed. I think it was his way to trap Jim and force him to keep his mouth shut," I said.

"I'm not following you."

"Why would Jim want to publish a story about his family's dirty laundry? It was a well-kept secret for so long. Why now? Why did Jim hire me?"

"Why do you think he hired you?"

I rushed to my laptop and googled the name of the newspaper in

Georgia and the editor who had referred me to Jim. I clicked the name of the editor with whom I interviewed. A bio popped up. "Here we go. Good old Nathaniel Brown, formerly an award-winning reporter for the *Washington Intelligencer*."

"Nathaniel Brown?" Richard said. "I remember him. He left the paper in disgrace."

"Why?"

Richard laughed so hard he almost gagged, but he managed to mutter, "Impersonating a woman."

"What?"

"Yeah, he was caught in Jim's office... Oh my God..."

"What?"

"He was wearing the wig and clothes Jim wore when he ran me off the road."

"I think Nathaniel found Jim's wig and dress and put it on for a lark. Then when Jim found out, he was scared Nathaniel would out him, so he fired him. I bet when I interviewed with Mr. Brown, he called Jim and told him if he didn't hire me he'd leak a story about Jim's cross-dressing. That's why Jim offered me the job."

"That's a huge leap of logic," Richard said.

"This may be far-fetched, but I think Nathaniel Brown knows a lot about Jim and the Jordans. I think Nathaniel knows the whole story. Nathaniel knew who I was when he interviewed me. I bet after the interview, he called Jim and told him I was trying to enter the world of journalism. I think Jim panicked at the thought that Nathaniel would eventually spill the beans about who I was. So Jim hired me to shut me up."

"And he shut you up by assigning you to write a story about Dorothy Hall, exposing the truth about your birth parents? That makes no sense."

I put my laptop in front of Richard and said, "I think this might change your mind."

"What?"

"Mr. Brown went to the University of Maryland at the same time Dan Jordan, Warren Keane, and my father were there."

"So?"

"So, I had forgotten he asked me if Andrew Lukins was my father. I was surprised and asked Nate how he knew my father. He told me they'd gone to college together, and although he kept in touch with a few mutual friends, he hadn't seen or heard from my father."

"Oh boy, Emarie, you've gone completely nuts."

"Well, I'll prove you wrong."

Richard handed me my laptop and rose from the couch. "I've got to go."

I escorted him the six steps to the front door.

"Good luck trying to prove me wrong," he said.

"My pleasure."

Once behind closed doors, I couldn't control my tears. I'd been duped. I didn't know who to trust. I decided to pay a visit to the two people I still trusted—Mom and Dad.

CHAPTER FORTY-EIGHT

T HE NEXT MORNING I WAS dressed by eight thirty. At nine o'clock, I headed to my parents'. I knew they would be home, and I knew they wouldn't be expecting me. I rang the doorbell.

I was nervous about confronting my parents with my theory. After all, it could cost me my relationship with them. I hoped to God I was wrong. After a few moments, I rang the doorbell again. No answer. Where could they be? Their car was in the driveway. I rang the doorbell again… and again… and again.

I started to shake.

Something was wrong.

I got out my key and opened the door.

"Mom? Dad?" I yelled.

I rushed through the house. Everything looked normal. Then I went from room to room and examined every detail. In my parents' bedroom, the bed was made. I went into the kitchen and checked the coffee maker. Ground coffee was in the basket, and the water tank was full, indicating the machine had not been turned on. I had visions of my parents held captive in the basement. I ran down the stairs so fast I nearly tripped and fell.

"Not in the laundry room," I muttered. "Not in the bathroom."

I rushed back upstairs and flung open every closet door. The coat closet was the only one that gave up any information. My mother's dress coat was missing as was my father's wool overcoat. That's when I saw something horrifying. My mother's handbag sat on the dining room table. She would never leave it there. They must have left in a hurry. A vision of masked men dragging them out of the house haunted me. I wanted to call 911. Instead, I called my father's cell phone number.

After several rings, he answered. "Hey, Emarie. How are you?"

"I'm fine," I said, trying to sound as normal as possible. "Are you home?"

"No," my father replied. After a short hesitation, he said, "Umm… we're at the doctor's. Your mother had an appointment."

"Oh… I think she mentioned that the other day. I'll call you tonight."

"Okay. Talk to you later."

I decided to not hang up until my father did. To my surprise, he stayed on the line. Then I heard a voice that sent shivers down my spine.

"Did she buy it," Dan said.

"Yes," my father said.

"Good. Then let's get this settled," Jim said.

I hung up and raced to my car. I drove like a crazy person. I wished the police would stop me but was relieved they didn't. Forty-five minutes later, I pulled into the parking garage across the street from the *Washington Intelligencer*. I tried to appear nonchalant as I approached the elevator.

"Hurry up," I nearly screamed out loud.

Ding. The elevator door opened. I was face-to-face with Liz.

"Emarie? It's wonderful to see you," Liz said as I watched the elevator doors close.

"Nice to see you too," I said.

"Are you paying us a visit? I hope so."

"No. Just returning something."

"Well… I hope you can stay awhile."

"Me too, but I've got to get back home. Work is waiting."

"Did you get a new job?" Liz asked.

"No... no. Freelance work."

"Oh, that's wonderful. I'm so happy for you. We miss you around here."

I had no reply. Her idle chitchat caused me to miss two elevators. My anxiety soared. Then Liz pulled me into the lobby ladies' room.

I yanked my arm away from her grasp and said, "What the hell is wrong with you?"

"Emarie, listen to me," Liz said. "Your parents are in Jim's office. So is Dan Jordan. If you want to ensure your parents' safety, you'll go home now. Do not go to Jim's office."

"Liz, are you protecting me... or are you protecting Jim?"

"Why you, of course. Why would I protect Jim?"

"I think you know why. Everybody knows about Jim and you."

Liz's face flushed. Beads of sweat speckled her forehead.

"Oh, Liz, please don't tell me you thought you'd pulled the wool over everyone's eyes with your sickening-sweet personality and innocent-little-girl voice."

Liz glared at me. I half expected her to slap me. Instead, she said, "You've been warned." Then she stormed out of the building.

I rushed toward an open elevator. As the door closed, I saw Liz through the lobby glass door. She was on her cell phone, watching me rise to the eighth floor. *Hmm, I wonder who she's talking to?*

I pushed open the doors to the office. I thought I heard someone gasp, followed by "Hi, Emarie. Good to see you." I ignored the comment and approached Jim's office. There they were. Jim, Dan, my parents and... Richard. To my surprise, they were laughing. My parents sat on the couch, looking relaxed. Jim sat with his feet propped on his desk. Dan and Richard sat in the chairs that usually faced Jim's desk but now faced my parents, creating a barrier between them and Jim's office door. What should have been a heated meeting of adversaries appeared to be a friendly gathering of old friends catching up on old times. *What the hell are they up to? Why are my parents so at ease? Whose side are they on?*

As I opened the door, Jim glanced at me and removed his legs from his desk. I felt energized and all-powerful. Anger was my ally. I stepped forward, only to discover my handbag was caught in the door. I nearly fell. In a nanosecond, my courage dissipated.

"Hello, Mom… Dad," I said as I yanked my purse free. "Jim, Dan… *Richard*? The plot thickens."

"Emarie, it's not what you think," my father said.

"And what is it I think?"

Jim got up and gently guided me by the arm over to the couch. "Emarie, please sit."

I refused.

"I know this doesn't look good—"

"It looks like a conspiracy to me," I said.

"What an imagination," Dan said. "It's just a little gathering of family and friends."

I scanned the room. Everyone was relaxed but me.

My father scooched closer to my mother and patted the cushion next to him. "Emarie, sit."

"No, Dad. I have something to say, and then I'm leaving."

"What's up, babycakes?" Dan said.

"I've got this whole thing figured out."

"Really?" Jim said.

I glanced at my father. He glanced at my mother. Now they looked scared.

"Do tell," Richard said.

"Before I do, where is my manuscript?"

Jim laughed as he pushed a shredder toward me. "I guess you could say we're having a manuscript-shredding party."

"We destroyed the tapes and everything else," Richard said. "And if you check your computer, you'll see the files have been erased."

"Well, you've confirmed my theory then," I said. "By the way, where's dear Aunt Vivian?"

"She's on her way to your condo to retrieve the background information you copied and kept."

I didn't flinch. "Well, here's my theory. Remember when I interviewed with Nathaniel Brown of the *Atlanta Herald*? He didn't hire me. In fact, he didn't even seem interested in me. But he did ask me a question that in retrospect is important. He asked if Andrew Lukins was my father. I told him yes and asked how he knew my father. According to Mr. Brown, you, Dad, went to the University of

Maryland with him. It seems you had mutual friends with whom he kept in touch, but you and he didn't see or talk to each other after college. That was pretty much the end of the interview. I didn't give it a second thought. But I was surprised when you, Jim, told me the editor of the *Atlanta Herald* referred me to you."

"So? We editors know each other. It's no biggie he referred you to me."

"But it is a biggie that Mr. Brown, a reporter for the *Washington Intelligencer*, was fired for impersonating a woman."

Jim leaned back in his chair and took a deep breath.

"Yes, Jim. It seems Nathaniel, better known as Nate, discovered your women's wear, and being a bit effeminate himself, he put it on for a lark." Images of Nate dancing around Jim's office singing "I Feel Pretty" nearly made me laugh. "You became enraged and fired him. I think you were scared to death he'd out you and worse, out your Uncle Dan. After all, everyone who knew Dan in college knew he was a cross-dresser."

"Your point would be?" Jim asked.

"Well… I was the missing link. I was Nate's revenge. When I showed up for a job interview with him, I think he hatched a plan to get back at you for firing him. One of the two college buddies Nate remained friends with was your father. I think they were more than just college buddies, I think Nate and your father were good friends. I think your father confided in Nate about my adoption. I think he was going to hire me for one reason… to write a story about your family, to out your Uncle Dan and the corruption in Darrington. He called you and told you about his plan. You begged him not to, knowing that your father, the Honorable Warren Keane, would be revealed to be less than honorable. Nate agreed to not write a story if you hired me. So you did. For the next two years, everything was hunky-dory. The family secret was safe. Until… your Uncle Dan did the unthinkable. As Dorothy, he killed Bull and your Aunt Patti. You became irate with all the cover-ups of your uncle's child-abuse behaviors, his disguise as Dorothy Hall, and the fact he pulled your father into an illegal adoption that could have tarnished his sparkling reputation."

Dan laughed, looked at everyone in the room, and gave the universal motion for "crazy."

Nobody else said a word, so I plowed ahead. "So *you* hatched a plan. You assigned me to write a story about Dorothy Hall, who had been accused of killing her twenty-five-year-old boyfriend. You dropped an envelope on my desk that contained little information with which to prepare a story. You told me you had assigned the story to Richard, but he refused to write it due to a lack of information. You knew I wouldn't refuse the opportunity to make a name for myself as a journalist. And to make things look legit, you demoted Richard for his refusal to take on the assignment. This was a ploy to enlist him to tail me because you were afraid I didn't have what it took to be a good reporter—"

"Emarie, this is totally ridiculous," Jim interrupted.

"I'm not done yet." I was about to continue but hesitated when I saw Richard give me a don't-even-go-there look and shake his head no. Nonetheless, I continued. "What you didn't predict was that Dorothy would reveal herself to be your Uncle Dan or that your Aunt Vivian would get entangled in the mess. Then, when you thought I knew too much, you got your Uncle Dan and Aunt Vivian to scare me, but it didn't work. Then you killed my story. I guess you thought I would pout and give up on it. But instead, I quit. When you found out I was writing a book about Dorothy, aka Dan Jordan, you panicked. And when you found out Richard had betrayed you and was helping me, you tried to kill him. And now you've pulled in my parents, who were completely unaware of the biggest secret of all… the fact that I am the child of your father, Warren Keane, and Patti Jordan."

My mother gasped. My father went pale. Jim, Dan, and Richard didn't move or utter a word. I wanted to run, but my feet felt like lead weights.

"Mom, Dad, let's go."

Jim sprang up and said, "They're not going anywhere… and neither are you."

"Get your hands off *my* daughter, Jim," my father yelled as he tried to rise from the couch.

Jim lunged at me, pushing me into his office door with so much force that it opened, giving me an easy escape.

I glanced at my parents from the opened door. My father mouthed, "Get out." I took his advice and bolted for the elevator.

The elevator ride to the lobby gave me a few minutes to calm down and think about what had transpired. *What did you just do, Emarie? You mouthed off and left your parents trapped in a room with crazy Dan and Jim.* But in my gut, I knew they wouldn't be harmed. On the other hand, sometimes my gut was wrong.

CHAPTER FORTY-NINE

B ACK AT MY CONDO, I checked my office. I opened the drawer in which my manuscript and backup materials were sheltered. They were safe and sound. But I didn't know if the same was true for my parents.

My heart raced as I dialed their number. "Please let them be home," I muttered.

"Hello."

"Dad, it's me. Emarie."

There was silence.

"Dad?"

"Hey, Emarie. May I call you back?"

"Sure. Everything all right?"

"Yeah, everything's fine. I'll call you later. Bye now."

My heart throbbed in my throat. Something was wrong. I began to pace. That's when a folded piece of paper, my name written in caps on the front of it, caught my eye.

My dearest Emarie:

You may not know this, but I've been a part of your life since the day you were born. I was present at your birth and every one of your life's major events, and I have the photos to prove it.

I watched you blow out the candles on your first birthday cake. Your little legs wobbled as your mother steadied you while your father captured the moment on film.

I watched you hold your mother's hand as you happily skipped your way to your first day of school.

I took pictures of your sixteenth birthday celebration at Indian River Inlet with your parents and your best friend, Laura.

I cried when I saw you graduate from high school, knowing you were no longer a child.

I clapped with pride as you accepted your diploma from the University of Maryland's College of Journalism, happy you were a beautiful young woman with a world of opportunity before you.

But the event that touched me most was watching the police gently carry you to an ambulance that whisked you away to a better life. Yes, I called the police when I discovered you were in danger in the care of Dorothy Hall. I regret I didn't know that Dorothy had you. But as you know, our family is held together by lies, deception, and corruption, of which I'm not innocent.

Nonetheless, I have loved you from afar for your entire life. Therefore, I will not thwart your greatness. Please publish your book so others can be freed from the control of Dan Jordan.

Love,

Aunt Vivian

I didn't know what to think or feel. I felt violated, elated, and set up all at the same time. I didn't trust Vivian. How could she have spied on me my entire life without my knowing? Did my parents know? Was this just one of their secrets?

My hands trembled. I eased onto the couch, hoping to relax and calm my nerves. No such luck. The phone rang. I bolted up and snatched the phone. It was my parents' number.

"Hello," I said, my voice shaking.

"Well hello, Emarie."

"Vivian?"

"Yes."

"What are you doing at my parents' house?"

"Just visiting with my old friends."

"Let me talk to my father."

"Okay."

"Emarie?"

"Dad, what's going on?"

"Nothing. We're just catching up on years of lost time with Vivian Jordan."

"I thought you didn't like her."

"You're confusing her with Patti Jordan."

"Oh."

"Did you get my note?" Vivian said, making me wonder if she had taken the phone from my father or if she was listening in on our conversation.

"Yes."

"And?"

"And what? You expect me to be thrilled that you've stalked me all my life?"

"I didn't know how you'd react, but I felt you needed to know. What about the last part about publishing your book?"

"I'll think about it."

"Emarie?" my father said, making it obvious he and Vivian Jordan were sharing my call. "Publish your book. Everything will be all right."

"You can't guarantee that, Dad. Jim and Dan could come after me."

"No they won't," Vivian said. "They're just two bullies with no bite. If they wanted to harm you, they would have by now. Besides, they'd have to answer to me."

"Okaaay." I wondered what kind of power Vivian had over Dan

and Jim. Desperate to end the conversation with Vivian, I said, "I gotta go. Talk to you later, Dad."

Relief that my parents weren't in immediate danger eased my anxiety, but I still needed reassurance. The best person for the job was Laura. I called her, and like a sister, she dropped everything and came over.

Laura and I sat on my couch, enjoying a glass of wine as we discussed my concerns about my parents' safety if I published my book. Although it was good to have my sister back, our conversation felt forced. Might as well tackle it head-on.

"Laura? Are you upset about something?"

"No. Why?"

"Come on. Things don't seem right between us, that's all."

"Well, since you asked. I've felt left out lately."

"Left out of what?"

"Your life."

"I thought you had a new life with Richard."

Laura sighed, rose, and walked into the sunroom. She stared out the window, sipped her wine, and said, "Richard and I broke up."

I walked over and put my arms around Laura's shoulder to comfort her. She jerked away from me.

I was hurt and confused, but I wasn't about to allow Laura's dismissive behavior to slide. "What's wrong?"

"Nothing... nothing at all," she said as she went back into the living room. "I guess I should go."

"Wait a minute." I turned Laura toward me. "You can't fool me. I'm your sister, remember?"

"Well, you haven't been much of a friend lately... let alone a sister. You're self-absorbed. You've let your little story consume you. No one else matters to you but you."

"Yikes. That hurts. And it's not true... but enough about me."

Laura smiled, which I took as permission to ask a question. "What happened between Richard and you?"

Laura huffed and puffed her way to the kitchen, slammed her wineglass on the counter, and yelled, "You. You're what happened between Richard and me."

"I don't understand."

"Of course not. You live in your own little world, and you won't let anybody in."

"Right now I don't understand you. We've always been open and honest with each other. We've always had each other's back."

"No. We used to be open and honest… until you let Dorothy, aka Dan Jordan, into your life and your head. Why couldn't you leave well enough alone?"

"Why don't you tell me what's really going on?"

"I just told you. It's Richard and you."

"There's nothing going on between Richard and me. In fact, I don't like him and I don't trust him."

Laura flinched. "Well, he sings your praises."

"Really?"

"Yeah, he says you're sitting on a story that will shake up Darrington and the Washington Intelligencer and make you famous. But you won't publish it because you're chicken."

"Please, Darrington isn't important outside of Darrington, and the Washington Intelligencer is too powerful to be brought down by a book written by an unknown author."

"Oh, Emarie," Laura said, her head down as if she was ashamed. "Please don't publish your book."

What was up with Laura's phony drama? Was she hiding something? I squelched the urge to blurt, Oh please, I know you too well to let your fake emotions fool me. Instead, I said, "Why would you, my best friend, not want me to publish my book?"

"Because Jim, Dan, and Vivian will harm you. I've lost Richard. I can't bear the thought of losing you."

I rolled my eyes like a teenager dismissing a parent. "You're being a drama queen. Nothing is going to happen to me."

Laura's eyes filled with tears. "Richard said they'll harm you. We had a terrible fight over it. That's why I broke up with him. I don't trust he has your best interests at heart."

"You got that right. He's trying to ruin me. He's playing both sides. I don't trust him as far as I can throw him." And I don't trust your crocodile tears either.

"You don't trust him?"

"No, I don't."

Laura quickly walked toward the front door. "I've got to go." With her hand on the doorknob, she turned and said, "Emarie, I beg you, do not publish your book. I love you, sis." Then she charged down the stairs.

"What a drama queen. Nobody tells me what to do."

Through the sunroom window, I spotted Laura standing on the sidewalk in front of my condo. A car pulled up, and she jumped into the passenger seat and hugged the man in the driver's seat. As the two of them sped off, I caught a glimpse of the license plate. My heart sank. My stomach churned.

Laura had lied to me.

CHAPTER FIFTY

F OR THE NEXT FEW MONTHS, I became a skilled actress. I pretended my book was the farthest thing from my mind even though it consumed my every moment.

Of course, after apologies from me for my self-centered behavior and forgiveness from Laura, we made up. I never told her that I knew she'd lied to me about breaking up with Richard. Was this maturity? Or had irreparable harm been done to our relationship? I'd have to wait and see. Despite my concern, our friendship returned to normal. We chatted on the phone nearly every day and met at TGI Friday's on Saturday evenings as usual. Sometimes Richard joined us. He didn't talk about work, Jim, or anyone else at the *Washington Intelligencer*, and he never mentioned the elephant in the room, otherwise known as my book.

I had dinner with my parents every week and talked to them frequently. The fact that I wasn't hustling for a full-time job with benefits worried them. To calm their nerves, I told them a partial truth or a partial lie depending on how you looked at it. I said I was unbelievably busy with freelance writing jobs. And in order to stay on top of my workload, I was working twelve hours a day, seven days a week, and even had to turn away work. For some reason, I blurted out my hourly rate, which I might have inflated a bit.

The look on my father's face was priceless as he said, "That means you're making more than three hundred thousand dollars a year."

Even I was impressed, and for a split second, I considered dropping my book for a lucrative freelance career. The truth? I scrambled for just enough freelance jobs to survive and spent the bulk of my time fact-checking, editing, and rewriting my book. That meant my annual income was more in the range of fifty thousand dollars a year. Oops! It was only a two-hundred-and-fifty-thousand-dollar lie.

After a monthlong search, I found a fabulous editor who thought my book had great potential. His name was Aaron, and he rapidly became my new friend and confidant. We contacted several agents and publishers. Months went by. No bites. Then one day I received a call from a publishing rep who had turned down my query. She said she'd left her job to work on a lifelong dream of owning her own publishing company.

"Has anyone picked up your book? Have you submitted to a publisher that requires you don't make other submissions for a specified time period or until you hear from them regarding your submission?" she asked.

When I said, "No and no," she seemed pleased. She asked me to read the submission guidelines posted on her website and submit my full manuscript for consideration. I immediately called Aaron and told him the good news.

"Sharon Plinkton?" Aaron said. "That name rings a bell."

"You know her?" I said.

"I'm not sure, but her name is familiar."

Aaron asked me a few questions about Sharon Plinkton's publishing company for which I had no answers. So I gave him the web address to check out the company himself. We simultaneously viewed her website and agreed it was impressive for a start-up. When I told him I was going to submit my manuscript, he wished me luck and hung up.

I was pretty sure my manuscript already met the requirements, but I printed the submission guidelines and checked them against each point. I wrote a thank-you e-mail, attached my full manuscript, and hit Send. Then I waited with bated breath to hear back. Nonetheless, life went on.

Aaron and I were definitely more than editor and author. As summer heated up, our relationship got hot. It was time to kick it up a notch.

"Aaron? Would like to join me at TGI Friday's and meet my friends, Laura and Richard?"

"Sure."

"Of course, you can't mention my book or the fact you're an editor."

"My lips are sealed."

Saturday evening, I introduced him to Laura and Richard. Aaron and Richard hit it off. Laura was happy. I was suspicious.

When we were seated and had ordered our meals, Richard said, "So Aaron, what do you do?"

"Uh… photographer," Aaron replied.

"Really? What do you photograph?" Laura asked.

"Crime scenes."

Laura glanced at me. I nervously replied, "And he's really good."

"Do you work for the police department?" Richard asked.

"Yep."

"Which one?"

"Fairfax."

"City or county?"

"County."

"What have you photographed lately?"

"I'm not at liberty to say."

"Do you like your work?" Laura asked.

"Most of the time… but some crime scenes are emotionally difficult."

"How long have you been a crime-scene photographer?" Richard asked.

"Hmm. Gee… it's been eight years already."

"Time flies when you're having fun," Richard said.

"Yeah, something like that," Aaron replied.

Just in time, our meals arrived and the conversation changed to food. I thought all was well until I heard Richard ask Aaron, "Read any good books lately?"

Aaron made a horrible mistake. He glanced at me as if to ask for help.

And stupid me, I answered for him. "He's not much of a reader."

Richard smiled.

Laura appeared clueless.

The evening dragged. Once we were in the car I said, "Crime photographer?"

"Yeah, I just edited a book on crime photography. I figured if anyone asked questions, I could at least answer intelligently. And why didn't you tell me Richard is Richard Bader?"

"You know him?"

"Well, duh. Journalists. Editors. It's a small world. I worked with him at a newspaper in Ohio. He was a gofer and I was a cub reporter. Neither one of us lasted long."

"Oh God." *It's a small world. Too small.*

The ride home was torturously quiet until Aaron broke the silence. "I can't believe he's still in the business."

"Who?"

"Richard."

"Why?"

"He was an ass kisser... a whiner... a conniver. He wasn't respected by anyone."

"I see he hasn't changed."

"If it wasn't for Jim Keane, Richard would probably be asking, 'Would you like fries with that?'"

"What about Jim Keane?"

"He's Richard's cousin... uncle... sister-in-law's brother... something or other."

I gasped. I couldn't breathe. I was in the throes of a full-blown panic attack.

"Emarie, are you okay?"

"No," I whispered.

Aaron stepped on the gas and raced to the Inova Healthplex emergency room. Two hours and one Xanax later, we were home. I immediately went to bed. Aaron made me a cup of tea, sat on the side of the bed, and held my hand. I had no idea he was such a sweet man. As I drifted off to sleep, I thought I felt him kiss me on the forehead and say, "I love you."

I awoke the next morning to my phone ringing. I answered and tried to pretend I wasn't half-asleep.

"Sharon Plinkton… from Plinkton Press."

"Sharon? Hi," I said as I shot up in bed.

"I reviewed your manuscript. I think your book has great potential. I'd like to schedule a time for us to meet."

"What's a good time for you?" I asked, barely masking my excitement.

"How about tomorrow at eleven o'clock?"

"Perfect," I said.

Click. I was the happiest person in the world. I jumped out of bed and ran down the hall to tell Aaron the good news. He was gone, and my heart was broken. He didn't even say good-bye. Was he mad at me? I called his cell phone. No answer.

I ran through the events of the previous evening. There was no evidence anything was wrong, yet my heart was heavy with worry. At that moment, I realized how much I loved him. Yes, I said "loved." The thought of losing him was devastating. I'd never felt this way before.

My home phone rang. I rushed to the kitchen, knowing it was Aaron. Nope—it was Laura.

I shared my good news about my meeting with Sharon Plinkton. Laura was cold and distant. "Laura? Is there something wrong?"

"You had one hell of a nerve bringing Aaron Aaronson with you last night."

"He's my boyfriend," I said.

"Well, Richard can't stand him. You should have—"

I hung up on Laura. We were now officially on the outs again.

I spotted a sealed envelope on my dining room table and picked it up. Was it a rejection letter? It was heavy. "He's returned my key. He's dumping me." My hands shook and my knees buckled as I tore open the envelope. Inside were a key (not my key) and a note. The note read, "My place. Six p.m. Don't tell a soul. And wear something special."

"Wear something special? What the hell does that mean? An evening dress? Victoria's Secret lingerie? My birthday suit?"

I decided to take all three.

CHAPTER
FIFTY-ONE

I LOOKED MARVELOUS. MY PERFECT little black dress perfectly hugged my curves. My necklace dipped to my navel and swayed with each sexy step I took. My makeup and hair were straight out of Glamour Shots. I hoped Aaron was as enamored with me as I was with myself. I tossed my little black overnight bag in the back seat of my car and whisked myself to my lover's house. My spat with Laura? Long forgotten but not forgiven.

I rang the doorbell and waited. Then I remembered Aaron had given me a key. "Honey, I'm home," I yelled as I walked in.

I was tackled, knocked to the floor, and kissed by Walter, Aaron's ten-month-old Lab. I struggled to get up, but Walter was determined to keep me to himself. He pawed at my hair, causing hairpins to tinkle on the tile like hail. He licked my face as if it were an ice cream cone. When I rose from the floor, he jumped on me again. I pushed him away. His nails snagged my dress and tore a huge hole in my pantyhose. But it was the sound of beads bouncing on the floor that made me cry. My grandmother's necklace, which had survived fifty years of family Christmases, engagement parties, christenings, weddings, and funerals, didn't survive Walter. Beads bounced across the foyer as tears ran down my cheeks. I wanted to kill Walter. He was lucky he was so damn cute. I turned around and was greeted by a woman.

"Hello, you must be Emarie." I wanted to die. The woman was the spitting image of Aaron. There was no doubt she was Aaron's mother. I tried to say hello, but I couldn't stop sobbing.

"There, there, dear," the woman said as she put her arm around my shoulder. "It'll be all right."

Then a man screamed, "Walter, what have you done?"

I looked up to see a handsome, sixty-something man. He had to be Aaron's stepfather. He grabbed Walter by the collar and dragged him into a room. A door slammed, and Walter whined.

I composed myself and managed a somewhat civilized introduction. "Yes, I'm Emarie."

"I'm Annabelle, Aaron's mother," the woman said. "And this is my husband, Louis."

Louis smiled, extended his hand, and said, "Nice to finally meet you."

I shook Louis's hand and said, "Aaron didn't mention I'd be meeting his parents this evening."

"He didn't?" Annabelle said. "Well then, I guess you had something else in mind for this evening."

I laughed. "Yes. Something else."

"Well, let's not spoil the evening. Let's get you fixed up so Aaron can see how gorgeous you looked before Walter mauled you."

I liked Aaron's mother already. We went to a back bedroom where Annabelle redid my hair, freshened my makeup, gave me a new pair of pantyhose, and undid the snags in my dress.

"Well, with the exception of my grandmother's necklace, I look perfect."

Annabelle smiled and said, "I think I have a little something that would look fabulous with your dress." She opened a drawer and slowly lifted a long string of beads.

I couldn't believe my eyes. It was the same necklace. She placed it around my neck as the two of us looked at me in the mirror.

"Where did you get this necklace? It's just like the one I was wearing."

"Years ago, I bought it for my grandmother. I thought it was beautiful. She loved it. Wore it to every special occasion. She even wore it to my wedding to Walter, Aaron's father. When my grandmother died, my aunt gave it to me."

"I can't believe it's the same."

"It was popular at the time. Almost every woman had one."

"I love it. But Walter destroyed it."

"You know, I haven't worn this necklace for twenty years. I thought of wearing it this evening, but I've changed my mind. It's my gift to you."

"Oh no… I couldn't—"

"You must. I can't think of anyone who would enjoy it more."

I turned and hugged Annabelle. "Thank you. I don't know what to say."

"Wear it in good health, my dear."

As Annabelle and I returned to the living room, I said, "Did Aaron name his dog after his father?"

"Yes. His father would be honored. He was a big dog lover."

Louis stood up to greet us, scotch in hand. "You look beautiful," he said, causing me to blush. "Aaron should have been home a while ago."

"He said he had to pick up something on his way home. Maybe he's—"

Aaron walked through the front door. He grinned and said, "I see you guys have met."

He kissed me on the cheek and said, "Sorry I'm late."

"That's all right," I said. "We've had an interesting introduction thanks to Walter."

"What did he do?" Aaron asked.

"We'll fill you in, son," Louis said. "Let's go. I'm starving."

Aaron took Walter outside to do his business as we ladies gathered our handbags and applied lipstick.

"I'll drive," Aaron said.

"Good," Louis replied. "Then I don't have to worry about my scotch consumption."

I sat in the front seat. As Aaron's parents got comfortable in the confines of the back seat, he leaned into me and whispered, "You look beautiful."

"You don't have to whisper," Annabelle said. "We all agree she's beautiful."

After thirty minutes of getting to know each other, debating politics, and Louis yelling at the crazy drivers, we arrived at the Washington National Harbor's Gaylord Hotel. The valet helped me out of the car as if I were a queen. Then Aaron rushed to my side and escorted me into the hotel lobby. A short elevator ride in silence and we arrived at the doors of the Old Hickory Steakhouse.

"Ah, Mr. Aaronson," the maître d' said. "Everything has been arranged. May I begin?"

"Yes. Please," Aaron said as he smiled at me.

Suspicious me wondered what he was up to. When we got to our table, I noticed two things—the beautiful view of the harbor and two extra chairs. *Hmm, that's odd. Who's joining us?*

"Did you get settled in okay?" Aaron asked his mother and stepfather, bringing me out of my head and into the moment.

"Of course, dear," Annabelle said.

"So what did Walter do?"

"Another time. Let's enjoy what promises to be a lovely evening."

"That bad, huh?" Aaron asked.

Just in time, the waiter arrived with our drinks—white wine for Annabelle, vodka tonic for me, and scotch for Louis and Aaron.

"Cheers," Aaron said.

"Cheers," Annabelle, Louis, and I said as we raised our glasses and then sipped our drinks.

I smiled at Aaron and took another sip. I felt happy. No, I felt contented. It dawned on me one of my wishes had come true. Instead of an evening at TGI Friday's being escorted to our table by a teenybopper, selecting the same meal from plastic-coated menus, and practically yelling at Laura over the deafening noise level, I was sitting in a white-tablecloth restaurant with leather-bound menus, dressed to the nines, having a normal-decibel conversation with the man I loved and his charming, sophisticated parents. Life as I knew it was over. Thank God. It was about time. I was relishing the ambience when an image in the window of two people caught my attention. Aaron and Louis rose to their feet as I turned to see my parents, accompanied by the maître d'.

"Mom... Dad," I said. "What a surprise."

They both came over and kissed me. My mother looked beautiful and happy. I swear she glowed. My father couldn't have looked more handsome.

Introductions were quick. As soon as my parents were seated, their drinks arrived. Then the six of us settled in for one of the most extravagant meals I'd ever had. The seafood tower and beef tartare appetizers started our evening's taste sensations—succulent steaks, a magnificent cheese plate, desserts worth every calorie, and wine to complement each course. We raved about the food. The evening was perfect.

"Well, this has been a wonderful evening with my favorite people," Aaron said.

"Hear, hear," Louis said, looking a tad looped.

"As special as this evening has been," Aaron said as he turned to me, "I hope it's about to get better." He reached into his suit-jacket pocket. "I have a little something for you."

No. No. It's too soon. This can't be happening, my mind screamed as my lips formed a smile. God only knows what my eyes said. *He's going to propose. I'm not ready for this kind of commitment.*

"Emarie Lukins?" Aaron opened his hand, revealing a small black velvet box. He flipped it open and said, "Will you marry me?"

I was stunned speechless.

"Cat got your tongue," Louis slurred.

"Louis." Annabelle admonished her husband.

I took a deep breath. It felt as if everyone in the restaurant was staring at me. "Well," I said, "this has been the loveliest evening of my life, despite Walter's attempt to ruin it."

Aaron took a deep breath and exhaled. My mother looked worried. Annabelle and my father smiled. Louis took another sip of scotch.

"And I can't imagine a better way to end this evening and change my life for the better than to say... Yes, Aaron Aaronson, I will happily marry you."

"Welcome to the family," Louis said as he raised his glass to toast the occasion and motioned to the waiter for a refill.

Aaron slipped the ring on my finger. It was the most beautiful ring

I'd ever seen—a two-carat pear-shaped diamond accented by two one-carat pear-shaped diamonds set in a platinum mount supported by a hand-etched shaft of eighteen-karat yellow gold. It was gorgeous beyond belief. I couldn't believe it was mine.

Aaron kissed me and said, "You've made me a very happy man."

Then I rested my head on his shoulder and cried. "I'm happy you asked. I hope you discussed this with Walter."

Louis, Annabelle, and I laughed.

My mother and father came over to me, and we hugged and kissed. My father even hugged Aaron, shook hands with Aaron's stepfather, and hugged his mother. Throughout the family celebration of our engagement, I couldn't stop crying.

"Are those tears of joy?" Aaron asked.

"No," I said.

Aaron looked shocked and saddened. "What's wrong?"

"The person with whom I've shared every major event in my life isn't here."

"Who?" Aaron asked.

"My sister."

"I didn't know you had a sister."

"Laura," I nearly yelled.

"Laura? Emarie, I didn't meet her until last night. It was too late to invite her. Besides, you texted me today and told me you two are on the outs."

"She's my sister. We're always on the outs." I laughed as I wiped my tears.

"I'm sorry. I promise to make up for my oversight."

"I'll hold you to that."

Champagne preceded our departure. I felt as if I were dreaming. I checked my left hand. I wasn't dreaming. I was engaged. It's amazing how quickly life changes; in this case, for the better.

As we exited the restaurant, the maître d' handed me a note.

"Thank you," I said as I put it in my purse.

The ride home was full of excited conversation about Walter's enthusiastic welcome and the destruction and reconstruction of my hair, clothes, and jewelry. Aaron and I dropped off his parents at his house and then drove my car to my condo. I pulled my overnight bag from the back seat and headed up the stairs.

"I see you came prepared," Aaron said.

"Well, you said to wear something special. I wasn't sure if you meant a dress, lingerie, or my birthday suit, so I brought all three."

"Well, I've seen the dress. What do you say we forgo the lingerie and go straight to the B-day suit?"

I smiled. I didn't have the heart to tell him I wasn't in the mood. I deliberately took a long time in the bathroom. It worked. When I got into bed, Aaron was sound asleep.

The next morning was pure bliss. After we rolled out of bed and shared a pot of coffee, Aaron said, "I have an idea. How about we invite Laura and Richard over for dinner? Then I'll propose again... just the four of us."

"That could work. Oh, I almost forgot," I said as I put my coffee cup on the counter and grinned at Aaron. "I have a meeting at eleven o'clock with Sharon Plinkton of Plinkton Press. She's interested in my book."

Aaron took a deep breath and walked into the living room.

"I thought you'd be happy for me," I yelled as I headed down the hall toward the bedroom.

"Of course I am," Aaron said.

I soaked in the relaxation of the shower's hot water as I reveled in my new life. I was engaged to a wonderful man, and I was going to get my book published. "It's all too good to be true," I mumbled. My words felt like a bad omen. I shuddered as the happiness of last night and this morning washed down the drain.

CHAPTER FIFTY-TWO

A T TEN FORTY-FIVE A.M., I sat in a brand-spanking new office, feeling antsy about my meeting with Sharon Plinkton and sweating like a pig. Her young assistant snapped gum and texted on her cell phone, oblivious to the fact she oozed a lack of professionalism that created a poor first impression for her employer and her.

To calm my nerves, I rummaged through my purse. I spotted the note the maître d' had handed me the previous evening. I'd seen this stationery before but where? As I ran my fingers over the fine paper, I felt embossed letters on the flap. "Oh God," I whispered. I hesitated to turn it over for fear of seeing the letters VJ, but I did it anyway. There they were.

I stood up, ready to bolt out of the office. The ring of the office phone stopped me in my tracks. The assistant snatched the receiver and quickly hung up. Head lowered, eyes on her cell phone, thumbs beating out messages, she said, "Ms. Plinkton will see you now."

I smiled and headed toward the door. I felt as if I were about to meet with a doctor regarding a terminal illness. Seconds later, I greeted Sharon Plinkton.

"Ms. Lukins, what a pleasure to meet you."

"Pleasure to meet you too," I managed to say in a surprisingly professional manner.

"Are you okay?" Sharon said, noticing my sweat-covered face. "May I get you some water?"

"I'm fine, thank you. I'm always warm in the morning."

Sharon motioned for me to take a seat as she sat in the chair next to me. I noticed her gorgeous desk and beautiful décor. *A little too perfect,* I thought. Something was wrong. Then it struck me. The bookshelf was decorated with knickknacks and art but no books. Strange for a publisher. And her desk was immaculate. Not one piece of paper. *What? No pile of manuscripts? Was this a rent-an-office?*

"Emarie? Are you sure you're okay?" Sharon asked.

"I'm fine. Just a little too much excitement last night."

"I hope it was fun excitement."

"Couldn't be better. I got engaged."

"Marvelous. Who's the lucky man?"

"Aaron Aaronson."

Sharon coughed. She looked pale. "Oh," was all she said.

"Do you know him?"

"Sort of."

"How do you know him?"

"I worked with him in Ohio."

"Oh. Then I suppose you worked with Richard Bader as well."

"Yes… but it was years ago."

"By the way, do you know Jim Keane?"

"Of course. I worked with him in New York before he went to the *Washington Intelligencer*. I was young. He was my mentor. We were a great team."

My gut screamed for me to leave. "I'm sorry, Ms. Plinkton," I said as I stood. "But I don't think I'm ready to turn over my manuscript for publishing at this time."

Sharon remained seated. "Emarie? Please… let's discuss this."

"There's nothing to discuss. I'm just not ready." I extended my arm in an attempt to shake hands with her. She stood but did not reciprocate.

"Well, please keep Plinkton Press in mind when you are," she said as she escorted me to the lobby.

As Sharon opened the lobby door, I said, "Thank you for your time." Then I walked away. Emarie had left the building.

I sat in my car as I tried to gather my thoughts and control my anger. I retrieved the note from my purse and tore open the envelope. I took a deep breath and read the note.

> *Dearest Emarie:*
>
> *Congratulations on your engagement. You looked stunning this evening. I wish you and Aaron a lifetime of happiness.*
>
> *Not to put a damper on your joy, but I hope you read this note before you make a horrible mistake. DO NOT trust Sharon Plinkton. She is not a publisher as she claims. She has been set up by Jim and Dan to get the rights to your manuscript and prevent your book from being published. And please, when you meet with her, don't let on that you know anything about her arrangement with them.*
>
> *I'll be watching.*
>
> *Love,*
>
> *Aunt Vivian*

I gasped. Rage consumed me as I sped home. Fortunately, Aaron had already left for work. I googled the publishing company Sharon Plinkton claimed to have left to start her own company. I dialed the number.

"Hamilton and Reeves Publishing. How may I direct your call?"

"Sharon Plinkton, please."

"Sharon is out of the office today, but she's expected back tomorrow. May I take a message?"

"No, I'll call back. Thank you." I hung up and paced. It was time to hatch another plan.

The room became cold. The hair on my arms stood up. I looked up and saw a familiar person standing in the corner. There was no mistaking the robed man. I watched him, but he remained motionless.

"What do you want?" I yelled.

Silence.

"If you're not going to talk to me, then get the hell out."

The robed man moved toward me. I was scared, but I stayed put. When we were face-to-face, he whispered something.

"What? Did you say publish or perish, or publish and perish?"

He disappeared.

"Damn you," I yelled. "If you're not going to help me, stop haunting me."

I sat in the sunroom, staring out the window, repeating "publish or perish… publish and perish." Which was it? What was the robed man trying to tell me?

I returned to the living room. A ghostly figure of a man—a black cape draped over his arm like a maître d' with a white cloth—stood before me. The moment I saw his face, I knew who it was—Warren Keane, my birth father. He motioned for me to look in the dining room, then moved to the table and pointed at my computer.

"What do you want me to do?"

The ghost pointed at the computer again. He didn't utter a word, but I heard his words in my head with a clarity I'd never experienced.

"Publish your book."

I glanced away. When I looked back, he was gone. I felt energized, happy, free, fearless. I knew exactly what I needed to do, and it had nothing to do with a publishing company. And no one, not even dear old Dan, could stop me.

My moment of pure joy was interrupted by the phone. It was Aaron calling to inform me that Laura and Richard would be coming to his house for dinner at seven o'clock but not to panic because he'd hired a caterer to handle everything.

The fact Aaron hadn't asked about my meeting with Sharon Plinkton raised my suspicion and hurt my feelings. I told myself he was probably busy and that was why he'd forgotten about something so important to me. Oh well.

The evening with Laura and Richard was lovely. Aaron and I reenacted our engagement, complete with champagne. I should have won an Oscar for my performance as the unsuspecting bride-to-be.

Richard and Laura congratulated us with hugs and handshakes. Laura oohed and ahhed over my ring and asked endless questions about our wedding date, honeymoon plans, and living options. In the meanwhile, Aaron and Richard discussed football and old times at the newspaper in Ohio. I was surprised the guys got along well. No animosity. No mention of Dan or Jim. No mention of my book.

Later, as Aaron and I slipped between the sheets, he said, "That went well."

"Yep."

Lights out. Walter wedged himself between us. Good doggie.

CHAPTER FIFTY-THREE

ONE MORNING, AFTER A NIGHT together at my condo and several days with no inquiry from Aaron as to my meeting with Sharon Plinkton, I casually mentioned I had decided to self-publish my book.

"Good for you," Aaron said. Then he kissed me on the cheek.

"You never asked me how things went with Sharon Plinkton," I said, my voice surprisingly whiny.

"I didn't have to," Aaron said before taking a huge gulp of coffee. "The fact that you said nothing spoke volumes. Obviously, it didn't go well."

"Not for her," I said.

"Good. I never liked her anyway. I can't believe she's still employed in any field associated with writing."

"Why?"

"She's god-awful. That's why." Aaron glanced at his watch. "Gotta go." Kiss on the cheek. "Get cracking on publishing your book."

"Already have," I said.

"I figured as much."

For the next two weeks, I studied the art of self-publishing. It was a lot of work with no guarantee of fame or fortune. But in reality, a traditional publishing contract guaranteed zilch. And because I'd have to turn over the rights to the publisher, I would have to relinquish control over the publication of my firstborn book. I guess that was Jim and Dan's motive when they reeled in Sharon Plinkton to play the eager new publisher. Ha! Not gonna happen. They can't fool me.

One afternoon, I got a call from a crying Laura. "Laura? What's up?"

"I got laid off."

"What? You work for your father."

"He had to lay off ten percent of his staff. He did it by expendable positions, not people. So I got axed."

"Maybe he'll hire you back."

"Doubt it. He told me it was time to flee the nest."

"Yikes… that hurts."

"Yeah, but he has a point." Laura took a deep breath and exhaled. "It's time for me to spread my wings and fly."

"Where to?"

"Heck if I know."

"Well, I can make you an offer," I said, almost instantly regretting that I opened my big mouth.

"What kind of offer? Cleaning your condo?"

"No. I was thinking more along the lines of you being my assistant."

"Your assistant what?"

"Well, I'm self-publishing my book. I need lots of help."

"What's the salary and benefits?"

"I can pay minimum wage, and the benefits are huge."

"How huge?"

"You get to work with me, your sister."

"Forget the pay. I'm financially secure for a while. And Richard is paying half the rent."

"Well, are you going to take me up on my offer or not?"

"Of course I am. The benefits are outrageous."

We laughed.

"When do I start?" Laura asked.

"What's today?"

"Friday."

"Your father laid you off on a Friday?"

"Yep. Evidently, there's some psychological benefit to being let go on a Friday. Your support team gets to suffer through the weekend with you and listen to you cry and curse."

"How's this. Meet me at TGI Friday's at six o'clock. We'll celebrate your layoff and our new partnership. And you can cry and curse all you want."

"Sounds great."

"Hang in there, little sister. You'll be fine."

"Thanks. See ya later."

"Oh, Laura?" Too late. She'd already hung up. I didn't get the chance to tell her to not tell Richard anything about my entering the realm of self-publishing. I thought about calling her, but my gut told me it didn't matter. She'd tell Richard no matter what.

I spent the rest of the day organizing my publishing plan and packing up clothes and personal items to keep at Aaron's. His house was quickly becoming my home. And my condo was becoming my office. Not a shabby setup.

I was happy to see Laura sans Richard. It felt like old times. We started with a vodka tonic for me, wine for her, and an order of our favorite appetizer. We chatted about her layoff, my plans, and her role in my new adventure. Then she leaned across the table and whispered something that nearly threw me into cardiac arrest.

"Vivian Jordan is sitting behind you. She keeps staring at me. And I swear she's taking notes."

"Aunt Vivian? Are you sure?"

"Yes. What's she doing in our neck of the woods?"

"Spying," I said.

"Why?"

"She's been spying on me my whole life."

"That's creepy."

I raised an index finger to my lips and whispered, "Shh." Then I sat back and said in a voice loud enough for Aunt Vivian to clearly hear me, "How's your job search going?"

Laura raised her eyebrows and widened her eyes as if to say, "What the hell do you want me to say?" "Um… not so good. Um… I don't have a résumé… and I don't have a clue how to look for a job online."

"Well, I can help—"

The server arrived with a tray containing two drinks. "Compliments from the woman at the next table," he said as he placed a vodka tonic in front of me and a glass of wine in front of Laura. I turned around to acknowledge Vivian Jordan. She was gone.

"Damn," I nearly yelled. "I'm sure she got an earful."

"I should have told you about her sooner," Laura said.

"It's not your fault." I tapped Laura on the hand. "Let's enjoy the rest of the evening."

We did.

We laughed.

We cried.

I realized how much I'd missed my Laura time.

"Laura? No matter how much our lives change, let's always get together, just you and me. No talk about husbands, babies, soccer games, work… Well, maybe work. Get my drift?"

"Yep. Just you and me talking about us."

I smiled at Laura, knowing as life changed, so would we and so would our conversations. I raised my glass and said, "To us."

Laura clinked her glass with mine. "To us."

We shared a moment of silence.

"What's the old song about sisters?" Laura asked.

"What old song about sisters?"

"You know the one about not coming between a sister and her man."

"The one from *White Christmas*?"

"Yeah. That's the one."

The lyrics to Irving Berlin's song *Sisters* rushed through my head as a chill crawled up my spine. Without saying a word, Laura had made it clear that I was banned from her and Richard's relationship. I felt like I'd been sucker punched.

The rest of the evening was awkward. Laura rattled on about what kind of job to pursue and her relationship with Richard. But all I could hear was that old song running endlessly through my head.

I'd been warned.

Feeling sick to my stomach, I made an excuse to leave. As we settled the bill, Laura appeared radiant.

On the way to our cars, she said, "See you Monday. I can't wait to start working with my sister."

I smiled as I watched Laura skip to her car. Why was she so happy? I didn't know, and I didn't care.

When I got to Aaron's, Walter and he were fast asleep in front of the TV.

"Great watchdog, Walter," I said as I petted the top of his head. Walter opened his eyes and looked at me, but he didn't move. I looked at Aaron, but for some reason, I didn't give him my usual hello kiss. Let sleeping dogs lie. As I got cozy, Walter joined me and the two of us fell asleep. A while later I was awakened by Walter licking my face. As I pushed him off, I looked at the clock. It was two a.m. I looked at the bed. No Aaron.

I wandered to the living room. Aaron was still asleep in the chair. His face was pale, bloodless. I panicked. I shook him so hard I nearly broke his neck.

He opened his eyes and looked at me. "Emarie, what the hell are you doing?"

"Are you okay?"

"Yeah. Why?"

"You look like death warmed over."

"I'm not surprised. I spent half the evening throwing up my dinner."

"Feel better now?"

"Yeah. Probably just food poisoning."

"Well, come to bed before Walter hogs the covers."

Aaron slunk to bed, obviously drained of energy. He crawled in beside me and quickly fell back asleep. I, on the other hand, was awake all night petting Walter and wondering what I'd gotten myself into.

CHAPTER FIFTY-FOUR

ALTHOUGH MY BOOK HAD BEEN thoroughly edited by Aaron, I had made some changes and asked him to take another crack at it. He reluctantly agreed. After a few heated discussions resulting in hurt feelings and the silent treatment, we decided that for the sake of our relationship, I should find another editor. Laura agreed and contracted with a top-notch editor, found an inexpensive yet talented graphic designer to design the book cover and the e-book version, and secured the ISBN code for the printed version. And because the control freak in me decided to publish the old-fashioned way, I contracted with a local on-demand printer. Everything was falling into place. Laura was working out swimmingly.

I worked on the editor's comments, some of which stung, but I took all into consideration and eventually agreed with most of them. I wrote the back cover synopsis and consulted with the graphic designer on the book cover while Laura continued working on everything else. In fact, she worked so hard I swore she wanted my book published more than I did. Of course, Laura's enthusiasm raised my suspicion. Who could I trust? I was becoming more paranoid every day. The book had taken over my senses.

I was obsessed.

Aaron was frustrated.

He pressured me endlessly to plan our wedding. I told him I would once I made my first million. He stormed out and didn't talk to me for two days. Fortunately, I had Walter to talk to. He lent an understanding ear and gave sweet kisses. Apparently, a dog isn't just man's best friend. And I was in desperate need of TLC.

One Friday afternoon, Aaron unexpectedly showed up at my condo, or I should say, my office. "Okay, Emarie," he said. "We're going on a little weekend getaway."

"Really? Where to?"

"It's a surprise, but it's somewhere you've always wanted to go."

"Paris?" I squealed.

"No. Save that for our honeymoon."

"Then where?"

"The Greenbrier."

"Don't tease me."

"I'm not teasing. Go pack."

I felt like I'd been asked to the prom by the cutest guy in school. I was so excited I could hardly pack fast enough. As I threw my things in a suitcase, I yelled to Aaron, "Where's Walter?"

"At my parents'. Just hurry up."

Suitcase in hand, I nearly glided down the hall. I stopped at the office door and said, "Laura, please lock up for me. My *man* is taking me away for a romantic weekend."

"So I heard," Laura said.

"Oh, and remember to lock *everything* in the safe."

"Done."

"See you Monday."

"Hope you two lovebirds have a good time."

"I'm sure we will."

I kissed Aaron, and the two of us left. "Where's your car?"

"I don't know. Maybe someone stole it," he said. Then he pulled out his cell phone, dialed, and said, "We're ready."

A limousine appeared around the corner. The car stopped in front of us, and the driver got out. He took my suitcase and put it in the trunk. Aaron and I settled in the back seat, and off we went.

"What's the occasion?" I asked.

"Well… I feel we've drifted apart. I thought a weekend in West Virginia's Sulphur Springs would restore our relationship."

I smiled at Aaron and held his hand. "I think you're right."

Three days later, back at my condo, I reminisced about the weekend of massages, gourmet food, relaxation, beautiful views, and romance. Yep, relationship restored. I felt like the luckiest woman in the world.

I looked at the clock. Laura was late. My weekend getaway faded away. I went into the sunroom and spotted her getting out of her car, carrying a large envelope. She looked up and waved at me. I opened the front door and waited as she climbed the stairs.

"I see your weekend went well," she said.

"Yes. And yours?"

"It was fine. Laid-back. Movies. Pizza. Jogging."

"What's that?"

"Galley," Laura said, smiling as she handed me the envelope. "It arrived right after you left. I almost called to tell you they were in, but I decided to wait."

"Why did you take them home with you?"

"They wouldn't fit in your safe, and I was paranoid someone, namely Vivian the spy, would know you were gone for the weekend. I was afraid she or someone else might try to take them."

"Oh… well… thanks." I scanned the envelope to make sure Laura hadn't opened it and, God forbid, shown the galley to Richard. Then I carefully opened it and pulled out the galley. I held it to my chest and took a deep breath, taking in the sweet scent of paper and ink. I spread it out on the dining room table and began to read. Then I got up and walked into the sunroom.

"Emarie, what's wrong?"

"It stinks," I said, holding back tears.

"A week ago you thought it would be a best seller. What's changed your mind?"

"A week ago it wasn't this close to production. I've spent the past eighteen months living this book. What am I supposed to do when it's finished?"

"Get married? Have babies? Start a new career? Write another book? Whatever you want."

"I don't know what I want. I don't even know if I want to get married."

"Why?"

"Because I feel like I'm losing me."

"But you're gaining a husband and a cute, hairy son."

"I know you're trying to make me feel better, but it isn't working."

"Okay, I'll be blunt. You're doing what you always do—undermining your success."

"No, I'm not."

"Yes, you are. Every time you advance in your career, you either quit, change jobs, or start a new career. I'm not going to let you do it this time."

I held my tongue and my anger, knowing she was right.

"You're onto something, Emarie. I understand you're scared to publish this because of the possible consequences, but you can't lose your nerve now. Do you think I put aside the past few months of my life to help my sister publish a book I didn't believe in? I believe in you, and I believe your book needs to be published. I, for one, want to see Dan Jordan get his just deserts."

I agreed.

I pored over my galley for hours. I had no idea what Laura was up to, but she seemed busy. Around three, I decided I needed a break. I went to the office door and caught Laura doing something surprising—looking at wedding dresses online.

"Is there something you want to tell me?" I said.

Laura twirled around in the chair. Her you-caught-me look was priceless. "No."

"Then why are you looking at wedding dresses?"

"Just passing time."

"Yeah, sure. Are you and Richard engaged?"

"No… not yet."

"Sooo, are you filling a hope chest?"

Laura clicked off the website and got up. I noticed paper samples on which words were printed. "What's that?"

"What?" Laura said as she turned to see what I was pointing at.

"Oh. Um… nothing. Just announcements for your book."

"You were never a good liar, Laura." I snatched an announcement off the desk and read it. "Did Aaron put you up to this?"

"Partly." Laura ran her fingers through her hair. I was well acquainted with that delay tactic. "He said he was concerned about you not taking an interest in the wedding. I took it upon myself to make recommendations."

"Like a weekend at the Greenbrier so he could stake out the amenities for, let me guess, our wedding reception?"

"Oh Emarie, you're so suspicious."

"I appreciate everything you've done to help me with my book, but you crossed the line when you put your nose in my wedding plans."

"Emarie, I—"

"Shut up. You betrayed me. Leave. Now."

Laura stormed out of my condo. I watched her from the sunroom window as she got in her car and slammed the door. But she didn't leave. She sat in the car. I saw her talking on her cell phone.

"She better not be talking to Aaron." I had a serious bone to pick with him. I decided to pick it now. I sat in a chair that I knew hid me from sight but afforded me a view of Laura in her car. I dialed Aaron. To my relief, he answered the phone. *So who was Laura talking to?* While Aaron and I made small talk, I watched Laura get out of her car, pace, and yell at someone over the phone.

"That's why you called?" Aaron asked. "You wanted to know if I'll take Walter to get his nails trimmed?"

"Yep."

"Why are you whispering?"

"See you later. Love you." Click.

Laura leaned against the trunk of her car. "You promised," she yelled. Then she hung up and cried. I wanted to run to her and make sure she was okay, but something about her behavior didn't make sense. Then she got in her car and drove away.

I went back to the office to check Laura's online activities. The search history listed wedding and bridesmaid dresses, invitations, flowers, and no surprise, the Greenbrier. But something else caught my eye—Laura had left her e-mail open. I sat in the chair, perched forward, hand on the mouse, struggling with the idea that I didn't trust my best friend and hoping what I was about to discover wouldn't ruin our relationship. Deciding there was no such thing as an accident, I clicked on the e-mail icon. Wow! She's popular. Then I saw it—an e-mail from Vivian Jordan Photography.

I didn't hesitate.

I clicked.

I read.

> *Laura,*
>
> *Thanks for alerting me to your evening at TGI Friday's with Emarie. Sorry about my abrupt exit, but I heard what I needed to hear. You're doing a great job of keeping Emarie focused on publishing her book. Keep up the good work. Needless to say, Dan and Jim are angry that her meeting with Sharon Plinkton didn't go as planned, and they're suspicious about Emarie's intentions. Of course, they hope she'll chicken out and can her book. I hope not. Her story needs to be told.*
>
> *Vivian*
>
> *PS: Emarie's wedding needs to happen soon. See if you can get her moving on that without raising her suspicion. I know that's easier said than done as the suspicion gene runs in the family. You can count on me to be her official photographer. Just give me the date, time, and location when you have everything lined up. Don't tell her anything until everything shakes out.*

I read the e-mail over and over. *Had Laura betrayed me or helped me? Was Vivian on my side? What made Vivian think I'd want her as my official wedding photographer? Was Aaron in cahoots with them? Damn it. Who can I trust?*

I called my parents. After a short conversation, it was obvious they knew nothing about publishing dates or wedding plans. My mother asked about the wedding date, and I told her I hadn't set a date yet.

Then she said something that haunted me. "Aaron's not going to wait forever."

I was furious. I wanted to call Laura to ask which date Vivian and she had chosen for my wedding. But I didn't. I wanted to talk to Aaron first. If I couldn't trust him to be honest, the wedding was off.

CHAPTER FIFTY-FIVE

I ARRIVED AT AARON'S TO an empty house.

No Aaron.

No Walter.

I guess Aaron had taken Walter to get his nails cut, per my recommendation. It was a good thing as I needed time to calm down and think through how to approach what I suspected Laura of doing without putting Aaron on the defensive. I was in the bedroom changing my clothes when I heard the front door open. Then I heard footsteps in the hallway. Next thing I knew, I was knocked onto the bed. Then the perpetrator jumped on top of me. I tried to push him off, but there was nothing I could do but surrender. So I let Walter lick my face until it was makeup free. He ran in circles on the bed, giving me a momentary reprieve. I tried to sit up, but Walter was relentless. He was all over me again. "Walter! Stop," I yelled, no longer finding his kisses humorous.

"Walter, off," Aaron yelled.

Walter stopped, sat on the bed, and looked at Aaron.

"I said off."

That time Walter obeyed and jumped off the bed.

"Good thing I got his nails cut, or he might have clawed you to death."

I grunted and went into the bathroom to wash Walter's slobber off my face. Then I changed into my favorite clothes—men's pajama bottoms and a T-shirt.

Aaron was in the kitchen preparing a martini. "Want one?"

"Sure. I think I could use one after Walter's lovefest."

We both laughed.

Martinis in hand, we went into the living room. Aaron sat at one end of the couch. I stretched out on the other end and rested my feet on his thighs. Walter sprawled on the floor, staring into the kitchen as if he was protecting something.

"Aaron," I said, then sipped my drink. "There's something I need to discuss."

"I don't like the sound of that."

"I just need to get it off my chest."

"Okay."

"Did you ask Laura to make our wedding arrangements?"

"No. Why?"

"Well, she's been a busy little wedding planner."

"Maybe she thinks she's helping."

"Well, she's not. What about the weekend at the Greenbrier? Did she recommend that?"

"Yes. I asked her about a good place to whisk you away for a relaxing, romantic weekend. She suggested the Greenbrier."

"It had nothing to do with scouting out a place for our wedding reception?"

"No," Aaron said as he popped an olive in his mouth. "What's the big deal?"

"Well, I… Laura and I are on the outs. That's all." I waited for Aaron to say something. Instead, he picked up the TV remote and turned on the news. "What do you want for dinner?" I asked.

"Oh, I forgot to tell you. I picked up Chinese on the way home."

"Sounds good," I said. Then I got up, stepped over Walter, went into the kitchen, and made myself another martini. Walter followed me and sat at my side while I leaned against the island and contemplated how to smooth over things with Laura. But the scent of my favorite Chinese food distracted me. Laura would have to wait.

To my surprise, Laura showed up for work the next morning. She looked like she hadn't slept a wink.

"Coffee?" I said.

"Please," Laura said. She took the coffee from me and started to cry. "Oh Emarie, I have something to confess."

"What?"

"I didn't get fired." Laura waited for my response.

I decided to let her suffer.

"I took a leave of absence, because... because Vivian Jordan wanted me to help you publish your book."

"How did she know I'd offer you an assistant's position?"

"She didn't. If you hadn't offered, I was to offer my help, and knowing you, you would have said yes."

"So what's she got to gain?"

"She wants Dan punished for what he did."

"That doesn't make sense, Laura. Dan's not the only one who could be indicted for what he's done."

"Who else could be in trouble?"

"Vivian," I yelled.

"Why would she be punished?"

"For God's sake, Laura, didn't you read my book?"

"Not all of it."

"So you've blindly followed the suggestions of a psychopath?"

"She's not a psychopath. She's a nice woman who wants to help you."

"Laura—she's using you. Cut her off now. I hope it's not too late."

"What do you think she'd do to me?"

"She's a potential killer."

"She didn't kill anybody."

"She helped Dan kill Patti. Then she helped cover it up. Plus she helped Dan, masquerading as Dorothy, cover up the abuse of seven children and the murder of Bull."

"I didn't know that. But now that you mention it, she made it clear she wasn't involved."

"Of course. That was her way of sucking you in."

"I believed her," Laura said as she went into the living room and sat in the chair. "What have I done? How do I get out of this?"

"I'll think of something." I paced the living room. "Laura? Did Vivian ask you to edit anything from my book?"

"No," Laura said, appearing to be lost in thought. "Oh... my... God." Laura shot up from the chair and stood next to me. "She asked for the name of the printer."

I ran to the dining and flipped through the latest version of the galley. I couldn't find what I was looking for, so I ran to the office and opened my manuscript file. I searched for the words "Vivian took photos of you and Dorothy." Found it. I noted the chapter number and ran back to my galley. It was gone. I flipped forward and backward. There wasn't one mention of Vivian, Vivian Jordan, Vivian Jordan Photography, or Aunt Vivian. I flipped to the chapter where Richard and I first met the red-haired lady at McDonald's, then at the house, and our conversation on the porch. She had changed that too. It now read "the black-haired lady." I immediately called the printer. I told him I needed a galley of the previous version immediately. He seemed confused but complied.

"I'm getting a new galley," I said to Laura. "It will be here this afternoon. We have to work fast. This book needs to be printed before Vivian Jordan gets suspicious. I don't have time to know every detail of what she asked you to do. Just pretend you're moving forward with her suggestions."

Laura nodded her agreement and said, "Oh, Emarie, I'm—"

"No apology required," I said. "Let's get moving."

I didn't know what to do with myself while waiting for the new galley to arrive, but Laura appeared busy. She had several conversations with Vivian, which I managed to overhear. I was surprised how cool, calm, and collected Laura sounded. I had no idea she was such a good actress.

It was getting late. I was getting worried. Then the doorbell rang. I rushed to the door and peered through the peephole. A young man bearing a large envelope was on the other side. I opened the door and snatched the envelope from him before he could say, "A-1 Printing." Then he held out a clipboard with a list of deliveries and asked me to sign for my galley. Below my name, I saw Vivian Jordan Photography/FedEx. I yanked him into my condo, picked up the phone, and called the printer. I smiled awkwardly at the courier as I waited for the owner to pick up.

"Emarie? John here."

"John, I don't think I mentioned that all instructions regarding my book will come from me and only me. And I don't want anything FedExed to Vivian Jordan. She does *not* work for me."

"I'm glad you told me because she's driving me crazy."

"Has she contacted you today?"

"No."

"Good. If she does contact you, please delay her without telling her I told you not to take changes from her. And don't tell her about the new galley."

"Of course."

"Good. It's very important. Just so you know, she's a dangerous person."

"Okay. I'll alert my staff. Sometimes she asks for Tammy directly. I'll make sure this is taken care of."

"Thanks."

"What about taking direction from Laura Simmons?"

"She does work for me, but from this point on, I'll be your only contact."

"You got it."

"By the way, have you spoken with Laura today?"

"No. Not a word."

"Thanks."

"Emarie? Let me talk to Calvin."

I looked at the courier. "Are you Calvin?"

"Yes," he said.

I thrust the phone at him.

John spoke to the courier, who turned over the second copy of the galley to me and crossed Vivian Jordan's name off his list.

Once he was gone, I compared the galley with the final manuscript like it was the Dead Sea Scrolls. Everything was there. For the next two days, Laura and I took turns reading the galley out loud, looking for typos and other errors. I wanted to send it to someone with no prior knowledge of my book, but I didn't know who that could be. I would have to trust that the editor, Laura, and I had caught everything.

The morning of the third day, I signed the galley and returned it myself to A-1 Printing. John and I reviewed the front and back covers. Everything looked great. I took a deep breath.

"It's good to go." As the words crossed my lips, a sensation of dread rushed through me. I chose to ignore it.

Nearly a week went by. Laura fielded calls from Vivian, who wanted to know why she couldn't get through to the printer regarding her copy of the last galley. Laura told her the printer was backlogged and that I'd told him it was okay to put my book on the back burner. In other words, Laura's hands were tied. Vivian was suspicious but appeared to accept this excuse. Then they continued to plan my wedding. It was the week from hell. Then it happened—a knock on the door.

It was Calvin.

"First run, Ms. Lukins," he said pointing to two boxes.

I signed for the delivery as Calvin moved the boxes into my condo. Then I closed the door and yelled, "Laura… they're here."

Laura emerged from the office, and the two of us stared at the boxes. "Well, open them," she said.

I went into the kitchen and got a steak knife. Then I took a deep breath and slit through the tape, opened the box and removed the Bubble Wrap. I nearly cried when I saw the book cover. I picked up a book, held it to my chest, and hugged it as if it were my firstborn child.

I looked at Laura and said, "What the hell have I done?"

CHAPTER FIFTY-SIX

A ARON PICKED UP THE COPY of my book I had conspicuously left on the coffee table. He reviewed the cover and scanned a few pages, but he didn't read it. In fact, he didn't say anything—not congratulations, good job, go to hell, nothing. His silence said it all.

"Okay, what's up?" I said.

"Nothing," Aaron replied.

"What are you thinking?"

"I'm happy for you. I know this is a big accomplishment, but I'm worried."

"About what?"

"Oh, Emarie." Aaron tossed my book on the coffee table. "I think it's obvious," he said as he got up and walked into the kitchen.

Anger and disappointment battled for my emotional attention. Anger won. "Don't walk away from me."

Aaron stood in the kitchen doorway, contemplating his words and controlling his emotions. "I'm afraid you're going to get hurt."

"Or killed?"

Aaron stared at me.

I waited.

"Are you prepared for that?" he said. "I'm not."

"They're not going to hurt me," I said, not completely believing my own words. "They'd be stupid if they did."

"Emarie, I don't want to stand in your way, but please consider that there are other people in your life. People who care about you and love you. People who would be devastated if something happened to you."

"So you're saying I'm selfish?"

"Don't twist my words."

"Pff."

"Just think about it," Aaron said. "I'm going to bed."

I did think about it—all night long. At six thirty a.m. I got dressed, took four copies of my book, and left. As I started my car engine, I looked at Aaron's house and said, "I hope you understand."

I drove away, not knowing if what I was about to do was sane.

Not knowing if I would come home.

Not knowing if I would ever see Aaron, my parents, or Laura again... and for some reason, not caring.

At eight forty-five, I pulled into the Darrington McDonald's. I ordered coffee and an Egg McMuffin. I looked around for the perfect table and noticed that the table where Richard and I had our first encounter with Vivian was empty. I sat down, unwrapped my Egg McMuffin, and started to cry. The events of the past year and a half rattled through my head. I missed Richard. I should say, I missed the Richard I thought was my friend. Then I thought about Aaron. I didn't want to lose him. I really did love him. Thoughts of Laura made me smile. We'd shared so much of our lives. Somehow I knew she'd understand what I was about to do. Then I thought about my parents and burst into tears. The thought of breaking their hearts was too much.

I sipped my coffee, but I couldn't force myself to eat. I sat for a few minutes longer. Then I got up, tossed my coffee and Egg McMuffin in the trash, and walked to my car where I sat, running my hand over the cover of my book, hoping the title wasn't an omen.

"Come on, Emarie," I said. "You're no wimp." I turned the key. The engine roared. The radio blasted Sara Bareilles's *Brave* as I sped out of McDonald's parking lot. Then I made two pit stops: one at the

Bingingham County Circuit Court and one at the Bingingham County Police station where I dropped off a package addressed to the Honorable Samuel Brown and Sheriff Tydings, respectively. Each package contained a copy of my book and a letter.

Then I headed to Dan and Vivian's house. I parked out front, sat in my car, and tried to muster the courage to follow through with what I knew needed to be done. My gut told me destiny was about to change, for better or for worse, I didn't know.

Books in hand, I walked to the front door and rang the bell.

The door opened.

My heart skipped.

"Emarie? Why do I have the pleasure of your company today?" Vivian asked through the screen door.

"I have something for you," I said. "Is Dan home?"

"No, but Dorothy is."

"May I see her for a moment?"

"Dorothy?" Vivian yelled. "Emarie's here to see you."

"Damn it. What does *she* want?"

"What do you want?" Vivian asked as Dorothy, clutching a bottle of her happy juice, appeared at the door.

"I have a surprise for you."

"I don't like surprises," Dorothy sniped.

"I think you'll like this one."

Dorothy walked away. "Let her in, Vivian."

Vivian opened the door barely enough for me to enter. I brushed by her and walked across the foyer to the family room where Dorothy had plopped herself in her favorite chair.

"Well, don't just stand there." Dorothy wiped happy juice off her chin. "Show me what you've got."

"Well, before I give you my gift, I want to thank you for being you," I said to Dorothy. "And you too, Vivian. Without you two, I couldn't have accomplished this." I thrust a copy of my book at Dorothy and immediately pulled it back.

"What the hell?" Dorothy yelled.

"Before I give you this gift, I have two more questions," I said. "First, did you kill your brother, Warren Keane?"

"Why do you ask?" Dorothy said in Dan's voice.

"Well, Jim seemed to be out to destroy you. And despite all the horror you perpetrated on so many innocent children, I wasn't convinced his hatred for you was because of them. No, his hatred of you was personal. In his father's obituary, one word piqued my interest."

"What word?"

"'Suddenly.' The Honorable Warren Keane died *suddenly*."

"So?"

"Well, you already shut up Bull and Patti. Therefore, your brother Warren was the only person left besides Vivian who had the scoop on you."

"I had to kill him," Dorothy as Dan yelled. "When he found out Bull and Patti were dead, he went on a rampage. He knew Dorothy killed Bull and I killed Patti. He threatened to reveal my secrets. So you see, he was a threat to Dorothy—the only woman I ever truly loved. Damn it. I had to kill him. It was hard as hell. After all, he was my identical twin. Killing him was like killing myself."

"Oh please, don't tell me you want pity?" Before Dan could answer, I said, "That leads to question number two: How did you kill him?"

"Are you nuts? I'm not going to tell you how I did it. But I will tell you that I made it look like a heart attack. Lucky for me, he was cremated. So my secret is safe."

"Why no autopsy?"

"He'd had two prior heart attacks. No one questioned that the third one killed him."

"Okay, next question. How did you kill Patti?"

"You said you only had two questions."

"I was mistaken. How did you kill Patti?"

"She drowned. That's the truth."

"Ah... then I guessed right."

"What do you mean?"

"Well, even though you're a big, strong man, I knew it was impossible for you to carry a three-hundred-plus-pound woman's body to the pond and throw her in. So I deduced Patti walked to the pond of her own accord and you pushed her in. And knowing she couldn't swim, you left her to drown."

"How did you come up with that cockamamie idea?" Dan said.

I pulled a document from my purse and waved it in his face. "Dorothy's… or I should say Patti's, death certificate. Cause of death, drowning. Therefore, Patti was alive when she was dumped in the pond."

Dan snatched the paper from me, tore it into pieces, and threw the pieces in the air. They floated to the floor like confetti.

I gave Dan a copy of my book. "It's all in here," I said, hoping he didn't notice my trembling hand.

Then I turned to Vivian and gave her a copy. "A signed copy for you too."

"You don't know what you've done!" Dan screamed.

I didn't answer. I was too busy watching Vivian flip through the pages. She stopped, looked up at me, and said, "You bitch."

"Is something wrong?" I asked.

"Everything's wrong," Vivian said. "You betrayed me."

Dan yelled, "You think you can get away with this?"

"Get away with what?" I asked.

"I'm an important man in this town. No one will believe this crap."

"Oh… but I think they will because it's the truth, the whole truth, and nothing but the truth, so help me God."

Dan stood and shook my book at me. "This piece of shit will be the death of a lot of people. You want that on your conscience?"

I pulled back as he put his face in mine and spit. I was disgusted, but I didn't move or say a word. Then he walked into the kitchen and made a call.

I overheard him say, "Hey, Judge Jordan here. Send a squad car to my sister's house in a half hour."

I watched him open a kitchen drawer and pull out something. A knife? A gun? I couldn't tell because I was distracted by something that hit me in the back. I turned and saw my book on the floor.

"Leave and take that piece of garbage with you," Vivian screamed.

Then Dan lunged at me from behind. I managed to pull away, causing him to stumble into the love seat.

He regained his balance and moved forward, waving a gun at me. "Get out before I kill you," he screamed.

With a pounding heart and shaking knees, I bolted for the door.

Bang.

I raced to my car.

Bang.

I stepped on the gas and never looked back.

EPILOGUE

I HELD AARON'S ARM AND rested my head on his shoulder as the two of us stood over two fresh graves—the footstones read: Dan Jordan, January 8, 1948–April 10, 2017; Vivian Jordan, March 12, 1952–April 10, 2017.

The sound of two gunshots echoed in my head as I remembered the day, just one month ago, when I brazenly gave a copy of my book to each of them, igniting Dan's anger.

"I can't believe Vivian killed Dan. When I heard the gunshots, I thought Dan shot Vivian and then himself. I never imagined it was the other way around."

"They both got what they deserved," Aaron said. "Dan was despicable, and Vivian was no angel."

"But there was another side to her. She didn't deserve to die."

"Vivian kept her mouth shut about Dan abusing six children, killing his son, framing Patti for the crimes, as well as her complicity in Patti's murder." Aaron pulled away from me. "As far as I'm concerned, she deserves to rot in hell with him."

"Yes, but I feel as if I were the judge, jury, and… executioner."

"No. You were a victim of Dan's abuse. You had a right to expose him for what he was."

Aaron turned and walked toward the car. But I was immobilized by the sight of the robed man standing next to a majestic elm tree. He looked straight at me, raised his hand to his face, and blew me a kiss. Then he sizzled like a sparkler and disappeared.

"Come on, Emarie," Aaron yelled as he held open the car door for me. "You've shattered enough lies for a lifetime. Time to start a new chapter of your life."

ABOUT THE AUTHOR

Joanne Hughson, the author of the *Idlebury Series* and *Shattered Series*, grew up in the Washington, D.C. area. She earned a bachelor's degree from the University of Maryland and a master's degree from Marymount University. While dabbling in writing books, she toiled through two careers—the first as an advertising copywriter/creative director and the second as a mental health therapist. She hopes her third career as an author brings enjoyment to many and that her readers have as much fun reading her books as she had writing them. She is married to a patient man who respects her writing time. And she is the proud "mother" of an active four-legged son who demands to play at the most inconvenient times.